CLOSE ENCOUNTER

Nora stepped back, her intent to slam the door in Jake's face. She tried, but his boot stopped it in mid-swing. "I want to talk to you."

"If you're still trying to warn me away from your brother, don't bo—"

"I figure that wouldn't make no difference. You're a stubborn woman and wouldn't listen to anything I say."

"You figured right."

They stood, each on opposite sides of the threshold, their bodies inches from touching. Nora realized their proximity, but she wasn't about to let this man cower her. This was her home and he was going to step back. Until he did, she'd face him and do it with all the courage she possessed.

"What do you want?"

Ah, at last a question he could answer. "You."

Nora felt her heart make a giant thud. She tried to draw a deep breath, but she couldn't seem to manage it. She couldn't seem to breathe at all. "Why?" Her voice was soft and low.

"Damned if I know. All I know is you're driving me crazy. I have to touch you."

"No." Nora tried to back up, but her feet refused to obey the commands of her mind.

"*Yes*," he said as he took the half step that separated their bodies. His arms reached around her waist and dragged her against him. "I can't stand it a minute longer. I have to have you."

PATRICIA PELLICANE

DESIRE'S GLORY

ZEBRA BOOKS
KENSINGTON PUBLISHING CORP.

To Timmy, Donna, Anthony
and the newest addition, Nicolle—
God Bless.
And to the real Nora Bowens,
the great-grandmother, I never met.

ZEBRA BOOKS

are published by

Kensington Publishing Corp.
475 Park Avenue South
New York, NY 10016

First Printing: December 1992

Printed in the United States of America

Chapter One

Long delicate fingers encased in heavy, leather gloves pulled hard on the reins, causing slender arms browned by a ceaseless sun to tighten with firm muscle. As the stubborn team of oxen came to a stop at last, Nora Bowens groaned and arched her back against the aching stiffness. The nostrils of a nose, perhaps a bit too short, flared as she breathed a sigh of relief. She flung aside her floppy felt hat and raised her arm, wiping at the perspiration that coated her forehead and cheeks.

Green eyes looked about with only a hint of despair. Between a double row of shadowed, weathered buildings, ran a wide dirt street that promised to turn into thick, swampy mud at the first sign of rain. Most every structure appeared ready to tumble to the ground at the first sign of a breeze. Nora tried to imagine it was the lack of light that brought about this first disagreeable impression. Still, Glory hardly resembled the small, but growing metropolis described in Mayor Dodd's enthusiastic letters.

Nora gave an indifferent shrug. That the mayor's letters were more than a bit exaggerated hardly mattered. Right now, she couldn't find it within herself to care about anything, except to locate the promised comfortable quarters chosen for herself and her exhausted family.

Nora smiled with gentle indulgence as she watched a lone drunk lurch wildly along an uneven, wooden sidewalk. By the meager light spilling from the window of a nearby building, she checked her timepiece. It was a little after eleven and most of the town lay in deep shadows. Nora imagined it to be well past the time when most decent folks had settled in for the night.

Her family's wagon had come to a stop some ten feet from the swinging doors of Glory's only hotel/saloon. Nora turned toward the sound coming from the two-story structure. Loud, raucous laughter and tinny notes played upon a harpsichord, reminded her that not everyone retired with sun in these parts. It was Saturday night. No doubt the revelry would go on for some time.

The street was dark, but a lantern hung above the doors of the building, enabling her to read clearly the boldly lettered sign. It read, "Fancy's Place." Despite her exhaustion, or more likely because of it, Nora laughed. She hadn't seen anything remotely resembling "Fancy," since the day of Sherman's infamous and inhuman destruction of Atlanta. And she certainly expected to see nothing of the sort within a hundred miles of this small town.

The sun had long ago disappeared behind a distant mountain, and cool, desert air chilled her skin. Still, Nora might have labored beneath the harsh rays of a noonday sun, for the effort to control the slow moving oxen had taxed her to the limit of her ability and had left her drenched in sweat. Now that she had a moment to rest, she found herself trembling and wondered if the involuntary action was due to the cold, or to her exhaustion. No doubt both played a role.

Nora had little time to consider either her chill or fatigue, for just then a low moan came from the back of the wagon. Her father, although he never complained, suffered most of all. Her thoughts centered on her parents and the need to find them decent lodgings without delay.

If she were to accomplish that feat, Nora knew she'd best be about the chore, for the night was darker than pitch and the desert air grew colder by the minute.

She was thankful, beyond words that the journey was finished at last. If she'd known at the beginning the toll such an expedition would exact on her small family, Nora would have begged her father to book passage on a ship and gain California by way of the Cape and then overland to Virginia City, Nevada. From there it was only a hard day's ride north to Glory.

Surely a sea voyage could not have elicited more in the way of hardship or danger than what they'd suffered during this horrendous trip: the shortage of water, the food gone bad, the constant, terrifying threat of hostile Indians, and worst of all the dust and endless heat. It was, to her way of thinking, nothing less than a miracle that any of the train managed

7

to survive.

Nora scrambled over boxes and barrels, into the dark interior of the wagon and checked her father. He slept. She breathed a sigh and bit her lip with worry, even as she prayed he would soon regain his health. From her father's symptoms Nora had initially believed that he suffered from consumption. But no, it had been an unexplained fever that had struck during the seemingly endless journey and laid the man low. Long and hard fought, it had left him totally drained of his usual strength and vigor. Nora knew it would be weeks, perhaps months, before he'd be himself again. She wondered at her optimism and prayed it wasn't just wishful thinking. She shook her head, determined now that the fever had finally gone, he would be well again. He had to be!

Her gaze moved to the lone figure, sitting primly, at the back of the wagon; her back straight, her dress and hair as always were in perfect order. "Mother? Are you all right?"

"I'm fine dear," came her mother's cheerful reply. "I do wish you would hurry, Nora. Marabel Langsley is coming for tea."

Abigail checked her timepiece. The beautiful piece of jewelry, edged in delicate filigree, was pinned to her bodice. It was the only thing of value left to them after five disastrous years of war. The fact that it was, if possible, even blacker inside the wagon than out, appeared not to matter in the least, for her mother remarked, "She'll be here in ten minutes."

Nora wanted to cry. Instead she answered through a throat tight with a mixture of exhaustion, worry, and fear, "I'll hurry, Mother. You'll be all right, if I leave you for a moment?"

"Of course I'll be all right. What a silly thing to ask. Hurry now and make yourself presentable. Why a pretty young girl like you feels she has to spend the day working in that god-awful hospital of your father's, I'm sure I'll never understand. Why, only just yesterday, I mentioned that very thing to Clara Westly and she said . . ."

With a weary slump to her slender shoulders, Nora slid over the tailgate and dropped to the ground, leaving her mother to ramble on about her daughter's decidedly odd habits. She moved toward the brightly lit saloon, hoping to find someone who might direct them to their new home.

In truth, to say she entered the establishment, would have been a bit premature. She never exactly entered it. More to the point, her hand had reached for the door when she found herself suddenly flung into the air and then sprawled upon the street, with a huge, burly, bearded man lying full length atop her.

His body seemed to have shot out from nowhere, taking hers with it as it landed upon the dirt street, in a cloud of choking dust. Nora never would understand how her feet had entirely missed the wooden sidewalk and the two steps that led to the rutted street. Propelled through the air, she nevertheless found herself apparently uninjured. At the moment, however, the near impossibility of that happening never entered her mind. All she could think of was the means to find her next breath, for the dust was indeed intense and the pressure upon her chest more so.

The dust settled before she noticed this fool of a man was grinning ear to ear. It was obvious by the look of delight glimmering in whiskey-glazed eyes that he imagined the Almighty had somehow thought to bless him with a woman positioned, of all places, directly beneath him.

"Lordy, Lordy, what have we got here?"

Nora nearly gagged on the full blast of liquored breath. She attempted to throw the man off. The problem was, the man might have been drunk, but he wasn't so deep in his cups that he became malleable. Quite easily and despite her struggles, he remained where he was.

Nora felt the beginnings of panic as memories came crashing back. Her body stiffened even as she fought to keep control. This wasn't like the last time. This drunken fool posed no danger, meant her no harm. All she had to do was keep her head and she'd soon be out of this situation. "I beg your pardon," Nora said, the effort to keep the fear from her voice no easy chore, as she labored in vain to free herself.

"No need to apologize, darlin'," the man grinned. Then suddenly, to Nora's absolute amazement, he lowered his mouth and began to nuzzle her neck. That he slobbered and snorted like a pig during this less than adept seduction was hardly noticed by his victim.

Nora had the wild thought that a few more minutes of his suffocating weight would surely find her as flat as one of her infamous pancakes. The thought brought a smile to her lips and a wild giggle, born of fatigue and fear, escaped her throat.

She heard the jingle of spurs some moments before the boots came into view. "I hate to break up so romantic a moment, but don't you think it would be a sight more convenient if you brought your customers to your room?" There was real laughter in that deep voice and despite the fact that Nora was the one pinned beneath this slobbering giant, she had to fight her need to join him in his merriment.

The shaft of light, allowed by the half doors of the saloon, clearly illuminated Nora and her newly acquired, if less than coveted, devotee. The man stood just outside the beam of light, and Nora found herself straining to see into the darkness. Her eyes narrowed with the effort even as she sent the man a pleading look for assistance. The effort was lost in the darkness, but her need to laugh was not. Despite the danger of the circumstances she suddenly found herself thrust into, Nora couldn't stop yet another giggle from slipping from her throat. The sound only contributed to the man's erroneous supposition.

Nora realized it was total exhaustion and the remnants of a terror she'd thought long put to rest that caused this unusual emotion to surface. But no matter her efforts, she couldn't seem to stop the ridiculous urge to laugh. She giggled again. "Can you help me get him off?"

The drunken fool was suddenly flung from her. Lying along the edge of the street, the man obviously decided the effort it would take to come to his feet again and stagger home was unnecessary, for this was as good a place as any to bed down for the night. He went immediately to sleep.

He was snoring quite loudly by the time Nora managed, with some assistance, to come to her shaking legs. The tall man facing her grinned. The movement of his lips tilted his dark mustache. His hand on her arm held her until she steadied herself. Oddly enough, now that he'd given assistance, Nora was somewhat bothered by it. She wanted to push his hand away and she would have, had she been able. Nora was suddenly seized with such intense exhaustion and relief, she could only wonder how she managed to stay afoot.

Light from the saloon slashed across his hard, handsome features. A white shirt, rolled over thickly muscled arms, emphasized darkly weathered skin. Over the shirt he wore a black leather vest. His legs were long, his hips slim, his stomach flat. His trousers were tight, perhaps too tight, for they clung shamelessly to certain intimate parts of his anatomy. For some unknown reason a shiver ran down her back, and Nora wondered why? Certainly the man was far from ugly, but even if he'd been pock-marked and of hideously twisted features, why would that matter to her?

The man grinned again and his eyes widened in apparent appreciation as he took in her dishevelled state. His mustache dipped crookedly, emphasizing the curve of well formed lips. "You Fancy's new girl?" And when Nora made no attempt to answer, he looked at the drunk snoring in the street and grinned again. "He musta' been a bit anxious." Blue eyes sparkled with laughter as he took in the sight of her. "I reckon I can see why. The next time you should get him to your room first. It's dangerous . . ."

The rest of his words were lost as Nora's eyes rounded. She finally understood the man's implication. Oddly enough, instead of anger, his supposition brought about full-blown hilarity. Nora's sporadic giggles turned into boisterous, near hysterical laughter. "The trouble is," she gasped as her body was rocked with spasms of uproarious merriment, "I haven't got a room."

"All filled up, eh?" he asked obviously referring to the rooms above the saloon, since his gaze moved in that direction and then back. "Then you should have taken him into the alley. Anything is better than the street where anyone can—"

"I'm sorry," Nora said, although she couldn't imagine why she was apologizing to this dolt. All she knew for a fact was she was out of control; she couldn't repress this absurd need to laugh. By all rights, she ought to be thoroughly insulted at the reception this town had so far chosen to give her and her family. Instead, she laughed until tears rolled down her cheeks. She wiped them away, unknowingly leaving muddy uneven streaks to coat her smooth cheeks. She had to master this need to laugh. She had lodgings to find and her parents to see to. She couldn't take the time for hysterics now. She cleared her throat and tried to bring her quivering lips together into a prim, somber line. But no matter her efforts, she couldn't manage the chore.

Jake Brackston stood opposite the tiny woman with the fiery red and wildly curling hair and wondered what it would be like to hold this one in his arms. She wasn't what one would call exceptionally beautiful. For one thing, her mouth was too full and wide, and her chin, even with its slight softening cleft, too strong. Jake knew a woman with a chin like that was likely to cause trouble.

She was obviously one of Fancy's newest additions and he made a mental note to ask for her the next time he came into town. After all, he could take a bit of trouble from a woman with a body like hers.

Jake felt a sudden sense of unease as he watched her try to smooth back her hair. For just a second he wondered if he hadn't been too hasty in his judgment here, but no. No decent woman had hair the color of dark flame, nor wore it unbound, cascading over her shoulders and looking as if she'd just come from a good toss. What the hell was Fancy doing allowing her girls to use the street to entertain their customers? Were all the rooms upstairs really filled, or was this one going into business for herself?

Jake frowned, puzzled as he noticed for the first time her attire. She wore a man's shirt, a brown, dust covered skirt and black boots. Thick gloves covered her hands and a soft felt hat lay in the street. She certainly didn't dress like one of Fancy's girls. But Jake had hardly a moment to think on that oddity, for her shirt was opened almost to her waist. A white, cotton chemise, thinly edged with lace and the full, soft, womanly curves rising above it had caught his full attention.

Her lack of beauty didn't matter none. Tiny and yet full figured, she'd attract her share of men. He wondered what color her eyes were. Her skin, what he could see of it, looked as delicious as sweet cream. Jake's mouth watered as his gaze took in the barely covered mounds of feminine flesh. He was imagining how skin like that would feel and taste, even as he wondered when he'd be able to get into town next.

Nora managed to explain, despite the hilarity that

14

bubbled in her throat, "I'm afraid there's been a mistake."

Maybe he wouldn't wait. Maybe now was as good a time as any to sample this little beauty. "Would you like to go to your room and talk about it?" Jake nodded toward the man snoring not more than three feet from where they stood. "We'd have more privacy there."

His words only brought on a new bout of convulsive laughter. Lord, when she was herself again, she was going to put this ignorant oaf in his place. Right now, she couldn't even garner the strength to successfully strangle her need to laugh. "The doctor," she forced the words and finally managed, "My father."

"Is he ill?"

Nora blinked at the question and took a deep breath as most of her absurd need to laugh was finally put to rest. "As a matter of fact he is."

"Is that why you're plying your trade? Do you need the money?"

A smile touched the corners of her mouth again. "Please," she said and held up a hand as if the action would stop the words and the unwanted effect they were having on her. "You don't understand."

"Don't I?" Jake reasoned a sickly father as good an excuse as any for what she was doing. And he'd be right pleased to give the little lady a bit of his hard earned cash. After all it was going to a good cause.

"Wait!" she said as he took a step closer. "My father is the new doctor."

Nora swallowed twice and bit hard on the inside of her lip trying to force aside the need to laugh again.

15

Lord, but she was so tired she could hardly stand. There was no way she could control her emotions. Idly she wondered if she had the strength to get her family settled for the night. "Can you tell me where I can find his house?"

Jake's look of disbelief was tempered with amusement. "Don't you know where your father lives?"

This was getting worse by the minute. If he said one more ridiculous thing she was going to collapse in the street and laugh herself to death. She cleared her throat, raised her chin a fraction, and controlled the nearly uncontrollable need to laugh or rail at this imbecile. She wasn't sure which. "We left the train five miles south of town and only just arrived." She nodded toward the covered wagon, standing ten feet beyond the saloon doors. "I'd be ever so grateful, suh, if you could direct us."

Jake's eyes widened and his mouth twisted into a scowl of distaste as he noticed her accent for the first time. A Southerner! God, but he hated that soft drawl. Silky smooth, sweet, inviting and . . . deadly. Flashes of the year spent in one of their merciless prison camps, at the hands of inhumane guards, came flooding back, along with all the pain and abuse he'd thought long forgotten, and all Jake could think was how much he hated that sweet talking bitch who had promised him help, only to notify the authorities instead. Because of her he'd been returned to camp. Because of her he'd almost died. Maybe he wouldn't be wanting a go at this one after all. He'd had himself a belly full of Rebels. Enough to last him a lifetime.

"There are rooms above the mercantile," Jake

nodded down the street.

"Thank you, suh," Nora said in a tone filled with as much courtesy as she could manage. Considering the curious stiffening of his stance and the flicker of disgust she imagined to flare to life in the man's eyes, it was no easy chore. She reached for her hat, dusted what she could of the brown silt from her skirt and made her way to her wagon.

It wasn't until Nora was again seated upon the wagon that she had cause to look down while reaching for the reins. She gasped with horror upon finding her shirt torn clear to her waist and could only pray the night was dark enough so that ridiculous man hadn't seen what she knew he had.

It took some time, but Nora finally managed to bring her father, mother, and a few of their lighter possessions up the long flight of stairs, that ran outside the two-story building and into the rooms above the mercantile. The rooms were ugly, dark, musty and obviously neglected. The walls were in desperate need of paint, while the rugs were worn, and every surface was in need of a thorough cleaning.

She lit the stove, knowing the heat would go far toward relieving the rooms of their damp mustiness, and stripped away the gray bedding. An hour later, she left her parents, settled in beds made up with clean sheets and blankets taken from their own trunks. With a weary sigh, she descended the stairs again, knowing the wagon couldn't be left apparently abandoned in the street. She directed the team to the back of the building, fed and watered the oxen. It was with the last of her strength, that she managed to climb the stairs again.

Coated with dust, streaked with dirt, still in the clothes worn since morning, Nora fell asleep sprawled upon a narrow, bare mattress, knowing tomorrow would be soon enough to see to her usual ablutions.

"How do you do, suh?" Nora said as she allowed Mayor Dodd to raise her hand to his thick lips.

"I can't tell you how happy we are to have you finally here, ma'am." He smiled, exposing tobacco-stained teeth. "And how is your father?"

"Not well, I'm afraid. The trip was taxing, in the extreme. He came down with a fever a month back and hasn't as yet regained his strength."

"But he will?" Mayor Dodd asked hopefully. The people in this town had gotten together a goodly sum to see that a new doctor was brought to Glory. What was he going to tell them if their money and efforts were spent for naught?

"He will, Mayor. But it will take some time, I think."

Mayor Dodd couldn't hide his disappointment. Glory needed a doctor, badly. "Not too much time, I hope. This town is in desperate need of . . ."

"I'm well aware of the fact that you need a doctor, suh, and I'd be happy to help."

The mayor's beady eyes widened in shock.

"Of course, I'm not a doctor, but I am well trained in medicine, having worked under my father's guidance during the war. I will lend any aid I can while my father recuperates."

Mayor Dodd's gray eyes widened further as he

18

shook his head. "I'm afraid that won't do at all."

"Pray tell, suh, why not?"

"Because . . . because, you're a lady, of course."

"Thank you, suh, but I hope I'm much more than a lady."

"Ma'am?" the mayor prompted, confusion narrowing already beady eyes.

"I have nursed many taken directly from the battlefield. There is little I don't know about—"

He cut her off with a distinct clearing of his throat. "I've no doubt. Still," Mayor Dodd grew obviously flustered and uncomfortable as color stained his round cheeks. His shirt appeared suddenly too tight and he slid a thick finger inside his collar as he went on, "The truth of the matter is there aren't that many women in Glory, except, of course, for those at Fancy's Place." He grew fiery red at the mere mention of the women who lived above the saloon. "A lady wouldn't . . ."

Nora bristled under what she considered obnoxious patronizing. "Of course, she would." She held her tongue as his eyes widened with shock. Nora fought back the need to tell this man a thing or two and instead softened her words into flattery. "I'm sure an intelligent man like yourself realizes that the war disposed of much of that archaic reasoning. Dorothea Dix and her corps of female nurses are well-known to have administered to men almost since the first shot was fired." She smiled. "Believe me there were many in the South who did easily as much."

Did this pompous buffoon think those nurses were blindfolded while doing their chores? Did he actually believe that a woman was so weak of spirit as to

19

swoon at the sight of an injury, simply because it was inflicted upon the male anatomy? And did he think Nora Bowens so sheltered as to have never heard of women whose moral fiber was less than what was deemed savory? What, she wondered in silently growing anger, would he think of the things she'd seen and done during the conflict which ended only two years back? "I've learned well these last years, thanks to my father's tutelage."

"I'm sure you have, but—"

Nora didn't care that she was being unforgivably rude. She cut him off again. "Surely gender hardly matters when one is in need of care." She smiled, a devastating flash of straight, white teeth. Mayor Dodd was so taken by the beauty of that smile, that he never noticed it didn't quite reach her eyes. Nora didn't like the pompous fool. It took all her strength to remain civil. She forced another smile. "Why don't we let the good people of this fine town make up their own minds?

"My father will be well shortly." She prayed for the truth of that statement. "In the meantime, the women, if not the men, will have ample medical care." She said those last words with a flippancy she was far from feeling. "Good day to you, suh."

Nora left the mayor's office, a tiny room at the back of the only bank in town. She silently promised herself if any were foolish enough to refuse her care based solely on the fact that she was a woman, she would simply allow them the opportunity to die.

"Jesus, God, call Doc Morgan. She's bleedin'

20

like a stuck pig!" a deep voice bellowed from the upstairs landing.

An instant later, a man came bounding from the saloon. Ignoring the curses of the two men he almost knocked to the ground and the danger of wagon wheels and horses' hooves, he darted straight across the dirt packed street and up the stairs above the mercantile. He was pounding at the door when Nora snatched it open. "Yes?"

"Mazie got herself stuck."

"What?"

"Tell Doc Morgan to get over to Fancy's Place. One of her girls got knifed."

Nora nodded, reached for her father's small black bag, and followed the man down the stairs. The moment she stepped inside the saloon, Nora became conscious of a number of disagreeable odors. Unwashed bodies, stale whiskey, cheap perfume assaulted her senses and over it all hung a powerful, choking haze of cigar smoke. The smell caused her eyes to tear and the back of her throat to itch. In the tight confines of an almost airless room, the scents were overpowering in the extreme and Nora figured it was nothing less than amazing that these patrons could breathe.

A large group of men gathered at the bottom of a steep flight of stairs. Nora could see nothing but their backs. "Where is she?" she asked no one in particular.

"Upstairs," came a booming voice. Nora wasn't sure if it was a man or a woman who called to her. She didn't take the time to find out, but ignored the crowd and the smell of the place as she moved

21

forward. "Up here," the voice added unnecessarily, for Nora had already cut a path through the men and was halfway up the stairs.

A moment later she was ushered inside a small room. Nora never noticed the gaudy, red velvet curtains, or thick rugs spread over scuffed, stained floors. She didn't see the grimy walls or dust coated furnishings, nor the long unwashed mirrors over the bed. She wasn't conscious of the tiny, many positioned, coupled figures that were carved into the bed's headboard. Her gaze took in only a very young woman lying amid a pile of red and pink satin pillows. Blood had pooled from a long wound that started just above and to the right of her left breast, ending at a white softly rounded shoulder. It soaked the bed beneath her. Nora issued a quick silent prayer that the wound wasn't deep enough to have damaged a lung. She could tell nothing in one glance, but she feared the worst.

Nora leaned over the terrified woman. "What happened?"

"It was one of those good-for-nothing Willis boys," came the same deep, resounding voice, that had called her upstairs. This time it came from behind Nora's bent figure. "I knew I shouldn't a' let his kind in here. The bastard went crashing out the window when he stuck her."

"He got scared when I yelled," the young frightened woman offered.

Nora smiled and then nodded in silent response, as she examined the wound. The injury wasn't as bad as first imagined. Actually, it had all but stopped bleeding. The knife at entry had hit a bone, but had torn a ragged length of destruction across her chest. The woman was going to carry a nasty scar for the rest of her life.

"Looks like he was a tad upset," Nora said; her sweet, soothing voice brought about an instant calming of her patient.

"You might say that," the injured woman gave what sounded like a giggle at her understatement. "I told him I wouldn't take no more of his beatin's. Don't matter now much money a man has, it don't give him no right to hit me."

Nora nodded at that comment. "I couldn't agree with you more." Her gaze moved to the woman's frightened eyes. "Mazie, is it?"

The woman nodded and then swallowed. The tears streaming over softly rounded cheeks grew in volume at Nora's obvious concern. She made a small sound of fear and Nora realized for the first time that her patient wasn't a woman at all, but a girl. A girl of no more than sixteen. "Am I gonna die?"

Nora smiled. "No, you'll be fine. But it appears you did lose a goodly amount of blood. After a few weeks of rest, you should be—"

"Weeks? What the hell do you mean weeks? I've got a business to run. I can't . . ."

Nora shot the snarling woman behind her a hard look of warning. It went far toward creating the silence she wanted. That was when Nora noticed for the first time, exactly what the woman was wearing. Her eyes widened with some surprise, for she had never met face to face a woman of this particular profession. At least not while so obviously dressed, or undressed as in this case, for work. The woman wore

23

only white stockings and frilly drawers that ended halfway between hip and knee. Above her waist, part of her torso, a very small part in fact, was encased in a tight corset. A corset, so sheer, that it displayed quite clearly her breasts and their large brown nipples. Like the rest of her, her breasts were far from small. Because they swelled above the confining material, their size was only emphasized. Around her plump shoulders hung a red feather boa. Nora turned back to her patient.

"If you'd like," Nora said, her eyes wide, her smile genuine as she forced aside any impulse to pass judgment on either woman, "you can stay with me. There are two empty rooms behind my father's office."

"Oh, I couldn't. I . . ."

"Of course you could. It would save me the trouble of coming here every day to check on you."

"Have you sent for the sheriff?" This she directed at the now silent, half naked woman at the foot of the bed.

"We ain't got no sheriff."

"What do you mean?" Nora frowned as she glanced at the woman again.

"I mean we ain't got none," the madam repeated. "The last one got hisself shot up bad. He died."

Nora gave a silent groan. Wonderful, just wonderful. What else did this town not have? Nora worked at cleaning the wound as she spoke, "Why hasn't the mayor appointed another?"

"'Cause nobody wants the job."

"Then who . . . ?"

"A marshal from Virginia City comes about once

24

a month."

"Send a telegram for him to come now."

"For this?" Fancy, Nora assumed the woman's name was the same as the establishment, looked astonished. "He won't come for this."

Nora nodded, disputing the woman's statement. "He'll come."

"You don't understand. She's only a whore."

"You don't understand, Fancy," Nora snapped back. "This girl is a citizen of this state and entitled to the law's protection." Her eyes narrowed with determination. "Send a wire. If he doesn't come, I'll know why."

Fancy's eyes widened in admiration. This small woman didn't weigh more than ninety pounds and stood not an inch over five feet, and yet she held such authority that Fancy wondered if there was a man in town strong enough to go against her. She chuckled at the thought of this little spitfire being let loose on the male population of this town.

God, she could have made a fortune with someone like her. For just a second, Fancy wondered if she could convince the girl that a change of professions would be beneficial to them both. She watched her for a long moment, noting the determined tilt of her head and the stubbornness of her jaw. No. Just by looking at those clear green eyes, Fancy knew the lady would not be inclined. She sighed and then shrugged aside the thought. It was a shame.

She flung her feather boa around her chubby neck and moved, uncaring of her half naked state to the landing outside the door. "Charlie," her deep voice boomed, while leaning over the railing, "Doc here

25

wants you to telegraph Virginia City for the marshal."

Fancy allowed the men below a good long laugh. But when the howls and guffaws turned into deep chuckles and then dwindled down to an occasional snort, she said simply, "Do it."

Chapter Two

Abigail Morgan left the family's dreary little parlor with a delicate rustling of stiff skirts and stepped daintily into the examining room to find her daughter closing the front door. "Have our guests left already, dear?"

Nora listened to her mother and sighed. Abigail was always expecting the arrival of guests. No matter who it was that came to their door, she imagined them to have come for a social visit. Nora turned to her mother and heaved yet another weary sigh at the blank expression that had greeted her since the last days of the war. She couldn't tell her mother that they hadn't had guests in years and weren't likely to receive any, until they got to know some of the townsfolk. Not an easy chore, since Abigail hardly ever left these rooms.

She bit back the retort, knowing the sharp words would do nothing but cause her mother greater confusion. "Patience," she silently repeated the word again and again. A moment later she met her mother's vague look. "That was Mr. and Mrs. Potter," she said, knowing there was no need to explain for Abigail had already forgotten her question. Still Nora went on, as she slid a copy of her list into her skirt pocket. "They very kindly stopped by to pick up my list."

"How nice, dear," her mother said vaguely.

Nora knew her mother didn't have a notion as to what she was talking about. This time she didn't bother to explain, for Abigail was hardly interested in the practice of medicine.

Mr. Potter was a rancher who lived near Glory. He and his wife, Mary, made two trips a year to San Francisco, to visit with their married daughter. Nora, hearing of the couple's forthcoming trip, imposed upon them to purchase a few badly needed supplies. Supplies that were impossible to obtain except in a large city.

The seemingly endless trip West, along with its many injuries and illnesses, had greatly depleted whatever supplies her father had managed to bring from Atlanta . . . which wasn't much to begin with. Worst of all, the medical closet offered no help at all. The shelves held little more than wood turpentine and herbal remedies such as green persimmon and red garden poppy. There was no way she could treat the people of this town without a decent supply of flint and bandages, not to mention quinine, chloroform, carbolic acid, alcohol, spirits, and so on.

During the war, the blockade imposed by the North had tightened until it shut off any means of obtaining supplies. Left with nothing, the doctors in the South had been forced to improvise with wild herbs and trees. Doctor Le Compte, a friend of her father's had managed to produce alcohol, silver chloride, sulfuric ether and more from native plants. Nora was thankful that those days were behind her, for she much preferred to use the original drug, rather than its substitute.

"Did we have tea?" her mother asked, just a bit upset at not being able to remember. Nora figured that was a good sign. At least she hoped it was. If Abigail wasn't happy with her indistinct thoughts and memories, maybe her mind was trying to get well.

"No, Mother," Nora smiled at the small, delicate lady. The two women looked enough alike to be mistaken for sisters. Both were small and delicately boned. Both had red hair and green eyes. But appearance was as far as the similarity went. Abigail was a refined and delicate lady, and hadn't nearly the strength of her daughter.

Nora sighed wishing she had her mother back, in mind as well as body. And cursed once again that horrible war and all the suffering it had wrought. Perhaps her father was right. Perhaps leaving Atlanta had been the best thing. Hopefully, without the skeletal reminders of a lost war at every turn, her mother would soon be well again. "Why don't we have tea now?"

"That would be lovely, dear," Abigail said as she allowed her daughter to escort her back to the drab parlor. Nora made a mental note to find white paint and perhaps an area rug. Something had to be done to brighten this room.

"Just let me check on Father and then I'll get it."

Abigail laughed. "Silly," she said referring to her daughter's offer to serve. "Jesse will get it." She gave the room another of her vague looks. "Now where did I put that bell?"

Nora flinched and wondered how much longer before Abigail remembered that Jesse, along with everything else she'd ever known and loved, was gone? "I saw Jesse outside. She's working in the garden," Nora said, knowing to tell this fragile, tiny woman the truth would only bring about a fresh bout of tears, and then her eyes would take on that vacant look again as her mind hid the truth away. "I'll do it."

Abigail nodded and smiled pleasantly. She lived more than five years in the past and nothing her daughter or husband did seemed to make any difference. Her mind wouldn't accept the fact that she had nothing left. Not son, not home, not belongings or status. Everything she'd known as a girl, as a young woman, as a new wife and mother, was gone. Somehow her mind had shut down to protect her from the horror of it all. Nora sighed as she left the room and wondered if her mother wasn't better off.

"How are you feeling, Father?"

"Better," her father said as he leaned back against the freshly fluffed pillows. "Much better. I think I'll soon have my strength back. I was up for an hour this morning," he said with a touch of pride at the achievement.

Nora's hand rested for a moment upon his forehead, for she was ever watchful for any possibility of a return of the fever. She smiled in obvious relief to find his skin cool and dry.

"I told you."

Nora grinned. "Just checking."

"Your mother and I had a nice visit. Where is she?"

"In the parlor." Nora's eyes clouded with worry. "Do you think she's . . ."

"Don't fret, child," he said, his hand patting hers. "It will take time."

"It's been years. How much longer?"

"For what, dear?" Abigail asked as she entered her bedroom.

As usual, her mother's dainty steps gave them no notice of her appearance. They both turned at the sound of her voice. "How much longer before Father decides he's had enough rest and gets himself out of that bed, permanently."

"Have you been overtaxing yourself?" Robert Morgan frowned.

"I'd hardly call the little I've done since we've arrived, overtaxing." Nora laughed. "Presently, we have one patient, who will be ready to leave us before the week is out." Nora sighed her disappointment. "It seems the people of this town don't have much faith in a female doctoring. The men in particular."

"They will. You're doing a wonderful job. Soon all hereabouts will know how good you are." Robert grinned. "Then they'll be asking for you instead of me and I'll have to take a backseat to my lovely daughter."

"Oh, yes, backseat, that reminds me," Abigail said, her words making sense only in her own mind, as she settled herself upon a chair near the bed. "You have a gentleman caller, dear."

Nora frowned wondering who that could be. Certainly patients were few and far between. After almost two weeks she'd only had three. Mazie, one little boy who had burned his hand, and a young girl who had cut her finger. Nora realized it was going to take some time before the people of this town trusted her, and there wasn't a thing she could do about it.

"Go ahead, Nora." Her father winked at her, knowing the man was most likely in need of medical attention, for Nora would have mentioned if had she a beau. "Show them what you can do."

Nora checked her appearance in the mirror that hung beside the door that connected the living quarters with the doctor's office, feeling ridiculously nervous for the first time in years. She forced aside the emotion, smoothed a stray wisp of hair into place, even as her hand reached for the door.

Her eyes widened for just a instant as they took in the man standing in the center of the room, his hat in his hands. He was dark, very attractive and had a smile that was endearingly shy. Nora had seen him in town before. He had spoken to her twice. Both times remarking on the weather. She wondered now what he was doing here? "Good morning, suh. Is there something I can do for you?"

Cole Brackston stood in a room that was lined on one wall with empty cots. On the other side of the room sat a large desk and three chairs. A huge cabinet almost covered the wall opposite the door. Cole imagined it housed a variety of medical supplies. His dark eyes twinkled with appreciation as he watched

Nora walk toward him and he grinned as he realized what she'd just said. Lord, a woman, especially a woman who looked as delectable as this one, should know better than to ask a man a question like that. His gaze moved from inquisitive, intelligent eyes to hair the color of fire. Parted in the center, it was drawn back and held with pins at the nape of her neck. The severe style did not lessen her appeal. If anything, it only emphasized her high cheekbones and wide green eyes. He watched as a curling, colorful wisp of hair fell from her tight knot to lie prettily against skin the color of rich cream, unmarred but for a sprinkle of freckles over the bridge of her nose.

"Are you the doctor?" Cole knew she wasn't, but he hadn't made any plans beyond seeing her and he didn't know exactly what to say.

Nora smiled charmingly. "No. My father is the doctor. At the moment, he's not feeling quite himself. If there's a problem, I could . . ." Her voice drifted off as she realized the intensity of his stare. "Are you ill?"

Cole shrugged. He wasn't a man who often lied, but he had tried before to get this woman's attention. Twice he'd made the effort to speak to her, only to see her hurry off, busy with some chore. When he'd come here, he hadn't had a plan. All he wanted was to get to know this woman. At the moment he was wondering if he shouldn't come up with some ailment. What better way to meet her?

Going slowly wasn't exactly the way Cole did things. When he saw something he wanted, he used every means at his disposal to get it. Right now, with her looking so soft and pretty, her cheeks high with color and growing more so the longer he looked at her, Cole knew he wanted to get to know her in every way possible. He wasn't about to lose his chance with her by being overly truthful.

Word had it her father was ill and her mother not quite right in the head. Cole figured that was a lot of responsibility to lay on shoulders so small. He figured that she could use a bit of fun. He sure as hell knew he could.

"Now that you mention it, I am feelin' a bit poorly."

"Now that *I* mention it?" Nora's brow furrowed in confusion. "You mean you weren't feeling poorly before I mentioned it? And yet you came to see a doctor?"

"Well, you see . . ."

"Why don't you sit down and tell me what ails you."

Cole sat in a chair by the desk. "It's my throat, I think." Cole figured he'd be safe enough with that complaint.

Nora murmured a low sound. The man had made the effort to come and see her, why then was he so reluctant to tell her the real reason? "You think it's your throat? Is it sore?"

"Some."

"Let's have a look," she said as she gathered her supplies from a small black bag that sat on the corner of the desk.

God, this woman's sugary, sweet voice did something to his stomach that no voice ever did before. She sounded as beautiful as she looked and that was saying something.

"Open your mouth," she said as she leaned down. Cole obeyed.

Nora looked inside, and pressed his tongue down a bit with a wooden depressor. After a few minutes, Nora said, "Your throat looks fine. It's not the least bit red. Your tonsils are pink, no inflammation." She came to her full height again, her eyes clouded and puzzled.

"Now that sure is odd, Miss Morgan."

"It's Mrs. Bowens."

"You're married? But I thought . . ."

"I lost my husband at Gettysburg, suh."

"Oh, I'm sorry." Cole said the right words but his voice was filled with relief, not pity. In truth he wasn't the least bit sorry to hear this particular woman was available.

"Is it giving you a lot of pain?"

"What?"

"Your throat."

Cole looked at her with some real puzzlement until he remembered his supposed ailment. "Oh, my throat." Cole smiled sickly. This wasn't working out at all. He never should have started this. He should have just told her he wanted to see her. He was a fool to chance her anger and now that he had, he couldn't do anything but forge on. Silently he swore he'd never do anything so stupid again.

Cole couldn't know that Nora already suspected his ailment to be nonexistent. He might have felt some hope if he'd known that she thought the situation mildly amusing and was at this moment wondering what she could do to teach him a well-earned lesson.

"Well, maybe not a lot, but . . ."

"It's bothersome?"

He nodded vigorously, thankful to find a way out. "Yeah, bothersome." And then despite his best intentions he heard himself say, "My . . . chest hurts too."

Nora bit her lip, trying to hold back her laughter. She put her stethoscope just inside the collar of his shirt and listened to the steady rhythm of his healthy heart.

"You want me to unbutton my shirt?"

Nora jumped at the sound of his voice loud and clear in her ears. She shot him a stern look. "I want you to be quiet."

She was close . . . so close he could smell her. His gaze moved over thickly fringed eyes, lowered for the moment in concentration. White teeth bit gently at her lower lip and Cole had to hold back a groan as he imagined it was his teeth sinking into that soft flesh.

He breathed deeply, trying to control the things her nearness was doing to him. Only breathing deeply had much the opposite effect. It drew in her scent and caused him to squirm uncomfortably in order to hide an unwanted arousal.

She smelled wonderful. Clean and sweet, not at all like Fancy's girls, who could have used less perfume and more soap and water. Cole's gaze moved to her throat. Her skin was the color of rich cream, smooth and unmarred by the harsh sun. He almost sighed his disappointment as he followed the length of her graceful neck until it disappeared into the high collar of her dress.

Her green eyes were wide, clear and guileless, filled

with none of the provocative sophistication he was used to seeing in his women. Thickly fringed with dark lashes, they brought to mind the most erotic thoughts. Cole couldn't help but imagine what they would look like when clouded with passion. Her nose was straight and small, her chin, just a bit too firm. And surrounding all that beauty was hair the color of dark flame. Cole held his hands tightly in his lap lest he give into the need to sink his fingers into its fiery thickness. She was beautiful and Cole couldn't imagine why the men in this town weren't banging down her door, trying to get to her. Unless they were scared. He grinned at the thought. They probably were scared. He forced back the need to laugh. Imagine grown men afraid of a tiny little thing like her, just because she was smart. Well maybe not as smart as he was, he reasoned cockily, but she had to be plenty smart to work at doctoring.

Nora listened for a long moment. His breathing was slightly uneven, but his lungs were clear and his heartbeat strong and steady. As far as she could tell, there was no reason why his chest should hurt. It wasn't until she raised her gaze to his that she noticed the humor in their dark depths.

"Are you laughing?"

Cole desperate to find a reasonable excuse, mumbled, "That thing is cold."

Nora's gaze followed his to the stethoscope. She made no comment, but simply put her equipment away. "Have you been coughing?"

"All night long," he lied. "I can't get any sleep." The last was partly true. He hadn't been sleeping much lately, but his tossing and turning had nothing to do with coughing. It had to do with thoughts of this lady.

"How long has this been going on?"

"A few days. Maybe a week."

Nora walked around her desk and sat. Cole wasn't happy to see her move away. He never thought to hold back his sigh of disappointment.

Nora's head snapped up at the sound. Her hand still positioned over the paper she was writing on. "What's the matter?"

"Nothing."

"You sighed. Something's the matter. What is it?"

"I can't tell you," Cole said, as an idea came suddenly to mind. Over the years, he'd spoken to many women about sex, but none of those women were anything like her. He wondered just how far he could push and realized that what he had in mind shocked even him. Cole wondered if he dared say it, and knew before the thought became clear in his mind, he would. "You're a woman. It might be better if I talked to a man."

Cole couldn't have known it, but he said exactly the right words. "Don't think of me as a woman. Think of me as a nurse. There's nothing I haven't heard before."

Cole almost grinned. He'd wager there were one or two things she hadn't heard yet. "All right then, I can't . . . you know." He forced his gaze from hers and stared at the desk, hoping he looked properly embarrassed.

Nora frowned at his cryptic reply. "Actually, I don't know," she returned. "You'll have to be more specific. What is it you can't do?"

"Women. I can't . . . Well," he shrugged. "I'm afraid I'll never be able to have children."

Nora felt her cheeks darken with heat. Lord, but this man was bold. It took her a moment, but once she recovered from her initial shock, she could see the tiny smile that teased one corner of his mouth. She had administered to all sorts of men these last years and not once had any one of them been so forward.

Cole saw the look of shock in her eyes and forced an innocence he was far from feeling into his gaze. "You said you're a nurse and that I could tell you."

Nora swallowed and prayed for courage. Oddly enough she felt no anger. Instead she found herself forcing back the urge to laugh. He was a devil and needed badly to be put in his place.

"Do you have something I could . . . take?" Cole watched carefully the sudden narrowing of her eyes. "Could you do something that would . . ." His gaze rested for an indecent amount of time upon her breasts. ". . . help me?"

Again his dark gaze moved to hers. What was she thinking? Did he dare hope that she would take it upon herself to cure such an ailment, with perhaps personal interest? His lip beaded with sweat at the thought, but Cole forced his gaze to appear wide and innocent as he awaited her response.

"I have just the thing," Nora said as she left her chair and moved to the medicine cabinet.

"Do you?" Cole asked in amazement. Actually, he didn't know there was such an ailment. He'd made the whole thing up.

"This should fix you up in no time." Nora said as she poured two fingers of liquid into a glass and

39

returned with the peculiar looking brew in hand. There was no way Cole was swallowing that.

"What is it?"

"It's medicine. It will help. I promise."

"I don't want it."

"Of course you do."

"I don't." Cole was speaking through clenched teeth as Nora held the glass to his mouth.

"Come on now. Be brave. One big swallow and it will be all over."

That's just what he was afraid of.

Cole gagged as the liquid was almost poured down his throat. He made a horrified face, clearly telling of his disgust. "What in the hell was that?"

Nora laughed at his dramatic reaction and placed the glass on the desk. "Mineral oil and a touch of blue mass."

Cole grimaced and then shuddered at the oily mixture still upon his tongue. "What's blue mass?"

"Mercury and chalk."

Cole forced back the need to gag. He shuddered again. "What's it used for?"

Nora grinned as she sat a hip on her desk. "Many doctors believe that open bowels are the beginning of good health."

Cole groaned. He had no need to ask, he knew the truth of it. "And you just opened mine."

Nora grinned. "No need to thank me. I was happy to do it."

"I thought I had you fooled," he groaned morosely.

"Why did you really come here? Your throat doesn't hurt."

Cole hung his head, managing at once to look properly chastised and devilishly appealing. His dark eyes twinkled wickedly as he remarked, "I should have thought of something else."

"I'd say you've thought of quite a number of things. Most of them improper, to say the least."

He controlled his need to laugh, but his eyes fairly danced with the emotion. "I had to talk to you."

"About what?"

"*Us.*"

Nora grinned as she returned to her seat. "Are you always this bold?"

Cole took heart at the laughter in her eyes. "Only when I see something I want."

"What is your name?"

"Cole Brackston. I'm twenty-three and I live ten miles north of town. I'm kind to children and animals. I've never raised a hand to a woman in my life and I promise to cherish the one I marry and give her as many children as she wants."

Nora's eyes rounded with surprise and a smile curved her mouth. "That's quite a speech."

"I meant every word of it."

Nora leaned back in her chair and studied the man opposite her. He had dark hair and eyes. His features were even, his skin not nearly as weathered as most of the men who lived out here. He was dressed in black boots, dark trousers, a blue cotton work shirt and black, leather vest. Even so casually dressed, Nora had to admit he was one of the best-looking men she'd ever seen. Nora couldn't deny she was flattered that he had gone to such lengths to make himself known to her. She figured there were better ways to go

41

about it, but she also imagined he'd probably learned his lesson. At least he most certainly would in a few hours. "I should be furious with you."

"But you're not."

Nora couldn't resist his smile. She answered it with one of her own. "I cannot condone what you did, Mr. Brackston, but no, I'm not."

Nora smiled and said as she rose from the chair and walked toward the door, "If your cough gets worse, please don't hesitate to come back. I can give you another—"

He cut her off. Just the thought of swallowing another dose of the wretched brew made him want to heave. "I'm sure I'll be fine."

Nora laughed again. "You're probably right. Still I could take another look at your throat, if need be."

Cole definitely enjoyed the notion, only he wanted her to look at more than his throat. His mouth went dry as a picture of her and him together, each taking in their fill of one another came to mind. Wisely he said nothing. At the door he paid her fee and just as he was about to leave, asked, "Would you like to go to the church picinc this Sunday?"

Nora blinked her surprise. A church picnic? Lord, it had been years since she'd last done anything so frivolous. "I hadn't heard . . ."

"The preacher is tacking signs all over town."

Nora smiled again and a light of anticipation entered her eyes. She wanted nothing more than to go to the picnic with this charming, if slightly wicked, man. She desperately needed an afternoon away from her responsibilities. But the moment she acknowledged the thought, the light in her eyes suddenly extinguished. "I'm sorry. I wish I could, but my father is ill and my mother," she gave a tiny shrug, "well she is . . ."

"I'll have one of the girls from the ranch sit with your father and we'll take your mother with us," Cole interrupted, easily dismissing her excuses. He gave her his most charming smile and waited as she wrestled with her desire to go and her obligation to stay.

Despite the fact that Cole had more than his share of confidence, when it came to women, he couldn't prevent a sigh of relief when Nora said, "I'd love to go."

Chapter Three

Jake Brackston watched with an indulgent smile as his six-year-old son Matt darted between tables, heavy with food. He'd been listless and feverish lately, and it was a relief to finally see him well again.

No sooner had the boy started running, then he was joined by two others, of about the same age. A minute later there were five children running in and out of the crowd, diving wildly beneath the tables.

Jake shook his head. It didn't take much to imagine that before long someone was going to get hurt, or at the very least one of those tables was going to be sent flying to the ground. "Matt," his father called out. "If you want to run, do it over there." Jake pointed to the flat field, of dry, waist-high grass, behind the church and all five boys took off. They ran as fast as small legs could manage; their exuberant cries of freedom, echoing loudly behind them.

Jake stood watching for a long moment, before he

joined the men at the barrel of ale. It was a good day. The sun was bright, the sky clear and much like his son, Jake was looking forward to an afternoon spent in the company of his peers.

Jake, a quiet man, was not one to socialize much. All of his time, spare or otherwise, was spent caring for his ranch and his son. There was little time left over to dally with neighbors.

Jake was a bit of a loner. Except for his son and his brother, he took no one into his confidence. Jake had been born in a brothel, the son of one of San Francisco's most infamous whores, the father unknown. The only schooling he'd had was of the flesh and that at the hands of well-practiced whores. He hadn't shunned their expert tutelage. Indeed, he'd enjoyed immensely those long lazy Sunday afternoons when the women had nothing to do but play with a young boy. Still, even as a boy, Jake was far from stupid. In truth he was smarter than most, for Jake compensated for his lack of education with inherent intelligence, sharp instinct, and a will to succeed.

And that he had. Starting with nothing, he'd taken a desolate piece of land and adding year after year, had made it into one of Nevada's largest and most prosperous cattle ranches.

When it came time to marry, he chose a lovely woman. A woman he believed at the time of high morals. It wasn't until his return from the war that he found out differently. It wasn't until then that he discovered Emma was about to leave him. She'd had enough of the loneliness of ranching and a neighbor's son, Miles O'Malley had convinced her to run off with him.

They had shouted terrible, unforgivable words that night and Emma had run from his black menacing rage, only to be thrown from her horse and died, all within a day of his return. There were whispered comments after that. Some believed he had killed his wife in a jealous rage. Others might have believed the same, but imagined a soldier returning home had the right to expect his wife to have remained true. Jake shrugged. It mattered little what folks believed. Idly he wondered if God, assuming of course such a deity existed, hadn't punished him for daring to pull himself out of a gutter and claim a life, a standing in the community, that he had no right to expect. He hoped not, because he was about to dare it again.

Lately he'd been traveling the ten miles that separated his home from town at least once a week. He'd been visiting Mary Cummings, a woman who had been widowed more than a year ago. Jake figured he'd probably marry Mary. Maybe he didn't love her, but she was a nice woman, easy to get along with and damn it, he needed someone. The nights were endless and empty after Matt went to bed and it had been so incredibly long since he'd held a warm caring female body close to his.

Sure he occasionally visited the women at Fancy's. He was a man after all and a man had certain needs, but he needed more than the easing of lust, over and done in an hour or so. He wanted a woman in his bed. Someone he could turn to at night, someone who would share his life, listen to his problems and bring him a sense of contentment.

As he gained maturity, sex became secondary to a greater need. He wanted stability and maybe another child. In order to have that, he'd have to marry again.

He'd gone off to war only a year after he and Emma had married. The day after he returned, he found himself alone again, only this time with a four-year-old son to care for. White Moon had done a good job seeing to the boy, but Matt needed a mother and he a wife.

It had taken the last two years to get his ranch back into shape. Cole had done what he could, but the ranch, despite the fact that it belonged equally to both brothers, wasn't Cole's chief love and all had been done in a haphazard fashion. Jake's mouth drew down and a crease furrowed his forehead as he remembered the endless work and loneliness. His expression showed not a glimmer of the joy he should have known at his decision. Yes, he would marry Mary. Besides his needs, Matt needed the softening influence of a lady in the house. The boy was likely to grow up too wild and rough as things stood now.

Nora couldn't remember the last time she'd fussed with her appearance. It had to be just before her wedding six years ago, she reasoned. Nora felt a tightening around her heart when she remembered that poignant day. Johnny had left the next day to join his regiment, only to die two months later during a skirmish so small and insignificant it hadn't justified a name. Nora's lips twisted into a humorless smile. Insignificant or not, it had been deadly enough to have left her a widow. They'd had only one night together, and she'd never seen him again.

If only . . . Nora breathed a long sigh and then put aside her sense of loss. This wasn't the time to think on what might have been. Today was the church picnic and a most handsome and enjoyable young man would be here within minutes to escort her. She'd forget for a few hours the responsibility that weighed heavily on her shoulders and simply enjoy this day.

Nora hadn't realized until now just how much she needed this day. Her eyes danced with excitement. She felt like a girl again as she smiled at her reflection and twisted her long, red hair into a slightly more elaborate knot than usual. She allowed a few tendrils of flaming color to fall around her face, the effect was a deliciously feminine picture. A frilly parasol took the place of a bonnet. Its pink satin trim matched her one and only gown. Petticoats flared out the material to a lovely circle at her small feet and emphasized the slenderness of her waist and back.

Nora wasn't aware of just how lovely a picture she made. All she knew was a sense of anxious excitement.

"Good God, you're gorgeous!"

Nora grinned at Cole's obvious shock and shot him a reproachful glance as she opened the door wider. "You needn't sound so surprised. It's not the least bit complimentary."

He couldn't stop staring. She was the most beautiful woman he'd ever seen, and Cole had seen plenty. Her dress was a modest confection of satin

49

and lace. To his disappointment, it came all the way to a neat demure ruffle at the base of her throat, but it hugged her body, thank God, and showed clearly her lush curves. Her breasts were fuller than he'd imagined, and Cole had done quite a bit of imagining on that score. All he'd seen her in thus far were loosely fitted calico dresses and aprons that hid her charms and only hinted at a tiny waist. She took a man's breath away. "I didn't mean . . ."

"Did you expect to find me in my usual gray or brown calico?" Nora usually wore the somber colors to inspire a sense of respect and confidence from those in need of her care. Besides, bows and lace were far from appropriate, when caring for those taken ill.

"I didn't know what to expect. Certainly not the sight of an angel until I reach heaven."

"And you expect that, do you? To reach heaven, I mean?" Nora's expression told him clearly her own doubts on the subject.

Cole laughed. "Now that I've been blessed with knowing what awaits me, beyond those pearly gates, I will. I promise you, I will."

Nora grinned and fluttered her eyelashes just as if she were a young girl again. "Verrry gooood," she said and dragged out the words with low, husky laughter, oblivious to the sudden pain the sound brought to Cole's gut.

It was only then that Nora noticed the young girl standing almost directly behind Cole. Cole saw the direction of her gaze and introduced the girl. "This is Mina. I brought her along to look after your father." Nora blinked her surprise. Mina wasn't as young as first supposed. Nora imagined her in her late teens.

Tall, lovely and delicately boned, she wore her long black hair loose to her hips. Her dark almond shaped eyes were raised timidly from tightly clenched hands at the introduction, but she barely returned Nora's smile. Nora imagined she knew the reason the moment the girl looked in Cole's direction, for her dark eyes took on a yearning so intense that Nora was left without a doubt that the girl was in love with this man. And by the way Cole spoke and looked at her, it was obvious he hadn't a clue to the girl's feelings. Nora imagined he rarely looked her way and if he did, probably never saw her as another might.

"Mother is almost ready. Why don't you come in, while we wait?"

Nora left Cole in the parlor as she introduced Mina to her father.

"Do you have much opportunity to use that charm around here?" Nora asked conversationally when she returned to the family parlor.

Cole grinned, his dark eyes moving with obvious appreciation over the curve of her waist and the hint of rounded bottom that the swaying, full skirt hardly allowed. "It's not easy, what with the lack of women in these parts, but I try."

"I'm sure you do more than try."

The two of them were still laughing when Abigail Morgan entered the room.

"I'm the most envied man here."

Nora smiled as she looked up at his grin. "Why?"

"I'm the only one with a beautiful woman on each arm," Cole said to the ladies.

Abigail smiled at the compliment. Today wasn't one of her better days. In truth, she appeared more confused than ever and Nora knew she'd make it a point to stay near her, just in case she was needed. "I don't see any of our friends, Nora. Where do you suppose everyone's gone?"

Nora shot Cole a worried glance. "I'm sure they'll be along soon, Mother. Why don't we make new friends while we have the chance?"

Abigail blinked her surprise at the outrageous thought. "Surely you're not suggesting we simply walk up to a stranger and introduce ourselves."

"I'll introduce you. I know everyone here," Cole offered helpfully.

"Would you? Oh, I'd be ever so grateful, Mr . . ." Abigail gave a helpless, vague smile.

"Brackston, ma'am. Call me Cole."

Her heart filled with gratitude, Nora gave Cole one of her sweetest smiles. He was a nice man. With patience and gentleness, he'd told her mother his name at least four times now. Despite his earlier disgraceful conduct and his obviously wicked tendencies, Nora had to admit that she liked him very much indeed.

Cole did as he promised and the two women were soon introduced to half the town's population. Not that either of them, most especially Abigail, would remember name to face. Nora reasoned all would come together in time.

"Are you confused enough, ma'am?"

"I think so, Mr. Brackston." Nora laughed at his teasing smile and the devilish light that forever shone in the dark depths of his eyes. "Is this your revenge

52

for my administrating the remedy?"

Cole shot her a wicked glance that promised all sorts of retaliation. "That was a purely evil thing to do. All I wanted . . ."

"Was evil things done to you."

Cole's eyes widened and he laughed as he realized the double entendre.

"Then you shouldn't be looking at me with vengeance, Mr. Brackston. After all, I was as evil as I could possibly manage."

"Lord, I can attest to that." His gaze told clearly of his suffering caused by her dose.

Nora laughed with genuine delight. Every man within hearing turned at the sound. It was deliciously low and sweetly seductive. Nora never noticed.

They stood near a tall man. His back had been to them, but at the sound of her laughter he turned. Beside him stood a woman who smiled sweetly, and Nora would later think quite stupidly, into his dark handsome face.

Jake watched his brother duck his head under a frilly umbrella, nod, and then move off leaving two women alone. Moments later he returned with lemonade for all three. Jake grinned and wondered when was the last time his brother had indulged in the nonalcoholic brew?

Cole noticed his brother's smile and escorted the two ladies toward him. "Mrs. Morgan, Nora, this is my brother Jake. Jake," Cole said, "I want you to meet my friends."

Jake's gaze moved from his brother to the women at his side. He neither noticed the older woman nor heard the introduction. Had he listened then, a great deal of misunderstanding might have been avoided.

Jake's eyes widened, as Nora moved aside her frilly umbrella. It was only then that Jake had the opportunity to see the woman holding onto his brother's arm. Had he taken a blow to his stomach, he couldn't have felt more breathless as his blue eyes met hers. God, but she was a beauty.

Despite the fact that Jake had first seen her cavorting in the street with one of her customers, there was no doubt in his mind that she was no ordinary whore. She dressed like a lady. One of Fancy's girls wouldn't be seen dead in a dress half so modest. Jake's brow creased into a puzzled frown. There was a time when he could spot a lady of the night on first glance. It came as a surprise that this one should make him question his first impression.

Still, his brother never accompanied decent women. She might not be so common as to work for Fancy, but she was something almost as bad. She was with Cole and Jake knew well enough what that meant. She was his woman.

His mouth twisted into a scowl and he felt an unreasonable spurt of anger as he imagined the two of them together. He felt his belly tighten and wondered why that fact should bother him? What the hell was going on here? What was he upset about? It didn't matter none to him who touched this woman. It was none of his business. His voice was little more than a husky hiss, "Ladies," he said, as he touched the brim of his hat.

Cole grinned at his brother's less than gracious

response. "You'll have to forgive my brother, Nora. The man spends too much time talking to his horse. He doesn't know how to treat a lady."

Nora smiled at Cole's teasing remark. She recognized the man as the one who had saved her from the drunk and smiled again. "We weren't formally introduced, but Mr. Brackston and I have met before. I'd like to thank you again for coming to my rescue."

"Rescue?" Cole said, obviously confused. His brother hadn't mentioned meeting Nora before.

"Yeah, I found her under a drunk, lying in the gutter."

Nora hissed a sound of shock as his unnecessarily harsh words registered. Her gaze moved to the older brother and she realized with some surprise the dislike in Jake Brackston's eyes. For just a second she wondered what she'd done to inspire that emotion? An instant later she shrugged off the question, ignored the man, and turned toward Cole as she explained. "The night we arrived in town, I was heading for the saloon, hoping to find someone who could give me directions to our quarters when a man came flying, quite suddenly, from inside the swinging doors. He knocked me to the ground and no doubt decided I was to be his mattress for the night. Your brother saved me."

Only half listening to her explanation, Jake's gaze never left her face, even as he wondered what kind of special magic his brother possessed. How did he always get the prettiest women to join him in bed?

Before either of them had a chance to go on, Abigail glanced at the woman standing almost directly behind Jake and her eyes widened with recognition. "Mary Standings?" A great smile curved her gentle mouth, and her eyes lost their usual vagueness. "Lord 'a mercy honey, what are you doing here? Why, last I heard you'd moved North with your new husband."

Mary smiled at her sister's friend. "That was ten years ago and it was North and then West. It's Mary Cummings, now." Within seconds the two women moved off in conversation. But it wasn't the sister of her mother's best friend that caught Nora's interest. It was the huge man who stood in a wide legged, arrogant stance before her. Nora never expected his next remark. "You Cole's woman now?"

Nora felt herself gasp at the outrageous words. She'd never before been the recipient of so blunt or so offensive a question. Therefore she found herself somewhat surprised by the ability to answer the man. "As a matter of fact, no, I'm not."

"Jake! What the hell's the matter with you?" And then he glanced at Nora and realized what he'd said. "Sorry, ma'am," he muttered.

"Nothin's the matter with me. I just know the kind of woman you keep."

The man was outrageous. How dare he assume that she belonged to anyone? "I'm afraid you're mistaken in this case. No one keeps me, suh." Nora was growing more upset by the minute. Just who did this man think he was? How dare he pass judgment on her?

"I reckon you're a lady, a true Southern belle," he jeered, his voice filled with disgust, for he knew the treachery of her kind. "Should I apologize?" he drawled in his Western twang. He didn't know why, but he couldn't stop his tongue from issuing the most insulting words. The truth of the matter was, he didn't like her. He wasn't sure why exactly, but her being a Southerner didn't help things any. Her eyes were green and glared at him with angry golden sparks. What color would they be, he wondered, when she was hot, soft and sobbing her pleasure beneath a man. Jake felt himself stiffen at the thought. What the hell did he care? He didn't want her, wouldn't have her if she begged to come to his bed.

"There's no need. I care little what you think of me, suh." Nora turned to Cole and while fluttering her eyelashes outrageously, instantly acquired the deepest accent any of the three had ever heard. "Why don't we watch the races, Cole, darlin'?"

Cole's body grew rock hard and his dark eyes narrowed with warning as he glared at the taller man. The words said might be downright insulting, but it was the look of hunger in Jake's eyes that bothered him most. Cole moved closer to Nora and cursed the fact that he didn't dare put a possessive arm around that tiny waist. "I guess I owe you," he said reluctantly.

Jake tried to remain unaffected by her gently spoken words. The problem was, he couldn't. She was the most beautiful woman he'd ever seen and all he could think was his brother was treating himself to her charms.

"It was nothing," Jake shrugged aside his brother's gratitude, while wondering how the hell he could live with himself if he tried to take this woman for his own? Even if he wanted her, and he didn't, his family meant more to him than any woman ever could. He gave a mental shrug. He didn't cotton much to redheads anyway. They reminded him too much of his mother.

They were standing at the edge of the town's only street, awaiting the beginning of the race. "Cole darlin', would you be a dear and refill this?" She handed him her empty glass. "My throat is parched."

Cole grinned at Nora's heavy drawl. He hadn't missed her sudden use of endearments either and rightly assumed it was because she was annoyed with his brother. Cole's eyes narrowed as he wondered what really happened that night. But at Nora's beautiful wide-eyed appeal, he grinned, "I'll be right back. You will watch her for me, won't you Jake?" Cole left without waiting for an answer.

"I reckon," Jake said so softly he might have been talking to himself. He stood rock still, saying nothing, while the tension between them grew to enormous proportions.

Nora had never felt so uncomfortable in her entire life. "There's no need, Mr. Brackston," Nora said as she decided that he was the most rude and uncommunicative man she'd ever met. "I assure you, I can take care of myself."

"Think so? Is that why I found you lying in the gutter?"

"That was a mishap, a misunderstanding. I was in no danger. I'm sure the man would have understood what was happening eventually."

"It was a stupid thing to do. No decent woman would think of goin' into Fancy's."

Another insult. It was obvious that this beast was

inferring that she was far from decent. Nora could feel her cheeks blaze with fury. She didn't know how she managed to control herself, but she knew she'd likely die before she'd honor his remark with a response. Nora turned away with an obvious snub. "If you'll excuse me . . ."

Jake caught her arm, holding her firmly in place. "What are you doing here with my brother?"

Nora's eyes widened incredulously at this man's unbelievable audacity. Her gaze moved to long, brown fingers wrapped firmly around her arm and then back to blazing blue eyes. For endless moments their eyes clashed, neither willing to be the first to look away. She wrenched her arm free of his hold. "Where I go and with whom I go with is hardly any of your concern."

"Everyone in this town is gonna' think—"

"What?"

"That you're his woman."

"Well then they'll be wrong, won't they?"

"He don't see none but the girls at Fancy's."

"Meaning, of course, that I must be one of them?" Nora spoke through her teeth and wondered how they didn't crumble into dust from the pressure her jaw was exerting.

He shrugged.

"If I were, how is it any of your business?"

"Are you?"

"As a matter of fact, I'm not."

"Then you're Cole's mistress. That's almost as bad."

"Meaning it's all right for a man to have a mistress, but not for a woman to be that mistress."

Jake grinned. The light in his eyes told clearly she understood the double standard.

"If you don't mind my asking, how can one be wrong and the other right?" She shrugged. "After all, a man can hardly participate in such a pasttime without a woman, now can he?"

Jake shrugged. "It's the way things are, I reckon."

Forget about her teeth. Nora figured her jaw bone was ready to crack from the pressure. "Yes, well, I reckon," she said amazingly calm as she mimicked his slow Western drawl, "your opinion is of equal value to a wart on a horse's behind."

Jake laughed out loud. His obvious enjoyment only made her angrier.

"Amazing," she said and as she tried to find yet another worthy insult, her gaze moved over his handsome face. Jake looked much like his brother, but harder, darker, more manly. Nora wondered why that fact should cause her stomach to tremble? Instantly she denied the thought. It didn't. There was no reason on earth why it should.

It hardly mattered what this man looked like. She didn't care that his hair was as dark as Cole's, longer and possibly thicker. What difference could it make that his eyes were blue, so blue in fact that despite her anger, Nora couldn't help but compare them to a summer sky? So what? She looked long and hard before she realized she was trying to find something wrong with that face. She gave up. It wasn't the face that repelled, but the man behind it.

His brows were heavy and black, as was his mustache. Shallow lines bracketed his mouth, his cheeks were slightly hollow, his jaw firm and square.

Nora ignored the fact that he was attractive in a dark, rough sort of way. At least he could be, if he ever allowed that scowl to leave his mouth. But Nora had seen attractive men before and none had ever caused her this extreme emotion. That's because none, handsome or otherwise, had ever been so openly insulting, she silently returned.

"What's amazing?"

"That you and Cole are related. Most often brothers are somewhat alike."

"I've been told we look alike."

"Indeed, but the similarity ends there, doesn't it?"

"Meaning?"

"Meaning, Cole is a very nice man."

"So I've heard," he returned dryly and then shot her a hard, sardonic grin. "I reckon it's in bed where he's nicest."

"While you can't even count on that," Nora snapped in return and then gasped at her thoughtless remark. Where had it come from? Certainly she had no idea whether he could or couldn't, and she wasn't the least bit interested in finding out.

Jake laughed, the sound so filled with arrogance that Nora's palms itched with the need to strike his face. For the first time since meeting her, Jake felt himself relax. She was mad, spittin' mad. He couldn't remember the last time a woman had so intrigued him. Maybe he didn't know how to sweet-talk a woman, but he sure as hell knew how to please one in bed. He and Cole were the results of his mother's chosen profession. Neither had known their fathers and both had come to manhood at the hands of experienced whores. No man knew more

61

about how to please a woman. "You're wrong." His thumbs hooked into his belt and his fingers curled in a relaxed pose, almost cupping the bulge in his tight black pants. His hips jutted forward just a fraction, and Nora felt her cheeks flame with color. She couldn't tear her gaze from his most improper stance, not until she heard his soft wicked laughter. "But if you're that interested, I could show you—"

"I'm not interested at all, thank you," she quickly interrupted, while silently raining every curse word she could think of upon this man's head. "And no, you won't be showing me a thing, and for that I'll be thankin' the Almighty every chance I get."

She was a spitfire. Jake could only imagine what it would be like with her in his bed. Damn, this one would probably rip his back apart. He felt himself growing uncomfortably hard at the thought.

"If you'll excuse me," she said as she made to step away from his disagreeable company, only to be stopped again as he had the audacity to again reach for her arm.

"I'd advise you, suh, to release me this instant," she said as she closed her umbrella and pointed it threateningly toward his midsection.

Jake grinned. He might not like this one's sugary speech or uppity attitude, but she sure as hell was a looker. And the angrier she got the better she looked.

"My brother asked me to watch over you."

Nora laughed. "Are you always this rude, obnoxious, and disgustingly arrogant when watching over someone?"

Jake lit a cheroot and squinted down as smoke

gathered beneath the brim of his hat. "What did I say . . . ?"

"You don't like me, for what reason I cannot fathom," she gnashed her teeth. "But you've made yourself abundantly clear."

"Why, Miss Nora," Jake said mimicking her accent, "I surely don't know what you're talking about."

Nora didn't bother to comment on his mockery. Her eyes narrowed with sudden insight. "You're upset. Why?" she asked knowing with absolute certainty that he was. It wasn't that he looked outwardly angry, but there was something deadly in his quiet, supposedly relaxed stance. "You look ready to murder someone."

"Do I?" he asked, "You don't look none too happy right now either."

"I wonder why?" she said sarcastically.

"Maybe you're hankerin' to find out if I'm better than Cole. That kinda' need sometimes makes for a prickly tongue in a woman."

Nora took two deep breaths before she dared open her mouth. What was the use? The man believed she and Cole were lovers. It seemed not to matter how strenuously or often she denied it, he was bound to believe what he would. Nora figured maybe he'd leave her alone if she allowed him to believe the worst. She took one more breath and smiled stiffly, "I'm sorry, but the thought never crossed my mind. No one could be that good."

Jake had never felt so intense a response to a woman in his life. His eyes narrowed as he searched her beautiful face. God, she was something. How had he imagined when he'd first seen her that she wasn't spectacular? Still, he'd seen beautiful women before. Why, he wondered, did just the thought of this one in Cole's bed make him want to rip his brother's throat out?

Because she belonged to Cole. He didn't have to hear her admit it to know the truth of the matter. He took a deep breath, trying to calm the almost insane need to take her in his arms, right here, before all these people. A second later he almost groaned aloud as her scent filled his being. Jake, his thumbs still hooked in his belt, leaned back, trying to control the things she was doing to his body. He said the first words that came to mind. "What do you want with my brother?"

Nora laughed with surprise. "Is that what this is all about? Are you upset because your brother is escorting me today?"

Jake snorted a sound that might have passed for laughter. It didn't quite make it. "I ain't jealous, if that's what you're thinkin'. You ain't got nothin' I want," his sneer turned his mouth down at the corners.

Nora's eyes remained fixed on that mouth for a long moment. She fought back the wildly insane thoughts that were suddenly careening through her brain. What, she wondered, would it feel like to have that mouth pressed against hers? Would it feel as hard as it looked? Would his mustache tickle? She gave a slight shake of her head and forced herself to remember the intensity of his words. They were hard and cruel, but they weren't true. Something was happening here. Something she didn't understand,

64

but she knew he was lying.

"You tryin' to get him in your clutches?" Jake asked.

As if she could. Nora almost giggled at the thought. She didn't know whether to be further insulted or consider his words a compliment. Certainly, she'd never considered the possibility of having such powers before. But whether she did or didn't was hardly Jake's business. "Cole is a grown man. I doubt that he would be pleased at your interference."

Jake was just about to tell her he couldn't care less if Cole was pleased or not, when he was interrupted with, "Papa?"

Both Nora and Jake looked at the little boy standing in the little space that separated their straining, angry bodies. Both wondered exactly how long he'd been there and what he'd heard?

"What is it, Matt?"

"My side hurts again," the boy said, while holding his open palm over the lower right side of his stomach.

"Does it?" Jake asked, concerned as he knelt before his son. Damn, he had hoped this illness was gone for good. Jake's hand reached for his son's forehead and found it a little warm. "Maybe you'd better sit down for awhile."

Nora's eyes widened as she watched his gentle concern. She'd never have believed the man had it in him. "Has it bothered him before?" Nora asked as she leaned over and pressed her hand to the boy's forehead.

Nora ignored Jake's sharp look that told her

clearly he didn't appreciate her interference. Because Jake had left her question unanswered, Nora leaned closer and asked the boy, "Has it bothered you before?"

Matt, the miniature of his father, grimaced and then nodded. His eyes were the same blue, his hair easily as dark. Nora felt a tugging in the region of her heart. He was a beautiful child and she was loath to see him in pain.

All anger toward his father was forgotten as she offered, "If you take him to my father's office, I'll be glad to look him over."

Jake growled as he shook her suggestion off. "Lady, it'll be years yet before my son'll be ready for your kind."

His meaning went over her head.

"What?" Nora straightened, her eyes wide with confusion. What was he talking about? "My father is a doctor. He's trained me well in medicine. I can help."

"Yeah, and I'm the Queen of England."

"But . . ."

"Besides, I've seen the way you Rebels care for the sick."

Cole had returned unnoticed with her drink. He stood now almost between the two combatants. "Jake! For God's sake!" Cole said, his whole body stiffening at the insult. "What's the matter with you today? She only wants to help."

"Yeah, I remember how those bastards helped me."

Nora took a step back as his hard features turned harder at the memory. She realized all at once what the matter was. Lincoln had accepted Nevada into the Union in '64, knowing they would fight against the South. Had this monster been one of the evil breed? She could well imagine it to be so. Her eyes narrowed with equal hate as she wondered if he was one of the rabble that had sacked and then burned her city to the ground? One of his cohorts had killed her husband, another had almost raped her. Lord, if anyone had reason to hate it was she.

Nora couldn't hold back the words, heavy with sarcasm, "While the North, on the other hand, has been acclaimed for their humane treatment." She watched as his gaze narrowed, knowing he was about to return words at least as harsh. She held up her hand, as if to stall his remark and continued in all honesty, "In truth, both sides were guilty of less than gentle treatment."

Jake couldn't argue with that. He might hate those who had caused his suffering, but he knew his counterparts suffered no less once captured. War made men into animals.

Was she really the daughter of a doctor? Jake swore it didn't matter. She was still sleeping with his brother. She'd said so herself. *And he didn't care.* All he cared about was his son and nobody, especially a woman with a Southern accent, was going to touch him. He knew it was unfair to hold her accountable for the horror that had been done to him, but his mind couldn't separate her from his tormentors. Not yet.

It never entered Jake's mind that the woman he intended to marry had come originally from Nora's hometown. He didn't consider her Southern, for

Mary no longer spoke with an accent. After ten years of living in the North and West, it was no longer in existence.

"Thank you for your concern, miss, but I'll see to my son."

Nora nodded at the stilted, if somewhat softened, remark and accepted the words as they were meant . . . an apology of sorts. Still, she was less than satisfied. Certainly the man had the right to thwart the intervention of others, but his child was in obvious need of care. His color wasn't good and he was in a great deal of pain. She couldn't tell, of course the source without an examination, but she knew it had to be serious. Especially since the ailment appeared to be recurring.

She watched in silence as Jake carried his son away. It was far from easy to accept his decision.

"Don't pay my brother no mind," Cole said. "He was in a camp for the last year of the war. He don't talk about it, but I reckon it was hard on him."

Nora nodded even though she was unwilling to give that incredibly nasty man the license to say the things he had. No matter what he'd suffered, it didn't give him the right. So he hated her for being a Southerner. Too bad. She had every reason to hate him as well.

Nora knew many, on both sides, held tightly to their prejudices. Perhaps they would for generations to come.

Suddenly she was sick of it all. What did hate accomplish, but to rot one's soul? She'd lost both her husband and brother, not counting her mother's mind, in the conflict, and yet she could well imagine those in the North suffering equally as much. Nora shook aside the horror of it all and faced the gentleman who stood watching her. "It's been ages since I've had a chance to enjoy myself. Why don't we forget about your brother today?"

Cole wiggled his dark brows and then grinned at her sudden burst of laughter. "My thoughts exactly."

Chapter Four

Nora dared administer the merest trace of ether and only when the pain was so intense it appeared impossible to bear. She needed this woman, if not alert, then at least in possession of most of her faculties. She had to listen and obey Nora's insistent commands. After almost twelve hours of watching Alice Bennett writhe in torment, Nora had begun to wonder if the child would make it. Worse yet, she began to doubt the mother's survival.

Covered with sweat, eyes pleading for release from untold agony, Alice made desperate, unintelligible sounds as she struggled to rid herself of this torment.

"Push!" Nora urged. "Can you hear me? Push!"

"I . . . I can't. Please," came the soft, decidedly weakened response. "I'm so tired. I can't."

"You must. Do it!" Nora was standing at the foot of the narrow bed. With one hand she forced the woman's legs farther apart. With the other, she reached for the protruding abdomen and waited for its next tensing. Beneath her hand, muscles tightened

71

as hard as wood, contracting inwardly in an attempt to expel from the body its agonizing burden.

Nora said over the woman's building scream, "It's almost over. Push! Now!"

Alice bared her teeth in a sneer, no doubt ready to tell this woman what she thought of her orders. Suddenly another scream, shrill and filled with horror, tore from her throat and then turned suddenly low, almost eerie and decidedly savage as if an animal grunted in pain. Mr. Bennett's eyes filled with terror. He'd never seen his wife like this. He'd never seen anything like this.

Alice had no control now but to obey the commands. She couldn't have stopped this if she'd wanted to.

From the head of the bed came more grunting, ferocious sounds as the birth canal widened. "I can see the baby's head," Nora offered, hoping to instill a moment's confidence that this ordeal was near its end and with that knowledge perhaps bring about a renewal of the woman's strength.

Alice sucked in a lung full of air and reached for the last of her strength as she bore down. Her body came up, almost to a sitting position, as she strained and then her hand moved automatically toward her body's opening.

"Hold her hands," Nora said to Mr. Bennett. "Don't let her reach for the baby."

Nora smiled as the head finally slid from the birthing canal. "It looks like a boy," she said knowing the words would give the mother the needed will to make her last effort. "I need you to push one more time." Again her hand rested upon the hugely rounded belly. Nora waited for the muscles to begin contracting again before she said, "Now! Do it now!"

Alice gave one final grunting push, her face turning almost purple with the effort, and then collapsed into a state of exhaustion she'd never experience again. She gasped for breath, her face, her entire body covered with sweat, she lay there totally helpless.

But a moment later, her exhaustion was forgotten as her face lit up with unbelievable pleasure at the sounds of a sharp, terrified cry.

Nora breathed a sigh of relief. The last push had gained the needed results. The child lived. It was nothing less than a miracle, considering the size of his mother's narrow hips. "I was right. You have a son."

By now both mother and father were openly crying, holding on to each other, rocking one another in relief.

The baby was small, but as far as Nora was concerned his size was nothing less than a blessing. Had he been even slightly larger, both mother and babe would surely have been lost. Nora smiled. He might be a tiny one, but his lungs, Lord, they were just perfect. She couldn't stop the tears from misting in her own eyes. It had been a long time since she'd heard such a happy sound as a newborn baby's cry.

Throughout the seemingly endless night and the long day that followed, Nora had hidden her growing apprehension behind a smile and gentle words of praise and encouragement. It was only after the baby's lusty cries had filled the small house that she'd realized how well she'd disguised her fears.

Mr. Bennett had been blissfully unaware of the danger. He never realized death hovered within touching distance. It wasn't that he was uncaring. Indeed, he'd been as anxious as any young husband might be, but had tempered well the pity he knew for his wife's plight with pride at her endurance. And his joy at the birth of his son had been beyond bearing. Tears had run freely and unashamedly over his whiskered cheeks as he bestowed untold adoration upon his exhausted wife.

It wasn't until Nora was preparing to leave that his joy had turned to horror. His face had grown sheet white when she'd told him exactly how close he'd come to losing both his wife and his son. The man had been terribly shaken. She knew the first thing he'd do would be to vow never to touch his wife again. Nora also knew the impossibility of such a pledge and silently promised a visit with Alice Bennett the first chance she got. The woman needed birth control and probably a trip to San Francisco to purchase it. Without a pessary, she'd be again with child inside of a year and the next time, she'd probably die.

It was late when Nora eased her weary body from the buggy and tied the reins to the hitching post, directly before her father's office. She leaned against the wooden structure for a moment, while trying to summon the energy needed to mount the stairs. It had been an endless exhausting two days. More than once Nora had to shake herself awake as she drove back to town.

Nora was roused from the thought of her bed, clean

74

and waiting for her weary body, by a sharp, if whispered, call. "Doc!"

Nora turned at the sound and watched the man stagger toward her. She wasn't a doctor. Everyone in town knew she wasn't and yet since the day she'd taken care of Mazie, many had called her doc. She answered to it without giving the title any thought. "What's the matter."

"It's Johnny. He's hurt."

"Where? Where is he?" Nora asked, her lack of energy forgotten.

"Down there," the man pointed toward the shadowed street. "Right by the alley."

Nora was on her way before the man finished his sentence. It was dark. Stores edged the wooden sidewalk, but they were closed for the night and offered her no light. She moved quickly within the shadows of the mostly covered sidewalk, guided only by moonlight. The sidewalk was uneven and she stumbled as the toe of her high-buttoned boot caught on a raised piece of wood. She might have fallen had not a man suddenly reached out from seemingly nowhere and caught her in his arms. "Oh," Nora breathed with no little surprise at finding herself suddenly thrown against this stranger. "I'm sorry."

"I'm not," the man returned with a wicked laugh as his arms tightened and he began to pull her into the alley that separated the post office and bank.

Nora was stunned. It took a long moment before his words and actions sank in. Too long. She was yanked into the alley before she thought to put up any kind of struggle. A sharp cry escaped her throat as she realized, too late, what was happening. The cry was abruptly cut off by a less than gentle hand slamming over her face. "I told you this would work," came the voice of her captor.

"I don't think we should do this," came another out of the dark.

"I don't give a shit what you think," the man holding her said. "Nobody ain't got no right to this more than me. Besides, I promised you my share of the next job, didn't I?"

Nora was hardly conscious of their whispered, stilted conversation, for the terror that overtook her left little room for much else. She was reliving the horror, the stuff of which nightmares were made. Lord in heaven, this couldn't be happening again. She'd killed him, hadn't she? No. Not this one. This wasn't the same man. This one wasn't a hated Yankee, come to her home, threatening to burn it to the ground, if she didn't give him what he wanted, only to offer her no chance to give, but tried to take instead.

From somewhere close by the low whimpering sounds of strangled fear mingled with the crashing throb of an anxious heart. It filled her ears. For a second she wondered who was making that sound? Whose heart beat as if it would burst? Was there yet another woman in this alley, suffering a fear as great as her own?

But Nora didn't have time to think on the plight of others. Her first and primary concern was to bring air into her straining lungs. Not an easy task since the man's hand held both her mouth and nose. She twisted her head, but his hand merely followed the movement.

In doing so it slipped just enough. Enough for her to take a much needed breath. And then her teeth took the opportunity offered and sank deep into the thick pad of flesh.

"Ow! Goddamn bitch! She bit me." The man released her mouth and instinctively sucked on the injury.

Nora screamed as hard and as loud as she could manage in the instant allowed. And an instant was indeed an accurate accounting, for her cry was cut off yet again, but this time by a fist slamming into the side of her jaw. Nora groaned and slumped against the man, dazed from the blow.

Jake rolled off the whore and groaned out his exhaustion, as he lay naked, staring up at the stained ceiling. It had taken forever. Not that it wasn't a pleasurable experience, but since when did it take him almost an hour before he found release?

"Lord, honey," Susie said as she cuddled against his side. "You're the best man I've ever had."

Jake took no notice of her remark, knowing all whores said as much. The truth of the matter was, he'd only pleasured her until she was half out of her mind, because it had taken him that long to finish the act. He hadn't wanted to drag out the coupling. All he wanted was a woman to relieve the ache he'd felt. An ache that had been his constant companion for weeks. What the hell was the matter with him? Why had it taken so long? And why had he been tempted to leave her in the midst of it all?

The only reason he'd stayed was because he knew

this one's tendency to gossip. Damn, she would have spread his lack of ability around town faster than the plague. And he didn't need no strange looks from the men around here. He'd had enough looks after his wife died. To this day, probably half the town believed he killed her.

Jake rolled to a sitting position and Susie knelt on the bed. Her hands moved over his back as he pulled on his drawers. "If you stayed, we could do it again."

Jake almost groaned aloud at the thought.

"I wouldn't charge you nuthin'."

"Next time," Jake said, knowing there wouldn't be a next time. "I gotta' get goin'."

Susie sighed her disappointment. She could have gone all night, especially with a man like this one. She walked naked to her dressing table and ran a brush through her dark hair, never noticing the black makeup that was now smudged around her eyes, making her look much like a raccoon. "Are you sure you won't change your mind? I could make it worth your while."

"Thanks," Jake said, as he reached for his shirt, vest, and gun belt. "But I have to be up early in the morning. I gotta go."

Jake sighed with disgust. The woman was pretty enough, he supposed, or would have been, if she went easy on the black around her eyes. Actually she was his favorite of all of Fancy's girls. She knew how to excite a man. She knew how to pleasure one like he hadn't been pleasured since he was a kid. She was tall, almost as tall as he was, and uncommonly full figured. Jake supposed that in a few years all that firm flesh would turn to fat. She'd be soft, too soft. He couldn't suppress a shudder.

He made a quick escape, with only one perfunctory, short kiss and left the saloon by way of the swinging doors. He stood on the sidewalk for a moment, clearing from his lungs the heavy smoke and heavier perfume that he'd breathed this last hour, trying to understand his deep sense of dissatisfaction. He had no cause to criticize the whore's cooperation, or performance. Indeed she had done all that could be expected. Above and beyond, if the truth be told. No, the fault didn't lie with her. It was him. And why after an hour spent in bed did he feel the need for something or someone more?

He was walking along the sidewalk, heading for the stable and his horse, when he heard the sounds of a scuffle. If he'd come across two men fighting in the street, Jake might have taken a moment to watch, but he wouldn't have offered either grappler his help, for Jake wasn't a man to butt into things that were none of his concern. But an *alley*. Who would choose to settle their differences in confines so close and dark? Only one who wanted the advantage of surprise, he reasoned. Someone was obviously in need of help and he couldn't simply ignore their plight. But Jake wasn't fool enough to enter a dark alley not knowing what he'd find. He stopped and listened for a moment.

"I thought you said nobody was gonna' get hurt. You said she'd be willin'," said a voice in objection.

"You oughtn't hit a lady, Johnny," another whispered, and Jake sighed, knowing there was no way he could ignore this and walk away.

"My thoughts exactly, Johnny," Jake said, his

voice coming soft, low, and filled with menace from the end of the alley.

"Jesus!" came a terrified cry as Nora was unceremoniously dropped to the ground and all three men began to run. Jake followed the faint shadows of movement, guided more accurately by sounds of running footsteps than sight. He figured he was within seconds of grabbing at least one of the men, when he tripped over Nora's prone form and found himself landing with a thud, almost on his face.

Nora groaned at the force of yet another blow, for he'd landed with breath-stealing impact upon her. The abuse she'd taken to her jaw had left her momentarily dazed, but his fall had brought her instantly to her senses again. For a second she imagined her lungs to be completely crushed and useless. They weren't. It took only a second before she took a deep breath, as deep as one could while lying beneath almost two hundred pounds of hard, unyielding man. She screamed a frightening sound of pure terror, only to have it cut off as a hand reached for her mouth.

She never noticed Jake's curses. He was trying to get to his feet and trying to do it without trampling her any further. Nora didn't, for a moment, know who lay sprawled upon her, nor what he intended to do. In the seconds where neither spoke, she imagined this one was yet another of her attackers, especially since he touched her where no man dared. She fought like one gone berserk.

Jake groaned when a fist suddenly came out of nowhere and landed with perfect precision against his left eye. He saw stars.

"God," he gasped as he leaned to one side, shook his head, and then rolled forward upon her again, while wondering if all the men hadn't run. Had one of them stayed behind and kicked him? He listened for a tense second. No, they were gone. The alley was silent but for the slapping sounds of the woman beneath him, beating him about his face and head. He grabbed her hands and pressed them to the ground. Yes, indeed this was a woman. A very soft, very comfortable woman in fact. He couldn't see a thing, but he could feel her. It was her breast he had inadvertently touched just before she'd started punching him. "What the hell did you do that for?" he asked looking down into the darkness.

"If you ever touch me again, I'll do more than hit you. I'll . . ." Nora grunted as his knee put some real pressure on her thigh. The dolt was obviously trying to get up, but for some reason he couldn't find his leverage.

The truth of it was, he was trying to move without hurting her, and without getting hurt himself. He released her hands and eased back, straddling her hips.

"Get off me!" she shoved him. All that managed to do was knock him off balance again.

"Calm down, I'm trying to help you." Jake smiled as he realized who it was he was lying on. His mind was gathering in all sorts of information at once: Nora, warmth, softness, clean woman. It caused his body to thicken despite his best intentions. She hit him again. And again he grabbed her hands. His eye was throbbing and his lips weren't feeling much better.

"You're trying to kill me," she grunted as her hips moved from the ground.

She was trying to buck him off and doing a mighty fine job of it, in Jake's opinion. So fine, in fact, that he forgot, for a moment, the pain in his eye and imagined he couldn't enjoy more the way this woman moved beneath him. But then her legs started kicking.

Jake grinned as he put his weight upon her flailing legs. Things were getting just a bit dangerous. There was no way he was going to let her kick him. "Nora, it's me, Jake."

"I know who it is, you imbecile!" She tried to kick him again. If she'd been half unconscious she would have recognized the low wicked laughter in his voice.

"Wait a minute. Don't move. I'll get up." His hands reached for her legs, to make sure that they'd remain still as he levered himself away. He heard her quick indrawn breath as his fingers touched bare skin and wondered if it were shock or desire that caused the sound. It didn't matter. Now wasn't the time or place to find out. He couldn't see a thing, but her dress had obviously risen above her knees during the fray. The hardest thing he'd ever done in his life was to pull his hand away. "Easy," he said, his voice low and soothing. "Easy now."

Nora wondered if this was how he spoke to his horses. She could well imagine most any living creature responding to that sound. His voice was low and gentle and caused a trembling somewhere in the pit of her stomach.

Ridiculous! What, in the world, was she thinking? Of course it did no such thing. If she trembled at all, which she doubted, the cold, her extreme exhaustion, and the events of this night were the cause.

A moment later he was helping her to her feet. "What happened?"

"Three men . . ." She shivered with revulsion, for she knew well enough what they were about to do. The last man who'd tried to do as much was buried in a shallow grave, beneath the burnt-out ruins of what was once their barn. Thank God she hadn't had to kill another. She felt the same nausea attack her stomach and bubble threateningly up her throat, as she remembered what had happened the last time. He'd come late at night, drunk, but with one intent. He'd have her or be damned he'd said. Well, she hoped his soul rotted in hell for the terror he'd caused and the fear that lingered still.

He'd forced his way into her home, and tore her nightdress in his struggles to claim her. It was only through the grace of God that he had backed her into the library and she'd had the sense to reach for the letter opener. The blood. God, she could still remember its sickly sweet scent, and the horrible wet warmth, as it coated both their bodies. Worst of all, she could remember his sobering shock and the last whispered words, "You killed me." For years they had haunted her nights and filled her soul with horror.

"What the hell were you doing here?"

The hard, clearly angry question brought Nora from her nightmarish memories. Her head snapped up and despite the darkness she glared, for his tone clearly told her he believed the blame for this near fiasco was hers. That he should dare to put the blame for this on her shoulders was more than she could take! She never realized her scowl was wasted. He couldn't see her clearly enough for any expression to make a difference. Besides, Jake wasn't the sort to be cowed into silence by a woman's anger. He didn't give a damn if she were angry or not. He was furious.

"A man said someone needed help."

"Who?"

"I don't know." She turned away, and began to wave her hand low to the ground. "Where's my bag?"

Nora was bent over searching the alley, when she was suddenly wrenched into a standing position. Jake held her by her upper arms, just beneath her shoulders and just short of the ground as he gritted, "You don't know? You mean you just went with a stranger?"

Nora blinked with surprise at the unleashed anger she heard in his words and felt in his less than gentle handling. What was he so upset about? "He said, 'Johnny was hurt,'" she returned defensively. "Put me down."

Jake ignored her last words. "Who the hell is Johnny?" he asked while giving her a sharp shake.

Nora gritted her teeth to stop the words her throat ached to release. She took a deep calming breath and then said, "I don't know."

Jake groaned and pulled her tightly against him. For a long moment neither said a word as he nuzzled his face into the sweetness of her hair and neck, greedily absorbing her warmth, her scent.

Nora never consciously admitted that he felt good against her. His arms were strong, but she didn't need the safety they afforded. And his scent. She shivered as her brain assimilated the clean, masculine smell with this man, and Nora groaned as she found herself fighting the need to melt against him. His voice was raw with emotion when he spoke, "If you ever do something this stupid again, I'll wring your neck."

Nora stiffened. How dare he? Who did he think he was talking to? She tried to break free of his hold. "No one tells me what I can and cannot do. No one!" She tried again to free herself to no avail. "If you don't put me down this instant, I'll blacken your other eye."

Jake grinned. Nora could just barely see the flash of white teeth. "I thought a doctor's pledge was to help the sick, not inflict pain."

"I'm not a doctor, and you're not sick. At least not so anyone would notice."

"Meaning?" As he asked the question he took the two steps that brought them up against the Post Office wall.

Nora felt the building press hard against her back, but mostly what she felt was Jake against her front. He held her suspended, hip to hip, belly to belly, chest to breast. An instant of panic flashed through her mind, for she had no doubt what this man was about. Her body stiffened with dread, and she wondered if she could ever again know the touch of a man without reliving this terror? She forced aside her fears and fearlessly faced this man. Referring to his question she said, "Meaning, some suffer ailments less of body than of mind."

Jake grinned again. "You tellin' me I'm crazy?"

"I haven't seen anything yet to judge otherwise."

Jake laughed and pressed himself more firmly

85

against her. "Then this shouldn't matter none. A crazy man can't be held responsible, can he?"

"What are you doing?"

"I'm gonna' kiss you, darlin'."

She would have slapped him. In truth she tried, but holding her arms just below her shoulders disallowed the needed movement. She awaited his assault, her mind racing to the obvious and horrifying conclusion. She tried to imagine that this man was not like the others, but his actions proved her wrong. He was no better than the worst of them. At least they didn't pretend otherwise.

Nora thanked the Almighty for the strength she needed, when she heard her voice come soft but even, almost as if she were bored with this nonsense. "If you plan to take up where the others left off, be quick about it. My father will be awaiting my arrival." She tried to shrug and remembered again her arms were pinned to her sides. "I wouldn't want to worry him."

Jake smiled at her bravery. This woman had spunk. She couldn't best him in strength so she used her wits, the only weapon permitted her. Even had he been of a mind to take her by force, he wondered if he'd have gone through with such a notion after hearing her almost disinterested remark.

He laughed at her brave facade, knowing she was anything but unconcerned. Her words might have been meant to imply indifference, but she couldn't deny the shallow, rapid breathing, or the stiffening of her body. "Darlin', I've never taken a woman by force in my life. There ain't never been no need."

He felt her stiffen again. "Not until tonight, you mean?" Lord, she was asking for trouble. Even to her the words sounded like a dare. Why couldn't she simply keep her mouth shut, or at the very least, try to talk some sense into this man? But no. All she could do was shoot him one snide remark after another.

"Not even tonight," he returned, all confidence. "If I wanted you, there'd be no takin', only givin' on your part."

"Why you insufferable, egotistical boor." Nora wondered why that remark angered her so. Did she want him to want her? Was she upset or was she angered, because he didn't want her?

Jake, wiser to the need of both men and women, found himself wondering much the same thing. She sure was putting up a fuss over a little kiss. Maybe, just maybe she wanted that kiss as much as he did. Maybe she wanted it more. Some women couldn't come right out and tell you what they wanted. Some dared you to find out for yourself.

"Easy darlin'," he said and she shivered again, only this time there was no revulsion involved. She hated to admit it, but even now she knew it was anticipation that caused her trembling and the fact that he felt so good against her. Her words were soft, almost whispery when she said, "Let me go."

His hands came to cup her face. Gently his thumb rubbed over her bottom lip. "I will . . . in a minute."

His mouth was soft against hers. Tentatively, gently, it brushed back and forth. His mustache teased her soft flesh, adding a measure of unwanted pleasure. His lips were warm, softer than she'd imagined, and were parted. That surprised her, because hers weren't. She'd been married. She'd lain with a man, and yet she hadn't realized that you could part your lips when you kissed.

She should have. That drunken Yankee had kissed her with his mouth wide open. Nora shuddered and pushed the memory from her mind. Now wasn't the time to think on that. Now was the time to . . . what? She didn't know. She couldn't think straight, not with the way his mustache tickled her mouth. She trembled against him and wondered why his kiss seemed to bring a tingling sensation throughout her entire body? Inside her high-buttoned shoes, her toes curled.

His mouth brushed by hers again, softening her lips, easing them into a more pliable state, and Nora gasped at the sensations that were rifling through her body.

She breathed in his scent. It was probably the wrong thing to do. She didn't want to smell him. There was no telling what might happen now that she felt him hard against her and breathed his scent as well.

"Jake," she said as his lips plucked gently at hers.

"Mmmm," he answered, his whole body concentrated on the things she was letting him do to her mouth. He ground his hips more firmly against hers.

"You probably shouldn't do this."

Only probably? Jake took hope in the less than decisive remark. "I have to."

"Are you sure?" she asked, even as she wondered why she was asking this most idiotic question.

"I'm sure."

"Oh," she murmured the soft exclamation and Jake almost grinned for she sounded like it was all right to do it, as long as he had to.

Jake deepened the kiss and listened with delight to her soft groan of pleasure. God, but she was delicious. Delicious and soft and sweet. A fleeting thought ran through his mind as Jake wondered how he could keep her this way forever. He forgot the thought almost as soon as it came, however, his mind centering on yet another as he wondered when she was going to open her mouth. He flicked his tongue against her lips and when that did nothing, he rubbed it back and forth, coating her with wet, delicious heat.

"Jake," she murmured weakly, her starved lungs causing her a distinct lightheadedness. At least she thought that was the cause. It had to be. What other reason, but lack of air, could cause her heart to pound her body to weaken to such a state?

"What?" he asked. They spoke mouth to mouth, neither thinking to create some distance so that their words might be more clearly heard. In truth, they seemed to have no problem understanding.

"You're licking me."

"I know." His lips smiled against hers as he continued the erotic assault. Was she so innocent that she didn't know what a kiss involved?

"Do you think you should?" Her tone was low and dreamy, and he knew she was further along in her passion that she'd ever admit.

"Mmmmm. Do you like it?"

"I don't know." That was murmured following a groan. "It's different, isn't it?"

"No. You're different.

"You're making me dizzy."

"Good."

89

"But this isn't a kiss."

"Yes, it is."

"You're eating my mouth."

"I know. Stop talking and let me do it right."

She did and so did he.

Despite the fact that, albeit for only one night, Nora had shared a bed with her husband, she'd never been kissed like this before. This was no gentle touching of mouth to mouth. Her husband hadn't known the technique of pleasing a woman. Her husband hadn't been tutored by the best.

Her lips were growing fuller, softer as she allowed this tutelage. Jake couldn't remember a mouth so sweet, so soft. He groaned a deep sound of pleasure as he managed to part her lips at last.

Gently, expertly he ran his tongue over the sensitive flesh inside and wondered if this wasn't the one woman who could cause him to forget all his expert teachings, cause him to lose his clear mind, for Jake always kept a clear mind, no matter how intense the pleasure. It didn't seem to matter that he had only minutes before left a whore's bed. He shouldn't have felt renewal of lust, this almost overpowering need. He should have been drained. But he wasn't. It came to him then that this was what he'd felt was lacking. It was this woman he wanted. It was because he hadn't been with her that he'd left Susie's bed unsatisfied.

He held her head steady as his lips, teeth, and tongue plundered her mouth. He couldn't get enough of her taste. God, even with all of his experience, he'd never imagined a kiss could feel this good.

He breathed heavily against her mouth. His need for more of her taste was just too great for him to move away. Gently he moved her hands from his shoulders to his neck and groaned as she wrapped them tightly around him.

His tongue moved deep into the honeyed sweetness of her mouth and he groaned again at her delicious warmth, her taste. God, but he had to have more. He had to have all she could give.

He left no part of her mouth untouched. His tongue was greedy as it plumbed and imitated the movement of his hips against hers. It was happening. He was close to losing all control. In another minute he wouldn't be able to stop.

Jake muttered a tortured curse as he tore his lips away. He shuddered as he realized just how close he was to taking her here, in an alley. God, this woman deserved better. This woman deserved all he could give.

He was breathing hard, holding her tightly against him as his mouth buried itself in the sweetness of her hair. He forced himself not to search out her mouth again. It was impossible to touch her luscious lips and keep hold to his control. His voice was tight against the strain he knew. "Don't go out at night again."

"What?" Nora asked dreamily, not yet herself, not yet done with this wondrous phenomena, caused by mouth against mouth.

"If you're needed, get someone to go along. I don't want you out alone again."

It took her a moment, but Nora came almost too quickly back to her senses. Her body stiffened and her face flamed as she realized her position. How could she have allowed this? What could she have been thinking?

No doubt it was the near rape and the resulting shock suffered that had caused her to let down her guard. Well it wouldn't happen again. She'd have to be out of her mind to allow a man like Jake Brackston a kiss, if one could call what he'd done to her mouth a kiss. He was the most aggravating, insulting beast, she'd ever had the misfortune to meet. And there he stood, in all his supposed glory, telling her what she could and couldn't do.

"Did you hear me?"

Nora wanted to laugh. Just who did he think he was to give her orders? "I heard you," she said. "Put me down."

"And?"

"And what?" she asked, ignoring the fact that her body trembled and her legs were as strong as strawberry jam and he had to hold her again lest she fall to the ground. A second later she brushed his hands aside and began again to look for her bag. If her hands shook and her legs were at present none too steady, Nora could only bless the darkness, for he never noticed.

"Are you going to listen to me?"

"I told you I heard you, didn't I?"

"But you didn't tell me you'd obey."

"Obey?!" Nora couldn't believe her ears. She stopped her search and glared in his direction. Jake knew she was glaring by her next remark. "Good God, are you mad?"

"Nora," Jake warned.

92

"It's Mrs. Bowens to you, and I'll thank you to remember it."

Jake grinned at the pompous, uppity words. "Norie, I want your word on this."

Norie! No one called her *Norie!* Nora tried for a calmness that refused to come. She had to gain control of this absurd need to do this beast bodily harm. If she didn't hit something, preferably his smirking face, and by his tone she knew he was smirking, she was going to go stark raving mad. She punched her thigh instead.

Nora wasn't accustomed to the fury that had come over her. It must be the result of what had happened with those awful men and the liberties she'd allowed this insufferably arrogant man. She couldn't take it *or him* a minute more.

"Where I go and what I do, Jakey," she emphasized the "e" in retaliation for what he'd done to her name, "is none of your business." She moved across the alley and continued her search. "Now leave me in peace."

"You're pretty cocky, now that you're safe."

"Am I?" she asked, more cocky than ever. "I didn't need your interference." They both knew that for the lie it was. "I didn't ask for it." At least that much was true. But even more true was the fact that had she known he was close by, she would have begged for his help. Stubbornly she kept that fact to herself.

Jake scowled. Is this the thanks he got? "You didn't, did you?" he growled, his anger more than apparent. "Well then, I reckon I should search out those fellas and tell them you waitin' for them. If you don't mind, maybe I could even watch. It should be good sport."

"Only you could think the brutalizing of a woman, sport."

"Tell me you think I did as much," he dared. "Tell me I forced you. Tell me I ripped your clothes and pinned you down and . . ."

"You kissed me," she interrupted his growing anger.

"Oh, and I reckon that's a hangin' offense."

"There's no need to be sarcastic, Mr. Brackston. The fact of the matter is, I never gave you permission."

"No, but you liked it well enough."

"I did not." She'd die before she'd admit the truth of that statement.

"Really? You mean all that moanin' and groanin' and strainin' against me was 'cause you were tryin' to fight me off?"

"Exactly."

"You're a liar, Norie."

"Don't call me Norie!"

"Why? I like it."

"Well, I don't.

"There are other things I like."

He was waiting for her to ask what. She could tell by the sudden teasing in his tone. Well, cows would fly first. "Good for you," she said and then moaned a low sound of disgust as she accidentally kicked over her bag and heard most of the contents empty onto the ground. A bottle of chloroform broke. The scent instantly permeated the still air. Nora forced herself not to breathe too deeply lest the scent bring about a drugging effect.

She was on her knees, her fingers gently moving over the ground searching for the bag's contents when she noticed him suddenly at her side. "What's the matter?"

"I knocked my bag over and . . ."

"Here, let me help."

"Don't!" she said, but the word came too late. She heard the sharp hiss and knew he knelt on the broken bottle.

"Damn!"

"I told you not to—"

"A little late, wouldn't you say?"

"Is it deep?"

"How the hell do I know? I can hardly see my hand in front of my eyes."

"Lower your voice. Someone might—"

"Right, we wouldn't want anyone to know that you stepped into an alley with me."

"I didn't step in here with you."

Jake almost grinned. He would have if his knee wasn't sending waves of pain up his leg. "No you didn't but that's not what people will think."

Nora scooped her things back into the bag and turned to face Jake's anger. He was sitting on the ground holding his knee. "If you come upstairs, I'll take a look at it."

Jake was just about to tell her to mind her own damn business, when he thought better of the notion. He figured it wouldn't be the worst thing in the world if the two of them were alone in a small room . . . with a bed.

Besides, he wanted to see for himself just what all

the uproar was about. Word around town had it that this woman was a miracle worker of the first order. He'd heard that some of the men had actually made up ailments just to see her. Jake never knew his own brother had been one of the first.

They moved along the wooden sidewalk, leaning mostly against each building they passed, almost hidden in the shadow of overhanging roofs. Jake leaned heavily upon her, his arm over her shoulder, his hand dangling dangerously close to her breast, as they staggered forward and then finally up the stairs. He grinned as he listened to her panting, never realizing his real need to hold on. Upstairs at last, her back was to his chest as she leaned him up against the wall beside the door. Not a bad position, he reasoned, although it wasn't necessarily the best. His arms moved around her waist, but he seemed to be having a bit of trouble holding on to his hands. Amazingly enough they couldn't find each other in the dark.

"God," she grunted as she used most of her strength to keep him in place. "You're heavy, aren't you?" Nora said a bit breathlessly as she reached for the door. How was she going to get him into the room? Without a wall to lean against, she was going to be thrown to the floor, probably with him on top of her again. "Are you all right?"

"Fine." The lantern over the door showed clearly his wolfish grin as he leered down at her.

Nora ignored his smile, knowing the cause. "Are you feeling a bit depleted?"

Jake blinked and grinned again. "What's depleted?"

"The opposite of clear minded."

"I reckon, I am a bit."

Nora nodded as if she had expected as much. "It's the chloroform. Some must have entered the cut." She sighed as she looked into the room, measuring the distance from the door to the first cot. She wished there was someone she could call for help. Her father, although gaining strength every day, was probably asleep, her mother, as tiny as the woman was, would be less than useless. Nora took a deep breath trying to garner the needed strength. "Don't worry. I won't let you fall. Just hold on to me."

Jake did as he was told. Was it his fault that he was so lightheaded? Was it his fault that she didn't have half the strength needed to hold him?

"Get off me, you imbecile!" came a muffled voice from somewhere beneath him. Exactly where, he couldn't tell. "I can't breathe!"

Jake gave a mighty yawn. The expansion of his chest nearly crushed her to death. Thank God the bottom of this cot gave a bit, or she'd be as flat as one of her infamous flapjacks.

"Jake."

"Mmmm."

"Jake, don't go to sleep."

"I won't, darlin'." His words were muttered in a seductive drawl. "I know what you want."

"Here's what I want you to do," she said as if speaking to someone of considerably lesser intellect. He never noticed. "Roll to your right side. Do you hear me?"

"Mmmm."

"Do it Jake. Move."

"Can't. Sorry darlin'," he drawled sleepily. "Next

97

time, I'll make it better for you. I'll . . ." the rest of his words became a low unintelligible mutter, and then to Nora's dismay, came the sound of a gentle snore.

Oh God, what had she ever done to deserve this? And how, in the world, had it happened in the first place? All she could remember was moving away from the wall and then suddenly she was lunging forward, totally off balance. In a moment she found herself crushed beneath this giant oaf. Lord, all she needed was for someone to come to the door now and find her stuck under his sprawled, sleeping body. If they found her at all that is, for he covered every square inch of her.

Her face was pressed hard into the canvas cot, and she had to concentrate on breathing, while that stupid man snored loudly in her ears. She could feel the rumble of his chest against her back and head.

Nora felt the sudden and absurd urge to giggle as her imagination ran riot. What if she were never found? What if he stayed right here forever?

Get hold of yourself. Don't panic, just wait a minute and he'll relax. Once that happens you can push him off.

Nora was trembling with exertion as she rolled him over at last. Lord have mercy, but he weighed a ton! She groaned a soft sound of disappointment as she tried to get up. Her skirt, almost all of it, was trapped beneath him, suspending her legs above the floor. How in the world was she supposed to get it out?

"Jake, can you hear me?"

"Mmmm," came the sleepy reply.

"Move your legs. My skirt is trapped under you."

"You feel so good," he said as his arms came around her and pulled him to lie against him.

"That's very nice, Jake," Nora knew it was the chloroform that made him talk like this. She had enough experience with men under the influence of the drug to know they didn't mean a thing they said. Not only didn't they mean it, but they didn't remember a thing once they awoke. It was ridiculous to feel a sense of disappointment at his muttered comment. She didn't. She decided it was best not to delve too deeply into what she was feeling right now. She was tired. That's what it was! She was tired and not thinking clearly. "I need you to move."

"I need you too."

Nora swallowed back the odd sensation in her throat. What in the world was happening here? Why did she feel like she was about to cry? She cleared her throat, took a deep breath and said, "Jake! Listen to me."

"What?" he said, sounding slightly annoyed, even as he moved his leg.

In an instant Nora was free and standing over the cot, her entire body trembling from the effort it had taken to get him up the stairs, not counting what it took to remove herself from beneath him.

Nora stumbled toward the medicine cabinet and retrieved her needed supplies. Within minutes she was bent over him again, this time working on the gash in his knee.

"Jesus, God! Are you crazy!?" Jake hissed the words, suddenly more alert than he would have liked. His body was stiff with pain and Jake reacted unkindly.

"Hold still."

"What the hell are you doing?"

"I'm cleaning out your cut."

"What are you doing it with? Acid?"

"Alcohol."

"That's enough." He gasped between clenched teeth as she coated the wound again.

"I'll be finished in a minute."

"Christ! You're killing me!"

"You're acting like a baby."

That made him mad. She was torturing him and when he dared to complain, she told him he acted like a baby. Probably he wouldn't have gotten so upset, if he hadn't already been in unbearable pain, but he was and he did. His hands reached for her shoulders and he brought her sharply up to where he could look into her eyes. The alcohol fell to the floor.

"Look what you did?" she complained as her gaze moved to the bottle and the wet stain it created.

"It ain't nothin' compared to what you did."

"What? What did I do, except try to help you?"

"Is that what you call it? Helpin' me? Lady, there are better ways."

"Oh? So now you're a doctor as well as an arrogant beast?"

Jake's eyes widened and he almost grinned at her name calling. "Is that what I am?"

"That's the best of it, I'm afraid," she said stiffly as she tried to free herself from his huge hands.

"You mean there's more."

"Most definitely. If you let me go, I'll tell you the rest." Jake grinned and then sighed as he watched half her hair slip from its pins and fall to one shoulder. The colorful red mass covered his one hand. For just a second he lost his train of thought. "Damn. You have the most beautiful hair. It feels like silk."

"Thank you," she said even as she reached to pin it up again.

He watched her hands move to her hair. The movement caused her breasts to rise and press against her dress. He couldn't for a minute remember what it was he'd been about to say. Why did that happen around this woman? Why when her eyes grew soft and as green as a dark forest couldn't he remember what the hell his name was?

"If you stay still for just another minute, I'll bandage your leg."

Jake looked toward the mentioned appendage, noticing for the first time that he was without his pants and his drawers were pushed up to expose his knee. Neither one was unaware of the sudden growing bulge above his legs. "I reckon I ain't a baby after all."

Nora's eyes darkened and then narrowed with menace. He didn't have to point out what was happening to his body. It had happened in her presence before, and she realized it was probably the same involuntary occurrence most decent men had tried to hide. But not this man; no embarrassed flush darkened his cheeks. He was almost proud of the erection. The man was a beast of the first order. "I didn't say you look like an infant, I said you were acting like one."

Jake grinned and lay down again. His hands were under his head as he watched her work over his knee.

All too soon she was wrapping a linen bandage around the wound. "Why'd you take my pants off?"

"Because the leg was too tight to rise up." She shrugged and cursed the fact that her fingers shook. She'd never before felt nervous caring for a man. Instantly she denied the thought. It wasn't nerves. She was tired. That's all it was. "It was that or cut one leg off."

"You sure that's the reason?"

Nora breathed a long weary sigh. "I have no design on your body, if that's what you're suggesting, Mr. Brackston."

"I wouldn't mind none."

"I'm sure you wouldn't," she said and if there was a note of sarcasm in her voice, Jake chose to ignore it.

"'Cause you're going to see me like this from time to time."

She shot him a puzzled glance. "Why? Are you expecting to get hurt every so often?"

"Nope. I'm expecting to have you every so often. And when I do, you'll see me in less than this."

"I'm afraid you're doomed for disappointment, Mr. Brackston," Nora silently cursed her shaking voice as she finished her chore and gave his knee a less than gentle pat.

"*Ow.*" He came to a sitting position and returned her glare. "You did that on purpose."

"Besides being an obvious boor, I see you are also astute," she said as she moved to the desk and returned with his pants and boots.

"Darlin', if you keep insulting me, I just might not make love to you at all."

Nora grit her teeth together. She tried, but she

couldn't think of anything bad enough to say.

"I could have had you in that alley," he taunted. Despite the fact that his statement was true, Jake knew the moment the words left his mouth, it was the worst thing he could have said.

"Not likely," she said as she flung the articles at his head. "Shut the door when you leave."

Before Jake could come to his feet, she had disappeared into the sancturary of the family's living quarters. She won't be able to hide for long, he swore. This woman was going to be his. He didn't care how she denied it, she wanted him and he was going to have her. And then he remembered Cole and cursed the whole time he dressed and all the way down the stairs to the stable.

She was Cole's woman. How the hell did he keep forgetting that fact? There was no way he could step in between his brother and her. Jake had never known frustration like this, in his life. He'd never wanted a woman he couldn't have.

He rode his horse over the uneven countryside at a breakneck pace, uncaring of the danger to both animal and man. He needed to vent his frustration and he did it with the only means at hand.

Chapter Five

Nora left Thorton's Mercantile with her packages and nodded a greeting to Jenny Simpson's mother. "How is Jenny this morning?"

"Oh she's fine, thank you," the young woman said. "It's a chore to keep her home. She wants to play with the other children."

"Exercise is just the thing. She'll be better for it," Nora said, knowing the child was overly sheltered and made to rest more than any child would have liked.

"But Jenny is such a delicate little thing."

"In looks perhaps," Nora agreed and then added, "not so in energy." Nora smiled again at the worried woman. "Let her play, Mrs. Simpson. Sunshine and fresh air will bring her no harm."

Mrs. Simpson made some comment about thinking on her advice, but Nora had no hope that Jenny would ever lead a normal life with an overbearing mother like that. Yes, the daughter tended to be a bit nervous and high-strung, but who wouldn't be with a mother like that?

Nora turned at the sound of her name. "Mrs. Bowens. Mrs. Bowens, watch us jump!"

Nora laughed in enjoyment as she watched the three little girls play jump rope. She knew all three and had seen two of them on a professional basis at her father's office. Mary and Jane Winters had both suffered bee stings, while on a family outing, half a day's ride west at the base of the Sierras. They had been ill for some time, and apparently had not forgotten her gentle care, for they came often to visit. "That's wonderful."

"Can you play?" asked Mary as she tugged on Nora's skirt. "Can you? Huh? Can you?"

Nora looked from the packages in her arms to the little girl's face. She didn't have anything pressing at the moment and supposed she could spare them a few minutes. "Do you want me to turn for you?"

The girls laughed with joy as they realized she wasn't going to put them off as would most adults, but was going to join them. "You have to jump first!"

"I don't know if I remember how."

"Try, try," came a chorus of laughter from the three little girls.

Nora put her packages down and tightened the strings of her bonnet, beneath her chin, even as the girls' laughter grew in volume. They couldn't believe that a grown-up was really going to play with them.

Cole couldn't believe it either. He pulled the wagon to a stop across the street and watched as her body swayed with the rhythm of the turning rope, readying itself to jump in. He smiled as he watched her bite her lip. Damn, that lip again. When was he going to get the chance to taste it for himself?

He laughed out loud as she waited for the moving rope to fly high above her head and suddenly ran into the center. An instant later she was jumping. The children were singing some kind of a rhyming ditty, while Nora laughed and jumped to the beat. More than one man stopped to enjoy the sight as her bonnet fell back and her red hair, gleaming in the sunshine, loosened and fell down her back. Cole wondered if their stomachs suddenly ached as his did. Were their fingers itching to feel that silky length?

Nora ran from the rope, her hand at her hair gathering up the red, waist-length curls and pinning the mass again to the nape of her neck. Within seconds she was taking a turn at the ropes while the children jumped.

Damn! That was hardly any better. Every time she raised her arm, her breasts pressed against the front of her drab, gray dress. Cole had an urge to wrap a blanket around her shoulders. Maybe then the men standing on the sidewalk would stop ogling her.

Cole jumped down from the wagon and did his best to glare the men into remembering what they were about and ignore the woman, but he couldn't stop all from looking their full. He imagined Fancy's girls were going to be busy tonight. He knew he'd be visiting one of them himself, unless he could get a fiery-haired lady to stop laughing at him every time he made his intentions clear.

She treated him like a kid, or worse yet, like a friend. The only trouble was Cole didn't want to be her friend. Friendship was the last thing on his mind when he was around her.

He was wearing out his horse coming into town to see her, and what did he get for his troubles? Nothing, that's what. Cole wondered how much longer he'd have to wait. He'd never met a woman like her before and he wanted her like he'd never wanted another.

"Having a good time?" he asked as he came up behind her.

"Oh Cole," she said, laughter lighting her green eyes. "I didn't know you were in town."

"Just got in. I need a few things."

She shot him an inquisitive look, while her arm kept moving.

"Supplies for the ranch."

She nodded and turned her attention back to the game, occasionally calling out to the girls, "That was very good. You try it, Sally."

"Everybody is watching you."

Nora laughed at his remark. Why would anyone be interested in children playing? "Don't be silly."

"You're gorgeous when you laugh," he said, his voice low and as sensual as he knew how to make it.

"Cole, stop it."

"Why? It's true."

"Because you'll make me blush and then everyone will think you're whispering naughty things in my ear." She shot him a warning look. "Step back, or hold the rope."

"I want to whisper naughty things in your ear. Only every time I try, you laugh."

Nora ignored his words and placed the end of the rope in his hands. He was turning it before he knew what was happening. He glanced quickly around. It was a good thing the men who watched were looking at him with envy, or he didn't know what he might have done.

Nora jumped again. This time only a few steps before the rope got caught around her feet. She was still laughing as she gathered her packages again, told the girls she couldn't play any longer, and thanked them kindly for the chance to jump again. She joined Cole on the sidewalk.

"That was a sneaky thing to do."

"What?" she asked, looking at him for the first time, full in the face. Her eyes were so green and so big, he felt his stomach quiver at her wide-eyed question.

"Men don't jump rope."

Nora smiled and before she thought to stop the words, she asked, "No? What do men do?"

"They kiss pretty girls."

Nora ignored his statement, knowing she'd left herself wide open for the flirtatious response. She was used to them by now and didn't take offense. Instead, she returned to his first remark, "I didn't ask you to jump. I asked you to turn while I jumped."

"You didn't ask. You put the rope in my hands."

Nora laughed. "All right, I apologize." And after a few minutes asked, "Do you have time for a glass of lemonade?"

109

Cole groaned. He couldn't remember how many glasses of the stuff he'd drunk these last few weeks, but he didn't think he could swallow another. "Do you have anything stronger?"

"Coffee?"

He sighed his disgust. He wouldn't have liked anything better than to while away the afternoon with this beauty, but he had to get back to the ranch. "Are you free tonight?"

Nora was always free, for Cole was the only man in town brave enough to try to court her. She didn't know it, but she was far too pretty and way too smart. Most men knew it and were intimidated by it. She nodded.

"Then I'll see you later. Jake is waiting for wire. We're fencing in the north section."

Nora ignored the sudden tightening in her stomach at the mention of the man's name. It didn't mean a thing. Well, that wasn't exactly true. It did mean something. It meant she couldn't stand the man and wished Cole would never mention him.

After that episode in the alley and his outrageous comments later, she'd been haunted by the man. Most every night he filled her dreams and she would awaken damp with sweat, her sheets tangled around her body, her heart hammering for another sampling of his kisses. It wasn't true, of course! She didn't want the man to kiss her. All she wanted was to be left in peace; yet Nora couldn't shake her mind free of him. She'd never before come across a man so bold and so arrogant. Nora prayed she never would again.

110

* * *

"It's a lovely night, don't you think?"

"Mmmm," Cole said as she joined him outside when it was time for him to leave. "When are you going to come to the ranch for dinner?"

"I don't think that's a good idea."

"Why?"

"Your brother . . ."

"What about him?"

"Well, let's just say, we don't get along."

"Why?"

"I don't know," she said, unwilling to tell him anything more than that. The truth of it was, she wasn't sure why, exactly. "He doesn't like me." At least she knew that for a fact.

"Oh, you mean that time at the picnic?" Cole waved aside her concern. "Don't pay him no mind. Besides, you're coming to dinner with me, not him."

"But he'll be there."

"I'll tell him to leave."

Nora laughed. "His own house?"

"Don't worry about him. Will you come?"

Nora gave a weary sigh and then nodded. "I'll come."

"When?"

"Soon."

"When?" he insisted, much like his brother might. "Tomorrow?"

"Tomorrow," Cole agreed. "I'll come by about six o'clock. Is that all right?"

Nora smiled at his hopeful expression. "Six

111

o'clock is fine."

"Can I kiss you good night?"

Nora looked up to his gleeful expression and wondered why she didn't feel anything but fondness for this man. He was appealing in the extreme; he was both kind and considerate. A woman couldn't ask for more pleasant company. What more could she want in a man? Nora didn't know. All she knew was she didn't feel the things he obviously did. She shook her head. "Cole, I don't think . . ."

"One kiss," he pleaded. When she opened her mouth to object, he asked again, "Just one. Please?"

Nora thought about his request for a moment and realized that perhaps a kiss would tell him more than mere words. Perhaps then he'd realize that what he was looking for was not her. "One."

Jake didn't know why he'd come into town. All he knew was the loneliness he'd suffered lately was getting worse as every day passed. During the day it wasn't so bad. He could work until he forgot the ache that constantly plagued him. The nights were the most tormenting. They went on forever, leaving him with no hope in sight for remedying the loneliness.

He should be visiting Mary. He owed her an explanation for suddenly disappearing from her life. He hadn't seen her at all in the last few weeks. Not since . . . He didn't want to think about Nora. She wasn't the cause of his trouble. She wasn't at the bottom of his frustrations. His loneliness didn't have a damn thing to do with her not being at his side.

112

Then what did?

Jake couldn't answer the question.

He headed his horse toward Mary's house. The thought of marrying her was out of the question now, and the worst of it was, he didn't know why. All he knew was he had to get his life back in order. And marrying Mary, or anyone, wasn't an answer.

His gaze moved automatically toward the rooms where Nora and her family lived. His teeth almost shattered, his jaw clenched in rage at what he saw on the landing just outside her door. She was in Cole's arms. Goddamn her! Goddamn her to hell!

From the constant ache in his midsection came a pain of startling proportions. It almost doubled him over in its intensity. So, it was all true. *She was Cole's woman!* He'd said it enough times, but there had always been that tiny doubt, that tiny hope. What the hell was he thinking? What was he hoping for? It didn't make no difference to him. He didn't care who sampled her charms. She was nothing to him.

Their mouths parted. Like a man possessed, drawn to the most excruciating pain imaginable, Jake couldn't pull his gaze away.

Cole's arms reached for her and brought her body to rest against him. Jake almost groaned aloud his torment, for he knew how she would feel. He remembered her softness, her scent, her taste. He remembered them until he was crazed with wanting to sample them again. He wanted to kill the two of them.

Nora rested her head upon Cole's chest. Her gaze dropped to the lone figure to her right and just

113

below, sitting silent and still upon his horse. Nora felt the breath leave her body when their eyes met. His gaze was filled with condemnation, hers with shock, as he twisted his lips into a cold wolfish grin, spun his horse about, and headed for Fancy's place. He shoved his way inside the swinging doors and Nora couldn't tear her gaze away until long after the doors grew still.

"Cole, I don't think this is a good idea."

Cole grinned. "If you're afraid of my brother, don't worry. He won't be there."

"I'm not afraid of him," she said, praying it was true.

"Then what's the matter?"

"We'll be alone. It's not proper."

"We won't be alone. Mina is there and so is White Moon."

"Who is White Moon?"

"Mina's mother and our housekeeper. She also takes care of Matt. And Matt will be there, too," he added as if he'd just remembered his nephew.

"But asleep?"

Cole laughed. "Not till later. Are you nervous to be alone with me?"

"No."

"You think I'll be a perfect gentleman? Even after knowing how good you taste?"

"Won't you?" she asked, her wide gaze filled with sudden unease. She hadn't imagined that she couldn't trust this man, but suddenly realized the kiss they'd shared last night might give him reason to believe she was open to more of his advances. That wasn't what she had wanted him to believe.

Cole laughed. "Of course I will," he said, even as his arm came around her and hugged her, in a brotherly fashion, against him. Cole wasn't under any delusion. He'd known almost immediately, well as soon as he got control of his emotions anyway, that the kiss they'd shared last night had meant a lot more to him than it had to her. He didn't mind. Cole had more than enough confidence. He knew he could convince her to love him. Why before long, he'd have her begging for his touch, his kisses. God, he could hardly wait.

The double "B" brand, strung between two tall posts, depicted the boundary of the Brackston ranch. Cole drove the buggy beneath the sign and then on for at least another mile before coming to a stop at the large ranch house. The house, like most of the outbuildings, was made of stone. It had a sloping roof that came all the way from its peak to the front porch. The house looked homey and comfortable. Nora wondered how a man like Jake could build something like that. To her mind, Jake was as far from homey and comfortable as a man could get.

Nora almost groaned aloud as she saw Jake come from inside the house at the sound of the buggy's approach. He leaned in a nonchalant pose, his arms folded across his chest, his shoulders against one of the posts that supported the porch roof. It was at least an hour before dark. Nora had no trouble seeing the look in his eyes. To say he was far from happy would not have been an exaggeration. The truth of the matter was, Jake Brackston looked furious. And all that fury was directed at one small woman.

Cole frowned. "I thought you were visiting Mary tonight?"

"Mary's busy," Jake returned, not having the least idea or interest in the truth of his statement. "Besides, why would I want to make myself scarce when such a lovely lady is visitin'?"

Nora groaned. The anger in his eyes did not lessen as the words were spoken. In fact, his blue eyes seemed to glow with the fire of rage. Nora wondered what she'd done this time? Why was the man always so furious in her company?

By the look of him, this evening would be a battle of wits, and she'd better prepare herself . . . *now!* Nora took a deep breath and reminded herself to keep her temper. He couldn't win if she stayed cool and unaffected by his taunts. She was much more likely to best him if she kept her mind clear and her temper under control.

Cole helped her from the buggy. His arms were still at her waist when he winked. Nora laughed and with renewed courage turned to face her antagonist. Mentally they squared off, each waiting for the other to begin. "Good evening, Mr. Brackston," she said as she came up the two steps to the porch.

Jake's blue eyes darkened with fire, but he only nodded in return.

"Is dinner ready?" Cole asked.

"White Moon will call out," Jake shrugged, "I reckon."

"Would you care for a drink while we wait?"

"I'd love one, thank you." Nora gave Cole one of her sweetest smiles in appreciation.

Cole was about to invite her inside, but knew from experience that it was at least fifteen degrees cooler in the shade of the porch. "We'd do better having our drinks out here." He guided her to one of the rockers. "Why don't you make yourself comfortable? I'll be out directly."

Nora smiled and settled herself as Cole moved into the house.

"I wouldn't make myself too comfortable, Mrs. Bowens. You won't be stayin' that long."

"I wouldn't be staying at all, except for the fact that Cole insisted."

"You mean you wouldn't have come, if I'd invited you?" he asked, each knowing the invitation would never have been extended if it were up to him.

"I think we both know the answer to that."

Nora felt the urge to fidget, but forced her hands to stay in her lap. He was staring at her; saying nothing, just staring. She took a deep calming breath and wished she was familiar with swear words. She never needed them more than at this moment. Lord, but this man was impossibly rude. The rudest she'd ever had the misfortune to meet. If it weren't for Cole, she'd still be standing before him. This was his home and yet he'd never suggested that she might sit, have a drink, or perhaps see his house. All he did was stare at her, his eyes filled with what Nora could only describe as a combination of annoyance and . . . what? Sexual interest? A neat trick. She wondered if

117

he looked at other women with quite the same contempt. She wondered if he kissed them the same masterful way. *No!* She couldn't care less how or who he kissed.

Nora felt a moment's unease and then knew only anger. This man and his obvious dislike irritated her more than she could say. What right did he have to hate her? He was the one who acted like an uncouth beast from their first encounter. He was a Yankee, for God's sake! A man couldn't get much lower than that! He was . . . she cut off her thoughts and dared him to keep his cool control with a taunting, "Is something the matter, Mr. Brackston?"

"Not a thing." A grin tipped his handsome mouth to one side. Nora fought against the need to groan as she remembered how that silky mustache felt against her skin. "Why?"

"I thought perhaps I might have grown another nose during the drive out here, what with the way you're staring?"

Jake grinned. "Not another nose, lady, just a real smart mouth."

"Thank you, suh," Nora said choosing to take his comment as a compliment, rather than the mockery in which it was meant.

Jake grinned again. Maybe he was going to enjoy tonight after all. This woman and her smart, sweet mouth certainly held his interest. "You know, instead of sassin' a man, a smart woman knows what to do with a mouth like yours."

For just a moment, Nora didn't know what he was talking about. But his wicked lopsided grin soon relieved her of any ignorance. He was obviously making some kind of sexual insinuation. Nora was glad not to have understood *exactly* what he meant. It was enough to know she was being insulted. "You truly are a beast, aren't you?"

Jake chuckled. "And here I thought havin' a Rebel at my table would make for a tryin' evenin'."

"If it weren't for Cole, I'd never have come."

"You've made yourself clear on that score."

Cole returned with drinks. There was fire in her eyes when Nora turned to Cole and smiled again.

Jake barely held back a feral growl. Despite the calm facade, he was just about ready to kill someone. Why did the sight of that smile directed at another drive him wild? He moved to sit in a chair across from them and gritted his teeth as Nora set out to ignore his presence.

"Have you finished repairing the fence?"

"This morning," Jake said before Cole could answer.

Nora shot him a derisive glance and then turned back to Cole again, her body leaning slightly closer than Jake deemed necessary. "It was terribly hot today. How can you stand working in heat like that?"

"He's used to it. We all are."

Cole grinned as Nora moved closer still. Maybe he should keep his brother around all the time. Nora was never so obviously interested in everything he had to say, until Jake was nearby. He had to admit he liked the attention. "The northern pastures are higher in elevation. It's actually quite cool up there."

"Then why didn't you build the house up there?

119

Wouldn't it have been—?"

"Because," Jake cut her off, ignoring the fact that she wasn't talking to him in the first place, "it's too cold most of the time. It's only the summer months when it's cool."

Nora shot him a "Who-asked-you" look and was rewarded with one of Jake's impish grins.

God, why had she agreed to come here? She couldn't stand this man. As of right now, she wasn't particularly fond of his brother either. What she wanted to do was claim a headache and leave, but she wouldn't. Even though she did in fact have a headache, a headache brought on by the mere presence of this disagreeable man, she was staying. She wasn't going to let this man know he had the power to drive her away.

"So," she said after a long interval where no one spoke, "why don't you show me the barn, Cole?"

"After dinner," Cole grinned. After dinner everyone would have left the place. He almost sighed at the thought of the two of them in the barn . . . alone. He had every intention of kissing her again, only this time, he wasn't going to settle for one. "Then we can take our time."

Not likely, Nora mused. After dinner she was getting out of here and she didn't care if that was rude or not. It would be a miracle if she managed to swallow a thing anyway, and her headache was growing worse as each silent minute went by.

"Are you interested in horses?" Jake asked.

Even though she hated to do it, Nora had no choice but to answer him. "Before the war, my father kept a

120

stable of thoroughbreds. I love horses."

"What happened?" Cole asked, never realizing the question was like putting flint to kindling.

"Most were given to the soldiers," her eyes darkened and moved accusingly to the man sitting across from her. "And the Yankees came and butchered all we had left."

"Butchered them? You mean for food?"

"I mean, for the pleasure of seeing a beautiful animal die," she retorted with all the remembered pain coming again to full bloom.

"That's ridiculous."

"Is it?" Her gaze shot Jake a look of hatred and disgust. "Too bad you weren't there then. Or maybe you were," she added suspiciously.

"I wasn't." Jake didn't believe her story for a minute and found himself denying the supposed carnage. No one could be that sick to find pleasure in watching a beautiful animal die. "There was always need for horses. We wouldn't have killed them."

Nora nodded. "I could have understood taking them, to keep for themselves. It was nothing but a waste for them to die."

"Maybe," Jake shrugged, seeing as how she wasn't backing down. "I reckon it was meant to show those Rebels just what they were up against."

"You mean monsters?" she asked almost pleasantly. "Oh, we already knew that."

"I mean the fact that they couldn't win."

"If we had the factories, we would have."

"But you didn't and you lost. We broke you to a man."

121

"Jake!" Cole had never seen his brother act like this before. Yeah, he was a bit rough around the edges, and tended to be a bit uncouth, therefore he usually kept quiet around the ladies. But the strong silent type only caused some of the women in town to try harder to get his attention. Still, he'd never seen anything like this. What was the matter with him? And what was the matter with Nora? He'd never seen two people dislike each other more.

Both Jake and Nora completely ignored Cole's shocked exclamation.

Nora knew gloating when she heard it. It was a miracle she manage to stay in her seat. All she wanted to do was lunge at this beast and inflict all the harm she could. Instead, she raised her chin just a notch and remarked in her most arrogant tone, "But you never broke our spirit. Never that."

"I reckon you're right about that. It didn't matter none how they suffered. I ain't never seen so many pompous asses in my life."

"No doubt, if you look in a mirror, you'll find the most pompous ass of all."

Jake's eyes twinkled with laughter and that damn mustache of his tipped again. Nora felt something plunge to the depth of her belly and tighten uncomfortably at the sight of it. What in the world was the matter with her?

Jake sure as hell liked it when she was mouthing off to him. But what he liked most of all was the feel of that mouth against his. If he had his way, she'd be in his arms right now. He knew it wouldn't take that much convincing to sample again the soft sweetness

122

of that mouth. But he couldn't do that again. Not as long as Cole wanted her. He gave a mental shrug. Mouthing off to him was better than her making believe he didn't exist.

Nora turned to a laughing Cole. His dark eyes beamed approval and pride. His brother was treating her in the most outrageous fashion, but she was giving as good as she got.

A slender Indian woman of indiscriminate age, Nora figured she was anywhere from thirty-five to fifty, came to the door to announce dinner was ready, just after Nora had said, "I'm sorry, but if you don't mind, Cole, I'd appreciate a ride home."

"Scared?" Jake taunted. He sure as hell didn't want her here. He would have rivaled his son in doing flips of joy if he never had to see her again. But for some reason, he couldn't stand the thought of her leaving. He grinned knowing by the fire in those green eyes that his softly spoken dare had worked.

Nora's head snapped back, her eyes narrowing with fury. "Of you?" she asked, the words filled with contempt, and she gave a decidedly unladylike snort. It was so out of character that Jake almost laughed out loud. "Not likely."

"Then why are you running?"

"Running?" the word dripped ridicule. "The truth of the matter is, we can hardly stand one another. I merely assumed you'd be pleased to see me gone."

"The truth of the matter is, we can't stand one another at all," Jake countered truthfully, "but I can take it if you can." Jake gave her a careless shrug,

123

hoping to infer that her presence bothered him not in the least. It was a goddamn lie. There wasn't nothing about the woman that didn't bother him. Maybe Jake couldn't understand it, but he knew it was true.

Nora came to her feet and looked at Cole. Both men knew she was thinking over his dare and both grinned when she straightened already straight shoulders and said, "Will you be so kind as to escort me to the table, Cole?"

Jake gave a startlingly sharp whistle and within seconds Matt came running from the barn to join them. He had to leave again to wash up, but returned with a perfectly washed oval of dirt missing from the center of his face, leaving the rest of his skin to his hairline ringed with dirt, almost like a picture frame. Nora wondered how he had managed to do that so evenly. Apparently the question was clear in her eyes and Jake explained, "First he splashes water and then he balls up a towel and rubs it over his face."

Nora grinned at the boy and asked, "No soap?"

"Naw. I wasn't that dirty," Matt said as he hungrily sank his teeth into a piece of fried chicken.

Dinner was the most unusual affair any of the three adults could ever remember. Matt never noticed. When Jake and Nora weren't at each other's throats, Nora divided all her attention between Matt and Cole. Jake was eaten up with jealousy.

"Has your side been giving you any more trouble?" she asked the boy while totally ignoring the father.

124

"Nope."

"Seems whatever it was it went away without doctorin'," Jake offered. He'd been real worried during the last two times that the boy had been burning with fever, but they hadn't had a doctor then and the pain went away. His son was as healthy as a horse. Thank God.

Nora knew it wasn't that simple. If Matt suffered from an inflammation of the appendix, as she suspected he might, he could appear recovered for a time. Then there was sure to be another flare-up. "My father's been working a few hours every day. Why don't you take Matt to see him, just to be sure?"

"Lady, if it ain't broke, why fix it?" He glared at her interference, never realizing how scared he actually was at the thought of Matt being sick. His fear took the form of anger. "I don't need anyone tellin' me how to care for my son. I told you he's fine."

Nora shrugged. The detestable man was the boy's father. All she could do was make the suggestion. After all, it was up to Jake to see to his care.

No sooner did Matt down the last of his meal and gulp his milk when he asked to be excused. Jake nodded and the boy was gone in a flash of excitement back to the barn. It seemed his dog had delivered a litter of puppies last night and Matt hadn't been able to drag himself from their side all day.

Nora promised the boy to visit the new mother before she left. Her smile was filled with fondness as she watched Matt run from the house.

"You like kids?"

She smiled at Cole's question. "I love children."

A snort came from the opposite end of the table. The sound brought Nora's head around, her eyes snapping fire. "You find something amusing in that statement, suh?"

"Only the fact that it's a lie."

Nora leaned back calmly in her chair and fingered almost lovingly the knife at the side of her plate. "Is it? Since when have you, suh, become privy to my thoughts, my likes and dislikes?"

Jake watched her fingers slide over the knife and wondered if she was angry enough to do what she most obviously longed to do. He almost laughed at the thought. He'd like to see her try. He'd like to shake her out of that sweet ladylike pose. This ought to do it. "If you like kids so much, why don't you have a passel of your own? You're already long in the tooth."

Nora closed her eyes and took a deep breath. If it weren't for the fact that her mother had drummed manners into her since almost before she could walk, she would have gladly emptied that pitcher of milk over this stupid man's head. "I'm twenty-four. Is that what you consider long in the tooth?"

"It's long enough. Why don't you have any of your own if you love children?" The last two words were said mimicking her drawl.

"Apparently it doesn't mean much to you, but *I* believe it's best to marry before one brings children into the world."

"So why ain't you married?"

Nora had reached the end of her patience. This

126

man was beyond all bearing. Her voice raised just a fraction in outrage. "Excuse me, suh, but how is anything I do your business?"

"It ain't. I just don't cotton to liars."

"Jake! That's enough."

Nora knew the man wasn't talking about this particular conversation. He was referring to her denial when reminded that she had enjoyed his kisses. Her eyes glared her dislike even as she allowed the sweetest smile she was capable of giving, while never realizing that the curve of her mouth twisted more than one stomach. Both men held back their groans. "Don't you? My, that is good to hear," she said feigning cheerfulness. If one didn't take into account the deadly glare in her eyes, Nora might have been suspected of enjoying herself. "I shall make it a point then to lie to you every chance I get."

Barely a second went by before she spoke to the room at large. "Oh, by the way, did I tell you? I received a note from President Johnson's secretary today." Her smile was radiant. "It seems he will be able to accept my invitation for a visit after all."

Neither man was absolutely certain that she was lying. After all, they didn't know her all that well and there was no telling exactly what her family connections might be. Both watched her closely, knowing there was just an outside chance that maybe . . .

"Have you ever met his wife?" She looked directly at Cole and then Jake, but didn't wait for an answer before she went on, "A lovely woman, wouldn't you agree? Of course," she said doubtfully, "there is

127

that habit of tobacco chewing. I've been told it tends to stain the teeth. Still, that hardly matters in this case, since hers are made of wood."

Nora glanced to her left and then her right, satisfied to find her audience astounded. She couldn't hold back her grin, nor the adorable soft giggle that accompanied it.

Jake laughed aloud. God, but she was precious! For just a moment he was able to forget that she belonged to Cole.

Nora cleared her throat and looked as prim as a Sunday schoolteacher as she admonished, "One mustn't laugh at the shortcomings of others, Mr. Brackston. It's terribly unfair, isn't it?" Her look turned from angelic to a significant glare. "Unless, of course, it's your shortcomings that are under consideration."

"Of which there are many, I assume."

"Ah," the word was almost a laugh and then a brilliant smile curved her lips as she continued, "Mr. Brackston, no doubt there's not enough paper or ink in the world should I attempt to enumerate."

Nora purposely turned her back to the man and flashed Cole one of her sweetest smiles. "Cole, would you—?"

Nora never got a chance to finish her sentence. Cole was already on his feet, an eager smile curving his handsome mouth. Nora had been about to ask him to take her home, forgetting her promise to see Matt's new pets, but Cole thought she was ready to see the barn. She almost groaned her disappointment when he said, "You'll love the barn."

Nora didn't correct his erroneous assumption. Not when her glance moved to the darker, older brother and noticed how tightly he held his mouth. How his eyes blazed with what? Fury? For just a second she felt a jolt of surprise. Why should Jake care if she walked through the barn with his brother? It was obvious he wanted nothing to do with her. Or did he? Could it be the man was jealous? Was that why he was always so nasty? Nastier than ever when she was with Cole?

It was a ridiculous thought, probably completely wrong, but Nora couldn't repress a sense of enjoyment at the notion. The truth of the matter was, if she could ever bring this man the slightest bit of pain she was more than happy to accommodate him.

Nora smiled at her dinner companion. "Why I'd love to see the barn. Thank you, Cole."

Chapter Six

Nora stepped into the dark musky smelling building and smiled as she watched Matt fuss over the five tiny puppies. "Papa said I can keep this one," he said, holding a black sleeping pup. Cole lit another lantern. The light exposed a long line of stalls. From each stall protruded the handsome heads of some of the finest animals she'd ever seen.

Nora turned her attention to the boy and the litter before him. "He's a beauty, Matt." She eyed the long-haired setter lying in repose, still ever watchful of this stranger. She licked occasionally at her offspring as they hungrily nursed, as Matt asked, "Wanna' hold one?"

"I don't think I should. The mother doesn't know me."

"Yeah," the boy nodded his head as he thought over her response. "Maybe you shouldn't. Spider don't like anybody 'cept me touchin' them."

"It's past your bedtime, Matt."

"Papa will whistle when . . ." The words were no

sooner spoken when a sharp whistle rent the air and Matt's small shoulders slumped. He breathed a sigh and put the puppy at his mother's side. A look of disgust twisted his lips as he looked at the two adults. "Guess I gotta' go. Night."

He didn't wait for a response, but was gone in a flash.

"Does he ever just walk?"

Cole grinned. "Not if he can help it."

Cole guided her toward the length of stalls.

"They're lovely, Cole. Just lovely," she said as she reached to pet the long neck of the first horse.

"That's Devil. Don't go too close." He pulled her hand back. "He's apt to take a bite of your fingers. He belongs to my brother. No one else rides him."

Nora's mouth twisted in derision. That was fine with her. She didn't want to touch anything that had anything to do with his brother anyway.

"Show me the rest."

"There are other things I'd like to show you."

"Behave yourself," Nora said with a tender smile. She didn't think she could stand another romantic encounter and prayed his mind wasn't thinking along those lines. Lord, not after the dinner she'd just suffered through. All she wanted was to go home and lie down. Nora couldn't imagine a stronger need to be gone from this place.

Cole faced her, leaning his hip against one of the stalls, while hooking his thumbs in his belt. He was very appealing, but Nora couldn't help but be reminded of much the same pose taken by his brother, upon her arrival. Why had her heart pounded then, but not now? Surely Jake was no more

132

exciting than his brother. Nora shook her head, unable to understand her thoughts.

"Don't you think it's a waste to have all this privacy and not put it to some good use?"

Nora laughed at his boyish, and yet wickedly charming, grin. "You are a devil, Cole. Do you often get the ladies to agree to your less than proper pleas with that smile?"

Cole shrugged, gentleman enough not to answer her question in detail, for he'd never found a problem persuading the ladies before. "All I want to know is, is it working now?"

"Cole, I—"

"I want to kiss you again," he interrupted.

"I know."

"Will you let me?"

Nora shook her head. "We'd better not."

"Why? Don't you like to kiss?"

Nora amazed herself with the need to tell him she liked kissing quite a bit, especially when in Jake's arms. The thought was ridiculous. She hadn't liked it at all, or did she? "Kissing is very nice, but I . . ." Nora heard approaching footsteps and knew without a doubt Jake was about to enter the barn. She'd never know what possessed her, and would feel nothing but a deep sense of mortification for weeks to come, but she took the needed steps that separated them and found herself suddenly in Cole's arms, her mouth raised to his kiss.

"Sorry to interrupt," came the sneering comment from the barn's door. "But I need my horse. I thought I'd visit with one of Fancy's girls for awhile."

Jake never bothered to mention the fact that he'd

been seeing quite a bit of Fancy's girls lately. Nor did he expound upon the fact that each time he did, it proved to be more of a chore than a pleasure. The worst of it was, he had no hope that tonight would be any different. "Want to come Cole? Susie was real good last night."

The man was the most egotistical beast! How dare he boast of his conquests, even if it was with a woman of less than usual morals. Nora turned her back on the two men, pretending the sudden ache that was centered near her heart didn't exist. She didn't care that the man made regular trips to town to visit with prostitutes. It wasn't any of her business what he did. She couldn't have cared less.

She made a show of checking her timepiece, even though the light gained from the distant lantern hardly offered her a clear view. "It's time for me to go anyway, Cole. I didn't realize it was so late."

"Yeah, that happens when you're having a good time," Jake sneered.

A good time? Lord, she couldn't remember a more uncomfortable, unhappy evening. But Nora only smiled and nodded her agreement. "Or when you're in excellent company," she said, her gaze on Cole. "But, I really should go."

Jake's horse sped out of the yard before Nora was seated in the buggy again. The man was certainly anxious, wasn't he? Nora raised her chin and fought aside the odd sense of despair. She couldn't imagine what was wrong with her tonight. Why did she have this ridiculous urge to cry? All she could think was the animosity between herself and Jake Brackston was so great that it filled her with the most confusing, ridiculous thoughts. She'd be fine again once she got home. She'd be fine forever if she never had to lay eyes on that man again.

It was late. Nora was dressed in her nightgown and robe, a kerosene light burned on the table near her chair as she tried to concentrate on the book in her hand. But the pages might as well have been blank for all her mind absorbed. The sounds of merriment down the street were fading. Most of Fancy's patrons were either upstairs with the women they'd chosen for the night or gone on home. Nora swore she didn't care that Jake was with one of them. It didn't matter in the least. He was hateful. No woman in her right mind would find him appealing. No woman in her right mind would feel this terrible loss just knowing he was with another.

There was a soft knock on the outside door. Nora was halfway expecting it. She and her father were sharing his practice now. The evening hours were usually given over to her. After a day of work her father was so tired, he could hardly stand. Still, he was a lot better and getting stronger every day. And if an emergency came where Nora needed his help, she knew he was but a calling distance away.

She put aside her book and came to her feet. No doubt another man had been involved in a scuffle and needed her care. It happened less during the week, but regularly on Saturday nights. The men would stagger up the stairs, bruised; occasionally one suffered a broken nose or a few missing teeth, but none so far had been badly hurt.

135

Nora entered the dark office and opened the door to the outside landing. She almost jumped at the angry voice that greeted her. "What the hell is the matter with you? Why'd you answer the door?"

She couldn't see his face. His wide-brimmed hat, pulled low over his face, cast his features into shadows, but she'd know this man anywhere. Her lips curled into a sneer. "Why'd you knock if you didn't want me to answer?"

"You could have asked who it was?"

"I should have," she agreed. "If I'd have known it was you, I would have ignored it altogether."

Nora stepped back, her intent was to slam the door in his face. She tried, but his boot stopped it in mid swing. "I want to talk to you."

"If you're still trying to warn me away from your brother, don't bo—"

"I figure that wouldn't make no difference. You're a stubborn woman and wouldn't listen to anythin' I say."

"You figured right."

They stood, each on opposite sides of the threshold, their bodies inches from touching. Nora realized their close proximity, but she wasn't about to let this man cower her. This was her home and he was going to step back. Until he did, she'd face him and do it with all the courage she possessed if it killed her.

"What are you doing here?"

Damned if he knew and for the moment he couldn't even come up with a good lie.

"Is something wrong?" she asked when her first question brought about no response.

Is something right? he silently countered. Damn it to hell, things hadn't been so messed up in years. Maybe they'd never been this messed up before.

Nora scowled at his continued silence. "Jake! What is it? What do you want?"

Ah, at last a question he could answer. "You."

Nora felt her heart make a giant thud. She tried to draw a deep breath, but she couldn't seem to manage it. She couldn't seem to breathe at all. "Why?" Her voice was soft and breathless, the question hardly more than a rusty squeak. Nora didn't know why his response should set her heart to pounding and bring her knees to the consistency of jam. All she knew for certain was, he wasn't with another. He was here, standing at her door, telling her he wanted her. It went beyond the realm of her understanding as to why those words should cause her heart to triple its beat and her body to tremble.

"Damned if I know. All I know is you're driving me crazy. I have to touch you."

"No." Nora tried to back up, but her feet refused to obey the commands of her mind.

"Yes," he said as he took the half step that separated their bodies. His arms reached around her waist and dragged her against him. "I can't stand it a minute longer. I have to have you."

"Oh God," she groaned as their bodies pressed together. "This isn't what I want."

"I know. It's not what I want either." His voice was almost choked with pain. "But I can't help it."

"You can't. Stop!"

"You're right about that. I can't stop." His mouth brushed her hair, her forehead as he groaned, "I

137

might never be able to stop."

And then his mouth was on hers and Nora forgot her promise never to let him touch her again, forgot her most recent and halfhearted refusal, forgot the reason why this shouldn't happen, forgot everthing but the taste and feel of this man.

His mouth was hungry, hungrier than she could have ever imagined and Nora melted into that insistent heat. Their mouths fused together as if neither would ever know life or happiness again until they experienced this one ecstasy.

She never noticed when he drew her inside, away from possible prying eyes. She never noticed that he'd leaned her up against the closed door, that her feet dangled in the air as their mouths came even. All she knew was that the taste and feel of him was heaven. Her hands reached for his shirt and a soft groan escaped her throat as it opened at her touch almost to his waist. Her hands skimmed the smooth muscles of his chest and sides, her fingers delighting in the roughness of his body hair. He was beautiful. It didn't matter that she was almost always angry at some nasty comment he'd made. It didn't matter that she came a lot closer to hating him than liking him. All that mattered was the lust she knew, the hunger for more of the feel of him. He was the most beautiful man she'd ever known and she had to know the taste, feel, and scent of him.

"Jesus, God, you're driving me crazy," he said even as his lips refused to part with hers. His hand reached for his hat and threw it across the darkened room toward one of the cots. Then it returned to his chest for one of her hands and drew it slowly down the length of his body. Palm open she cupped his arousal and Jake thought he'd explode. Nothing had ever been like this. No woman had ever driven him half out of his mind with need for her.

"Norie, God, Norie, let me please," he said as he shuddered uncontrollably into her exquisitely erotic and yet shy caress.

His hand was beneath her gown, sliding deliciously over her naked thighs, even as his face pushed aside her robe and took the tip of a full, soft breast into his mouth. It hardly mattered that her nightdress barred him from touching her naked flesh. He couldn't take the time to open the buttons of her chaste gown. It took all the control he had not to rip it from her body.

She made a low sound, almost a wailing of pain, as he sucked her deep into his heat. His teeth nipped at the tip, causing her to squirm against him. He was driving her out of her mind with this teasing and she had to have more.

She cried out in protest as he tore his mouth from her breast, but then sighed with greedy, almost hedonistic, delight as his lips found her mouth in the dark again.

The instant his lips covered hers, Nora gasped and was rocked to the core of her being, for at that exact moment his hand found the sweet enchantment between her legs. Long, strong fingers slid past the soft curls to penetrate the hot, moist tightness. Their mutual cries of delight echoed softly around them as each found their own measure of dizzying pleasure.

She was tight. "God," came a low guttural groan.

As tight as a virgin and the knowledge that he'd been wrong, that she and his brother weren't lovers nearly drove him to madness. It escalated a desire that needed no intensifying. He was already mad with this longing, crazy for it, in fact, or he wouldn't be here now, pressing her up against a door, ready to take her without a gentle word spoken between them.

"Darlin'," he said as if to rectify the lack of tenderness in his assault. "Darlin'," he repeated as his lips sucked away her breath and left her helpless but to withstand the onslaught of a hunger she'd never imagined.

Less than gentle in their need, they clawed at one another. His hips moved wildly into her hand. His pants strained at the seams with an erection so huge and hard he couldn't imagine living unless he found release. He couldn't deny it any longer. The only release possible was in her. Deep, deep within the hot folds of her body. Only then would the pain ease. Only then would he sleep again, laugh again, live again.

His hand left her waist and joined the other beneath her nightclothes. He cupped her bottom and slid his fingers between her legs from behind. His mind swam dizzily at the softness, the burning heat he encountered. God, she was luscious. Soft, giving and sweet. He'd never known pleasure like this before.

His arms trembled as he fought for reason. Weakened with the yearning that controlled his every movement, he couldn't stop her from sliding lower and he didn't care. In another minute they'd be on the floor, the cots not three feet from them, entirely forgotten.

They were on their knees now, mouths still clinging, hands still hungry to explore. "Open my pants," he murmured against her lips. "Hurry," he said knowing he couldn't hold on much longer. He'd been right. She was the one woman to make him lose control. He was almost there now. He couldn't wait.

He pushed her to her back and spread her legs, her gown was raised to her waist, his hands moved at will over her exposed flesh. God, she was so warm, so soft, Jake wondered if he'd live through this ecstasy. He could imagine how tightly her body would hold him. He could imagine it squeezing him, sucking at him, willing him to give her all he had.

He couldn't stop the sudden need to know all of her. His mouth was on her, his tongue sliding through the protective curls, even before he realized what he was doing. He heard her soft cry of alarm, felt her body stiffen with surprise, but it was too late. He couldn't stop. He had to know her . . . know her as no man ever had.

She tasted of woman. Clean, moist, slightly musky, heavenly. His tongue drove as deep as he could, even as his fingers explored her delicate softness. He heard her cry, but it wasn't from shock now. It was a deeper sound, an urging sound, a sound of longing. *She wanted more.*

Her hips raised from the floor, her legs parted farther, enabling him greater, easier access. Jake had never known such wondrous delight. It was almost as good as finding his own release to listen to her sounds of wonder, of joy, of hunger.

141

"Jake, oh God, Jake."

"Does this feel good?" he asked, between gasping breaths, knowing it felt better than anything she'd ever known before.

"Jake, please."

His mouth left her, but not his hand. His finger, expert in bringing pleasure, rotated the tiny hard bud, even as his mouth took hers again. He felt her straining toward him and increased his pace. Her arms were around his neck and she pulled him closer, opening her mouth at the slightest prodding of his tongue, demanding from him all he could give.

"Let it come, darlin'. Let it come," he whispered, his mouth against hers.

She strained against him, her body growing stiff in anticipation of the coming delight. Her nails bit deep into his back. He wondered if she hadn't ripped his shirt. He'd been right. This one tore at him, wild in her desire, in her pleasure.

Nora had lost all sense of reason long before he pressed her upon her back. All she knew was the heaven she found in this man's arms. All she wanted was more.

She never noticed the raising of her nightdress. She never felt the chill of night air against her bare flesh. She heard his voice urging her to do something, but she couldn't make her mind understand.

And then the most amazing thing happened. He kissed her, but not on her lips. Her body stiffened and her mind cleared just a fraction. No one had ever done that before. She hadn't imagined anyone ever doing that.

She gave a sharp exclamation of shock, but

amazingly enough, within seconds, the shock lessened and then disappeared, leaving only pleasure in its place. Pleasure the likes of which she'd never imagined to exist in this world. Pleasure she couldn't resist. Pleasure she couldn't deny.

She was unaware of the soft sounds she made. She never knew they only spurred him on, to discover yet greater heights of delight. And then the pleasure eased, or changed, or something. She didn't know what, but she was suddenly suffering under the masterful manipulations of his tongue and fingers, tormented, aching, for . . . what?

Her body grew harder, stronger, as her need grew more urgent. She tugged him closer, mindlessly pleading, demanding that he ease the discomfort he'd brought about.

She heard his low words, "Let it come," but didn't know the meaning behind them. He had to do something, something that would fill this void, this need.

"Easy, darlin'," he said again. "Easy, just let it happen."

Only it wasn't easy. It was torment. It was agony. Nora knew it would tear her asunder and yet she ached for the tearing. He was killing her and all she wanted was to die in his arms. "Jake, help me," she managed, although she couldn't have said how. She couldn't breathe, she couldn't think as her body strained higher toward the delight of his moving fingers.

He should take her now, he thought. Now, while she was wild with this wanting. But he wouldn't. He had to witness her desire, know this enchantment first. He had to feel her shudder against his hand, know her pleasures, listen to her cries of ecstasy and know he was the only man to have known this woman so intimately.

Despite the fact that she was a widow, no man had ever touched her like this. He knew it by her shy touch, by the stiffening of her body when he'd brought his mouth to her most intimate parts. Jake couldn't begin to comprehend the feelings that flooded his being. He'd never known anything like the tenderness that gripped his soul.

And then it happened. It was beyond her power to stop it. His mouth was on hers, stealing her breath, absorbing her cries as she stiffened and then bucked into his hand. He felt her body shudder. His fingers slid inside and he felt the powerful almost crushing waves of pleasure for himself. Jake imagined the sensation surrounding his sex and shivered with a need that was beyond anything he'd ever known. His hands reached for his belt. He couldn't wait a second longer. He couldn't resist. He had to feel her squeeze around him or go mad.

"Doc!" came a voice from the other side of the door. "Doc! Open up," the voice insisted as a foot pounded against the wood.

Jake tore his mouth from hers with whispered curses so vile Nora didn't recognize them. Within seconds he brought her to her feet and leaned her dizzy form against the door. "Someone wants you," he said, his mouth close to her ear, breathless and aching with unfulfilled need. He steadied her wobbly legs. "Do you understand me?"

Nora blinked and then nodded.

"Answer it," he said even as he left her.

Nora turned to the pounding as she pushed back her wildly curling hair and straightened her gown and robe. Reluctantly she reached for the knob. How in the world was she going to explain her appearance? What would the man say or think when he found Jake here?

Nora didn't know and tried not to think about it. She couldn't ignore the man's call for help. No matter if everyone found out what they'd been about, she couldn't.

Nora wrenched open the door and saw two men holding another between them. The men naturally assumed she'd been in bed. "We're sorry to wake you up, Doc, but Charlie here had an accident," one of the men said.

Nora took a step back, allowing them entrance into the room. Her shaking hands reached for a lamp near the door. Within seconds the room was awashed in soft light. "Put him on the cot," she said, without looking up.

"Jake!" one of the two said in surprise. "You all right?"

Nora followed the man's gaze as it moved to the occupied cot. Jake was lying there, under a blanket. Even to her he looked as if he'd just awakened. Nora blinked her surprise.

"Got kicked by a horse," he said. "The doc here said I shouldn't ride till morning." Jake was rubbing his ribs as he spoke and acted as if it were an effort to sit up. There wasn't a doubt in Nora's mind that these two men believed his story. If she hadn't just spent the last few minutes alone with the man,

145

suffering the most erotic and delicious encounter imaginable, she might have believed it too.

Nora moved to the injured man. He was unconscious. A large red stain was slowly spreading across his midsection. "What happened?"

"Charlie and that Willis kid wanted the same girl. It was a fair fight."

Nora knew there was little hope that the man would live. She could operate, but there was no telling how much damage the bullet had done. There were a dozen organs it could have hit and injury to any one of them could prove fatal.

Her lips narrowed at the waste. "What's the matter with Fancy? Why doesn't she hire someone to protect her people?"

The marshal had come to Glory, looking for Willis, but the boy had been warned of his imminent arrival and had disappeared. The marshal had stayed for as long as he could, but it was a big state. He couldn't stay in one small town indefinitely.

"All right, leave him. I'll see what I can do." The two men were backing out of the door when she asked, "Does he have any family?"

One of the men nodded. "His wife lives—"

"You'd better get her. There's no telling if he'll . . ." Nora shrugged even as she reached for her apron and began to wrap it around her slender form. "Is it bad?"

"Wounds to the abdomen are always bad," Nora said without looking up from the injured man. She didn't bother to add that wounds to the abdomen were almost always hopeless.

The two men left, each wondering how they were

going to tell Charlie's wife that the man was near to dying because he'd been wanting another woman.

Jake felt a twinge of jealousy as he watched her move around the room, readying herself and her equipment for the impending operation. How the hell had she forgotten what had just happened between them? He might as well not be here, for all the notice he was getting.

For just a moment Nora considered waking her father, but she knew he had been exhausted tonight. He had been up longer than usual today and by the time she'd returned from dinner with Cole, he hadn't been able to get to bed on his own. Nora knew it would be hours yet before her father would be able to help her. She also knew she couldn't wait. If she operated, the man was almost sure to die. If she did nothing, the prognosis was the same. She had to try.

Nora made the decision, one she prayed she wouldn't be sorry for. "Jake, bring me some light." Even as she said it, Nora shook her head, knowing this wouldn't do at all. She couldn't work while the man lay on a cot. "Put him on the desk," she ordered without thinking. And then she shot Jake a questioning look. "Please?"

Jake nodded. Within seconds Nora had swept the desk clean of papers, pens, and medical paraphernalia, and Charlie was placed on it. A lamp hung over the desk. Jake gathered more lamps from around the room and placed them on each corner of the desk, while Nora gathered the needed supplies.

Jake stood nearby, not having the least idea what to do. Nora turned to him and handed him a clean square of cloth. "I need you to hold this over his mouth and nose. Every few minutes put two drops of chloroform on it."

She was as bossy as hell. If Jake had the time to ponder it, he would have realized he liked his women a hell of a lot less confident. Still he couldn't help but admire the way she went about her business.

He watched her dip her hands in a bowl she'd filled with alcohol. A few instruments were then laid in the same bowl. With clean cloth she bathed the area around the injury and then without further hesitation, she took a thin bladed knife and slit the man's stomach open. Blood streamed over the cut, blocking most of her vision. Still, without a flicker of disgust, she pulled at the opening, parting the thick flesh as far as possible.

Jake watched in amazement as she automatically wiped away the blood and searched out the wound with a giant pair of tweezers. Jake knew most women would have fainted dead away. His own knees weren't feeling as strong as they should, but Jake forced aside the weakness. He couldn't faint. Not now, not ever in this woman's company.

Jake was a strong man. He'd seen much suffering in his lifetime, been a party to a lot more than he cared to remember. It wasn't the blood that made his stomach queasy, it was the way her hands held the bloody flesh as she probed for the bullet. He swallowed against the nausea that churned in his stomach and shook his head, trying to force aside the sudden light feeling.

He shouldn't look and yet he couldn't stop himself from doing just that. He made a small sound and

Nora's gaze moved quickly to his horrified, white expression.

"Do you know Mary Parker?"

Jake could hardly hear her over the humming in his ears. The room swam before his eyes as he hung on. He was going to disgrace himself and there wasn't a damn thing he could do about it.

Nora continued on, seemingly unaware of Jake's suffering. "She's one of six children. Lives south of town, about five miles."

Jake muttered a low sound of acknowledgement. He knew the one she spoke about and forced his thoughts away from what Nora was doing to the tiny girl and her five rambunctious brothers.

"Her father brought her in today. She and two of her brothers decided there was no reason why someone as small as Mary shouldn't be able to fly. They figured that if their kites could do it, she should be able to do the same, since she isn't all that much heavier.

"So the three of them climbed to the hayloft in the barn and then out to the roof. The two boys laid a sheet across Mary's back and tied each end to her hands," Nora chuckled, "Apparently they were trying for a pair of wings and Mary almost got a real set of her own." She smiled and shook her head as if imagining the little girl and her brothers. "Anyway, they finished the costume off with a kite tail, tied around both feet." Nora grinned at the comical sight that must have made. "I imagine it was a bit of a shock to all three, especially poor little Mary, when they shoved her off the roof. Instead of flying, she fell like dead weight, face down into a pile of hay. Lucky

149

for her the hay was there. Unluckily, it wasn't quite big enough. She broke her leg." Nora smiled and again shook her head at the children's antics. "It could have been much worse."

Jake swallowed and refused to look in her direction as she spoke. He knew what she was doing. Still, the fact that he had very nearly disgraced himself before her, did not sit well. Not while Nora spoke as calmly as you please, completely unaffected by the fact that she had both hands inside a man's belly, while blood squirted everywhere.

There was nothing he could say, nothing he could do that would ease his acute embarrassment. His dark skin flamed at the realization that he didn't have the stomach of this tiny woman.

Still, he needn't have worried what Nora would think of him. Nora understood that most couldn't take the sight of this, at least not at first. She had almost fainted herself when watching her father operate for the first time. Actually what she'd done was to empty her dinner into the first slop pail she'd come across while fleeing from what she'd believed to be a most gruesome sight. Her full attention was still on the wound and she smiled as she located the bullet.

"I've got it," she said, sparing Jake the smallest of smiles with a glance that didn't see him at all.

"Give him more chloroform," she said, this time never looking up from her work. "I don't want him to wake up now."

A moment later the bullet was out and Nora was wiping yet again at the blood. "Can you give me some pressure here?" she asked while showing him

150

how to hold a thick piece of folded cloth in place. She moved away and prepared the needle and thread to be used to close the wound.

Jake, with wobbly knees and shaking hands, did as she asked. A moment later she was back, edging him out of her way.

A few minutes later, Nora placed a clean bandage over the closed wound and looked at Jake. "You can stop now," she said, suddenly so weary she had to hold on to the desk for support. She poured water from a pitcher on the dry sink into a bowl and washed her hands.

Neither mentioned the fact that Jake had nearly fainted. In truth, Nora had forgotten it. But Jake wouldn't be forgetting it for a long time.

His weakness didn't bother him so much. What bothered him was that he'd shown that weakness in front of Nora and she had gone on stronger than any man he'd ever come across. Oddly enough, the knowledge that she had that kind of strength angered him. He wanted to be the one who was strong. A man was supposed to be the stronger of the two. How else could he care for his woman?

"I reckon you did a mighty fine job."

Nora turned, a puzzled expression in her eyes. The anger in his voice was unmistakable. Now what was the matter? What had she done to anger him this time?

"What's the matter now?"

"Not a thing."

"Then why are you angry?"

"I ain't."

"Yes, you are. Why?"

151

"I told you, I ain't."

Nora tried to remember what had happened these last few minutes. For the life of her she couldn't remember doing anything that would cause him to be upset. Nora knew she had a tendency to order people about when in the midst of an emergency. Had she done that? Had she somehow offended him in doing so?

"I'm sorry if I acted badly," she sighed. "Sometimes, when I'm in the middle of an emergency, I tend to bark out orders." Her gaze moved to his. "Was I nasty?"

Jake grinned and realized she'd forgotten what had happened. Obviously it meant less to her than it had to him. He was tempted, but he couldn't allow her to take the blame for his own failings. He admitted on a soft sigh, "I almost fainted."

"But you didn't." Nora shrugged. "I know. Most everyone does, the first time."

"Did you?"

"No, but I was fortunate enough to find a slop pot nearby." Nora smiled as she remembered how she had suffered that first day. "I didn't think I'd ever be able to face another operation. I went home crying."

"But you came back."

Nora nodded. "So did you."

Jake moved toward her, stopping only inches from her. "You were wonderful."

"Thank you," she smiled, "but I was far from wonderful." She shrugged as her gaze moved to the man still lying on her desk. "I'm not sure he'll live. His breathing is bad." She shook her head. "There's no telling how much damage was done." Her green

152

eyes filled with trepidation as they moved to his. "A bullet travels once it enters the body. There are a dozen organs it can destroy."

Jake knew his anger had stemmed from feelings of inadequacy. He'd been wrong in thinking she was so strong. She wasn't. All she did was what she'd been trained to do. It made her no less a woman, no less delicate, or in need of protection. This woman was something special, more special than he'd so far imagined. Tonight's outcome didn't matter; what mattered was that Nora had the courage to try and save him. Jake couldn't have felt more in awe. "You should be a doctor."

She shrugged. "There was a time when I wanted that, more than anything. But women weren't accepted in medical school."

"And now? What do you want now?" His hands came up to frame her face.

Nora smiled at the rare softening of his gaze. "A good night's sleep."

He was going to kiss her again. He couldn't help it. Never in his life had he come across a woman so brave, so strong, and yet so enticingly soft and sensuous. His mouth was lowering to meet hers when they heard the sounds of running footsteps. They moved apart only seconds before the door burst open and Charlie's wife, along with the same two men who had brought Charlie in, came into the room. The woman gave a short, horrified cry and then instantly crumbled to the floor at the sight of her husband upon the desk. The two men beside her groaned and clutched their stomachs at the sight of Charlie's blood soaked shirt and the many bloodied rags that had yet to be cleared away.

Nora shook her head in dismay as she quickly moved to discard the bloody evidence. If this kept up she'd have all the cots occupied tonight.

Nora sighed tiredly, her gaze filled with compassion and perhaps a touch of humor as she asked the two men, "Would you put her on one of the cots?"

Chapter Seven

"Have you gone and lost your mind?" Jake snapped as he reached beneath Devil's belly and pulled tight on the cinch. The horse snickered in sharp disapproval at the force used and turned his head to butt the big man away. Jake never noticed his rough treatment and shoved back. All he could think about was Cole and Nora. Goddamn it! There was no way he could live here if Nora Bowens became Cole's wife. Just the thought of it nearly drove him into a rage. How was he supposed to share a house with a woman who refused to leave his thoughts? . . . Who caused him endless sleepless nights? . . . Who he wanted like he never wanted another living soul?

"And where do you figure on livin'?" he asked, while praying it was anywhere else but here.

"Here, I reckon. For a spell, at least." Cole sighed at the stiffening of his brother's back. "Jake, I know you don't like her, but—"

"You love her," Jake sneered his contempt.

"Besides, the obvious reason, you want to tell me why?"

Cole shrugged. "Why does anyone fall in love? She's sweet, smart, and beautiful. I can hardly keep my hands off her."

"Not that you try," Jake returned with a grin that was as devoid of humor as any Cole had ever seen. He shrugged. "Look, you're a big boy. Why tell me?"

"I figured I might build us a house on the western pastures."

"What are you lookin' for? Permission? Do what you want." Leather creaked as Jake mounted his horse and turned the stallion in a half circle. He stopped, forcing the nervously pacing animal under control. "Only you'd better get the lady to agree first."

Cole grinned. "I'm wearing her down." And then with his usual confidence, he added, "Don't worry, she'll agree."

Don't worry?! Damn, it would be nothing less than a miracle if he could do anything but worry. God almighty, there was no way that he could live like this. It was bad enough that she was always on his mind, but to have her for a sister-in-law, was asking too much.

He'd help Cole build his damn house. It would be bad enough knowing they shared the same bed. There was no way Jake could stand living with her under his roof.

Nora piled the paper wrapped parcels on a chair

and then helped her mother seated across from her. Nora smiled at the beautiful lady, noting the flawless skin that hardly showed a line and belied the fact that she was a generation older than the woman sitting across from her. Nora gave a silent sigh. The loss of one's memory did one thing at least. It kept the sufferer, in appearance at least, in a continual state of youth. "You're not tired, are you, Mother?"

"Not at all, dear," Abigail returned as she watched an aproned serving girl come toward their table. "What are you going to have?"

"Just tea, I think. It's too hot to eat."

It was mid afternoon and the two women had been shopping most of the morning. Shopping was a luxury they hadn't been afforded in six years, and both women thoroughly enjoyed their time spent at the mercantile and the dress shop. They might have to be conservative with their funds, for they'd never again be well-to-do, but the practice Nora had begun and now shared with her father was doing quite well. The town's doctor and his young daughter were much in need. And if their rates were sometimes bartered for goods rather than cash, and the cash received equivalent to the low income of the townsfolk, at least they made up for the low fees in quantity.

Nora sipped at her tea, as she glanced out the window. Her green eyes followed the big man who brought his horse to a stop some two doors down the street. She watched his muscles bunch as he dismounted. She watched his smile soften his hard features as he watched his son do much the same.

Father and son tied their horses to the hitching post and walked into one of the stores.

"What is it?"

Nora realized her cup had been raised to her lips for some time and she had neither drunk nor lowered it to the saucer. She gave her mother a weak smile. "Nothing. Why?"

"You were watching someone. Who was it?"

Nora's smile was weak, her lie even more so. "One of the children playing."

"Did you see Johnny?"

"Mother," Nora sighed. She'd been through this a dozen times. Johnny was dead. When was her mother going to remember that? "No, it wasn't Johnny."

A moment later Jake, having completed his business, walked into the little restaurant, his son at his side. Nora couldn't stop her cheeks from gaining color as he stood for a long moment at the doorway, his blue gaze immediately finding hers and holding. It had been a week since that night in her father's office. A week in which she'd hardly slept and when she did only to dream again of the things he'd done to her. The things she'd let him do. The things she'd urged him to do.

He was coming toward her and Nora felt a wild urge to get up from the table and run. She couldn't talk to him. After what she'd done, she couldn't face him ever again. "Afternoon ma'am," Jake said while touching the brim of his hat. A moment later he was holding it in his hands.

Nora cursed the fact that she was suddenly breathless, while he acted as if there had never been a moment of intimacy between them. He might have acted the part, but his hungry gaze told her clearly he remembered every delicious moment. "Good afternoon, Mr. Brackston." Nora smiled in greeting as she looked at the young boy at his side, "Matt."

Nora introduced her mother to the two and then watched in amazement as Matt sat himself at their table. Jake muttered something about not bothering the ladies, when her mother invited them both to sit. Nora decided there wasn't anything she could do about the invitation, but she didn't have to talk to the man, just because he was sitting at their table. She directed all her conversation toward the young Brackston. "What are you doing in town?"

"Papa had to order some nails and stuff. He said if I came with him, I could get candy and then a piece of chocolate cake."

"Candy and chocolate cake? All in one day?"

Matt shrugged and then rubbed his bulging pocket covetously. "Papa says, I have to save the candy for tomorrow."

Nora smiled at the boy. He was a tintype of his father, but a thousand times more agreeable. His father just sat there staring at the cup of coffee he'd ordered, saying nothing as he occasionally raised his gaze to Nora and then back to his cup.

When Abigail realized Jake was Cole's brother, she had nothing but praise, for Cole was not only a very likeable man but excellent company, as he'd come to her home near every night for the past few weeks. Her praise only caused Jake to grow quieter than ever as his lips tightened with what Nora imagined

159

to be displeasure.

At last, finished with their tea, it was time for them to leave. Nora couldn't get away from this rudely silent man fast enough.

She breathed a sigh of relief as she stepped outside, only to hear her mother say, "Mr. Brackston is very much taken with you, Nora."

Nora almost dropped the packages in her arms as she turned to her mother in shock. "Whatever made you think that?"

"The way he looks at you." Abigail shrugged. "Too bad he hasn't the charm of his brother."

Thank God, you mean, she silently mused. If the man had his brother's charm along with . . . she gave a mental shrug . . . whatever it was he did have, they'd be no hope for any woman within a hundred miles of Glory.

Johnny Bowens sat astride his horse and watched his wife's slow progress as she headed the black buggy toward town. Two years after the war he had finally come back home, only to find his wife and her family gone. It had taken another four months, but he'd finally found her again.

He grinned beneath the neckerchief which was pulled up to cover the bottom of his face. Wouldn't she be surprised to find out her long dead husband was still alive and well? Johnny shrugged as he remembered his decision to fake his death. He'd figured, after that first bloody battle, that fighting for a cause that was doomed to fail before the first shot was fired was a damn fool thing to do. No, if he was going to fight, he was going to do it for his own profits.

And he had.

He'd taken up with two others and later joined the Confederate renegade William Clark Quantrill. Damn, but the memory of those days was good. There was nothing he couldn't have, nothing he couldn't do. Later, after the final raid in Kentucky and Quantrill's death, the three of them had drifted West.

Johnny made a low sound of imminent satisfaction. Yeah, his little wife was going to be surprised all right, but that bit of news could wait a while yet. What couldn't wait was his need to have her again.

It had been six years since he'd touched her. Johnny hadn't remembered until he saw her again, just how beautiful she was.

If she hadn't bitten his hand that night in the alley, he would have had her then. It didn't matter that he'd chanced recognition in the act. All he wanted was to feel that warm soft body under his.

He'd seen that fool mother of hers twice now. Christ, yesterday she'd almost walked right into him. She'd recognized him, of course, even with his beard, but he'd heard the rumors. Abigail had probably gone and told Nora, but he doubted anyone would believe her.

Johnny looked over the wide empty land, knowing there was no privacy for what he had in mind. The thought of taking her out here in the open didn't bother him none. He had Pete and Dan to watch out for any cowpoke that might come along. He'd like to take her back to camp and keep her there for a while, but Johnny knew that was too dangerous. No. He'd have to be satisfied with a little now. He smiled beneath his bandanna. It wouldn't be long before he had all he'd ever wanted.

Word in town had it that Cole Brackston was sweet on her. Johnny figured Nora would marry Cole. What neither of them realized was that maybe a month or so after the marriage, Cole would meet with an accident. And then Johnny would suddenly be there to claim his wife's share of the Double "B" spread. Half owner at first, but not for long. If he could take care of one brother, the second one would be no problem. No problem at all.

Johnny grinned at the thought as he spurred his horse forward. The two men with him followed close behind.

Nora was far from her usual good humor today. Despite her best effort, despite her father's as well, Charlie had died last night, just one day short of the two weeks since he'd been shot. The fact that the man had hung on for two long weeks made losing him all the more difficult. It had allowed all to hope, even though everyone knew it was nearly impossible for anyone to survive a gunshot wound to the mid-section.

Lost in thought, she directed the horse and buggy along the rutted, dirt road back to town. She'd been called out to the Simpsons' place, early this morning. The message had implied that Jenny was, at very least, hovering near death. As it turned out, Jenny suffered from nothing more dangerous than a case of sniffles and could have easily been brought to town. As it was, Nora would waste a good part of the day driving the sixteen miles round trip.

She shook her head in dismay and wondered again how the poor child was ever going to make it to adulthood with a mother so overprotective?

The subject of mothers brought Nora's mind to her own. When was she going to get better? she asked for at least the thousandth time. How much longer would she suffer her delusions? Just this morning Abigail had remarked, almost offhandedly, that she'd seen Johnny the day before.

This wasn't the first time Abigail had reported the sighting. The truth of it was, Abigail thought she saw her dead son-in-law at least once a week. At first, Nora had ignored the comments. But this morning, after losing Charlie only hours before, she couldn't seem to hold back her frustration. She blurted out before she thought, "Mother, that's impossible and you know it. Johnny is dead. You couldn't have seen him."

"Johnny is not dead, Nora," her mother said with certainty. "I did see him."

Nora hd turned to her father, her gaze pleading for help, but his steady blue eyes had only asked her to let the matter drop.

The distant sound of gunfire, echoing over the vast empty and silent desert, broke Nora's musings.

163

Hardly an instant later her horse leapt suddenly into the air. For an endless moment he wavered, balanced precariously on his hind legs, pawing the air before him, whickering shrill, terrifying sounds. Nora wondered for a fearful moment if he wouldn't fall back and crush her and the buggy as well.

Wide-eyed with shock, Nora watched the buggy suddenly lurch forward. She was soon barreling over the rough, rutted road, as her horse gained his footing again, jarring Nora to where she almost lost her grip on the reins. She had to hold tightly on to the seat, or be flung free of the small vehicle.

Thankfully, she kept her wits about her and the reins firmly twisted around her hands. It took her some time, but she finally managed to bring the horse under control. The buggy came to a stop at last. Nora wasted not a moment, but leapt from the seat. "What is it boy? Are you all right?" she asked as her hand ran over his long smooth neck.

Cinnamon, so named for his reddish brown color, was making the most god-awful sounds. "What is it? Are you hurt?"

Nora was running her hand over Cinnamon's legs. She could find nothing wrong. She hadn't really expected to find anything. His legs were obviously fine or he wouldn't have been able to run like that. Perhaps he'd seen a snake. A snake, coiled and ready to attack, was sure to spook a horse. Nora sighed. There was no telling what might have been the cause behind his odd behavior.

Cinnamon was obviously still agitated and paced nervously in place, shaking his powerful head, while grunting the most horrific sounds. Nora couldn't imagine what was wrong. Couldn't imagine that is, until she saw the blood.

It created a small, neat puddle beneath him, staining the brown dirt to a dark muddy red.

Quickly Nora circled the horse and then gasped at the sight of the wound. Someone had shot her horse just above his right hind leg. Good God, who could have done something so ghastly?

Nora looked to her left and then her right. Her gaze moved over the vast emptiness. Nothing. There was nothing out here, nothing but outcroppings of rock, sagebrush, cactus and of course the ever present brown dirt. Her brow creased with a puzzled frown. Why would anyone shoot at her? Why would anyone want to harm a horse?

Nora petted the animal, knowing her efforts went little toward easing his fear and nothing at all toward relieving him of his pain. Nora only wished she could do more, but she didn't have a notion as to what might help. She gave a low cry of dread as she watched his hind leg suddenly collapse. He was losing huge amounts of blood. The puddle beneath him was growing at an alarming rate. His leg gave way again and he struggled to remain standing. He couldn't make it. With a terrified cry, his huge body went down in a cloud of thick, choking brown dust.

Nora jumped back knowing a moment of pure panic as she watched him writhe in agony. He shuddered, his dark brown eyes seemed to plea for help. What was she going to do? How could she help this animal? There was only one answer. In her heart she'd known it from the first moment she'd seen the wound. He had to be put out of his misery. Did she have the courage to do it?

Tears ran down her cheeks as Nora walked numbly to the buggy and reached beneath the seat. Returning to the suffering animal, she held a rifle in her hands.

She had found him as a colt a year before the war had ended. Secretly, she'd kept him hidden in the thick woods beyond her burnt out home, woods already searched and imagined to hold nothing for Sherman's troops to confiscate. She'd watched as he'd grown into a beautiful stallion. Tied to the back of their wagon, she'd brought him West. He was the last thing she had from home. The last thing to remind her of what there once had been.

Blinded by tears, shaking with sobs, she forced her hands to remain steady, lest she miss her mark and cause him still greater pain. The blast of the rifle was loud, louder still as Cinnamon's cries were silenced forever. Nora wiped her eyes with the sleeve of her shirt. Unable to bear looking at the damage done to what had been her pet, she turned blindly away. Tears streamed over her rounded cheeks, her rifle clattered to the ground unnoticed, as she began the long walk back to town.

She never noticed the distant cloud of dust to her left, kicked up by three charging horses. Nor did she see the lone rider, racing like the wind across the uneven ground to her right. She raised her head, looking at the sky as she blinked back still more tears, and tried to swallow down the lump in her throat.

166

She wouldn't think on it. Except for that Yankee, she'd never killed a living thing in her life. Even the Yankee's death was more an accident than an intentional killing. She'd picked up the letter opener without thinking. She'd only wanted to get the man off her.

Nora shook her head and tried to control her emotions. Lord, there was no need to get this upset. Cinnamon was only a horse, after all. She'd done what had to be done. She'd find another. The thought flickered through her mind that finding another would be no easy chore. Her family might be on the verge of doing well financially, but buying another horse would surely cripple their meager funds for a time.

It was easy enough to say, but the words couldn't keep at bay the terrible loss nor the aching sobs that tore at her throat.

Nora turned at the sound of a horse galloping toward her. She blinked her surprise and almost smiled at the deep sense of relief that suddenly flooded her chest. For just an instant she forgot what she'd just done. Jake! Thank God! She hadn't realized until just this minute how frightened she'd been. Someone had shot her horse. Even though she couldn't see a sign of anyone, someone had to be out there. Someone who no doubt watched, even now.

It had been a week since he'd joined her and her mother at the restaurant. Two weeks since the humiliating experience in her father's office. She didn't have to think on why he'd made himself so scarce. She knew the reason behind his absence well enough. She'd disgusted him by her actions. She didn't blame him for feeling like that. No man wanted a wanton in his arms. No man appreciated a woman who lost every bit of her control once his mouth joined with hers.

Her cheeks colored brightly at the thought, but an instant later her timid expression turned to one of pure shock as she watched him come barreling down on her. He wasn't stopping. Good Lord, what could the man be thinking? He was headed straight for her. In a second his horse would trample her flat.

Nora spun on her heel. In a panic she ran as fast as her legs could carry her. Directly behind her came the sounds of pounding hooves. She could hear the harshness of his horse's breath, Jake's muttered curses and her own heart slamming against the walls of her chest. She screamed as a steel-like vice caught her around the waist and she was suddenly lifted into the air.

Nora was flung face down over his saddle, the breath knocked from her lungs. Beneath her, heavy muscles surged and the horse took great jolting leaps as the ground sped by at a dizzying pace. She was horribly bounced as Devil fairly flew over the rough terrain. She could feel Jake's thighs pressing into her side, his hand flat on her back, holding her in place.

Her hat was lost along with most of her pins and her hair tumbled forward. She looked through the red tangled strands at the moving ground and reached wildly for the flying black mane, a scream bubbling in her throat. She clung tightly to the horse, curving her body over his back, holding on for dear life.

Jake neither stopped, nor changed direction, but continued across the road and up the steep grade of a sloping hill. He brought the horse to a stop only when he gained the summit and then the opposite side of the slope. The horse paced nervously, flinging its long, black neck and beautiful head, even as its sides expanded and receded as it gasped for much needed air.

Jake dismounted in a flash. Instantly Nora was standing at his side. The world spun by. She swayed, almost falling, before being caught against him. With one arm around her, Jake pulled his rifle from the saddle. Without a word spoken, she was being pulled, or dragged, behind him, as he retraced Devil's steps and crawled toward the peak.

Nora had yet to regain her senses, but she managed to mutter a sharp, "Are you insane?" as she was hauled along.

Jake made an unintelligible sound that might have been a curse.

"Why did you do that? What's the matter with you?"

Jake ignored her question. His eyes narrowed as he watched the distant cloud of dust grow closer. They were too far to get a clear shot, but even from this distance, he could tell there were three.

Jake cursed as he looked around. There was no protection. The back of this hill only sloped out to still more desert. Nothing except his rifle and handgun was going to stop these men from coming on. If they were smart, they'd circle the hill and come at them from both directions. Jake prayed they didn't have the sense. "Take my horse and get help," Jake said as he closed one eye and lowered the other as he watched their progress.

"What?" she asked, still more than a little breathless after that harrowing ride. She rubbed her midsection, silently promising that this bully of a man was going to pay for his abuse. "Help for what?"

"There are three of them. I might not be able to hold them off."

"Three of what? What are you talking about?"

"Three men. The ones who shot your horse."

Nora gasped and then tried to look over the rim of the hill, only to be abruptly yanked down again. She glared at the man, her gaze silently accusing him of unnecessarily rough treatment. "Why would anyone want to—"

He cut her off with a quick, "How the hell should I know? All I know is they did."

"If you saw them, then why didn't you stop them?"

Jake turned to glare at her. "'Cause they were too far away. Besides, I didn't know what they were up to till I heard the gunshot and saw your buggy. Now go get us some help."

"Where?"

"Town, where else? We're too far from the ranch."

"We're too far from town, too." Nora mentally calculated that the ride would take her thirty minutes or more there and back, and came to an instant decision. "I'm not leaving you." Jake couldn't have been any more surprised than Nora at the vehemence in her voice. She didn't know why, but she knew she couldn't leave this man to go up against the others alone.

Jake turned to face her. For an endless moment their gazes locked. Nora felt her heart pound louder, harder than ever. She had to remind herself to breathe. "Why?" he asked, his voice low, coaxing the truth from her.

Nora answered before she had a chance to think. Her voice faltered as the protective words tumbled free, "There's no telling what might happen if I left." And as a warming light came to life in the depths of his eyes, she swallowed and added weakly. "To me, I mean."

Jake watched her for a long moment before he smiled and returned his attention to the oncoming men below them. "I don't suppose you have a gun."

She looked around her, wondering what had happened to the weapon and then frowned, obviously puzzled. "I must have dropped it."

Jake nodded. "Then keep your head down."

Nora did as she was told. His order was easy enough to obey. What wasn't easy was trying to understand her impulsive actions. Why had she stayed? What could she hope to accomplish? She didn't even have a weapon. It wasn't completely true that she was afraid to ride alone back to town. She was, but she was more afraid to leave this man alone. It was a foolish thought. What could she do that he couldn't?

Nora sighed, knowing only a state of utter

171

confusion as she waited in silence. Her gaze moved over the big man crouched at her side. She watched his blue eyes narrow as they followed the progress of the men below. Blue eyes that could penetrate her soul. Eyes that could sometimes read her thoughts. Eyes that knew things she couldn't, wouldn't ever be able to, admit.

She couldn't leave him because she couldn't bear the thought of something happening to him. There. She'd admitted the truth of it. Now, all she had to do was figure out why.

Her gaze grew puzzled as it moved over his long form. He wore a blue shirt, tight black pants, a gun belt and black dusty boots. Nothing unusual about that. Nothing she hadn't seen a dozen times, a hundred times since coming West. Then why did the stains of sweat under his arms and down his back cause her mouth to go dry? Nora shook her head. *It didn't.* Why, because his shirt was only buttoned to mid-chest, did his black curling chest hair cry out for her touch? *Of course it didn't!* She tore her gaze away feeling suddenly weak. *Not true.* She couldn't be feeling weak because of that.

His shirt sleeves were rolled to his elbows and exposed hard, brown, hair-smattered, muscled arms. Arms that had the strength to control an almost wild horse, or hold her tenderly against him. Nora swallowed at the thought. Certainly he was an attractive man. There was no denying that fact, but she felt no tenderness for the man. Did she? Of course she didn't. How could any woman feel tenderness toward a man so uncaring of her feelings? A man so

172

rude, so arrogant, so impossible.

The fact that he could kiss her to oblivion didn't matter in the least. There was more to relationships than kissing, wasn't there? And that night two weeks ago, in her father's office . . . the night when he'd introduced her to almost unbearable pleasure and showed her things about her body that had left her in a constant state of embarrassment . . . Nora forced aside the memory.

It was sex. Lust. Not an easy thing for a woman to admit to, but nevertheless, she wanted this man. She'd never before believed herself capable of the emotion, but she wanted to know his body in every possible way.

No, it wasn't that she felt any tenderness for him. She lusted for him, plain and simple. Only she wasn't about to give into that emotion. She was a lady and ladies didn't give into carnal desires. Ladies weren't supposed to have carnal desires.

Nora forgot her train of thought as the gun in Jake's hand suddenly exploded with sound. She ducked lower and pulled her knees into her chest, as it fired again and again.

She thought she heard a cry, but the noise of the gun was so close, so deafeningly loud, she couldn't be sure.

Below them one of the three riders called out in alarm and pain as a bullet caught his chest, almost mid-center. He slumped forward, his horse almost falling as it slid backwards down the hillside. The other two turned the moment the first shot rang out. Jake thought he might have gotten one more. He couldn't be sure, but it looked like the man had taken a jolting blow just before he urged his horse to greater speed.

Within seconds the three men were little more than distant specks of dust on a sweeping landscape, as they ran for their very lives.

"They're gone. I got one of them. Maybe two," Jake said as he turned toward Nora. "You all right?"

"I'm fine," she said, knowing only at that moment that her statement was true. She was all right and she hadn't for a minute been afraid. She couldn't begin to fathom why that was. "Thank you."

Jake narrowed his gaze. Every trace of his former tenderness was suddenly gone as his eyes glared and his features grew rock hard. Nora knew she was going to be the recipient of yet another of his angry tirades. She didn't know what she'd done this time, but she wasn't about to listen to a word this man said. "Don't start."

Jake, of course, ignored her words. "Lady, you've got to be the stupidest female in these parts." He was up on his feet walking to his horse as he went on, "What the hell is the matter with you?"

There was no way Nora was going to lie there and listen to this abuse. She too came to her feet. She never realized she was following him until he turned on her so suddenly it made her jump back. "Can't you listen to a man?"

"What man?" she glared her anger in his direction. The effort was lost as he turned his back to her again and slid his rifle into his saddle.

"Me!" He turned on her again. His face was dark

174

with fury, the veins in his neck stood out as he shouted. Actually, roared would have been a more accurate accounting. "Didn't I tell you to take someone with you when you go out?"

"Who the hell are you?" Nora's mouth dropped open and she blinked in amazement. Never in her entire life had she used such a phrase. Lord, what was there about this man that constantly had her emotions in an uproar? Why couldn't she simply ignore him?

Jake grinned at her use of profanity, his anger gone as suddenly as it had come. "Lady, I'm the man who has twice saved your ass."

Nora snorted a most unladylike sound, even as her cheeks grew pink at his indelicate wording. "Beast, you mean. If you were a man . . ."

"I'm a man all right. If it wasn't for my brother, I'd show you exactly the kind of man I am."

"Your brother?" What in the world was he talking about now? Nora felt almost dizzy at the sudden change in conversation. She blinked in confusion. "What has Cole to do with this?"

"Cole loves you."

Nora's mouth dropped open with shock at hearing the words so casually said. Actually they were far from casually said, they were very nearly yelled into her face. "Of course he doesn't," she finally managed. "Don't be ridiculous. Besides, what has that to do with—"

"Cole loves you, lady. I don't know what the hell he sees in you, you bein' a Rebel and all, but you've managed to get under his skin." He glared at her,

175

filled with impotent rage, knowing the words were out and out lies. He'd have to be dead before he couldn't see why his brother was in love with her. Maybe he couldn't name the exact cause, but there was something about this woman that brought erotic thoughts to any man at the first sight of her. He knew that for a fact. "If he didn't, right now I'd have your skirt flipped up and my mouth where you want it most."

Nora felt her back grow stiff with shock at the bluntness of his words. She knew her cheeks were flaming with color, but willed away her embarrassment. She had to be mistaken. She couldn't be hearing what she thought she was hearing. No one, not even a man as rough and coarse as this one, could be so indelicate. "What?" she asked, her voice breaking on the word.

"You heard me."

"Why you obnoxious . . ." she never finished. The loud sound of flesh hitting against flesh brought to an immediate end anything she was about to say.

Huge hands reached for her, just below her shoulders, lifting her from the ground as easily as if she weighed no more than a pillow. "Why you little spitfire. I ought to—"

"Why don't you try it?" she taunted bravely as she glared her hatred and tried to punch his chest. She couldn't reach, with her arms held as they were, so she kicked him instead. "Why don't you just try it and see what I do next?"

"Ow!" Jake groaned as he rolled them both to the ground. It took him a minute, but he finally managed to still her wildly flailing arms and legs. He pressed his weight over her, holding her firmly beneath him. Her hands were pinned above her head, her body almost crushed into the hard earth at her back. "So far, you've slapped my face, punched me in the eye, kicked me, poured alcohol over a cut and then slapped it. If I didn't know better, I'd say you didn't like me much."

"Only a horse's ass could imagine anything else." She grunted as she tried to throw him off.

"A horse's ass or the man who held you beneath him in a doctor's office two weeks ago."

Nora grew completely still. She could feel her cheeks grow red again as she tried to gather her wits and explain. "That . . . that was . . ." Words escaped her. There was nothing she could say. Nothing that wouldn't make everything worse. She tried to buck him off. Her efforts were wasted. Curse this man to hell for being so big!

"The best thing that ever happened to you," he finished for her.

Nora groaned in her rage. The man was impossible. She couldn't beat him in strength. She couldn't beat him in anger. What she had to do was keep her temper, and never let him know just how close he came to the truth. Her chin raised a notch as she managed to control her anger at last. "If it soothes your ego, then by all means believe what you wish."

"Am I lyin'?"

"You're mistaken. Now get off me."

"And if I don't?" his mouth curved into a teasing

177

smile. God, this man could switch moods with more danger and speed than a twister racing over the prairie.

"Mr. Brackston," she swallowed and took a deep breath, trying to keep her voice calm. "I can't imagine what I've done to cause you to treat me so unfairly."

Jake could have told her what she'd done. He could have told her that he'd been lying awake night after night remembering the delicious taste of her, the softness of her lips and the feel of her body beneath his. "Tell me you don't want this. Tell me your heart isn't hammerin' right now, that your body ain't aching to feel mine inside you."

"It's not!"

Without warning, his hand covered her breast and a slow smile curved his mouth at the pounding against his palm. "You're lyin'. Your heart is jumpin' faster than a jackrabbit."

Her eyes glared her contempt. She felt no expected revulsion, only anger that he would dare to push his cause. "And what do you expect? Am I supposed to remain calm when a man is about to abuse me?"

"Is that what you think? That I'm gonna take what I want?"

Her lips twisted into a sneer. "Won't you?"

Jake shrugged. "Never had to take a woman by force before."

"Till now, you mean." Nora almost groaned at the words. They were a dare if ever she'd heard one. Lord, why couldn't she keep her mouth shut?

Jake grinned. He couldn't understand all the

178

things she caused him to feel, her being Southern and all. He felt nothing but hatred for her kind, but he couldn't deny the fact that he wanted her. Despite what she was, he wanted her like he'd never wanted a woman in his life. "I reckon maybe we should try it and see."

"What? See what?" The words sounded on the edge of panic.

"See if you're willin' or not."

"There's no need. I can tell you right now that I'm not."

Jake ignored her words. He remembered clear enough how she melted in his arms the last time. No matter her denial, he knew it would happen again. All he had to do was kiss her and she'd be begging for more. He held her face still with his free hand, as his mouth lowered to hers.

"Don't," she said, the word soft and breathless.

"I won't hurt you," he promised. "Just let me kiss you." She tried to turn her face away. "One kiss," he coaxed and Nora was helpless against the ecstasy promised in his deep, husky voice.

His tongue flicked out to run along the curve of her bottom lip and Nora made a low sound that was oddly close to a groan. A shiver raced up her spine. Was it fear or anticipation? She couldn't for the moment tell the difference.

And then his mouth sucked at her, drawing her lower lip into wet delicious heat, as he rubbed his tongue along the soft flesh. She groaned again. Lord, couldn't she stop those sounds? Couldn't she simply bear this torment, forcing her mind to the moment

179

when she'd be free again?

Nora tried. She truly did, but despite her denials there was something about this man. Something that caused her to forget how much he annoyed and aggravated her, something that caused her to forget his arrogant manner. For the moment she only knew she wanted his kisses. Didn't she? She was probably hysterical. That's what it was! She was hysterical and only imagined that she wanted his kisses. God, she could barely tolerate the man. There was no way she could want this.

The only thing Nora knew for a fact was that she was more confused than she'd ever been in her entire life. She didn't want him to kiss her and yet she'd never known such intense longing for him to complete the act.

She made another soft sound as his tongue slid between pliant lips and bathed the soft sensitive flesh inside with his taste. He hadn't as yet actually kissed her, but instead was treating her mouth to the most erotic sensations imaginable.

She softened beneath him and squirmed just enough for him to know she was ready, hungry for his kiss, almost as hungry as he was to give it. His lips coaxed hers to part and both groaned a sound of near torment as he brought their mouths together at last.

He ate her. His tongue and teeth were never still as he tried to absorb into himself her taste, her textures, her scent. Nora had been kissed by him before, but she'd never been subjected to a hunger like this. Her mind, her reason fled and she knew only a deep sense of longing that each movement of his mouth only intensified.

He sucked at her; drinking in her sweet taste; groaning at the glory of this ecstasy. He stole her breath and replaced it with his own. Nora had never known that a kiss could be so intimate, so knowing, so all-encompassing.

She hadn't the strength to fight this. She stopped thinking of fighting this. All she knew was an almost unbearable hunger for more. His body was hard against hers. His hips cushioned in the soft cavity beneath him, and Nora knew a dizzying unreality as he moved his hips, rubbing himself against her.

He released her hands and she wrapped them around his neck, dragging his mouth against hers, unable to think but needing to have more. No longer was she simply a recipient of his hunger and need. Nora knew a sense of her own hunger. *She had to have more.* She had to have all he could give.

Her blouse opened beneath his hands as if by magic. Nora never felt his anxious fumblings as his mouth held to hers, bringing her entire being to a mindless state of crazed yearning.

She cried out and felt her back arch as his hand covered her bare flesh. Only it wasn't a cry of revulsion. It was a sound torn from her throat in mindless ecstasy. She felt overwhelmed at the pleasure, and the hunger intensified. It drummed in her ears and throat. She had to have more. She had to find the answer to the ache he instilled.

Her hands reached between their bodies. His shirt tore from its buttons as she struggled in growing urgency for the feel of him. Warm flesh, hard, unyielding. Nora shuddered as her hands moved at will through the crinkling chest hair that had so beckoned, and then down over his flat belly.

Her mouth opened wide, wider as he delved deep into heaven, his body rock hard as he imagined the softness surrounding his sex. He couldn't wait much longer. He had to make this woman his. No matter what she was, she had to belong to him.

He'd never known wanting like this. He'd never suffered this yearning, this almost insane intensity. His hands reached beneath her skirt. He groaned a sound of torment as he felt her warm and moist through her drawers. She was ready. He knew she'd be wet and hot beneath his fingers. He knew she'd be tight and blazing with heat once he entered her slim body.

Jake tore his mouth from hers. He wasn't going to make it. Not while thinking thoughts like this. He had to regain his control before it was too late, before he lost it all.

"Wait, Nora," he said into her mouth, helpless but to allow her to drag him back. "I can't . . ." he groaned, but Nora wasn't paying attention to his distress. All she knew was the longing he'd caused her to know. All she knew was he had to bring her to release.

And then the shudders overtook him. Mindlessly his body jerked against her, his hips rotating wildly against hers as a cry was torn from the depths of his soul.

Jake groaned in humiliation. Not since his first

time with a woman had anything happened like this. He'd always been so cool, so careful, so calculatingly controlled and unaffected. Why had he lost it all with her? Jake cursed a sound of torment unable to believe this had happened. God, he didn't stand a chance in hell against this woman.

He couldn't leave her like this. He'd never be able to face her again if she discovered what had happened. His one saving grace was her innocence. She'd never suspect what had happened if he brought her to her own release. His hands reached beneath her drawers, determined to prove that she had no more strength against him than he had against her.

He groaned a low sound of pleasure as he found her exquisite softness. She was as hot and wet as he'd suspected. His hands slid deep into her warmth, bringing her unimagined pleasure. Only he didn't stop there. He kissed her long and hard, willing away her reason as she clung desperately to him, aching and hungry for more of his mastery. He felt her body tighten again, surging toward him, squeezing around his moving fingers, even as her hips raised from the ground and pressed wantonly into his hand. He heard her cry. It started deep inside and came as a tearing sound of searing torment. Her body bucked wildly beneath his hand.

Jake breathed a long, gasping sigh as he collapsed upon her. He shuddered again; his pleasure in watching was almost as great as her own. He groaned in aching frustration as he felt the last of the tormenting, aching waves of near madness soften into delicious ripples of pleasure. And he knew only helpless, fascinated longing as he imagined it was his sex that was absorbing her pleasure.

He'd never known a woman so hot, so greedy, so demanding; he closed his eyes and moaned again, so soft and giving.

Nora blinked as his dark face came back into focus. She took a deep breath and bit her lip, wondering what was the protocol? What did one say to a lover after the moment had passed? She lowered her gaze and stared sightlessly at a nearby cactus, while wondering what in the world had come over her. This wasn't the first time this man had reduced her to a quivering mass of mindless flesh. How did he do it? And worst of all, how did she allow him to do it?

Jake rolled to his side as he saw her eyes mist with unshed tears. He muffled a curse as he rubbed a hand over his face, wishing he could wipe away the tempting sight of her soft and dishevelled, with her hair wild and loose around her shoulders, with her eyes glazed with passion. God, but he'd never seen anything to compare. He glanced her way and his lips tightened as he remembered his brother. Jesus, what the hell was the matter with him? How could he have touched her knowing she was his brother's love? Family had always come first, his brother and son being the only family he'd ever had. And now he'd gone and touched her, even knowing she was the woman Cole wanted to marry.

He was lower than dirt and yet he knew, given the opportunity, he'd do it again. There was only one answer. He had to keep his distance. He'd make sure

184

he'd never again be alone in her company.

His voice was rougher than he expected when he came to his feet, turning his back on her as if he'd forgotten her very existence. "Come on," he said gruffly, "I'll hitch Devil to your buggy and get you back to town."

Chapter Eight

Johnny Bowens muttered a gutter word as he watched Dan breathe his last. It wasn't so much that he hated to see Dan die. The truth of the matter was, the gurgling sound of his breathing made Johnny's skin crawl and he was glad to hear it finally end. The words he uttered were merely an automatic reflex. He never noticed the coarseness, for coarseness had long ago become second nature.

He frowned in frustration. This was the second time she'd been taken from his grasp and he didn't like it one bit. She was his wife, wasn't she? Didn't a man have rights?

He'd been waiting a long time. Even while he rode with Quantrill, he'd been waiting. Waiting for the day when he could go back. Only when he got there, there was nothing left but a city in ruins.

His wife was gone. He smiled even as he remembered his disappointment. Nora and her family had been right to come West. There was nothing for them in Atlanta. Johnny grinned. She didn't know it, but they'd soon be rich here. And he wouldn't have to do anything more than kill one man to get everything he'd ever wanted.

"I got to get to town. My arm is killin' me."

Johnny looked up from Dan's silent body to his last remaining partner and the bloody arm that hung limply at Pete's side. Jesus, the bastard who'd shot at them had done a mighty good job of it. A sly grin twisted a thin, mean looking mouth. "Maybe Glory's new doc 'll have herself a look at it."

Pete smiled; even through his pain a light of anticipation entered his eyes as he realized Johnny's meaning. "Yeah, maybe she will."

Johnny shrugged. It didn't bother him none knowing that others lusted for his wife. He never was the jealous sort, never would be. Besides, he knew Nora wouldn't give Pete a second glance.

From their camp high upon a rocky ledge, deep in the Sierra Mountains, Johnny shoved Dan's body over the edge to the gorge below. He watched as it fell to the floor of the dry riverbed. Later he'd go down there and cover it with rocks. Maybe.

He'd added to the fire and was pouring water into the pot when he spoke again. "Bring back some coffee, will ya? We're runnin' low."

Pete came to his feet. A sly grin twisted his too full lips. "Maybe I won't be back for a day or so. I might be too sick to ride."

Johnny grunted as he sat by the fire, waiting for the coffee to boil. He grinned at Pete's hopeful look. "I wouldn't get my cock all primed and ready if I was you. Nora ain't the sort who'd give someone like you a second's notice."

188

"Every woman likes a bit 'a sweet talkin', and I know how to give it."

Johnny snorted his disgust at his partner's obviously lecherous intent. He didn't worry none. Nora was a lady. He'd known her since both of them were children and knew a man like Pete Smithers, rough and coarse, could never hold her interest. Nora would always prefer a gentleman. He'd been a gentleman once. Before the war, a lifetime ago. "Yeah, and maybe you could piss into the wind and stay dry."

Nora spun at the sound of his cry and then gasped in stunned silence as the bucket of whitewash slipped from atop the ladder and fell, splashing most everything in the room. The fact that it coated one entire side of his face and body nearly brought a giggle from her lips. The truth of the matter was, even before the spill, he'd painted more of the floor and himself than he had the walls. She gave a mental shrug. No matter. The floors could be scraped clean and partly covered with new rugs. Having him here was certainly better than if she tackled this job alone, no matter the mess he made.

"Cole!" she said, while biting her lips in an effort to keep the threatening laughter at bay. "I told you it's the walls that need painting, not you. You're white enough."

"Smart," he said, his dark eyes narrowed with warning. Nora could see it coming, but she wasn't fast enough. She spun on her heels, but managed only one step. From the corner of the room he lunged at her knocking her down, rolling her beneath him.

"Just for that . . ." he threatened, but never finished what he'd been about to say, for Nora squealed and hit him full in the face with her brush in retaliation.

Cole grinned, despite the fact that he now looked as though he'd dipped his head into the bucket. Nora bit her lip, while laughter danced in her eyes. "I always had a soft spot for a painted face woman," Cole said as he rubbed his face against her. The two of them were covered in white paint and laughing at the mess they caused, when the door to the office opened.

Jake gave a silent curse. How many more men was he going to find this one under? He cleared his throat and watched Nora and his brother scramble to their feet. They were a mess. Both of them smeared in white and laughing at the fine job they'd done of it.

"We were painting . . ." Cole looked at Nora and started laughing again. "Each other."

"So I see," Jake returned without a shred of humor. His arms were folded across his wide chest, his blue eyes dark with recrimination when he nodded over his shoulder. "You've got yourself another patient. This one has a gunshot wound. I'd be careful."

Nora's eyes widened. "Is it . . . ?"

"I don't know." He shrugged. "Said it was an accident."

Cole looked from his brother's dark scowl to Nora's wide eyes. "What are you talking about?"

Nora turned to Cole. "I told you about the men who shot my horse. Jake might have hit one."

Cole turned to his brother. "You think he's one of them?"

190

"I think it don't hurt none to be careful."

"Don't leave her alone. I'll be right back." Cole grabbed a towel and wiped some of the whitewash from his face, just before he ran from the room.

Despite the fact that he'd silently vowed to keep his distance after this morning and the intimacy they shared, Jake didn't have any intentions of leaving her alone. They'd driven back in strained silence, for Jake couldn't bring himself to say he was sorry. He hadn't been even though he had no right to touch her. She belonged to his brother and yet their time together had been the best thing that had ever happened to him. Even now, his body ached for more.

Hours went by and still Jake lingered in town in the hope of seeing her just one more time. He had long since used every excuse he could think of and was cursing himself for every kind of fool, when he mounted his horse and turned toward his ranch. He'd been just about to leave when he'd spotted the man riding in. The man was obviously injured, and in need of care. He rode slumped in his saddle, while blood soaked the sleeve of his shirt and ran in a steady stream over his hand to coat one side of his horse. It was Jake who had brought the man to Nora's office.

Nora knew she looked a mess, but had little choice in the matter. She had to care for the man despite her less than professional appearance. Her father and mother were taking tea with the preacher and his wife, leaving Nora in charge of the office for the afternoon.

She wiped what she could of the excess, leaving

streaks of white along her cheek and jaw as she moved toward the office door.

"I dropped my gun and it went off," Pete said, his gaze wary as he glanced at the big man standing behind the tiny doctor. Pete had been hoping for a bit of time alone with her, but the man didn't seem inclined to leave. Instead, he sat his hip on the desk across the room, arms folded over his chest and stared at him until Pete was sure he'd been recognized. He shook away the thought. There weren't any posters of him. No one knew he was wanted.

"The bullet passed through," Nora said as she cleaned the wound. She pressed the meaty part of his arm, testing near the injury for any sign of a broken bone and nodded. "I don't think it did much damage." She prepared to stitch the wound closed as she spoke. "It'll be sore, but all right, I think.

"There's whiskey in the cabinet." Nora said as she raised her gaze to Jake. "Get him some. This is going to hurt."

"Why? You didn't give me none."

Nora's gaze held to his for an endless moment. Her stomach tightened and her hands trembled at the hunger she read in his eyes. She felt heat rush to her face. Had it only been this morning when she'd lost all control in his arms? Could it be that he wanted her yet again? So soon? It wasn't until the man on the cot made a small sound that Nora forced her attention back to him. "I didn't have to. You were half out of it, remember?"

"I wasn't half out of it and I remember everything

192

you did in this room," Jake said as he moved to the cabinet.

Nora knew he wasn't talking about the night that she'd cared for his cut knee. He was talking about the night they'd nearly made love on the floor, right in front of the door. She remembered the hunger, so intense at the time, that neither had given a thought to possibly being found out. Her cheeks colored at the mortifying thought.

Nora had tried for weeks to free her mind of that particular happening. She bit her lips, bringing them into a thin line of disapproval. It hadn't helped matters any to fall into his arms again this morning.

Afterwards, she'd never known so intense a degree of embarrassment and his silence on the ride back had only intensified the emotion. Lord, when was she going to learn to keep away from this man?

Nora went about her work on pure instinct. Later she wouldn't remember how she'd managed the chore. She was tying a clean bandage over her stitches when Cole came rushing back, with a star pinned to his paint-splattered leather vest.

"What the hell are you doing?" Jake's voice thundered in the small room.

"I asked Dodd to swear me in temporarily. At least until we can find a permanent sheriff."

"Jesus," Jake muttered as he ran his hand over his face. He'd never known a man to go to such lengths to impress a woman. He didn't have to be told that Cole had done this for Nora. Obviously his brother had some ridiculously romantic notion that this would make her see him in a more favorable light. "And who the hell is going to do your job at the ranch?"

"I will."

"I reckon you'll be the only man in history to be in two places at one time, then."

"I'll do my share. Don't worry. Mostly the town only needs a sheriff on Saturday nights." He shot Nora a tender smile. "And I intend to be here anyway."

Cole and Nora were smiling at one another. No one noticed Jake's less than happy expression.

Pete watched the happening from across the room. Christ, this was all he needed. A sheriff. The guy was bound to ask him questions and he hadn't as yet come up with a decent story. He'd known the town didn't have a sheriff and never thought he'd need one. And his pockets. Damn, his share of the money from that last job was still there. And the wrapper around the small bundle would be all the evidence they'd need to hang him.

"If you're finished with him, sweetheart, I'd like to ask him a few questions."

Jake muttered a low curse and reached for his hat. There was no way he was going to stand here and watch his brother make cow eyes at her, the one woman who had brought him more aggravation than any he could remember. He'd had enough of this. Enough of sleepless nights. He wished to hell he'd never laid eyes on her.

Jake was walking toward the door, when from the side of his eye he saw it. Pete sat up and in one unbroken movement, reached for his boot. Jake had

194

taken Pete's visible gun when they'd entered the doctor's office, but Jake knew what reaching for his boot meant. He came to an instant stop. Just as he'd known it would, the expected gun appeared, dark and deadly in the man's hand.

Jake reached for his own gun and drew as fast as any gunslinger, even as he shoved Nora out of harm's way. The explosion of gunfire in the small room was deafening. Nora screamed.

Pete's eyes widened in stunned surprise. He reached for his throat, what was left of it anyway, while Cole and Nora stood paralyzed with shock, neither able to believe what was happening.

The gun slipped from Pete's lifeless fingers and clattered to the floor just as he keeled over upon it and lay flat on his face in a growing puddle of his own blood.

"What the hell?" Cole muttered helplessly. It was over in seconds. Over before Cole knew it was about to begin.

The acrid scent of gunpowder filled the room along with a heavy, total silence. Nora swallowed down the nausea at the sight of the dead man. She'd seen hundreds die, but none so violently. The violence had always been done before they were brought to her. She took a deep breath. Her voice was surprisingly steady as she broke the stunned silence and remarked almost offhandedly, "You could have saved me some time if you did this before I sewed him up."

Jake's blue gaze moved to her white face. He grinned. Lord, but she was a cool one, no feminine hysterics for her, no swooning or fainting spells. It

195

was clear that she was shaken but except for her coloring, she gave no outward sign of it. Jake's eyes darkened with approval. "If I'd have known he was going to pull a gun, I would have."

He looked at his brother, humor lighting his eyes. "I reckon you volunteered just in time. Need some help carryin' him out?"

Cole didn't need help. There were a half dozen men suddenly at the door, alerted by the sound of gunfire coming from of all places, the doctor's office, and trying to see what had happened.

Nora left the men to see to their own business and moved into the family's quarters to change her paint-splattered clothes and tidy herself. Moments later she returned to the office, her intent to clean the floor where the man had fallen.

"I cleaned it," Jake said as he sat behind the desk and watched her reenter the room. Her gaze moved from him to the empty cot and the wet spot on the floor beside it.

"Thank you," Nora said as she gathered up her supplies and replaced them in the cabinet. "I didn't know you were still here."

"Or you would have stayed inside?"

Nora didn't respond to his taunt, but shot him a long, hard look.

"Afraid?"

Her eyes narrowed. "Of you? Hardly."

Jake grinned at her look, but his smile didn't last but a second as he remembered her and his brother rolling over her parlor floor. "He's calling you sweetheart now," Jake said as he came around the desk and leaned one hip on its corner.

Nora shot him another hard look. "Not that it's any of your business, but I assume you're referring to Cole?"

"Are you gonna marry him?"

"I told you before I don't love your brother."

There wasn't a doubt in Jake's mind that she spoke the truth, but she hadn't told him before. Jake felt a heavy heart lighten. He couldn't stop the smile from curving his lips. "No, you didn't."

Nora turned away and forced herself to concentrate on the suddenly complicated task of replacing the soiled sheet. The way his mustache tipped when he smiled did strange things to her stomach. Things she didn't want to think about. "Well, I'm telling you now. Besides, I hardly think you and I could manage to live in the same house."

"You mean because of what we feel for each other?"

Nora shoved the stained sheet, she'd taken from the cot, into a basket and turned to glare at him. "Hatred doesn't usually make for a peaceful environment, wouldn't you agree?"

"Are you telling me, you hate me?"

"No, I'm telling you, *you* hate *me!*"

"What do you feel?"

Nora almost told him. Her mouth actually opened and it was only by the grace of God that she thought before she blurted it out. Lord, what could she be thinking? There was no way this man could be trusted with her feelings. No way she could allow him to be privy to her thoughts. The truth of the matter was, she didn't know her thoughts. She wasn't sure what she felt for him. If one didn't count shameful lust and almost constant anger. "What I feel is none of your business."

"You want me."

Nora snorted a derisive sound. "It's amazing that you can find a hat to fit a head so swelled."

Jake grinned. "Why are you denying it?"

"I'm not denying a thing. Your comment simply isn't worth a response."

"Then you admit that you want me?"

Nora heaved a heavy sigh and rolled her eyes toward the heavens. "Lord."

"What are we going to do about Cole?"

Nora shot him an incredulous look. "Do about *him?* More to the point, don't you think, what am I going to do about *you?*"

Jake grinned. "I could show you, but first answer me."

Nora turned away. She couldn't look at him and keep her thoughts together. Not when he grinned like that. She forced her shaking hands to remain steady. He could show her and she wouldn't be able to stop it. She hadn't as yet been able to stop him from doing the most outrageous things. Not that she'd tried. Nora knew a sense of horrifying embarrassment as the truth made itself known. She hadn't once tried.

Nora wisely ignored the first part of his statement and quickly answered the second. "Nothing. I'm not going to do a thing."

"What do you mean you're not going to do a thing? He loves you."

"He hasn't told me that."

"Well, he's told me that."

"Jake, go away. I don't want to discuss this with you."

"I want to know what you're going to do."

"Why?"

"Because I want you and I can't do anything about it until you stop seeing my brother."

"Can't do anything about it," she ridiculed in obvious disgust as she continued straightening up the room. Her thoughts returned to this morning and what had happened between them. If that's what he called not doing anything . . .

Jake knew well enough her train of thought. He hadn't been able to think of much else since it happened. "Things got out of hand this morning," Jake said, almost as an apology. "I'm not sorry it happened. I just don't want it to keep happening until you tell my brother."

"What? Tell him what?" she asked in exasperation.

"That you won't see him again. That you and I are . . ."

"What?" she snapped, when it became obvious he wasn't about to finish. Nora was unable to decide which of them upset her more: Jake for his insistence or herself for listening to this drivel. "That we lust for one another? That we're in love? Tell me what I should say."

Jake stiffened at the mention of love. Christ, why did women always have to complicate things by mentioning love? Why couldn't they simply accept the fact that men and women both had certain needs? Love. Jesus, there was no way. His voice was harsh, his eyes cold as he nodded. "Lust is good."

Jake knew, even as he said it, it was the worst thing he could have said to a woman like her. But there was no way he was going to lie. It was lust he felt and he might as well get things out in the open. It would benefit neither of them if she thought he offered more.

Nora walked to the door and almost wrenched it from its hinges before it finally opened. "Maybe, but not good enough. Get out!"

Her eyes were blue, instead of green, and her hair a disappointing gold, not luscious, fiery red. She'd come to him in the dark of night; her voice soft, lilting, sweet and . . . deadly. Only he hadn't known it at the time.

He'd been so incredibly thin. So thin, in fact that he'd had no problem sliding through the tiny cellar window. Only his shoulders had given him a bit of trouble, but he'd hunched them in and managed to squeeze them through.

The cellar was dark, damp, and cold. He shivered, wondering if he'd ever know warmth again. He'd run through a field of frozen grass with no shoes. He couldn't feel his feet.

Damn, but he was tired. If he slept a year it wouldn't be enough. How was he going to get away? He had to have rest first. And food. God, if only he had something to eat.

His stomach growled, a constant happening. For months he'd been living on tainted meat and bread pies, as he and the others called them, for they held their own meat. Fat juicy worms. At first he couldn't

200

get the bread down, but it wasn't long before he waited anxiously for their one meal a day and ate as fast as any.

On his hands and knees, he crawled to a corner, a place darker and cooler than the rest, but maybe safer. He could hide here. Maybe he could hide forever. Maybe he wouldn't have to come out until the war was over. He shook his head. No. He had to come out. He had to find food. Later, he thought. He'd look for food later, after he got some sleep.

She was standing over him, a candle in her hand. She had the bluest eyes he'd ever seen. The candle-light made her hair look like spun gold, as golden as an angel. She looked like a fairy tale princess to him, so beautiful he was afraid to move lest the vision disappear.

"I won't hurt you," he said at the widening of her eyes. "Don't be afraid."

And she had promised she wasn't.

Her blue eyes were filled with compassion as she brought him blankets. He huddled beneath them and smiled as she offered a jar of peaches. Peaches she'd put up herself. God, had peaches ever tasted so good?

She was so kind. After the peaches she'd brought coffee. Hot and delicious. He couldn't believe it. He hadn't tasted real coffee in months.

He snuggled deeper beneath the covers, his body so emaciated, it appeared lost in the heavy folds. Warmth. God, when had he last felt warm?

He dozed, wrapped in the thick folds of the blanket, unable to remember when he'd known such comfort. He'd leave here soon, he promised, but not too soon. He had to get his strength first.

Strong hands were pulling at him. In his sleep he shrugged them aside, but they insisted. And then they were more than pulling, they were punching. He groaned with pain and lights flashed, as one meaty fist contacted with his eye.

He was jerked to his feet and dragged up the stairs. He passed her at her front door. Her eyes were no longer soft and filled with compassion, but hard with spite, her mouth twisted in hate.

"Keep the slime where he belongs," she said as he was carried kicking and screaming curses from her house.

Green eyes and red hair. She laughed as he was returned to the torture.

With a muffled cry of agony, Jake sat straight up in bed. Eyes wide, his body slick with sweat, his breathing labored, his heart pounding. Had he screamed? Had he called out? Damn, but it had been months since he had that dream.

He lay down again, his eyes open in the dark room, his body not yet ready to return to sleep. He shuddered as he remembered again and groaned, knowing he couldn't stop the memory.

He'd taken sixty-three lashes that night. At least sixty-three, after that he'd lost count. Afterwards he awoke in the dungeon, with no blankets or bedding. He stayed there a month, although at the time he would have sworn it was closer to a year. And all that time he prayed for death. Despite his prayers he'd eaten their maggoty bread and drank the none too clean water that the guards had pissed in. No matter

202

what his mind said, his body had wanted to live.

When they came for him, he was covered in green mold and only half conscious and still he didn't die. Instead he'd hung on to the hatred. It was all he had to live for. The only thing that kept him alive.

Jake shook away the memory. He'd forgotten to let it go. He'd hated for too long. In his dream blue eyes had turned into green, but it hadn't been Nora who had turned on him. He couldn't blame her for what had been done to him. She wasn't the one at fault. At last he found himself able to admit to that. He'd bet his soul that she wouldn't have done the same.

Her voice was just as soft, just as sweet, but he knew there was no hatred hidden in the throaty depths. In truth that soft, sweet drawl was most pleasing to the ear. Low and husky, it brought a stirring to his body. A stirring he couldn't control or deny.

Even now, it only took the fleeting thought of her to bring his body rock hard with need. Cursing he rolled over, knowing even as he moved the uselessness of trying to squash the yearning, along with his body's reaction to it. It wouldn't work. Nothing ever did.

The women at Fancy's had tried, but even they couldn't ease the torment of wanting her. Lately, he'd given up trying and had instead reverted to a most basic means that hadn't been needed since he was a lad. His hand reached between his body and the bed, his fingers closing around his erection. There wasn't a chance of sleep unless he freed himself, at least momentarily of the ache.

His hand moved mechanically, unthinkingly. As

he did what needed to be done, his mind went again to the woman who tortured his thoughts. She was everything a man could want in a woman. Smart, sweet, soft and so damn sensuous, she could drive men wild with wanting her. No wonder his brother was so taken with her. And that was the crux of the problem. His brother loved Nora. It hardly mattered that she didn't love him in return. She would in time. And Jake would suffer in his own silent wanting, never to have for his own the one woman that refused to leave his mind.

Chapter Nine

Jake muttered another curse. He'd been doing a lot of cursing lately and figured he'd better ease off some. Matt would be following his example before he knew it. His mouth tightened into a deep scowl as his blue gaze moved over the rough terrain and up the slope of the mountain, searching out any strays.

He tried to keep his mind on his work, but damn it, she was always there. He hadn't seen her in more than a month, hadn't dared go into town lest he come across her by accident. Still she wouldn't leave his mind.

He could remember, like it was yesterday, the smell of her, the taste of a mouth so lush, so sweet and hot that a man could lose himself in the ecstasy. Her skin, creamy white, smooth and so delicate he could see smudges of blue veins at her jaw and temples. And her scent! God, when had a woman ever smelled so clean, so good?

His body shuddered at the memory and he wondered when this torment would leave? When would he forget? When would he look at another and not find her lacking in comparison?

It was worse than anything he'd ever known. She'd stolen his peace of mind and there wasn't a damn thing he could do about it. He sure as hell didn't want to think about her, but no matter how he tried, she was always there.

He wanted to hate her. A month ago he could have. She was Southern and uppity and beautiful and everything he'd once despised in a woman. Jake's lips twisted into a wry grin. Bull! He'd been kidding himself even then. She was everything he wanted in a woman. Despite her being Southern, despite the fact that he'd never taken to red hair, she was so damn perfect and so far above him, he didn't stand a chance.

He possessed no skills, no finesse. He didn't know how to sweet-talk a lady. Yes, he could bed a woman with the greatest of skills, but he couldn't talk to one worth a damn. He had none of Cole's charm. Nora would have laughed at him if he'd tried. He was nothing but an ignorant cowboy who didn't know anything except ranching. And she was a lady. A refined lady at that.

The more he remembered how she worked over Charlie, how without hesitation, she'd actually dipped her hands inside the man's body, amid all that blood and destruction, the more amazement he felt. She didn't think it was beneath her to soil her hands while aiding and comforting the sick. He hadn't realized a lady would do such a thing.

Ladies, to his way of thinking, were creatures too delicate to face so monumental a task. Most ladies would faint or have the vapors at being forced to perform such a chore. But she hadn't. Just as if it happened every day, she went to work over the man and tried her damndest to keep him alive. She was a lady, no doubt. Her walk, her speech, her mannerisms all testified to the truth of that fact, but she was more. So much more. She was strong, capable, and brave. Jake had never met a woman like her. He doubted another existed.

People compared her to an angel. Cole never stopped in his regaling of her accomplishments. How she had sewn up Mary Lou Jenkins's cut. How she had taken care of Mrs. Applebee's warts. How she had set Tom Logan's leg.

Rumor had it that she'd worked side-by-side with her father during the war. Jake could well imagine what it must have meant to any man to see that face upon awakening. It was a wonder the North had won, for she alone could have garnered the morale needed to win.

God, but she had every right to hate his guts. Jake's face grew warm as he remembered how from the beginning he had attacked the woman and her character. He smiled as he remembered her nasty comebacks. She never let him get away with a thing. The woman had guts. She'd faced him down. The trouble was, every encounter had left her more appealing than the one before.

And there wasn't a damn thing he could do about it . . . except suffer. The woman belonged to Cole. Yeah, she might respond when he took her in his arms, but it was Cole that was going to have her. It was Cole who made it his business to go into town every damn night. Even if he'd had a chance, there was no way he was going to cut in on Cole. He had only one option and that was to leave her alone.

Damn, he wasn't accomplishing a damn thing mooning over the woman. It was growing dark, he couldn't find the missing calf and he was worried about Matt. He'd thought, he'd hoped, that whatever it was that had plagued Matt was gone for good, but he'd been wrong. Matt had been better this morning, but last night he'd been feverish and moaning in pain again.

He needed a doctor. Jake couldn't deny it any longer. Robert Morgan was well again. Between Nora and her father, Jake knew Matt would be in good hands. Tomorrow he'd bring the boy to town. Tomorrow he'd see Nora again.

Jake turned his horse toward home. It was cold in the mountains, but the calf should be fine for the time being. Tomorrow, after he got back from town, he'd look again.

Jake entered his home, a sprawling one-story, u-shaped structure that had at its center a large family room, dining room, and kitchen. At each side of the main room were halls that led to bedrooms. White Moon, the woman who served as his housekeeper since he'd first settled here and a nanny for his son since the boy was born, was wiping her hands on an apron. A fire was already set in the grate and the house was warm against the chill of a desert night.

Jake hung up his hat and gun belt on a hook behind the front door. He was taking off his spurs, when he asked, "How's Matt?"

The older woman shook her head. There was real

fear in her black eyes. Worry etched her thin lips. "We send for medicine man. He take out evil spirit."

Jake frowned. He would have liked to have told her what he thought of her primitive suggestion, but White Moon loved his son like he was her own. Jake wasn't about to hurt her. Still, there was no way he was going to let one of those medicine men near his son. What the boy needed was a doctor. Despite his denials, it couldn't be put off any longer. "I'll send Cole into town. The doctor's been workin' some. Maybe, he can ride." And if he couldn't then he'd see Nora for the first time in a month.

Robert Morgan was much stronger. If the boy was brought to town, he would have been able to see to him. "Tell your brother to bring Matt to town."

Cole shook his head. "He's too sick. He can't ride. I don't think he should be moved."

Nora had no choice but to go. There was no way she was going to allow her father to chance a relapse by overdoing it. Still, she was uncomfortable with the thought of facing Jake again. She put aside her feelings and concentrated on Matt. "Is he still suffering the same pain?"

Cole nodded. "It's somethin' fierce. He has a fever. Somethin' must be festerin'."

Nora nodded and left Cole as she went to see her father.

She paced nervously as she explained the problem.

Robert's gaze widened, perplexed at his daughter's sudden attack of nerves. "Nora, you've seen me do it a hundred times. You've done more than a few yourself. It's a simple enough procedure."

"But I haven't done one in years."

"You want me to go?"

"No." Nora felt a shiver of anticipation. "No. I'll go."

"You'd best not drain it. It will only fester again. Take it out."

Nora nodded as she gathered the things she'd need. She wasn't sure she wanted to do this. Did she want to go to that man's home? Did she want to face him, remembering all the things that had happened between them? Nora knew she had no real choice. Her father was nearly recovered, but had not as yet regained all his strength. Perhaps he never would.

An hour later Cole brought the small buggy to a stop before Jake's front door. Jake watched his brother hand her down. His gut wrenched at the familiar and possessive handling. How the hell was he going to stand this? "You took your sweet time. Where's the doctor?"

"My father isn't strong enough to make the ride. I'll have to do."

"Well, you won't do." Jake couldn't believe what he was hearing. What the hell was he saying? In his heart he knew it was Nora he wanted here. He'd been aching to see her again and now that she'd come he was practically ordering her from his house.

"Fine," Nora said as she turned around and sat herself again in the buggy. "I didn't want to come here in the first place." And she hadn't. She hadn't seen him in weeks and until now hadn't realized how peaceful her life had become. He was nasty, sometimes even cruel. She didn't want to see him. She didn't want to be near him. Lord, she didn't want anything to do with the man.

"Jake! What the hell is the matter with you?" Cole turned to Nora. "You know Matt needs her." After a long moment of silence as the two tried to stare each other down he said, "There's no one else."

Jake stood for a long moment and watched Nora glare in his direction. Well he'd fixed things up just fine this time. She just might be the only chance Matt had and he'd gone and started up all the old anger again. Damn!

"Sorry," Jake swallowed his pride and murmured barely above a whisper. "I'd be obliged, if you'd have a look at him, ma'am."

Nora again descended from the buggy and walked past Jake into his beautiful home, ignoring him as if he didn't exist. Nora never noticed the comfort or cleanliness, she turned on her heel and almost smacked against the man's chest. "Where is he?" she asked as she took a quick step in retreat.

Jake almost grinned at how fast she moved. She looked almost as nervous as he felt. He might have laughed if he hadn't been so worried about Matt. "This way," he said as he walked to the right of the parlor and down a long hall. At the first door he stopped and entered a room. Nora followed.

Matt looked so small, lying in that big bed that Nora's heart twisted with pity. His skin was hot to the touch, his face flushed. She prayed that if there was one person she was able to save, *"Please God, help me do it now!"*

Nora took her hand from the boy's forehead. "He has a fever. Has he been nauseous?"

White Moon, who stood at the foot of the bed murmuring some foreign-sounding words that Nora

211

assumed were prayers, answered with a nod.

"And the pain?"

"It's worse." This came from Jake who stood at the opposite side of the bed, staring at her. His blue eyes were filled with a combination of frustration at his inability to help his own son and pleading for her to do what he could not.

Nora pushed the sheet to the boy's hips. Carefully she pressed her hand along the length of his abdomen and nodded as the boy cried out.

She turned to White Moon. "I want you to wash the kitchen table and cover it with an ironed sheet."

The Indian woman left the room. Nora's gaze moved to the boy's anxious father. "Get all the lanterns you can find and bring them into the kitchen. I'll need plenty of light."

Jake nodded and was just about to leave the room when he came to a sudden stop. "What are you going to do?"

"It's his appendix. It has to come out."

His body went stiff with terror. It showed clearly in his eyes. "If you think I'm going to let you cut him, you're out a' your mind."

"If you don't, and his appendix ruptures, he'll die."

"You're not a doctor."

Her green eyes flashed. "I'm the next best thing." Silently she dared him to do better.

"Have you ever done this before?"

"Yes. And I've assisted my father a dozen times."

Jake was filled with fear, almost to the point of panic. If he gave permission, his son might die. If he refused, his son might die. What the hell was a man supposed to do?

She hadn't been able, no matter her skill and dedication, to save Charlie. But this wasn't a gunshot wound. This was different. Wasn't it? Jake looked at the tiny woman standing before him, eyes narrowed, her hands on her hips, waiting impatiently for his decision. Could he trust her with his son's life? Yes, she was good at taking care of burns, scrapes, and cuts, but did she know what she was about in this case? He gave a silent groan. No father should have to make a decision like this. His words were hard, born out of fear when he finally said, "Lady, you'd better know what the hell you're doing."

Nora's back stiffened at his harsh words and what was clearly a warning in his eyes. "Mr. Brackston, I work better without threats."

Jake had never felt so helpless in his entire life. He muttered a curse and left the room.

"Where do you want your things?" Cole asked as he stepped into the bedroom.

"Bring them into the kitchen. When the table is ready, come back for your nephew."

Nora stepped into the kitchen and opened the bags she'd brought along. "Get me a basin," she said, only glancing at Jake's emotionless face as she spoke to Mina. The girl did as she was told. Nora soaked her apron in carbolic acid and wrapped it wet around her body. Her shirt sleeves were pushed up and her hands, washed first in soap and water, were then dipped in alcohol. The sheet was just being slid over the table when Cole brought Matt into the now brightly lit room.

"Iron two more," she said and White Moon

nodded to her daughter who ran to do her bidding.

The boy groaned as he was placed on the hard surface. His eyes were wide as he watched everyone go about their designated chores. He clearly was in pain and terrified, obviously too scared to ask why he was on the table. A small whimper escaped his lips and Nora glanced in his direction. There was no denying the fear in his eyes. "Don't be afraid, darlin'," Nora said soothingly.

"I ain't afraid," Matt said bravely and Nora's heart fairly ached that a boy so small could possess courage so great. He looked at his father who stood at his side holding his hand. "Papa said you'd fix me up."

"And I will." She smiled into his frightened eyes. "I'm going to give you something to make you sleep." She smiled again hoping to bring the boy a measure of comfort. "When you wake up, you'll be all better."

"Promise?" His voice shook with fear and Nora saw the tears slip from his eyes into his dark hair.

"I promise." As she gathered her supplies and readied herself for her task, she asked conversationally, "I'll bet you're just plain tired of being sick all the time."

Matt nodded, his eyes huge and solemn. "I can't run any more. My side hurts when I run."

"That can't be any fun." Nora commiserated. "Can you ride?" she asked, hoping to get his mind off what was about to happen, for his eyes had widened to enormous proportions when he saw her take her instruments from the bag and lay them on the table.

"Papa taught me." His voice was tight with fear. Nora smiled again. "He did?" she asked pleasantly, knowing this conversation benefitted both of them. She too needed something to keep her mind off what was about to happen. "Are you good at it?"

Matt nodded proudly. "I don't have to hold on anymore."

"How old are you?"

"Six."

"Imagine that," she said gravely. "Six years old and you don't have to hold on. I was almost ten before I could ride without holding on." It wasn't true. Nora could ride by the time she was four, but Matt didn't have to know that.

"You're a girl."

Nora shot the boy's father a pointed look and frowned at his grin. It was obvious where she put the blame for Matt's prejudice. "Do you think girls can't ride as well as boys?"

"Papa says boys are better at things like riding than girls."

"Yes, I'm sure he does," Nora remarked, her voice only slightly annoyed and that annoyance was fully directed to the father. "Well, what would you say if I told you, you'll be riding again in a few weeks."

"That long?" he asked obviously disappointed. Nora had forgotten that a few weeks could seem like an eternity to a child.

"Aw, sweetheart, that's not so long. It's going to take a little time for you to heal, that's all."

"But then I'll be able to ride again?" he asked hopefully.

"Honey, in a few days, your papa won't be able to keep you in bed."

Matt grinned in anticipation and Nora laughed.

She moved to the head of the table and stood just behind him. "Now this stuff smells pretty bad, but I want you to breathe it in anyway. Just breathe like you always do. All right?"

The boy nodded.

Nora placed a clean piece of cloth over his nose and mouth. She let a few drops of chloroform fall to the cloth. Matt choked.

"Breathe easy now," Nora said as she brushed his dark hair from his forehead. "Easy."

She turned to Cole. "Can you stay? I need someone to keep this up."

Cole swallowed and nodded. His eyes were bigger than Nora had ever seen them. She could tell he didn't want to do it, but there was no way she could ask Matt's father. She'd never seen a man more terrified in her life. He might have smiled a few minutes back, but that was the one and only time she'd seen anything but fear in his eyes since she'd walked into this house.

"Just put a drop on the cloth every few minutes. There's no need for you to watch me."

"Thank God," Cole groaned and Nora smiled at the sound of his relief.

Again she bathed her hands in alcohol, her instruments as well. "Take off his nightshirt and cover him with that sheet to his waist. Put the other one over his hips," Nora said to Mina as she nodded toward the two ironed sheets.

Mina quickly did as she was asked.

Nora's gaze moved to Jake, who stood opposite her, holding his son's hand. "If you step outside, I'll . . ."

His face was hard, his emotions held tightly in check, except for the flicker of fear in his eyes. "I'm stayin'."

Nora shrugged. "It's different when it's your own." They both remembered the last time he'd assisted her. "Most can't take the sight of it."

"I won't look."

"If you faint you'll just have to stay there. I can't stop in the middle and help you."

"I'm stayin'," Jake repeated, this time a bit more forcefully.

"Fine," she said and then ignored the man. "Matt? Can you hear me?"

No response.

Nora pinched his toe. The boy slept.

"I need you to wipe the blood," she said to White Moon. "Can you do it?"

The woman nodded, and Jake knew only unbound relief. He couldn't have done it himself. God only knew what he'd do if he'd seen his son cut and bleeding. He didn't want to think of the terror he'd surely know.

He felt enough of the emotion as it was. He couldn't leave and yet he couldn't watch. His eyes stayed on Nora's heart-shaped face as she leaned over his son, a thin bladed instrument in her hand.

Jake swallowed down his nausea and shook aside the light-headed sensation that was overwhelming him. He couldn't faint. No matter how hard this was to bear, he had to go through with it. He had to stay. He had to be here. He knew something terrible would happen if he left.

He wished he knew how to pray, for he never in his

life needed prayer more. He begged God to take care of his son. Was that praying? Were special words needed? If only he knew for sure. Silently he swore he'd learn. He'd do anything, if only God would let him keep his son.

Nora felt a moment of anxiety as she mentally prepared herself for the task set before her. Her hands trembled and her heart raced as she glanced at the boy's white face. She couldn't allow herself to think. She had to remove from her mind how terribly important it was that every thing should go right. She had to forget the little boy and his anxious, terrified father and do what she'd been trained to do. A silent prayer filled her mind and her fingers moved automatically to do what they must.

The room was silent except for the soft, steady sounds of five adults and one child breathing. So silent in fact that Jake swore he could hear his son's steady heartbeat. He prayed to hear it always, even as he fixed his gaze on the woman across from him. She held Matt's life, his future, in her small hands. He prayed she was equal to the chore.

It was a textbook case. Within fifteen minutes, Nora had removed the inflamed, tiny organ and was sewing up the small incision. She bathed the area with alcohol and covered it with yet another ironed sheet torn into strips.

Nora moved to the head of the table and removed the cloth and chloroform from Cole's trembling hands. "You did wonderfully." She smiled at his weak, if grateful, look.

"Take a bit of fresh air. When you come back, you can carry him to his room."

Nora stripped off the wet apron, threw it in the sink and washed her hands again. All the while Jake stood silently holding his son's small hand, leaning weakly against the edge of the table.

"Is he all right?" he asked, watching the rise and fall of the small chest.

"He's fine. He'll sleep for a bit. When he wakes up he'll be in some pain, but that too will pass."

A few minutes later, Cole came back in and she followed him and Matt down the hall. They were standing on opposite sides of the bed, looking down at the sleeping child, when Jake walked into the room.

Nora smoothed a sheet and blanket over the boy's shoulders and turned away. "Would you like to stay with him for a while?"

Jake only nodded. He never glanced in her direction, but pulled a chair close to the bed and again took his son's hand.

White Moon and Mina busied themselves in tidying up the kitchen again, while Cole escorted Nora outside. They were sitting on the porch. In the distance, alongside the barn, stood a lean-to. Inside the three-sided enclosure, a blacksmith stood wielding a giant hammer. Muscles bulging, he slammed it upon a glowing piece of metal taken from the fire.

"What's he doing?"

Cole smiled as he followed the direction of her gaze. "Looks like he's fixin' to replace a shoe. The horses throw them every so often. 'Specially when we

219

ride into the mountains. It's rough country up there."

Nora nodded as she watched the man work. At home they'd had a blacksmith. Old Thomas had died just before the outbreak of hostilities. Moses, his son, who was learning the craft well, ran off a week after the fighting began. No one had taken his place.

Idly Nora wondered where Moses was now. And Jessie and the rest. She breathed a heavy sigh and closed her eyes. Having grown up with slaves and knowing nothing else, she hadn't realized the horror of one human being owning another. To Nora and her family, along with most of the South, it had been a natural occurrence.

Her family hadn't treated their people poorly. Indeed, the slaves at her small home were treated better than most. And still they had run off. At the time, Nora couldn't understand why they were so eager to leave behind all they'd ever known. It wasn't until the war ended and she felt for herself the real threat of living under another's rule, that she came to realize with shame what she and her family had done.

"You were wonderful, in there. You're wonderful all the time," he clarified. "I'm in awe."

Nora smiled, her eyes still closed as she teased, "You needn't stop on my account, Cole. A lady can never hear too much flattery."

"It's not flattery. I'm honestly honored to know you."

Nora's eyes opened wide at the declaration. She turned a smile in his direction. "Cole, how nice. Thank you."

"Nora, this probably isn't the best time, or place,

but I want to ask you to be my wife."

Slightly flustered, Nora's eyes widened at the unexpected proposal. Her voice was very small when she answered, "I don't know what to say."

His dark eyes watched her carefully. "You can't claim surprise. Surely you've known for some time my feelings for you."

"Yes, I knew." Lord, she didn't want to hurt this man. He was so good, so kind, and so very handsome. Why couldn't she feel what he did? And what in the world was she to say? "I've never encouraged them, Cole. I hope you know that."

"Are you telling me you don't love me?"

She couldn't bring herself to say it, not with the way he looked at her, not with hope shining in his eyes.

Her silence was an answer in itself.

"Is there someone else?"

"No," she answered honestly. "There's no one else." *Except maybe Jake* came a secret, startling thought. Nora felt nothing but amazement that such a ridiculous notion should come to mind. Still, she couldn't help but wonder what her answer would have been if Jake had done the asking? Wisely she refused to linger on the supposed scenario. Her thoughts were confused enough where that man was concerned.

"You could learn to love me, you know. It could grow into something wonderful."

She shook her head. "You'd be cheating yourself."

"Let me make that decision."

"But—"

"Wait," he held up his hand, hoping to stop any

221

further rejection. "Don't say anything. Just give it time. Promise me you'll give it time."

"Cole, I—"

"Promise me, please?"

Nora breathed a tired sigh. It wasn't going to do any good. She couldn't love this man in any way but as a dear friend. In her heart she knew the truth of it. Still, she heard herself say, "All right. I promise." After a few minutes she continued on with, "You know, Cole, maybe you should look closer to home, if it's a wife you want."

His brow creased into a frown. "What does that mean?"

"Mina. She's—"

"A child. I'm not looking for children. I want a woman."

"How old is she?"

"I don't know." He shrugged. "She's been around here for years. I remember her mother giving her a bath and rocking her to sleep."

"She's not a child any more, Cole. Look at her."

Cole shot Nora a puzzled glance, as his mind went to the woman inside. For the first time he realized Nora was right. Mina was full grown. How had he missed that? How could a man live in the same house with a woman and never see that the little girl who had come here all those years ago was all grown-up? He looked at Nora's soft knowing smile and shook his head. "It won't make any difference. It's you I want."

Jake chose just that moment to step outside. His mind was filled with worry over his son and his less than happy disposition wasn't improved any listening to his brother's declaration. His eyes were filled with both anxiety and anger. His voice was abrupt and hard when he spoke almost accusingly, "He's in a lot of pain."

Nora nodded and returned to the kitchen. She mixed a few grains of opium into a glass of water.

"Hurry," Jake said, standing at her back; his presence crowding her, imploring her to hasten her movements.

Nora followed the anxious father back to Matt's room.

"You said I'd be better, but I'm not," Matt accused in a low voice filled with pain.

"I know you're sore, darlin', but you'll be well again, very soon. All you have to do is rest and you'll heal up just fine."

Jake carefully raised the boy into a sitting position. Matt made a horrific face when Nora held the glass to his lips and he swallowed the liquid. "Yuck," he complained in a childish whine.

"I know," she nodded consolingly, "but it will take away the pain."

It took less than two minutes before the boy started drifting off. Jake shot Nora a grateful glance. Suddenly he wanted her to stay, to sit with him while Matt slept. Only he knew that she wouldn't want to stay with him and even if she did, he didn't know how to ask.

"I'll sit with him later."

Jake nodded. "Get some rest. Tell White Moon I said to give you the room next to mine."

It was hours later before Nora came again to check her patient. She wore no shoes, and a borrowed robe covered her chemise and stockings, having taken off her blouse, petticoats and skirt before she lay down. Cole was taking his turn sitting with his nephew. They exchanged a smile as she left the room. The boy slept on, but Nora knew he would soon need another dose of laudanum. While she waited for him to awaken, she moved through the silent house out to the porch. She stood at one of the posts that supported its roof and sighed tiredly. Her mind returned to the proposal she'd gotten this afternoon and her rejection of it. The truth of it was, he hadn't allowed her to reject it. But she knew it didn't make any difference. She wouldn't marry Cole. Idly she wondered if she'd made the right choice. Cole would have made a good husband, and she knew she couldn't help but love him in time. But Nora needed something more. Something she couldn't put a name to.

From the shadows at one corner of the porch came a deep voice, tight with fear. "Is he all right?"

Nora had thought she was alone. She made a tiny sound of alarm as she spun about. She hadn't noticed the scent of his cigarette in the still night. She hadn't seen the movement in the shadows as he came to his feet. She nodded and then in a voice oddly breathless, she said, "He's sleeping."

Jake flicked his cigarette into the air. It made a red blurring arc as it fell to the hard packed ground. He moved toward her, stopping only when he stepped into the light cast by the opened door. For a long moment he simply stood there. Twice his mouth opened trying to find the words. What could he say? There were no words that could describe the

MORE PASSION AND ADVENTURE AWAIT... YOUR TRIP TO A BIG ADVENTUROUS WORLD BEGINS WHEN YOU ACCEPT YOUR FIRST 4 NOVELS ABSOLUTELY *FREE*
(AN $18.00 VALUE)

Accept your Free gift and start to experience more of the passion and adventure you like in a historical romance novel. Each Zebra novel is filled with proud men, spirited women and tempestuous love that you'll remember long after you turn the last page.

Zebra Historical Romances are the finest novels of their kind. They are written by authors who really know how to weave tales of romance and adventure in the historical settings you love. You'll feel like you've actually gone back in time with the thrilling stories that each Zebra novel offers.

GET YOUR FREE GIFT WITH THE START OF YOUR HOME SUBSCRIPTION

Our readers tell us that these books sell out very fast in book stores and often they miss the newest titles. So Zebra has made arrangements for you to receive the four newest novels published each month.

You'll be guaranteed that you'll never miss a title, and home delivery is so convenient. And to show you just how easy it is to get Zebra Historical Romances, we'll send you your first 4 books absolutely FREE! Our gift to you just for trying our home subscription service.

BIG SAVINGS AND FREE HOME DELIVERY

Each month, you'll receive the four newest titles as soon as they are published. You'll probably receive them even before the bookstores do. What's more, you may preview these exciting novels free for 10 days. If you like them as much as we think you will, just pay the low preferred subscriber's price of just $3.75 each. *You'll save $3.00 each month off the publisher's price.* AND, your savings are even greater because there are never any shipping, handling or other hidden charges—FREE Home Delivery. Of course you can return any shipment within 10 days for full credit, no questions asked. There is no minimum number of books you must buy.

4 FREE BOOKS

TO GET YOUR 4 FREE BOOKS WORTH $18.00 — MAIL IN THE FREE BOOK CERTIFICATE T O D A Y

Fill in the Free Book Certificate below, and we'll send your FREE BOOKS to you as soon as we receive it.

If the certificate is missing below, write to: Zebra Home Subscription Service, Inc., P.O. Box 5214, 120 Brighton Road, Clifton, New Jersey 07015-5214.

FREE BOOK CERTIFICATE

4 FREE BOOKS

ZEBRA HOME SUBSCRIPTION SERVICE, INC.

YES! Please start my subscription to Zebra Historical Romances and send me my first 4 books absolutely FREE. I understand that each month I may preview four new Zebra Historical Romances free for 10 days. If I'm not satisfied with them, I may return the four books within 10 days and owe nothing. Otherwise, I will pay the low preferred subscriber's price of just $3.75 each; a total of $15.00, *a savings off the publisher's price of $3.00.* I may return any shipment and I may cancel this subscription at any time. There is no obligation to buy any shipment and there are no shipping, handling or other hidden charges. Regardless of what I decide, the four free books are mine to keep.

NAME

ADDRESS _____ APT _____

CITY _____ STATE _____ ZIP _____

TELEPHONE ( )

SIGNATURE _____
(if under 18, parent or guardian must sign)

Terms, offer and prices subject to change without notice. Subscription subject to acceptance by Zebra Books. Zebra Books reserves the right to reject any order or cancel any subscription.

gratitude he knew for this woman.

It was all there in his eyes. Nora knew he was having a hard time of it and offered, "You don't have to say anything. I understand."

"Yes I do." Jake looked like he was about to collapse. He was weak with relief and leaned heavily against the porch railing. "He's all I've got." His voice was choked and tight with emotion. "I've never loved anyone the way I love him. God, I was so damn scared."

Nora nodded, not knowing what else to do. The haggard look in his eyes made her forget her resolve to keep her distance. She moved closer and reached out to touch his arm. "He's all right now," she said, touching him in a comforting, soothing gesture, one much like she'd offer anyone who had suffered through these last fearful hours. There was nothing sexual in her touch, nothing but compassion for the torment of a fellow human being.

It was a long time before Jake got himself under enough control to trust his voice. "The things I said . . ."

Nora shook her head. "Don't. Not now."

He looked down at her. God she looked so soft, so sweet, he knew he wasn't going to be able to resist the need to hold her. With a low, almost anguished groan, his arms reached around her and brought her against him. He had to touch her or die, he had to feel her softness against him or go mad. "Just let me hold you," he groaned against her neck as he felt her stiffen. "God, I need to hold you," he said softly as he rocked their bodies back and forth.

Chapter Ten

Nora forced back the need to laugh as she watched him expose three of a kind and two pairs to her pair of threes. "Are you sure you wouldn't rather play hearts?"

"Poker's more fun."

"Does your father know you play?"

"Sure," Matt's dark head bounced back and forth as he knelt on wide spread knees above the covers. "Uncle Cole taught me. Only I don't get to win when I play with them."

"I feel like I'm contributing to the delinquency of a minor here," she said as she reached for the cards and began to shuffle again.

"Naw," he said and then cut himself off with, "What does that mean?"

Nora laughed. "It means that little boys shouldn't play poker."

"Why not?"

"Because they beat ladies and that makes the lady feel very foolish indeed."

Matt laughed and fell back on his pillow. Nora was having a time of it keeping the boy in bed, never mind still.

"Stop bouncing before you fall off the bed."

Matt eyed Nora and then the floor with undisguised hunger. The idea sounded pretty good to him. If he bounced hard enough and fell on the floor maybe she'd let him . . .

"No. If you fall out of that bed, you'll stay in it another two days."

"How did you know?" Matt asked, his eyes wide with surprise that she could have read his thoughts.

"Because I know little boys can be very tricky."

"What about big boys?" Jake asked from the doorway.

Nora felt her cheeks warm with color. She hadn't heard him enter the house, nor seen him for more than a few minutes at a time during the last week and never alone. Feeling suddenly awkward, she forced a smile. "Big boys are even worse." Nora felt her cheeks warm at Jake's smile and changed the subject. "You should be ashamed of yourself teaching a six year old to play poker. It's a disgrace."

Jake grinned and ruffled his son's dark hair. "I didn't teach him, his uncle did." He looked to his son and asked, "Did you win?"

"Sure," the boy answered in all confidence. "She was easy."

"I wish she was," Jake muttered, almost but not quite beneath his breath.

"What?" Matt asked.

Nora's cheeks grew warmer. Silently she cursed her fair complexion and the fact that this man could so

228

easily bring embarrassing color to her cheeks.

Jake watched her purposely avoid his gaze as she continued to shuffle the cards. This was the first time he'd seen her without her usual poise. The fact that she couldn't seem to still her hands and refused to meet his gaze convinced him that she'd heard what he'd said. Jake grinned at the thought of being able to fluster this woman.

"What are you laughin' at, Papa?" Matt asked, wanting to be included.

"What am I laughing at?" Jake repeated as he sat at his son's side and then placed the boy on his lap. He was brushing aside the hair that fell over Matt's forehead as he went on, "Let's see. Could it be I'm laughing because a certain boy of mine is almost ready to get out of bed?"

Matt beamed at his father's words and gentle caress. "You haven't got any other little boys. I'm the only one."

"So you are," Jake said in feigned surprise.

"If you got another one, then I would have someone to play with."

"Would you like that?"

Enthusiastically, Matt nodded his entire body. His hair flapped against his forehead and his blue eyes opened wide. "I could be a big brother."

"First we'd have to find you a new mommy." Nora's hands grew still. Her heart pounded and her breath quickened. She'd never known a greater need to run and yet she forced herself to remain in place. He was looking at her and she, coward that she was, couldn't raise her eyes to meet his. There was a moment of intense silence before Jake's silky voice went on to tease her senses. "Do you know anybody who could do it?"

"Sure."

"Maybe you should whisper her name in my ear."

Nora had never known discomfort so great, as she listened to this conversation and felt Jake's bold look move over her.

Matt made a show of whispering in Jake's ear, his eyes never leaving Nora's face. His whisper was as clear as if he'd spoken the words aloud and only brought Nora's cheeks to still a rosier shade.

"Would you like that?" Jake responded.

Matt nodded again, his blue eyes still on the woman in question.

"You think she likes me enough?" Matt wondered.

"I think she does, but she'd have to like me too."

"Why?" Matt asked as he looked at his father, truly puzzled.

"Because in order to be your mother, she'd have to marry me," Jake said, his gaze moving again to Nora.

Nora had had enough. She almost bolted from the chair in her need to be gone from a conversation which featured her as the subject and yet, oddly enough, had not included her at all. She groaned as the chair fell back against the floor. She bent to straighten it as she spoke, "I'll leave you two to visit." Her hands shook as she put the assembled cards on the bedside table. "Matt should take a nap before dinner." She couldn't get out of the room fast enough. Jake grinned at her haste, but before she had a chance to close the door, she heard Matt's loud, conspiratorial whisper, "Why don't we ask her?"

Nora shut the door harder than she would have liked, knowing the moment she did it she gave away her distress. She shook her head in dismay and leaned against it as she breathed a deep sigh. It didn't matter. Jake would have had to be blind not to know she was upset.

She shouldn't have stayed. The truth of it was, there'd been no need. After three days, it was obvious that Matt was well on his way to recovery and yet she had put off leaving. Why? Nora shrugged as she straightened her thoughts. There had been no need to hurry back. Her father might be unable to travel, but he was well enough to care for the townsfolk. And Matt had proven to be such an adorable little boy. Could she be blamed for lingering on longer than what was deemed necessary?

It didn't matter, her reasons. The fact was Jake had gotten the wrong impression. Nora swore he had no influence on her decision to stay. For six days she'd ignored the man almost to the point of rudeness. He had to know she wasn't the least bit interested.

And still as casually as you please, he'd hinted at marriage.

Had he meant it? Was Jake truly considering asking her to marry him? And was he doing it to find a mother for his son? Nora denied the sensation of pain that squeezed at her chest. She was sure he'd only been teasing. Jake wasn't the sort to look for a wife just so Matt could once again have a mother. If that was the case, he would have married again, well before now.

Yes, of course, he'd been teasing. He didn't mean it. They were just silly words.

Two offers of marriage inside of a week and neither satisfied, especially not the last.

"She said she'd think on it."

Jake felt his heart leap with hope. She'd think on it. Would a woman who believed herself in love ask for time before giving her answer. Didn't that mean she wasn't sure? Didn't that mean she wasn't in love?

"What are you going to do about it?"

The two men leaned back in their chairs, rolled and lit cigarettes as they sipped at expensive brandy. Cole's gaze moved to Mina as she cleared the table. Ever since the night, more than two weeks ago, that Nora had pointed out the fact that Mina was no longer a child, Cole hadn't been able to get her out of his mind. His brow creased with confusion as he wondered why. Why did his gaze search her out the moment he entered the house? Why did he find himself following her every movement? He wondered what the hell was happening here? Since when did the tall, willowy woman appear suddenly so fetching? Why hadn't he ever noticed before how her dusky skin glowed flawless in the lamplight? Or how her long, midnight hair gleamed with shining light? And when had her slender fingers grown as graceful in movement as her pair of beguilingly slim hips? Cole felt a distinct, familiar tightening in the pit of his belly.

This couldn't be happening. It was Nora he loved. Wasn't it? Then why had her refusal, or attempted refusal, left him without a trace of the heartbreak he should have known? And what the hell was he doing

232

watching another while he waited for Nora to accept his proposal?

"Cole."

"What?" he said, tearing his gaze from the young woman who had long since left childhood behind and had done it without his notice.

"I asked you what are you going to do about it?"

Cole shrugged. "Wait, I reckon. What else can a man do?"

"Are you going to see her tonight?"

Cole again dragged his gaze from Mina to meet his brother's puzzled gaze. "No, I think I'll stay home tonight."

Jake's eyes widened with surprise and he looked quickly behind him. Was it his imagination, or had Cole, for the last two weeks, been looking at Mina in a whole new light? Jake watched the two of them look quickly away from one another. "You haven't seen her in days."

Cole shrugged. "So another won't hurt."

Jake frowned. Cole hardly sounded like a man lost in the throes of love. Nor, for that matter did he act like one. Not with the way he was watching Mina. Jake came to a decision. "I'm going into town."

"Why?"

"I want to talk to Nora."

"Nora?" Cole repeated with some surprise. Jake had never before used her Christian name. Until tonight he'd always referred to her as Mrs. Bowens. "Why?"

There was a long hesitation before Jake finally returned, "She left so suddenly, I didn't get clear instructions on Matt's care." The excuse was so feeble, even Matt would have recognized it as a lie. It had been two weeks since she'd left and only now did he think to ask for instructions?

Amazingly enough, Cole felt not a flicker of emotion. Two weeks ago he would have been mad with jealousy. He tried for the emotion now and realized with some surprise that it didn't exist. "She gave them to White Moon two weeks ago."

Jake nodded. "I know, but Matt wants to ride again. I want to know if it's all right."

"You sweet on her, Jake?" Cole asked, a sly grin curving his handsome mouth.

"On who?"

"Nora."

"Look if seeing her bothers you, I can wait till tomorrow. When you see her you can ask her for me."

Cole shook his head. "It don't bother me none." His gaze moved again to Mina and his next words convinced Jake his interest in Nora was waning. "And, I reckon I won't be seeing her for a spell."

Johnny grinned at the whore who had sidled up to his side and rubbed the biggest breasts he'd ever seen along his arm. Her gown was tight and slit up one leg to her hip. It was red and came low enough to let a man see what he was buying. Johnny grinned at the sight of her pink nipples peeking through the black lace that trimmed the edge of her bodice. Her hand moved between his legs and she openly caressed him, uncaring that anyone in the place only had to look at her to see what she was doing. Johnny felt himself spring up, ready for action. Damn, he liked it best when they were dirty. If there was one thing he couldn't stand it was a prissy, sly whore, who pretended not to like what you gave her.

It had been a long time. He needed a woman real bad and figured he couldn't have found a better, or more willing, piece in the state of Nevada.

"Buy me a drink, honey?"

"Sweetheart, I'll buy you a bottle, if you can find us a private place to drink it."

"Sure, honey. Casey," she said to the bartender, "give me a bottle."

The bartender reached beneath the narrow lid of the bar and brought out a bottle. Johnny didn't much care that it had been opened already and was probably half water. His mind was on the whore who was tugging at his arm, pulling him through the crowded room toward the stairs.

A few minutes later the door closed behind them and he sank into a soft mattress, his boots, gun belt and hat still in place. He leaned back against satin pillows and put the bottle to his lips.

The whore ran her hand down her back, releasing its buttons and the dress fell to her feet. She stepped out of it, naked except for a pair of frilly drawers and black stockings held up by fancy red garters. She picked up the dress, laid it over a chair, and stood with her hands on her hips. Facing him, she smiled as she watched his gaze move over her near naked state.

Johnny grinned at the sight before him, his gaze holding to her chest. He wasn't disappointed. They were even bigger than he'd supposed. Damn, but he liked them big, the bigger and softer the better.

"Here, honey, let me help you," the whore said as she knelt over his legs, her rear facing him as she tugged at his boots. They both knew it would have been easier if she'd stood at the bottom of the bed, but then he wouldn't have been able to slide his hand under the lacy drawers, if she'd done that. A long finger felt its way between the folds of her body before sliding into her soft, wet flesh. She moaned. It could have been playacting. He'd been with a few that figured the more they groaned the better the pay. But she wasn't acting. This one was hot for him. He could feel himself growing hard and shifted trying to find a comfortable spot.

"Turn around and open my pants," he said, and smiled as Susie anxiously did his bidding.

Johnny put the bottle on the floor and leaned back as she knelt over him. Her breasts were hanging between his legs. He reached out and played with them, enjoying their jiggling as he pinched her nipples.

Johnny'd always known, there were whores and *then there were whores!* This one was the kind that would be happy enough to take care of a man and wouldn't complain when he was too tired to have a go at her. This one would take care of herself. He could tell by the way she was rubbing herself on his leg. He'd enjoy watching that, he thought, and then a moment later he couldn't think at all.

Damn, but she was right up there with the best. Johnny looked at her with new eyes just moments after his entire body eased its shuddering. He smiled as she lifted her mouth from his groin. She'd given him the best ten minutes he'd ever known.

With her smile still in place, Susie moved to lie down at his side. The man was a pig and knew as much about pleasing a woman as a boy during his first time, but he was a man and Susie couldn't complain about the size of him. She was anxious to feel him plunge deep inside her, but figured rightly that she'd have to wait a bit for that. She shrugged. In the meantime, there was no sense in depriving herself of a little fun. He sure as hell didn't offer.

She took a sip from the bottle and without the least bit of self-consciousness, pushed down her drawers, and kicked them free of her feet. She looked up at the mirror over the bed and smiled at her naked reflection. A moment later she was watching her hands move down her body as she spoke, "You staying around for a spell?"

"Maybe," he said as he raised the bottle to his mouth again. It never hurt none to keep a woman guessing. "I 'spect to come into some money soon."

"Really?" Susie said, as her hands played with her breasts. They all said the same thing. Next he'd be asking her to go away with him as soon as he got it. But Susie had been in the business long enough to know that a man's talk changed fast enough once his feet hit the floor.

He was watching her in the overhead mirror. She spread herself with one hand and slid her fingers inside. A small smile curved her rouged lips as she saw his member start to stand up on its own.

But Susie was enjoying her own ministrations too much. She didn't want a man right now. As far as she was concerned, men never knew exactly what a woman wanted. Most were either too rough or too timid.

Her fingers were slippery wet as she massaged her tiny arousal and Johnny grinned turning on his side to watch her. "You sure know how to enjoy yourself."

"I've had enough practice at it," she said honestly. She might be a whore, but most nights ended like this. Men came and went, finding their own release and usually leaving her as frustrated as hell.

Her hand moved faster. Her breasts were jiggling like crazy now and Johnny reached a fingertip over to play with the bouncing nipple. "Damn, but I like these big."

Susie's laughter was slightly breathless as she prepared for the coming pleasure. "Then you should love me, honey."

He reached over and bit her nipple hard.

Susie smiled. It felt good.

She was breathing hard, her legs were spread, her body wet. He pushed her hands away and leaned over her. A second later he sank himself deep inside her body.

Stupid bastard made her lose the whole damn thing. Still, what he gave her wasn't bad. Susie imagined she could wait till later to finish.

He was done in seconds and once again had robbed her of a climax. Susie silently rained all matter of curses upon the fool's head even as she tightened her body around him, leaving him with the impression that she too had found release. She gave him her most sensuous smile.

The sounds of her perfectly performed *uhs* and *ahs*

were still ringing in his ears when he said, "I reckon you ain't never had a man like me before."

Susie would have loved to have told him the truth of the matter. That he was no different than the dozen or so she'd had this week. Not once had she found release with any of them, and she figured she wasn't likely to find any tonight either.

His hands were on her breasts and he kneaded the soft flesh as he leaned himself up against the headboard and spoke. "You know, I meant it before when I said I was coming into some money."

Her nipples were getting sore. "Did you?" she asked, not having the slightest idea what she was supposed to say to that. She only smiled again.

"Yup," he nodded and was silent for a long time.

Their time almost up, Susie was just about to leave the bed, when he spoke again. "You know the new doc?"

Susie shook her head. "Hear he's been sick. I haven't seen him yet."

"No, I mean his daughter."

"Oh. Yeah, I've seen her a couple times."

"Cole Brackston still sweet on her?"

She shrugged. "I seen them together a few times. Why?"

"Just wonderin' is all." Johnny chuckled. "It don't pay none for pretty little girls to ask too many questions."

Susie had a lot of steady men she liked and some she didn't like all that much, but this one, despite his enormous size, came in on the bottom of her list. He wasn't bad to look at which was the reason she'd gone up to him in the first place, but as far as she could tell there wasn't nothing else good about the man. She didn't like the threat she heard in his voice. She didn't like the sly, almost crazed look in his eyes. And Susie started wondering why he should be asking questions about Nora Bowens.

She shrugged. Maybe he'd seen her in town and asked someone who she was. Maybe he thought she'd give him a minute's notice. Susie had to bite her lips to keep back her laughter.

"I gotta get downstairs," she said as she came to a sitting position.

"You sure do," he said as he pushed her face back to where he figured a woman's mouth did the most good.

Jake rubbed the toe of his right boot along the back of his left pant leg and then did the opposite with the left boot, until he was satisfied that both were free of dust. He straightened his collar, squared his shoulders, swallowed, cleared his throat, took his hat from his head, smoothed his hair back and forced his hand to knock at her door. Damn, but he couldn't remember the last time he'd been so nervous. His heart was pounding in his throat and he wondered if he was going to be able to talk once she opened the door.

He needn't have worried. A man, almost as tall as himself, but a good twenty years his senior and slightly hunched over, smiled as he opened the door. "Can I help you?"

Jake knew he had to look like an overaged fool come calling. Jesus, he felt like an overaged fool as he stared into the man's smiling hazel eyes and felt his mouth go bone dry. Why had he stopped to pick a fistful of wild flowers? They were damning evidence of what he was about.

He never expected her father to answer the door. That was stupid. The man wasn't an invalid any longer. He should have known there was a good chance that her father would be up and around.

Robert Morgan tipped his head as he waited for the man before him to speak. He hadn't seen him before, but the man looked to be in fine shape. Too fine a shape to be visiting a doctor's office. Perhaps he was new in town and had come to the wrong door. "Are you looking for someone?"

"Nora." Jake cursed the croak that had suddenly become his voice. He cleared it, but it didn't sound any better when he asked, "Is she in?" Now he didn't only look the fool, he sounded like one as well. What the hell was he doing here? Things weren't settled between Cole and Nora. Maybe she had all intentions of accepting his brother's proposal. Why was he rushing things? Why hadn't he waited?

For just a second Jake had the impression that the man was going to ask him what he wanted with his daughter. The wildest thoughts were careening through his mind. He could just hear himself saying, "I want to kiss her until she's all warm and soft against me. I want to bury my body in hers and maybe never come back to the real world, sir." Lord, a'might, he was losin' it fast. The best thing he could do was mumble his excuses and get out of here.

Robert Morgan smiled again. "And you are?" he asked waiting for Jake to tell his name.

"Jake. Jake Brackston."

"Oh, Cole's brother," Robert Morgan said with a smile, recognizing the resemblance. "Come in. Come in. I'll get her."

Jake did as he was asked and watched the door close behind him. He ran a finger inside his collar. Now, why should the door closing remind him of a lid on a coffin? God, he'd better pull himself together here. He watched the man move at a tired gait toward the family's living quarters. It was easy enough to see by the deep lines that ran from the man's nose to bracket his mouth that he was drawn and tired. Jake figured that after an illness some folks just never get back all their strength. Silently he hoped this man wasn't one of them and then found himself wondering why he should care.

He shook his head, unable to understand his thoughts. He hadn't made much sense since Nora came to town. Why start now?

"There's a man to see you honey." Robert's eyes twinkled as he teased, "I'd be gentle with this one. He's a shy sort."

"Did he say who he was?" Nora asked as she took a final sip of her coffee.

"Jake Brackston."

Nora's look was incredulous. Jake, shy? Not likely. She'd never in her life met a bolder man. Fear suddenly caught in her throat. She felt her breathing grow ragged and her heart twist. Something was wrong. If Jake was acting oddly, something had to be wrong. "Matt," she muttered as she ran from the room. In an instant Nora was rushing into the office, her green eyes huge with worry. "Is something

242

wrong with Matt?"

"No. Matt's fine."

Nora breathed a deep sigh of obvious relief and she pressed a hand to her pounding heart. "Thank God. You gave me a scare."

Jake hadn't seen her in close to a week, ever since she'd left his house. His gaze moved hungrily over her small form, taking in the slenderness of her shoulders, the swell of her breasts, the curve of her tiny waist. God, he'd missed looking at her. Graceful fingers smoothed back curling wisps of red hair as she waited for him to say something.

Nora looked at his stiff, formal stance, his spotless shirt, his hat in his hand and polished boots. She frowned. "Is there something wrong?"

"No," Jake said knowing even as he said it that it was a lie. *Everything is wrong and I want to put it right, but I don't know how.*

"Is there something you want?"

"No." Lies, lies. There was something he wanted all right. Damn it. What was the matter with him? Why couldn't he think of a thing to say?

"Then why are you here?"

"To see you, of course," he said slightly annoyed. Lord, he couldn't be more obvious, what with his polished boots and the flowers still in his hand and yet she'd had to ask him straight out.

"Oh," she breathed softly. "Of course."

He almost shoved the flowers into her hands. She smiled.

He smiled. Jake had never felt so uncomfortable in his life. If her family wasn't in the next room, he would have reached for her. As it was his fingers

243

itched for the feel of her.

"Would you like to come inside? We were just finishing our dinner, but we have apple pie for dessert."

"No," Jake said feeling himself backing away and unable to do a damn thing about it. There was no way he could sit with her family. God, he was uncomfortable enough with just her. He'd probably dump the pie in his lap and dribble coffee over his chin. "I . . . I gotta go."

"Oh."

He looked up from the floor. Was that disappointment he heard in her voice?

His gaze held to hers and watched her confused, almost flustered smile. "It was nice of you to come by."

It was damn ridiculous, you mean, he silently countered. "Yeah, well, I was in town."

Nora reached for the door knob. "Tell Matt I said hello."

"When are you coming out to see him?"

Her eyes snapped to his and widened with fear. "You said he was fine."

"He is. He misses you." Jake said, knowing no one could miss her more than himself.

Nora bit her lip. "I don't know. Why don't you bring him in here to see me?"

"You could come to dinner." There was a long pause before he went on. "Matt would like that."

"I . . ."

"I was thinkin'," Jake interrupted. "Maybe you'd like to go on a picnic sometime with Matt and me."

"A picnic?" she asked in amazement. Jake didn't

strike her as the picnic type.

"Sure. We go all the time." Another lie. Christ, he hadn't done anything but lie since he got here. Is this how men and women got to know each other?

Nora's smile grew wide. It lit up her face. Jake felt his stomach tighten with the pain of wanting her. He wasn't going to make it. He'd wanted her for too long. "That would be nice."

"This Sunday? After church?"

Her eyes widened again in surprise. Obviously he didn't seem the type to go to church either.

He looked slightly embarrassed, his grin sheepish. "I started goin' after Matt got sick." He shrugged. "Figure it can't hurt none."

"Indeed, it can't, Mr. Brackston."

He shook his head. "Jake."

She smiled again. Jake noticed she'd been doing a lot of smiling in these last few minutes. More than in all the time he'd known her. He never realized he was doing the same. A grin spread across his mouth when she nodded and said, "Jake."

"Well, good night," he said as he stood beneath the light just outside her door. He seemed to hesitate, as if he didn't really want to go.

"Good night," she returned and then gasped when he suddenly and without warning reached for her shoulders and pulled her against him. He kissed her, hard and quick, as if he didn't trust himself to hold her for too long.

He pulled away, and left her to stare after him. Nora shut the door and leaned against it, trying to sort out what had just taken place. What in the world had come over him tonight? What was he really doing here? He'd asked her to come for dinner, to visit his son, to go on a picnic. He'd actually asked her to go on a picnic! Why he'd acted like . . . like a man . . . her eyes blinked as the whole of his actions came together to form one conclusion. Good God! Could it be true? Was Jake Brackston courting her?

Nora laughed aloud at the foolish thought. But he'd looked at her like he was. He'd sounded like he was. He'd kissed her like he was. She spun around in a circle and laughed again. It sure enough felt like he was!

Chapter Eleven

"Matt," Jake said over his shoulder to his standing son, "I told you to sit still."

The wagon rumbled over the rough road, making its way toward the distant tree-lined mountain base.

"When are we goin' to get there?" Matt complained.

"If you fall out of this wagon, we won't get there at all."

Matt whined unhappily, and in a sulk muttered, "I'm hungry." A moment later he gave into his father's insistence and sat on the wagon's floor.

"We'll be there soon," Jake offered as he snapped the reins trying to hurry the horse along.

"It can't be much fun for him to sit back there. We've been driving for almost an hour."

Jake shot Nora a dark look of warning. "Are you complaining, too?"

Amusement filled Nora's eyes. "I wouldn't dare."

A teasing light flickered in Jake's eyes as he returned. "Oh you'd dare, lady. I know that for a fact."

Nora chuckled softly. The sound tore at Jake's heart. "All right. Maybe I'd dare, but I doubt that it would do me any good."

This wasn't turning out exactly like Jake had planned it. Gradually his son had grown out of sorts and Nora didn't appear quite as excited as she had upon starting this outing.

Jake had ridden to the base of this mountain more times than he could count, but the journey had never taken this long. Of course he had been astride his horse at the time, not encumbered by a slow moving wagon. He should have suggested they ride, but if he had, then Nora wouldn't be sitting this close, falling against his side every time the wagon hit a bump or rolled into a rut. No, a long, jarring wagon ride was worth the discomfort. Anything would be worth it just to have her beside him.

They hadn't even gotten there yet and Jake was already looking forward to the ride home. It would be dark by the time they got back. Maybe he would put his arm around her, guarding against a possible fall. Maybe he should do it now.

No. He'd better not. Nora seemed at ease in his company as long as he treated her with courtesy. If he got too familiar, she might freeze up on him again. He wouldn't chance it.

Just as Jake made up his mind to keep his hands to himself, the wagon hit a particularly deep rut and lurched to the right. It came to an immediate stop as his hands dropped the reins and instantly reached out for her, holding her around the waist, saving her from a nasty fall. "Are you all right?" Jake asked looking behind him at his son who lay sprawled upon the wagon's floor.

Matt nodded and came to a sitting position again while Jake brought his attention back to Nora. He brought her closer, his arms trembling as he realized just how close she'd come to being thrown free of the wagon.

"Are you all right?" he asked, his voice decidedly lower and more intimate as he directed the question to the woman in his arms.

"I'm fine. Thank you," she said, his arms still around her, holding her closer than what Nora deemed necessary.

"You're welcome," Jake returned, his warm breath across her mouth caused her stomach to flutter.

"You can let me go now," she said when it became apparent that he had no intentions of doing so on his own.

"Suppose the wagon hits another rut?"

Nora smiled at his obvious reluctance to release her. "Maybe I should sit in the back with Matt."

Matt heard her suggestion and instantly took her up on it. "Yeah, sit back here. Come on, Nora, sit back here."

Jake frowned at the notion. He didn't want her in the back. He wanted her here at his side. "I thought I told you to call her Mrs. Bowens?"

Nora put her hand on Jake's arm and shook her head. "Nora's fine," she said allowing his son the use of her Christian name. A moment later she was on her feet, stepping over the seat. "If you don't mind, I think I will sit back there."

He did mind, but unless he was willing to wrestle her back to his side, there was little he could do about it.

Jake waited for her to settle herself before he again took the reins and snapped them over the horse's back. The muttered curses that he murmured over the clicking sounds as he urged the horses to move out were not remarked upon. Nora noticed that his back was now stiff, and that he didn't speak again for the rest of the ride. She smiled knowing he was annoyed that he hadn't gotten his way.

It wasn't that he was angry, well maybe just a little. The truth of it was, Jake was quiet because he couldn't think of a thing to say. From the moment he'd helped her into the wagon, just like the night he had come to her place, Jake had grown suddenly tongue-tied. He'd never been particularly comfortable in the presence of a lady, but this was worse than anything he could ever remember. Jake put the blame squarely on Nora's shoulders. He wondered how this woman was able to make him revert back to the insecurities of his flustered, bumbling youth.

She was everything a man could want in a woman. She was sweet, giving, kind, beautiful, and smart. And he didn't stand a chance.

God, he couldn't even talk to her. The only things he could think of to say were things that couldn't be said in front of his son. Damn, he should have known better. He never should have suggested this. He wanted to shine in her eyes and instead felt like a fool and probably looked like one as well.

The moment the wagon came to a stop, Matt, anxious to be gone from his enforced confines, headed for the trees and the wondrous discoveries they were sure to hold. "Don't go far," his father called in warning.

"Are you over your sulking?" Nora asked as he helped her down from the wagon's tailgate.

Jake didn't answer, but allowed himself the pleasure of watching her bend over reaching for the blankets.

Nora stood at his side, blankets in hand; a puzzled expression in her eyes as she wondered what had gotten the man's attention. She would have blushed cherry red if she'd known it was her small, rounded rear. "Well? Do you expect me to carry it all?"

Jake took the heavy basket that White Moon had packed for them, and the heavier jug of apple cider. Together they searched out a shaded place for them to sit.

Jake watched as Nora spread the blanket under a thickly branched pine. The air smelled wonderful out here, clean, crisp with just a hint of fall. Tonight it would be cold going back. Jake held to some real hope that the ride back would be better than the one coming.

"Well, are you?"

"What?"

"Over your sulking."

"Is that what I was? Sulking?" Jake asked settling himself on the blanket. He stretched out on his side before her, his head resting upon his hand, as she leaned back against the trunk of the tree. He grinned. "Where did you learn those hand games?" Jake asked, referring to the rhyming phrases she and his son had repeated while slapping their hands together in a series of complex movements.

"From when I was a child, of course. All little

girls play them."

"Do they?" Jake asked as his gaze wandered over her face and hair. He didn't want to stop there, but knew she'd only grow uneasy, possibly angry, if he looked at what he really wanted to look at. "I don't know much about little girls."

Nora smiled, unable to resist, "No, I imagine big girls are more your specialty."

Jake grinned knowingly, but let the comment pass. "What were you like as a child?"

Nora laughed at the question and shrugged. "Like any child, I imagine."

"I don't think so."

"Don't you? Why?"

"'Cause you're different from any woman I've ever known. You would have had to be different as a child."

Nora shrugged. "Why, because I wanted to be a doctor?" She shook her head and a heavy curl slipped from the knot atop her head. She was repinning it when she spoke again, "I wasn't one to sit and read while others played, if that's what you mean."

"I never learned to read. Never went to school." Jake stiffened and then silently cursed his fool tongue for blurting that out. He didn't want to appear less in her eyes but rather more. What the hell had ever possessed him to let that slip? Now she'd know him for the ignoramus he really was.

Nora made no show of surprise. It wasn't uncommon to find a grown man unable to read. Still, he'd aroused her interest. "Why didn't you go to school?"

"Had to work." Jake wasn't about to tell her why.

He wasn't about to tell her that his mother was a prostitute and didn't care if either of her sons went to school or not. He didn't tell her that from as far back as he could remember, he'd been responsible for Cole and that unless he worked and tried to make a life for them both, the two of them would have likedly ended up in jail.

Nora could see he was embarrassed. No doubt he was sorry he'd mentioned his lack of education. Jake would have been amazed if he'd known the tenderness that filled her heart at that moment, for Nora believed no child should ever be denied the right to go to school. She wanted to ask him why he had to work but from the shuttered look in his eyes decided that explanation could wait.

"I could teach you, if you'd like."

He shook his head, dismissing the subject. "You don't have the time."

"It wouldn't take that much time. Practice would take the time and you could do that on your own."

"When?" he asked. Nora didn't miss the flicker of hope in his eyes just before he dropped his gaze to the blanket, tugging in a supposedly disinterested fashion at a few pieces of loose threads. The truth of the matter was, he was anything but disinterested. However, he had learned long ago to never let anyone know how badly you wanted something, or you'd be sure to lose your chance at it. He shrugged. "I wouldn't want . . ."

"Anytime you'd like. You could come into town on Friday or Saturday night. No one would have to know why."

His gaze sought hers and he smiled, feeling again

at a loss for words. She didn't ridicule him for his inability, but offered instead to correct the failure. "Would you do that?"

"Of course."

"People would think I was courting you," he said almost as a warning. He wondered why it had come out like that. Courting her was exactly what he wanted to do, and he didn't care who knew it.

"Would that bother you?" Nora tilted her head as she awaited his answer.

With the exception of exposing his ignorance, Jake couldn't have cared less about what anyone thought. He grinned, "You don't know me, if you have to ask that. But how would you feel about it?" His heart almost stood still as he watched her, waiting for her reply.

Nora teased. "I imagine I could stand the scandal."

Encouraged at her reply he ventured, "Suppose I was really courting you?"

"Was it courting you had in mind the other night?" Her gaze was soft, sweet, inviting; Jake took hope. He came up from his sprawled position near her feet and moved to her side. Facing her, he balanced himself with an outstretched hand and Nora found her legs trapped between his hip and his hand.

"I reckon it was," he said, his cockiness restored.

"Then why did you run off. Why didn't you stay?"

"'Cause, I felt like a fool."

"Did you? I wonder why? You didn't look like a fool."

"No? How did I look?"

She shrugged. "A little nervous maybe, but very nice."

"A little nervous? I was shaking with fear."

"You? Afraid? I don't believe it."

"Believe it. I thought you'd laugh at me."

"Then I would have been the fool, wouldn't I?"

Nora wanted to ask him why he had decided to court her, but was afraid of his answer. If he told her he was only seeing her because he wanted her, and judging by the look in his eye right now he just might, she would likely hit him with something.

Jake leaned closer. "You didn't answer me. Suppose I was really courting you? Would you like that?"

Nora's eyes twinkled with laughter, even as she gave an elaborate shrug and a long sigh meant to depict a degree of suffering. "I imagine I could get used to the idea."

Jake chuckled as he watched her fight back her laughter. "You mean you could learn to tolerate it?"

"I'm stronger than I look. I could bear the strain."

"You're a wicked lady."

"An even match for you, then, wouldn't you say?"

More than even. Jake knew he wasn't on equal footing with this woman and never would be. He'd never hope to be. Still, her teasing allowed him to dare, "I'd say we should kiss to seal the bargain."

Nora laughed. "I wasn't aware that we'd struck a bargain."

"You promised to teach me to read."

"And you believe that promise is deserving of a kiss?"

Jake grinned, "I was thinkin' you deserved

somethin' for your troubles."

Nora chuckled. "A kiss would probably lead to its own form of trouble."

"It wouldn't. Kisses are good and lead to better things." He glanced up through the tree's branches at the sky.

Nora smiled, obviously not unhappy at this turn of conversation. "Does that innocent look usually work?"

"What innocent look?"

"The one you're using now."

Jake's grin tipped his mustache and Nora's heart thudded. He watched her closely, knowing he'd never been so tempted. All he had to do was lean forward a few inches and her mouth would be under his. Still, he held back somehow; enjoying, even more than a kiss, this intimate conversation.

Nora chuckled, the sound low and enchanting. "Perhaps a handshake would do for now."

"If we're goin' to be courtin', I have to tell you now, you can't be stingy with kisses."

"I wouldn't think of it."

"Good, 'cause I like kissin'."

"You like kissing, or you like kissing me?"

"You."

Jake was lowering his mouth to hers. Nora could feel the warmth of his breath whispering over her lips. Her heart picked up its rhythm in anticipation, only to hear his groan as Matt called out in a voice heavy with disgust at finding the food still packed away. "Papa, are we gonna' eat?"

Matt rolled his eyes with enjoyment. "Mmmm, this is good. Why don't we always go on picnics?"

Jake cursed and felt his cheeks grow warm at the question. It didn't help matters any when Nora shot him a startled look that turned gradually into one of amusement.

Jake didn't know how to get out of it. He'd told Nora he and Matt always went on picnics and now his son had just showed him up for the liar he was.

"Yeah," she said, obviously enjoying his discomfort, "why don't we?"

"We will." He almost choked, the damn chicken caught in his throat. "All the time."

Matt was climbing over the wagon and then jumping off the tailgate with a loud roar, as if pouncing upon an invisible opponent and then climbing up again, after he'd wrestled the unseen foe to the ground. The two adults finished their fried chicken, cheese, and freshly baked bread, and sipped from glasses of apple cider as they watched. "Did anyone ever tell you that it's a sin to lie?"

"When did I lie?" Jake asked. He'd been wondering when she was going to call him to account.

"You told me you and Matt always picnic. Why?"

Jake decided it was best to make a clean breast of it all. Anything else was sure to get him into trouble. "Because the idea seemed to shock you."

"It did." And at his questioning look, she laughed and said knowingly, "I knew when you asked me, you didn't look the type."

Jake's eyes widened in surprise. "Is there a particular type? I didn't know."

She shook her head and declared, "Dark, dangerous men don't go on picnics."

"No?" His eyes danced with humor and, if

possible, even more confidence. The fact that she thought him dangerous obviously added to what Nora considered an already overinflated ego. It was a good thing she didn't say handsome as well, or there'd be no abiding the man.

"What do dark men do?" he teased.

"They pirate ships. They hire out their gun. They run off with the lady of the manor and maybe hold her for ransom after they've had their way with her."

Jake's eyes lit up with interest. "The last one bears considerin'."

Nora bit at her lip, the effort didn't stop her smile. "I thought it might."

He shrugged, his look almost one of disappointment, as if he were considering the options and found then wanting. "Well, I hate to be the one to tell a lady she's wrong, but there ain't no ladies of the manor around here. No ships either. And I can't draw fast enough to hire out my gun. So, I reckon a picnic will have to do."

"I saw you draw your gun. You're fast."

Jake seemed to hesitate. It was only an instant, but long enough for Nora to know he was about to lie. "Not fast enough." He came to his feet and offered her his hand. "Come on, let's explore."

Matt ran along ahead of them, scaring away rabbits and startling birds from their nests with his high-pitched shrieks. Jake and Nora held hands, saying little, content simply to look and smile at each other now and then.

Nora knew it had to be her imagination. He hadn't hesitated or acted oddly when denying that he could draw fast. The man wasn't a gunslinger. He was a rancher. He had a son, a home. Gunslingers didn't have that, did they? It had to have been her imagination.

"All right, but the two of you have to promise not to look." She glared at the silent, grinning father as Matt jumped with excitement. "We won't. We won't."

"Well?" she asked, her hands on her hips.

"The first one to find you gets a kiss."

"Aw Papa, that's not how you play," Matt said, his voice heavy with disgust.

"Matt's right. That's not how you play."

"It's the way I play."

Nora tried to look stern, but she couldn't stop her lips from quivering as she fought back her smile. "If you can't find me, you have to call out that you give up, or I'll never come out."

"I never give up," his eyes echoed the promise, and Nora felt a sense of warmth wrap around her heart like a luxuriously thick blanket.

"Turn around and count to fifty."

Father and son obeyed and Nora, without hesitation, dashed into the underbrush.

She could hear Matt calling out the numbers and chuckled when he got mixed up, "Ten, eleven, sixteen, eighteen, twenty-teen. Twenty-one-teen."

Nora ducked into thick underbrush, rolled into a ball, and gathered her dark skirt around her legs. The leaves were thick enough to close out almost all light. She grinned. They'd never find her.

They were calling as they searched out the immediate area, as if they expected her to answer. Nora chuckled a tiny sound. Boundaries had previously been set. All knew she had to be hiding nearby.

She could hear their thrashing, and stifled a laugh.

"You look over there," Jake said to his son.

A moment later Nora heard heavy footsteps moving closer and then nearly called out as he stepped over her. Lord, this was more dangerous than she'd first thought. She could have been squashed flat. She hugged herself into a tight ball and waited. Nothing. She continued to wait. Silence.

Where had they gone? Why couldn't she hear their calls, their movement? Had they gone off and left her? Had they forgotten the boundaries?

Nora waited. It felt like hours and was probably no more than five minutes, but she heard nothing. They must have forgotten the boundaries.

Nora stiffened. Was that a snicker? She listened, straining to hear something other than the chirping of birds and the hum of a bee. Nothing. Where were they?

Nora started. Something was crawling over her ankle. She jumped, gave a startled screech, and then scrambled free of the brush only to find Jake and Matt sitting side by side, with Jake holding a long stick. Obviously it was the stick she felt on her ankle. Matt burst out laughing, rolling onto his stomach and kicking his feet in his glee.

"Papa said we could make you come out."

"Oh, he did, did he?" Nora said as she eyed the villain in question. "Your papa doesn't know how to play this game, does he?"

Matt laughed again. "Sure he does. He found you right away."

"I could see your hair."

"Oh," Nora said as she reached down her back for the fallen tresses.

"It's my turn," Matt said as he dashed into the center of the clearing.

"Don't," Jake said coming up behind her, his hands stopping her from repinning her fallen hair.

"What?" she said, turning to face him.

"Don't pin it up. It's beautiful down."

"It's a mess."

"Don't pin it up."

Slowly Nora's hands came from her hair and Jake pocketed the rest of her pins. His mouth lowered to hers, his eyes dark and hungry as he whispered, "You owe me a kiss." An instant later he was in the clearing calling out for Matt.

Matt was asleep wrapped in a blanket in the back of the wagon. It was almost dark, the last of the sun reflected in the sky behind them as they traveled back toward town. Nora sighed, feeling tired but good. She allowed Jake's arm to curl around her waist tugging her closer to his side. She leaned against him, his chest a cushion for her head, and breathed deeply of his scent. Nothing and no one smelled like this man. Nora relaxed in his embrace, and never realized how she snuggled closer.

They had climbed the mountain, or what felt like a good part of the mountain; played ball; eaten until they couldn't swallow another bite; played hide and seek; and talked and laughed. Nora couldn't have had a more wonderful or exhausting day.

"Did you have a good time?"

Nora made a low, soft, wordless sound. Then she asked, "Are you sure you never went on a picnic before?"

He shook his head. "Never."

"You're very good at it."

"Thank you."

"You should do it more often."

"I intend to do it every chance I get."

"Really?"

"Mmmm," he murmured, with perhaps too much anticipation.

Nora raised her head from his chest and shot him a wary glance. "Are we talking about picnics?"

"Oh, is that what we're talking about?"

Nora chuckled and slapped his arm. "I suppose Matt will lean toward these wicked tendencies when he grows up."

"Why?"

"Because his father and uncle—"

Jake pulled back and brought the wagon to a stop. "What about Cole?"

"What do you mean?"

"Did he . . . ? Did you and Cole . . . ?"

"No he didn't!" Her eyes narrowed with outrage. She pulled out of his arms and shivered as the night air closed around her. She smoothed her skirts and moved to the opposite end of the seat, furious that he should even hint at such a thing. "And I'll thank you to mind your own business."

"Then why do you have a tick up your rear?"

She looked down her nose at him and Jake almost grinned. Only a few weeks ago, that very action would have set him into a rage. He wondered why it looked so adorable now. "Is that your delicate way of asking if I'm angry?"

"Are you?"

"I am."

"Why?"

"Because you have no right to—"

"I reckon I have every right, since I'm fixin' on marryin' you."

For just a second, Jake wondered who the hell said that. It was the first he'd heard. Jake couldn't have been more shocked at his sudden declaration, and it showed clearly in his dazed expression.

Nora burst out laughing. "If you could see your face." She giggled, trying to hold back the rest of her laughter. "I imagine you couldn't be more surprised if I did the proposing."

Jake wasn't about to deny his shock. He was surprised, but now that he'd had a minute to get used to the idea, he surely was taking a liking to the notion. "Get over here."

"No."

"Nora, I just asked you to marry me. The least you could do . . ."

"No you didn't."

"I did."

"Well, you didn't mean it."

"I mean it."

She looked his way again. The poor man looked as if he'd been poleaxed right between the eyes.

"Why else would I be takin' you on picnics and

actin' the fool by courtin' you?"

"Is that what you think? Only a fool would court me?"

"Of course not. Damn it!" He ran his fingers through his hair in frustration. "Don't try to twist my words."

"Then why are you doing it? And don't you dare tell me again that you want me, or I'll walk the rest of the way back to town."

"But, I do want you," he said almost helplessly and then grabbed her hand as she came quickly to her feet. She was about to jump from the wagon, but he yanked her onto his lap before she took a step. "I love you." Oh God, he was a goner. There was no hope. He couldn't stop the words from tumbling out. The worst of it was, it was all true. He'd gone and fallen in love with a woman who had the power at her fingertips to destroy him.

"No, you don't." She sat stiffly in his lap.

"How do you know I don't?"

"Because you wouldn't look so surprised if you did."

"I would if I just realized it myself."

She turned to look at him. "Have you?" her voice was soft, her eyes glittering in the fast fading light.

"What?"

"Just realized it?"

"It took me awhile to figure it out, but I reckon I've loved you for some time."

"Jake," she said softly as she reached her mouth to his. Her kiss was soft, sweet, wonderful. He felt his insides melting. This was the first time she'd ever brought her mouth to his, and Jake couldn't absorb the wonder of it. For the longest moment he just sat there like a great big dummy and let her kiss him. But not indefinitely.

Once he'd gotten over the shock of feeling her mouth against his, he took control of the kiss. With a low groan he tilted his head and deepened the kiss. And then he was forcing her lips apart and his tongue was delving deep into her sweetness.

God, had a woman ever tasted like this? Was there another alive who was half as soft? Or smelled as sweet? He had to have more.

One hand moved from around her back to cup her delicious softness and Jake trembled with the knowledge that he could have had her here and now.

He could have, if they'd been anywhere else but sitting in the middle of nowhere, where anyone could stumble across them. He could have if Matt wasn't sleeping in the back of the wagon.

His fingers undid the buttons of her dress and he pulled the fabric aside, cupping her naked breast in his hand. But when he tore his mouth from hers at last, the sun had finally fallen behind the mountain and the light was gone from the sky, leaving all in dark shadows.

He didn't care. He couldn't resist the temptation. His mouth took her deep into burning heat and Nora made a sound that told clearly of her yearning. It very nearly matched his. Her hands grabbed his shirt, pulling it into small fists, bringing him closer, as she arched her back, silently asking for more.

"We've got to stop," he groaned against her.

Nora muttered something unintelligible.

"Norie, honey, we've got to stop."

"No," she pouted as she clung to him, holding his mouth against her.

"Matt's asleep in the wagon," he reminded.

Nora stiffened. He heard a small gasp as if she'd just realized where they were and what they'd been doing. "Oh, God, I'm sorry," she said and tried to pull away. From her tone of voice it was obvious that she was embarrassed.

"No," he said as he felt her draw away. "Don't be sorry." He tried to lift her face from his chest. She refused to face him. "I wish we never had to stop."

"I can't understand what comes over me when . . . I can't believe I did this again. You must think I'm . . ."

"I think you're wonderful, hot, sweet, and delicious. I can't wait to take you to bed." He felt his body shudder at the truth of that statement.

Nora adjusted her clothing. They kissed a few more times, kisses that didn't transport them to the edge of madness. Instead they brought solace, tenderness, and sweet delight to both their souls. Then he started the horse moving again.

It wasn't until later when Jake lay tossing in his bed, remembering the night and the feel of her in his arms that he realized she'd never said she loved him in return. He smiled in the dark. Little witch. He'd bared his soul and she'd kept her feelings to herself. Well, almost to herself. After the way she acted in his arms, he knew she loved him.

A flicker of doubt made itself known. She did love him, didn't she? A woman wouldn't cling to a man like that unless she loved him. Women weren't like men. They didn't want a man just for the pleasure of it, did they? Jake sat up in bed, his eyes trying to see more than the dark room. He tried to see past her words, her actions. A frown creased his forehead. He couldn't be sure.

With a muffled oath, he fell back upon the pillow again. Silently he swore that no matter what she felt now, she would love him. He wasn't about to settle for anything less.

Chapter Twelve

Nora pulled the borrowed horse to a stop, dismounted, and tied the reins to the hitching post. She'd yet to find a replacement for Cinnamon and had been using the horses from the livery when she'd needed to leave town.

The sound of a jiggling spur captured her attention and Nora looked up with some surprise to find Jake walking from the house. Coming to a stop directly above her, he leaned his shoulder against a porch support beam. For the space of perhaps ten heartbeats, he watched her in silence and then a slow, deliciously wicked grin curved his mouth and hunger darkened his eyes.

His boots were shined to a soft glow, his clothes freshly laundered and pressed. In his hand he held his hat brushed clean of the day's accumulated dust. His hair was damp and combed neatly back. Obviously he hadn't just come in, but was on his way out. Nora felt an odd tightening somewhere around her heart at his smile. It didn't take much effort to imagine that he was thinking about last night. Nora couldn't stop thinking about it herself. "Couldn't keep away from me, eh?" he asked with cocky assurance. He didn't bother to mention the fact that he was just on his way to her place. "I didn't expect to see you till tonight."

Nora's green eyes narrowed and then glowed with warning. "What are you doing here?"

Jake looked slightly taken aback at the question. Laughter lurked in the depths of his eyes. "I live here."

Nora knew from the week she'd spent here that he never finished working this early. Usually, he didn't come in until after dark. She had expected to be gone long before he finished for the day. "Why aren't you working?"

The events of last night kept repeating themselves in his mind. They could hardly have come closer, their needs more urgent. How the hell could any man be expected to work with the memory of her scent, the feel of her in his arms, uppermost in his mind? Jake grinned. "Because I almost killed myself and figured I'd better stop before I—"

"What?! Are you all right?" she took a step toward him, but only a step and then looked around, conscious of the few men riding into the yard.

He nodded and smiled again, his heart filled with delight at her obvious concern. "My mind wasn't on work today."

She knew what he meant. She hadn't been able to think of a thing but this man all day. "Are you sure you're all right?" she said the words again, her voice breathy and soft.

Jake forced aside the impulse to go to her. He knew

270

she'd be embarrassed if he kissed her in front of the men. And there was no way that he could be near her and keep his hands to himself. "Fine. I'm glad you came. I've been thinking of you."

"I didn't." She shook her head. "I mean, I didn't come to see you. Is Cole here?"

Jake frowned, knowing at the mention of his brother's name what her mission was. "Nora you don't have to . . ."

"Yes I do. I owe the man my answer."

Jake watched her for a long moment. He didn't have to ask what her answer would be. Not after last night. He nodded toward the barn. "Are you stayin'?"

"No, I should get back."

"But you don't have to?"

Nora shrugged. To stay after the confrontation with Cole would make for an uncomfortable evening. No matter how she might want to stay, Nora knew she wouldn't. "It would be better if I left."

Jake nodded and watched her go. She might not be staying, but she wasn't going anywhere without him. Jake almost ran inside, calling to White Moon as he did. He'd have to hurry if he wanted to be ready by the time she came back.

Nora stepped into the dim, cool barn. No lanterns had been lit as yet, even though it was fast approaching dusk. The pleasing scents of horse, straw, and leather permeated the air. Nora smiled for the scents of a barn always brought to mind the days of her youth when she had spent endless hours with her father's horses.

She hadn't taken five steps before she heard a low

271

moan come from one of the stalls. Nora hurried forward. It sounded as if someone were in pain.

She must have made a sound, for Cole sprang suddenly from the barn's floor. Within seconds he was on her side of the stall. Nora took a startled step back and gasped with surprise, "Cole, are you all right?"

He looked awful. His dark hair was mussed, his bottom lip swollen, his shirt torn. He looked as if he'd been in a fight. "I'm fine," Cole said, even as he grabbed his opened shirt, pulling the sides together and moved quickly away from the stall.

His intent to bring her attention from the stall was obvious, perhaps too obvious. Nora couldn't help glancing back. Her eyes widened farther with surprise when she saw Mina stand up, straighten her clothing, and brush hay from her long, dark hair.

"What?"

"Nora, let me explain."

The pieces fell neatly into place and Nora smiled as relief flooded her. She hadn't realized until this moment just how nervous she'd been. "I see why you've been so scarce lately. So, you took my advice after all."

"Nora, I—" he began guiltily.

She cut him off, not interested in his explanations. "Do you love her?" she asked softly.

"I think so."

Nora had come here today to tell him she wouldn't be marrying him. Before she'd left town she'd decided she'd spare the man's feelings and not tell him why. After all, there was no need to hurt him further. To tell him it was his brother that she . . . well to tell him about his brother would be asking a bit much of any man.

For just a second it crossed her mind that she should be angry. After all, she'd been torn with anxiety. Cole, the beast, had asked her to marry him and less than a week later he was cavorting in the barn with another. Nora decided not to waste the emotion. She was too happy to be angry, too excited at the prospect of not having to hide the feelings she knew for Jake.

Cole was nervous. Obviously he didn't want her to make a fuss. And, from the protective way his arm slid around Mina, he was afraid this moment might turn embarrassing for all involved. He needn't have worried.

"That's good." She grinned at his surprise and then her grin turned into a soft peal of laughter. "That's better than good, that's wonderful." Nora kissed both Mina and Cole on the cheek, leaving the startled couple to stare at her flying skirts as she almost flew from the barn.

"Did you know?"

"About Cole and Mina?" Jake replied.

Nora nodded. He was standing where she'd left him. Nora never noticed that his horse was still tied to the hitching post, but was now loaded with food and a variety of goods that would make the small shack on the west range comfortable for the night.

"I suspected. He's been giving her some pretty hungry looks lately," Jake observed.

"And you didn't say anything?"

Jake shrugged. "I didn't know for sure. Are you disappointed?"

Nora gave a short laugh, her eyes sparkled with delight. "Not exactly."

"You wanna' show me what you are, exactly?"

"Here? Now?" she bit her lip and allowed a sly grin that brought an ache to Jake's gut.

"Get on your horse."

Nora's eyes widened. "Are you telling me to leave?"

"I'm telling you to get on your horse." As he spoke, Jake left the porch and mounted his own horse.

"Are we going somewhere?"

Jake grabbed the reins from her hands the moment she settled her skirts around her legs. Within seconds the two of them were racing out of the yard. Jake didn't slow the horses until both were heaving with exertion and a small dilapidated building came into sight.

Nora glanced at him as he brought the horses to a stop before the structure. "Why did you bring me here?"

She knew well enough why, and Jake was aware of that knowledge. Still, he figured he had to say something. "Since there ain't no lady of the manor for me to have my way with, I figured I'd take the next best thing."

"To have your way with?" she asked brazenly.

His eyes glittered with fire. He didn't answer her, but said simply, "Get off the horse."

Nora felt excitement leap to life and pound in her veins. Her heart hammered against the wall of her chest. Her voice was barely a whisper as she dared,

"And if I won't?"

"Aw, darlin', I was hopin' you'd say that."

Nora gave a tiny shriek as he grabbed her waist and hauled her off the horse. She was laughing by the time he slung her over his shoulder. "Beast," she said as she punched his back. Slowly he allowed her body to slide from his shoulder, down the length of his. Her voice was softer, more breathless than ever, as their mouths came even. "Why were you hoping I'd say that?"

"'Cause I wanted you in my arms."

"You could have got me there by asking, you know."

"Maybe, but I ain't a man to do much askin'."

"You're not? Then how will I know what you want?" she asked, her supposed innocence marred by a wicked grin.

"Oh, you'll know," he said as he brought her high in his arms. "I promise, you'll know."

Jake shoved the door open with his foot and carried her inside. His mouth sought hers in the darkness, with an impatience that told of his desperate need. He allowed her to slide to her feet and kept his arms around her, holding her steady against him. He felt her soften against him and he groaned.

Nora clung to his shoulders and moaned a soft sound of pleasure as he pressed his hips against her belly. He gasped as he tore his mouth from hers. "I've been wanting to do that since I saw you ride up to the house."

"What took you so long?"

He chuckled. Nora could feel the sound of his laughter rumble in his chest. God, how she loved being held close to him like this.

"I figured you'd be a mite upset if I kissed you in the yard, what with the men getting an eyeful and all."

"You could have," she began dreamily and then promptly forgot what she'd been about to say.

"You mean you wouldn't have minded?"

"Of course I would have minded. You could have invited me inside. You haven't kissed me since last night."

Jake grinned, shook his head. "In the house we would have been interrupted. I figured if I got you up here, I could kiss you all I want."

"Mmm, good figuring."

"I figured too, that while we were here, I could touch you," he said as his hands came from around her back to cup her breasts. His thumbs moving over their tips brought a low groan from her lips.

"That sounds interesting," she said, obviously having difficulty keeping her voice even. Her hands moved against his chest.

"And then when we both had enough of touching, I figured we could make love."

"You figured that, did you?"

Jake made a sound of agreement. Nora made no comment.

She was soft and warm in his arms. Her arms had circled his waist, holding him close, her mouth moving over his neck, but Jake wanted more. He wanted to hear her agree to his plans. "What do you think of my idea?"

"It's a little hard to think while you're touching me, but offhand I'd say it has possibilities."

276

His mouth closed over hers again and his hands moved to the buttons of her shirt. One by one they came undone and Nora shuddered with building need as he pushed the fabric aside. She was bare to the waist, her arms trapped at her sides by her sleeves and the straps to her chemise.

Slowly his hand moved to her shoulders. Palms flat against her they slid down, until she filled his hands to overflowing.

He was shaking when he tore his mouth from hers again. "If I don't stop now, I won't be able to stop at all."

Nora leaned against his hands and groaned as he gently twisted the tips between his fingers. "Don't stop."

He leaned her against the opened door and stepped back, obviously as shaken as she. "Wait here," he said and then cleared the huskiness from his voice. "I have to see to the horses."

The cabin was dark, eerie, and it smelled musty from long periods of disuse.

She heard a rustling sound and instantly adjusted her clothing, even as she moved quickly to follow him outside.

Jake was almost finished rubbing down the horses. She waited in silence as he brought them to a lean-to at the side of the building, fed and watered them. At last he slid a long piece of wood into place behind them, creating a tiny stall and grinned as he turned to see her watching. "Can't keep away from me?"

Lord, the man was so full of himself. Nora glared at him, which produced a low chuckle.

He took the bundle of bedding and supplies that

277

had been tied to his saddle and gave her a smacking kiss just before he entered the cabin again.

Nora followed close on his heels but stayed at the doorway as he searched out the small, dark room for a lantern.

"Jake."

"Mmm," he returned as he moved about the shack, banging into things and then cursing as he struck his shin on the bed's wooden frame.

"There aren't any *things* in here, are there?"

"Things?" A match flared to life between long callused fingers and he grinned from across the room. "What kind a' things?"

"Animals. You know, mice, lizards, spiders . . . things."

A lantern was finally located, of all places, under a table. Jake put the match to it and a soft glow soon illuminated the tiny room. It was a bit larger than Nora had first imagined. Across from her the wall was lined with tackle, ropes, shovels, pitchforks and various other supplies. On the floor amid the pile of equipment sat a saddle. Against the wall to her right stood a narrow bed with a distinctly unsavory mattress. The center of the room held a table and two chairs. All three pieces looked so rickety that Nora wondered if they wouldn't collapse under the weight of an inch of dust. Jake dropped his hat and gun belt on the table, and Nora realized it was sturdy enough. On the wall opposite the bed was a large black, mostly rusted stove. "Why don't I look the place over while you make the bed?"

She looked toward the bed and the cobwebs that hung like bed curtains from the ceiling to the four short wooden posts at each corner. "Why don't I look the place over while *you* make the bed?"

Jake caught the direction of her gaze and chuckled. "Mmm, so you don't like spiders, eh?"

She shook her head, looking very small and very serious.

"Maybe I should think things over a bit. A rancher's wife would have to tolerate a spider now and again."

Laughter came back to her eyes. "A rancher's wife would have to tolerate you. I figure that's enough."

He grinned. "Well now, I wouldn't want to rush into anything here."

"Me neither."

"Suppose I ask you a few questions before I . . ."

"Have your way with me?"

Jake shot her a dark look and ignored her giggle. "Do you know how to make a bed?"

"Of course. That's the first thing you learn when you work in a hospital."

"Can you sew?"

"Naturally," she said, sounding slightly affronted. "I sewed your knee together, didn't I?"

"Can you make a fire?"

She shrugged. "When necessary."

"Cook?"

"Well," she shifted nervously, her eyes downcast.

Jake thought she looked adorable. "You can't cook, can you?"

With a defiant glare, she looked up from the floor. "I'll have you know, my pancakes are famous."

"For what?"

A smile teased the corners of her mouth before she

said, "For giving a stomachache to anyone who . . ." He grabbed her and laughed as she screamed. They both fell across the bed.

But Nora wasn't the least bit interested in the playful teasing Jake had in mind. Her gaze fastened upon the spider that was dangling over Jake's head, and she fought like a woman gone berserk. "Let me up!" she demanded. And when he didn't move, she warned, "Jake, I mean it!" Actually, she never gave him a chance to move, but shoved all two hundred pounds of him aside and scrambled from the bed.

Jake watched her, his eyes wide, filled with nothing less than amazement that a woman so tiny could find the strength to fling him aside as if he weighed little more than a feather. Her entire body shuddered. "There's a spider over your head."

He grinned as he leaned back on his elbows. "All right. I reckon I could clean up the place a bit."

"It better be more than a bit."

Jake shot her a dark look as he came to his feet. Cleaning this cabin wasn't exactly what he'd had in mind when he'd brought her here.

"I can't stand bugs." She shuddered again.

Jake looked at her, clearly astonished. Imagine that. He'd watched her work over a man. He saw her put her hands into an opened belly without flinching, watched blood squirt over her apron and neck, knowing she hadn't even noticed. Yet, she shuddered with disgust at the sight of a spider. Who would have believed it?

Jake took the broom from beside the door and within minutes cleared the room of cobwebs and any spiders he found along the way.

"I heard rustling sounds before," she said as she watched him finish the chore.

"Oh, that's probably just a mouse."

"A mouse! Oh lord," she cried as she fairly flew toward the bed. In a flash she was standing on the soiled mattress. "Get it out." And when he simply stood there staring at her, she jumped up and down on the bed and yelled, "Get it out!"

Jake mumbled a series of frustrated curses as he yanked the bed away from the wall, with her on it, and ran the broom behind it. Nora screamed, scaring him half to death as a family of mice darted from under the bed and across the floor. She made a low sound of horror and Jake wondered if she wouldn't faint. Judging by her already white face, she was close to it.

At her nearly hysterical insistence he went after the tiny creatures. A few minutes passed, punctuated by Nora's sharp commands: "There's another one," or "I saw it go behind the pot!" Finally he shooed the last of them out the door. He slammed the door in place and leaned against it. "Satisfied?"

"I think so," her response was tentative at best.

"You think so?" he repeated in bewilderment, while looking around the cabin. Barrels lay on their sides, cans of food had rolled away from the wall. Pots, frying pans and wood for a fire had all been torn from their place under the sink and beside the stove, and left scattered in a pile at the center of the room. The place was in shambles and she wasn't sure if she was satisfied? Jake grinned at the woman with the huge, frightened eyes. She was still on the bed. "I can guarantee, the only things left living in this place are you and me."

Nora nodded slowly and even more slowly came down from the bed. She shuddered again and lifted huge pleading eyes to his. "Are you sure?"

"Aw, honey, don't be afraid," he said as he took her in his arms. "I got them all."

He held her for a long moment, feeling her trembling ease before he finally asked, "Better?"

She nodded again.

He smiled at her, his heart melting with tenderness at the sight of her fear.

He cleared the emotion from his throat and held her an arm's length away. "Here's the deal. You make the bed. I'll keep my eyes out for crawling things, put this stuff away, and cook supper and breakfast."

Nora nodded and turned toward the bed. "Take the mattress off first. I want to see if anything is under it."

Jake did as she asked. When Nora was satisfied that nothing clung to its bottom and the floor was empty beneath the bed, her spirits returned. She made up the bed with the clean bedding he had brought from home, while Jake returned the things he had scattered to their rightful places.

He was starting a fire when she realized what he'd said and spoke again. "I can't stay the night. My father will expect me back."

"No, he won't. I sent word that you're stayin' the night at my place. One of the men is sick."

Nora shook her head in reproach, even as she chuckled. "Very tricky. Just for my own information, which one?"

"Me."

Nora laughed. "You don't look sick to me."

Jake reached for a frying pan, wiped it out with the towel tucked into his belt, and placed it on the stove. He joined in her laughter. "You'll have to look closer then."

"Do you have any particular place you'd like me to look?" she teased.

He reached for the knife and a slab of bacon. "You'd better watch that smart mouth of yours, lady. I wanted to eat before we—"

While he worked, Nora quickly made the bed up with fresh linen. She smoothed the comforter in place and then gave into her wicked impulse, even as she wondered at her daring. She'd never in her life stood naked before another human being, not a servant, not even her husband, so she couldn't bring herself to discard the last of her clothing. Her dress and petticoats and drawers lay over the bottom rail of the bed and she stood clothed only in the thin chemise.

Would he be shocked? Would he be disgusted by her obvious eagerness? Nora almost lost her nerve at the thought and reached for her dress, but then reconsidered. No, if she disgusted him, so be it. She wanted to do this. She wanted this man. She wanted him to see her. She ached for him to look. And if it meant that he wouldn't want her afterwards, then at least she'd know now, before it was too late.

Nora cut him off with, "I thought maybe we could . . ." she allowed a long moment to pass before she went on, "try out the bed, *before* we eat."

Jake turned to look at her and nearly choked at

finding her standing there, except for the cover of her chemise, almost naked. He couldn't breathe. Thank God the stove wasn't hot yet, for his knees buckled and he found himself leaning weakly against it.

A strap slid from a creamy soft shoulder and the material slipped a few inches exposing most of one milky white breast. His eyes darkened with unbearable hunger as he watched her allow his gaze. The soft cotton material had been washed many times and had grown thinner and more transparent with each washing. The shadow of dark pink at the tips of her breasts would soon be his to see. The hint of golden red curls at the juncture of her thighs would no longer have to be imagined. He had touched her a number of times, but it had always been in the dark. He'd never seen anything more than vague yet enticing shadows, but he'd wanted. God, how he'd *wanted*. His mind raced ahead to the next few minutes. He tried for a deep steadying breath but couldn't manage it.

A slow deep blush began somewhere beneath the thin garment and worked its way up her throat to her cheeks. She was embarrassed at his staring, but Jake didn't have the strength to pull his gaze away. He almost smiled. He would have if his face hadn't been frozen with hunger, for despite his almost constant thoughts on the subject, Jake hadn't ever imagined beauty like this.

"It looks awfully comfortable, doesn't it?"

Jake couldn't tear his gaze from her. She was incredibly lovely. Her hair was loose and had fallen down her back and over one naked shoulder, almost hiding her breast. He swallowed. Her breasts were large with soft pink nipples, too large perhaps for a woman so small. Her chest was slender, her waist impossibly narrow. Her hips were full and her legs gorgeous and smooth. Jake had seen more than his share of women, in every stage of dress, but none could compare to this.

"Doesn't it?" she repeated. Not having the slightest notion as to what she was talking about, he nodded.

Nora smiled. "You didn't look."

"I can't stop looking," he said weakly. "My God," came a low husky groan that sounded closer to torment than pleasure. He felt his body's instant and helpless response to the sight of her. His gaze moved to hers and he looked almost apologetic. "I didn't want to rush you."

She moved toward him and smiled. "You're not. I think I'm rushing you. Is it all right?"

"Lady, you can do anything you want to me."

"Am I too bold?"

"No." His voice broke. He couldn't get enough of looking at her. "Jesus, no." He wrapped his arms tightly around her and pulled her against him, unable to resist the temptation any longer.

"We have to go slow, darlin'." He spoke into the side of her neck as he fought back the need to crush her to him and take her now without any further enticement.

"Why?" the word was muffled against his shoulder.

"'Cause I want to make it good for you."

"Being here is good for me."

"You're gonna' have to marry me soon."

285

"Why? Are you in a family way?"

He looked down at her grin and frowned. "You little monster. 'Cause you're driving me crazy, that's why."

"I can't marry you. My father only met you once."

"I'll come every night, I swear it." His mouth grazed her cheek, her jaw, and he groaned as it nuzzled the soft skin of her neck.

"And sit with all three of us and have tea?"

He moaned, far from happy at the thought. "Yeah."

"And we'll have a big church wedding?"

His eyes were glazed with the scent of her, the feel of her against him. "If that's what you want."

"With a huge party afterwards?"

Another groan. "Yeah."

"And you'll buy me the biggest diamond anyone has ever seen in these parts?"

Jake looked down at her, a flicker of confusion in his eyes. "All right."

"And new clothes? Lots of new clothes? And horses and a new carriage? A fancy new carriage?"

His glazed look slowly faded and dark brows came together in a frown. "Is that what you want?"

"No. I was just wondering how far I'd have to push before you woke up."

A grin tipped his mustache. "You little witch. You'll pay for that."

Nora giggled, her arms slid around his neck, holding him close as she bit his jaw. "You got something particular in mind?" she asked cockily.

He shuddered. "I'll think of somethin'."

Her fingers slid over his chin, his jaw, his lips. She

touched his mustache and closed her eyes with the exquisite pleasure of being able to touch him. "I've wanted to do this for so long."

"Then you shouldn't have waited."

"You mean you wanted me to do this?" she asked as if surprised by the notion.

His eyes promised retaliation and Nora laughed. "Why did you shave?"

"I was coming to see you."

"I like the feel of your beard against my skin. It scratches, but it feels good."

"Then I'll try to hurry and grow it back."

Nora laughed low and throatily. The sound added to his aching stomach.

"Oh God," he said as she pressed her hips against him. His gaze moved toward the bed, but Jake knew he didn't have the strength to get her there.

"You have too many clothes on," she almost whined.

Jake's fingers reached between their bodies and tore his shirt apart. An instant later he was lowering her chemise, freeing her breasts of its tantalizing confines.

"That's good," she said at the feel of his warm hairy chest against hers. "Oh God, yes, that's good," she moaned already lost in the delight as she rubbed her breasts wantonly against him. Jake wondered if he'd live through the ecstasy.

He almost didn't.

Chapter Thirteen

The tremendous force of raw, aching passion that raced through his body left him helpless and trembling. She was fumbling with his belt, her knuckles brushing against his belly. It excited him almost beyond his power to bear, as her mouth rained a hundred exquisite, hungry kisses over his chest and belly. He wasn't going to make it. Jake forced his mind from the touch of her hands, her mouth. Damn it, not this time. This time, they were going to take things slowly. This time, he was going to enjoy every delicious minute of her in his arms.

His hands at her shoulders urged her descending form to straighten. "Easy, darlin'," he murmured against her forehead, praying the words would bring the needed sanity to the situation. "Easy."

With his fingers beneath her chin, he brought her face from his chest. My God, she felt so good! Jake couldn't imagine where he got the strength to deny himself this pleasure. But one look at her passion-dazed eyes and he knew there was no way he could deny himself further. With a soft groan he joined his mouth to the sweet temptation of hers.

His arms tightened, lifting her slightly; he was desperate to feel the length of her against him. His mind swam and the yearnings grew to untold proportions as she allowed him total control of her mouth. He heard her soft, breathless whimperings and growled with hunger as his tongue reacquainted itself with every texture and taste of a mouth so deliciously hot it threatened madness.

Unable to ease his hold, he walked her to the edge of the bed and sat her before him. Jake was desperate to retain control. He took several deep, hopefully calming breaths as he willed away the temptation to ravage her without further ado.

Nora never realized his struggle, as her eyes came level with his stomach. His breathing was ragged and his stomach moved with each breath taken, causing a slight hollow to form between waist and pants. Intrigued, she again reached for his belt, bringing again a low aching groan from his throat.

His erection was throbbing; harder, hotter, than he'd ever known it to be. Straining against his pants, he felt ready to explode, and swore if she continued touching him, he'd die. He couldn't take another second of this agony and remain sane. And yet he hadn't the strength or will to take her hands from him.

"Norie, God," he groaned as she spread open the material and slid his long underwear and pants down his hips. Her palms ran along each side of his arousal, from his abdomen to his thighs and back again. "Jake, my God, Jake."

His name held a breathless, trembling quality. Jake frowned at the sound. Was it fear he heard in the low groaning of his name? Did the size of him frighten her? Surely she'd seen a man in arousal before. She'd been married after all. His fingers reached beneath her chin and tipped her face so he might see her expression better. "Don't be afraid, Norie. I swear to God I won't hurt you."

"I'm not afraid."

"Then what? What is it?"

Nora's hands moved at will over his body, from neck to belly and thigh, her eyes hungry for all she could see. Gently her hands came to cup him and slender, faintly timid fingers moved over his length. "It's just that you're so beautiful."

He groaned in torment, the sound telling clearly the pleasure she wrought. Braver now, she urged his body closer and pressed delicate kisses upon his belly. God, he was dying.

Jake felt a surge of emotion clutch at his heart. His eyes stung and he closed them lest he allow unmanly tears. At that moment every wall he'd so carefully created crumbled to dust and his heart was laid bare, exposed and vulnerable to the pain she could so easily inflict. Yet, he knew no fear or pain in loving her. He could trust his soul to this woman.

"Norie, my God," he growled helplessly as he crushed her against him. It couldn't go on. He'd waited too long to allow this caress. She was breaking down every barrier, as always with her, his usual cool

291

control was a thing of the past and she was forcing him ever closer to madness.

With gritting teeth, he pulled himself from her gentle hold, his breathing harsh and shallow. His arms reached around and beneath her. He stripped away her already lowered chemise. He brought her to the head of the bed and came down on one knee beside her, even as she reached for him again.

"Come here," she said in soft entreaty.

"Nora. It won't be any good for you, if you don't listen to me." He took her hands from him. At the end of his control, he didn't know how much longer he could hold back from sinking his body into the blazing heat of her.

"Come here," she simply repeated, and Jake knew all was lost. He hadn't the strength to stay away.

"Witch," he muttered as he lowered his mouth and body to hers. She reached for him again and his mind shut down, allowing only the ecstasy. Searing heat! God, he was drowning in her mouth, dying at her every touch, pressing his hips forward, begging for entrance even as he tried to hold back.

Damn it, if she kept this up, he was going to be finished before she had a chance to begin. He pulled away, taking her hands in his and holding them high above her head. It was bad enough being this close to her, but having her touch him was more than he could endure.

As she raised seeking lips to his, he said, "Darlin', I swear I'm going to make this good for you."

"Jake," she cried, her voice desperate and pleading, her body anxious as it moved frantically, urgently beneath him, silently begging for him to take what she offered. Her mouth brushed his jaw and his lips; her tongue ran over his mouth, seeking entrance and Jake trembled with answering need, knowing he was lost.

His mouth opened wide taking her probing tongue deep into his mouth. He sucked at her, drinking in her heat and her taste as his body slid into heaven.

God almighty, she was tight, as tight as a virgin. Jake's body trembled with the wonder of knowing this perfection. He heard her soft gasp and prayed to God it was from pleasure, rather than pain, because there was no way on earth that he could stop now. His body plunged deep into hers, slowly at first and then faster, growing more desperate with each movement.

Again and again he moved against her, in her, even as he tried to hold on. Ragged breathing and low moans filled the otherwise silent room and each muttered sound only brought them both closer to the edge. Sweat glistened upon their bodies and allowed delicious movement. No woman had ever felt like this.

Think! Think of something. Think of the ranch and that piece of fencing that needs mending. His mind repeated the words, but his body wouldn't listen.

"Damn it," he groaned in a gust of heaving, gasping breath. "I can't," he cried, his eyes tightly closed, his teeth set together in a grimace. His body was lost in the ecstasy of this woman. He couldn't stop and it was too soon. But it wasn't.

Despite the ache that had taken hold. Despite his trembling, he could feel the first almost crushing waves of pleasure come over her. It squeezed at his sex, greedily drawing him farther in, taking from him all he could give, his life and his very soul.

And he gave and he gave until there was nothing left but delirium.

"Damn it, Norie," he breathed against her neck as his shudders finally eased and he collapsed upon her. He was totally replete and more exhausted than he'd ever been in his life.

Nora sighed beneath him and snuggled her face against his damp neck. She made a sound that might have been a laugh. "You do have a way with words, don't you?"

Jake groaned, hardly able to breathe.

"Do you always curse at your ladies when you make love to them?"

He groaned again and pressed himself deeper into her.

She moaned a soft sound as another shock came to rock her body, leaving her trembling and exhausted. "That was . . . that was . . ."

Jake grinned as he rolled them both to their sides. "Left you speechless, did I?" He laughed at what sounded like a grumpy groan and pulled her closer, tucking her head under his chin. Happily exhausted, he closed his eyes, delighting in the feel of her against him and wishing they never had to leave this bed again. "Yeah, I've been known to do that on occasion."

294

His arrogance was a bit more than she could take. "Have you? Did you leave Susie breathless?" Nora shoved him off and tried to leave the bed.

Jake frowned as his arm snaked around her waist and hauled her stiff form back against him. "What's the matter with you and who the hell is Susie?"

"The woman you went to see the night I came to the ranch for dinner."

Jake remembered the things he'd said that night and cursed his fool tongue. "No, I didn't make her speechless. I didn't even see her that night. I only said that to make you mad." Jake wisely refrained from telling her about the nights he had seen Susie and the relief, even at culmination, that was forever out of his grasp.

"Why?"

"'Cause you were with Cole and I was crazy jealous. It was you I wanted. It was you who was drivin' me out of my mind. For months, since the first night you came to town, it's been only you.

"I tried to stay away from you, but I couldn't. I hated myself, knowin' Cole was sweet on you, but I couldn't think of anything but having you."

"You are a beast." The words were muffled against his neck. "I knew it from the first."

"And you are a darlin'," he breathed into her hair. "I was afraid of that from the first."

Nora's eyes widened at the compliment. "Were you? Why?"

There was a long moment of hesitation before he finally admitted. "I'm not sure. All I knew was that you were the most beautiful little thing and I was scared to death."

Nora pulled back, her eyes filled with disbelief. "You were not!"

"I was."

"Why? What could I do to you?"

He shrugged. "A man doesn't like to know he has no strength against a woman. Until you came along I was happy enough with the way things were. I knew the first time I saw you that things were going to change."

Nora hugged him closer, delighting in his admission. "And you're not much for changes?"

He grunted a sound. "I ain't much on love."

Nora smiled and rubbed herself against him like a warm, soft kitten. "I'd say you're very good at it."

Jake chuckled at her compliment. "And that reminds me. I told you last night that I loved you and you didn't say a thing."

"Of course I did."

"Yeah?" he asked in disbelief. "What did you say?"

"I said . . . I said . . . Jake I must have told you I love you."

"You didn't." He shook his head. Nora felt the movement above her head. "I reckon I would have remembered something like that."

"Are you sure?"

He nodded and grinned. A few minutes went by when neither spoke. "Well," he asked impatiently, "are you going to say it now?"

"Say what?" Nora teased.

Jake growled as he rolled her to her back and gave her his most threatening glare. "Say it."

Nora giggled. "You're the most impossible man, but I do love you."

Jake beamed, unable to control the joy of his relief. "Why?"

Nora screwed up her face, her eyes danced with laughter. "I wish I knew the answer to that myself."

He gave her a little shake. "Tell me."

"What?"

Jake's voice was low with warning, *"Nora."*

"All right, all right. I love you because . . . because you're . . . you're . . ."

Jake laughed. "You little witch. Can't think of one thing to say?"

She grinned. "Well, you are . . . attractive."

"That's it?" he said, trying to sound affronted, but unable to resist smiling at the compliment.

"No, that's not it. You're very attractive."

"And," he prompted.

"And I like your hair, the way it falls over your forehead. And your mustache, and your lips. And the way you obviously love Matt. The fact that you tried, despite one or two failings. . . ." She winked at him. Jake couldn't have been more amazed. "To do the honorable thing, when you thought Cole was in love with me. The way you look at me. And the way you keep coming to my rescue, even if you do yell at me afterwards."

"What do you expect? The thought of you riding around the countryside with no one to protect you

297

scares me to death."

"If I don't count you, no one has bothered me in weeks."

"That's not funny."

"Jake, I'm sure whoever it was, is long gone."

"When we get married, your gallivanting will stop."

"You mean if we get married?"

"You tryin' to tell me somethin'?"

"You won't own me just because—"

"I reckon I will. And nothin' ain't never gonna' happen to you. Not if I can help it." Jake felt a wave of panic at the very thought. His arms tightened without realizing and Nora felt herself struggling to breathe.

She made a soft sound and felt his hold relax a bit. There was no sense arguing with this man. If he was set on seeing her escorted about her business, Nora wouldn't object. Still, it galled her to give in to his demands, so she simply changed the subject.

"Your hair is scratchy."

"I'll shave it off."

Nora pulled him down upon her. "All of it?"

"All of it," he agreed.

"Don't." She rubbed her leg over his, delighting in the differences their bodies offered. "It feels good."

"I'll grow more."

A low chuckle sounded from beneath him. "You certainly are agreeable today." She kissed his chin. "If I'd have known, I might have . . ."

"Jumped into the sack when we first met?"

"Hardly," she sighed. "You were unbelievably arrogant then."

"And I'm not now?"

"You are," she nodded, "but I'm able to overlook it now."

"Because you love me?"

Nora breathed a sigh. "I never should have said anything. Now you'll only nag and pester wanting me to say it all the time."

Jake grinned at her petulant act, "Can't see how it's so hard to tell a body you love him."

Nora grinned. "Then be my guest. If you're so good at it, tell me you love me and why." Her eyes narrowed with warning. "And you better not mention one word about wanting me. Loving and wanting are two different things."

Jake tried to get his thoughts in order and then groaned. "Damn it woman, you've got me scared to open my mouth."

Nora giggled. The idea of this big man fearing someone as small as she was laughable indeed. Deliberately seductive, she rubbed herself against him, her eyes warm with laughter and love. "All right then, why don't you show instead. You can always tell me later."

Jake growled, even as he delighted in her obvious hunger for more of his loving. "Witch. If you keep this up, we'll probably starve to death."

"Would you mind?" she asked as she rolled him to his back and pulled herself over his body.

He groaned a low aching sound, knowing he didn't have the strength to deny her. Her hair fell forward creating a small private world of fragrance and touch that he couldn't resist. His hands buried themselves in the silky softness. It was a long time before either thought to satisfy any other hungers.

Jake filled the two plates with eggs and ham. On the table sat chunks of bread and butter along with two mugs of hot coffee. "Wake up, darlin'," he said as he brought the table to the side of the bed.

Nora moaned a low sound of annoyance at being forced to awaken.

Jake grinned, sat on the side of the bed, and rubbed her hip. She cuddled deeper beneath the quilt. "I'm not hungry."

"You've got to keep up your strength."

"For what? I'm not going anywhere. Let me sleep."

Jake raised the corner of the quilt and slid his head under it. A second later Nora gave a startled cry and was suddenly sitting up, rubbing her bruised backside. "Damn it, Jake, that hurt!"

Jake grinned. "All I did was give you a little bite. Come here and I'll make it better."

"Go to hell," she grumbled.

He chuckled. "I think I like it when you sass me."

"Then I'll have to remember to always be sweet."

"Like now?"

Nora glared at his grin, pulled the covers over her breasts, and tucked them under her arms. "Shut up and eat."

"Come out from under those covers." Jake had very definite ideas on how he wanted to share this meal. He'd been thinking about it the whole time he was cooking. He wanted to watch her sitting on the bed naked and he wasn't about to be denied looking at her. He wasn't going to let her turn suddenly shy. Not after the hours of loving they'd just shared.

Nora ignored his command and tried to ignore as well the fact that he was sitting facing her Indian-style, stark naked. She tried not to look at him and found the chore impossible. She licked her lips as her gaze moved over his chest. The man was fascinating. She could watch him for hours and never get her fill. From his waist up his body was darkly tanned. Obviously he worked long hours without a shirt. His shoulders were wide, his chest broad, his arms muscled. Nora felt small just looking at him. She studied the dark hairs that grew across his chest and ran into a narrow line that bisected his flat belly and then where it grew thicker surrounding his sex. He was magnificent. She licked her lips again and swallowed as her gaze moved over thickly mus-cled thighs and then back to the region just below his belly before moving quickly to his humorous gaze. She blinked, realizing only then that he'd been watching her slow perusal of his body. Hot color suffused her cheeks. Her voice was a soft scratchy whisper. "Don't you think you'll get cold like that?"

He shook his head. "It's hot in here. Take off the covers."

"And sit here naked?" she asked with some surprise.

"And sit here naked," he repeated and then leaned back on one arm, offering her an even more enticing view of his body.

"Jake, I . . ."

The covers were torn from her and thrown to the floor.

"Jake!" She reached for their one pillow. With one quick tug it followed the quilt to the floor. "Bastard!" Nora's mouth dropped open with shock, for she'd never in her life said such a thing.

He laughed as he tackled her upon the bed. "If you keep insulting me, Miss Nora, ma'am, I just might not make love to you again."

Nora blinked her surprise and then her eyes took on a wicked glow. She bit her lip trying to hold back her grin at his threat. "You said that once before. It was a lie then too."

"You tryin' to tell me I'm easy?"

"I'm trying to tell you, they don't come any easier."

Jake laughed. There was no sense denying her accusation. She was one woman he could never deny. He leaned back, his gaze moving over her naked length. "I want to see you."

"You saw me already."

He shook his head. "I was busy. I didn't get a good look."

"Tough." Nora struggled to throw him off.

He laughed. "Nora, I am going to be your husband," he reminded. "And a husband has certain—"

"Maybe," she grunted.

"Whatdaya mean, maybe?"

"I mean, I just might change my mind. First you bite my . . . rear." Jake laughed at the hesitation. "And then you pull away the covers."

"And the pillow," he reminded.

"And the pillow. Is this what I'm to expect once we get married?"

"This and more," he said as his dark head dipped and his lips took her pink nipple between them.

"Are you sure?" she asked, her voice growing slightly breathless. She was fast forgetting her annoyance.

"Very sure," he murmured, the words muffled against her pale, smooth skin.

"The food will get cold," came only a halfhearted protest.

"No it won't. We're going to feed each other, darlin'," he said as he raised himself on one arm and reached for a plate.

A moment later found them half reclining against the wall as they fed each other with their fingers. Nora giggled a sound of pure happiness as crumbs were dropped, perhaps deliberately, and Jake was forced to lick them away. "You don't have to do that, you know."

"I reckon I do," Jake said as his tongue paid particular attention to her left breast. "I don't cotton to crumbs in my bed." His glance was filled with glee as he accused, "You sure are a sloppy eater, lady."

She grinned. "I think it's the fork."

"I ain't usin' a fork," Jake said as he slipped a piece of ham into her mouth.

"I meant the lack of one."

Despite the simple fare, Nora couldn't honestly say when she'd enjoyed a meal quite so much. Never before had she realized just how sensuous greasy fingers could feel when rubbed against lips, when trailed down arms, when spread over eager flesh. She'd never believed the simple act of eating could be so carnal. Her body trembled with awakening desire, despite the fact that she had only moments ago felt totally replete. Her fingers brought a small amount of scrambled egg to his lips. And when a piece fell to his chest and another to his belly, Nora dutifully removed it with her mouth.

They were sipping from their cups, their stomachs full, another need clamoring for release, when Nora asked, "And you say, I'm to expect this once we marry?"

Jake nodded, his dark gaze moving over the length of her.

"Every day?"

"Every Sunday. I won't have time to feed you during the week."

"You've convinced me."

Jake grinned. "To what?"

"To marry you."

Jake looked surprised. "You mean you've only just decided?"

Nora nodded.

"Why?"

"Because I need a man who can cook."

"And . . ." Jake prompted.

"And I love you."

Jake swallowed against the sudden intense emotion that tore at his throat and blinked away the burning behind his eyes. He cleared his throat from the huskiness the words caused and swore, "Lady, you ain't never gonna' be sorry you said that."

Chapter Fourteen

"My mother was a whore."

It was mid-morning and they were dressing, sort of. The truth of it was every time Nora put an article on, Jake somehow loosened it, shifted it, or simply took it off again. He was standing behind her, his mouth nuzzling the curve of her throat, his hands playing with obvious delight upon the softness of her breasts when he spoke.

Nora's entire body grew stiff at the horrible announcement. Her green eyes glared daggers at the man. "Jake! For God's sake. That was a terrible thing to say."

Jake shrugged and silently agreed it was a terrible thing to be true. He'd never in his life ever told anyone the truth of it, but figured he might as well get it out in the open now. He wanted no secrets between them and if that meant he'd have to suffer her disgust, so be it.

"Maybe, but it's—"

"Maybe?" she gasped at his offhanded remark, almost dumbfounded that the man, that any man, could so degrade his own mother. "I can't imagine any man saying worse. You should be ashamed."

Damn it! He never should have said anything. He should have carried his secret to his grave. He'd hoped she'd be different. He'd been a damn fool to think the truth wouldn't matter to her.

Jake gave a silent sigh of remorse as he stepped away from her and continued on with his own dressing. He watched as she angrily pushed her foot into a boot.

"I thought before we got married you had the right to know."

"Married! I seriously doubt that—"

"Damn it to hell!" he interrupted. "I should have known it would make a difference. I should have kept my mouth shut."

"You certainly should have. If you'd slander your own mother, what would you say of a wife?"

"What?" he looked again in her direction, a puzzled frown creasing his forehead. She was pulling her chemise back into place. "You mean *you?* Why should I say anything about you?"

"Why should you say such terrible things about your mother?"

"'Cause they're true."

"Jake!"

His lips were pulled thin, eyes shuttered, allowing no emotion, even as his heart was ripping apart. Jake wondered if he'd survive this pain. He'd lost her, all because he'd been fool enough to trust her too much.

Jesus, when was he ever going to learn?

"Jake," her voice was suddenly softer, slightly puzzled as she saw the pain he couldn't quite hide in his eyes. Her heart thundered in her breast, but she forced aside the fear. "Jake, tell me."

He smiled the old, wicked, cool, hard grin that hid his innermost emotions. Nora limped with one shoe on toward him. "Tell me."

Why not? It was over anyway. She could never deny the disgust he saw in her eyes. He should have known no decent woman would ever want him. He might as well get it over with. He breathed a long sigh and began, "Her hair was red, like yours." He grinned again, his gaze hard with pain. "Only she got hers from a bottle." He shrugged as if it were of no consequence, "Word had it she was the highest paid whore in San Francisco." He shrugged again. "She was the busiest, anyway. Cole and me never got to see her much. She didn't want her customers to know about us, so we mostly stayed in the kitchen."

"My God," Nora breathed. The horror in her eyes could not be denied and Jake felt the last of his hope shrivel up and die.

"It wasn't so bad. We didn't have anyone tellin' us when we had to go to bed, or where we were allowed to go, or even if we should go to school. And on Sunday afternoons, the whores took pity on us. It was their slow time, anyway, so they showed us ways to please a woman. Somethin' that was a hell of a lot more important than readin', they said."

"Jake," Nora's hand came to her cheek, her eyes wide with horror never left his. Nora knew she'd

309

lived a sheltered existence, at least until the war had ripped her life apart. She couldn't believe any child could have grown up like that.

He saw the pity and found himself growing angry. "No need to feel sorry for me, I made it just fine."

There was a moment of silence before Nora could gather her thoughts. "I don't feel sorry for you. I feel sorry for the little boy you were. And, you made it better than fine." Her eyes gleamed with admiration . . . and love. Her voice was soft and breathless as she went on, "You are truly outstanding. Only a man of enormous strength of character could have come so far."

Jake felt astonishment at the unexpected declaration. Could it be? Dare he hope that his less than savory beginnings made no difference? "What do you mean?"

"I mean, I love you more than you can imagine," she said as her fingers moved to his shirt and slowly opened the buttons.

"What are you doing? A minute ago you were fussin' 'cause I wouldn't let you dress in peace."

"Was I?" Nora smiled as she backed him toward the bed. "Well, then it appears I've changed my mind. What does another hour or so matter?"

"An hour?" Jake's heart was near to bursting with happiness. He could hardly speak. The love he knew for this woman came close to strangling him. "What do you think we could do for an hour?"

"It's not *we*, it's *me*. I want to make love to you."

"Do you? Why?"

"There's no need to ask why. I love you."

"You're not feeling sorry for me?"

Nora laughed with surprise at the question. "Sorry for you?" Her tone suggested the notion to be obviously ridiculous. "Sorry for an arrogant, obnoxious beast? Sorry for a man who took himself out of disreputable circumstances and created a decent life for himself, his brother, and his child?" She laughed again. "Hardly."

"Aw, darlin'," he said, biting his lip, his eyes downcast, his voice filled with obvious reluctance. "Seein' as I told you that much, you'd best know it all. Then, if you want to change your mind . . ." Jake swallowed and then shrugged, apparently unable to finish that one sentence, unable to think of the possible consequences his words might bring about. "You were right about my being fast with a gun."

Nora said nothing. She simply waited for him to go on, knowing as he did, there could be no secrets between them.

"I was around eighteen when I joined up with some fellas that. . . ." He shrugged again. "We hired out our guns, did a few jobs for anyone who could afford to pay our fee. Made something of a reputation for ourselves." He was silent for a long moment. "And then a man in California got in touch with us." He bit the inside of his bottom lip. "It had been a dry couple of years. Seems he needed guns 'cause the land north of his place had the water rights he needed for his land. Instead of negotiating for it, he figured it would be cheaper in the long run to get the three

311

families off the land for good."

"Did you?"

"I tried at first," he said honestly, while praying he wasn't ruining every chance he'd ever had with this woman. "But when I realized what the hell I was doing, me and a few of the men kinda switched sides."

Nora nodded as if satisfied with his decision. "Did you kill anyone?"

"I won't lie to you, Nora." His eyes were dark and serious and Nora felt a moment of panic. "There was a gunfight. A lot of guns were firing at once. I don't know if I killed anyone or not."

The expression in his eyes grew distant as if he were remembering the happening in detail. He shook his head as if to dispel the violent scene. "When it was over, I figured I was in the wrong business. I didn't cotton much to a man takin' whatever he wants, just 'cause he was strong enough, or rich enough to manage it. Still don't. And they were the only ones who could afford my salary."

He cleared his throat, not daring to look in her direction, terrified of the disgust he might find in her eyes. "Anyway, during those few years, I got myself a little set aside. When it was over, I came out here and bought a small piece of land. Every few years after that I managed to add a bit to it." A long moment of silence followed before he finished with, "Now you know the whole of it."

Nora wasn't all that surprised. He was unusually fast with his gun. She'd remembered how he'd drawn against the man in her father's office. Drawn and killed him faster than a flash of lightning. The man had hardly gotten his gun in his hand and he was already dead.

Oddly enough the notion that Jake had once worked on the edge of the law did not repel her. After all, he hadn't been an outlaw. He hadn't been a murderer. No, the news of his dangerous past did not bring a measure of disgust. In truth, it only confirmed her suspicions and attached a certain sense of mystery to the man. "So, you were a gunslinger?" The expression in her eyes mingled a number of emotions, not the least of which was excitement. "For the good guys."

"Not at first. At first I was only interested in makin' money." His statement didn't dim the light in her eyes. She was building this up to be something it wasn't. Jake shook his head. "You're mistaken if you think there was something excitin' or romantic about bein' a hired gun." His words appeared to have no effect. "It was a lonely and hard life."

Nora ignored his last statement. "I knew it. I knew there was something dark and mysterious about you."

"I'm not proud of some of the things I did, Nora. What I want to know now is, does it make a difference?"

Nora smiled, the glow in her eyes soft and sweet. Jake felt a soothing balm ease around his soul and closed his eyes on a sigh of relief as he felt her hands reach for his shirt.

"Now where were we?"

Jake felt the last of his insecurities dissolve away at

her words. "You were about to make love to me." His voice shook just a little when he asked, "Do you know how to make love to a man?"

Nora shrugged, her gaze lifting to his. "How hard can it be?"

Jake's grin was pure devilishness. "*It* can get very *hard*."

Nora giggled as she cupped his arousal through his trousers. "So it seems," she said as she ran her hand with aching slowness up and down its length.

"Should I tell you what to do?"

"Only if I don't do it right." She eased his pants and long underwear down his legs and tugged them and his boots away.

"It don't seem fair," he said as she pushed his shirt from his shoulders, "that I should stand here naked and you should—"

"Then sit."

Jake did as he was told. "Bossy little thing, ain't ya?"

Nora smiled as she knelt between his thighs. "Do you really think a man in your position should be complaining?"

"Me?" Jake shot her a look of supposed amazement that she should imagine such a thing. "Complainin'?" Jake leaned back on his elbows, dazzled with the thought of this almost magical happening. "Darlin', I didn't say a thing."

The truth of it was, Nora had no notion as to how to go about this actual seduction. Even though her man was more than willing, there was the glaring fact of her inexperience. She remembered the things he'd done to her on the floor of her father's office and the things he'd done all through last night. How hard could it be if their roles were reversed? Nora forced aside the uncertainty of actual mechanics and decided that she'd simply allow her love for this man to show her the way.

It was easy enough once she started, for his kisses took her out of herself and when her mouth drifted down his neck and over his chest and belly it seemed like the most natural thing in the world.

His groans of pleasure spurred her on to further daring. She took liberties, never before imagined. The fact that she'd never done anything like this before only excited him further. In truth, skill was not needed here. The fact that her initial explorations were shy did not go unnoticed. Because they were so obviously timid, they only succeeded in filling his heart beyond bearing.

Nora's love for this man caused her to forget her insecurities. The taste of his body, the scent and warmth of him, were enough to incite the imagination. Her natural reserve was soon a thing of the past as she went about this most delicious chore. Realizing the power she wrought over his body, she took him beyond reality to a world where only magical pleasure existed. It wasn't long before Jake was gasping and shuddering, his fists balling clumps of the sheet in desperation. His body strained forward, hard as steel and on the edge of breathless release. He reached for her face, pulling her mouth from him. "No, Nora, don't," he said. "It's too much. You won't . . ."

Nora hardly heard his words, for her mind was dazed with the passion of loving him. Her mouth only lowered again, intent on continuing this exquisite assault.

He cried out her name as the helpless waves of ecstasy came and attacked his body, causing him to convulse wildly beneath her wondrous mouth. He was spun into a heretofore unknown delirium.

Nora nuzzled her face against his now soft groin and sighed her delight at being able to pleasure this man so. "Did you think I wouldn't love you simply because of where you came from?"

"I reckon the thought did cross my mind. A decent woman ain't likely to find that appealing." His voice was choked with emotion. Never in his life had a woman loved him like this. He couldn't believe this adorable, delicate lady had given him this pleasure and devotion. What had he ever done to deserve her?

Jake was lying back upon the bed. His feet were on the floor as Nora crawled up his body. He was staring at the ceiling, never bothering to wipe away the tears that had slid into his hair. Nora never mentioned them, but wiped them away with loving fingers and sweet kisses. "That was a silly notion."

His heart was so full that it threatened to burst with the love he knew for this woman. "I know that now."

"And you'll remember it always?" She kissed him and he could taste himself on her lips. He groaned as he rolled her beneath him, devouring her mouth. It was nearly impossible to believe a woman so unselfish, so sweet, so understanding actually existed. "I'll never forget it."

And as his hand began to slide up her leg Nora trembled in anticipation, knowing the delight his moving fingers could bring her. It wasn't until they were both lying naked, their bodies still joined but relaxed as the last of their pleasure enveloped them, that Nora said, "It galls me to admit this, but those whores should be thanked. They taught you very well indeed."

Nora's eyes widened with delight as she watched Jake walk stiffly into the parlor and take a seat upon the sofa. Her father sat in one chair, her mother in another, while Nora sat on the opposite end of the couch. True to his word, he had come to visit with her family. Nora hid her grin and wondered how many more nights he'd suffer through one of these strained visits before he carted her off to stand before the preacher?

To say Jake was not exactly a conversationalist was certainly putting it mildly. He was normally a quiet man. When they were alone he opened up quite a bit, but here, in front of her mother and father, he was positively mute.

Nora received more than one puzzled glance from both her mother and father as questions were answered in monosyllables. Finally Nora asked, "Would you care for tea or coffee?"

"Uh, yeah. Coffee would be fine," Jake said. And as Nora came to her feet, Jake did likewise. "I . . . I'll help you make it."

This brought more strange looks from her parents and both silently agreed the man was not at all like his brother. Cole had come often to visit and had always been pleasant and enjoyable company.

Nora, reading their thoughts correctly, smiled as she led the way to the kitchen.

The moment the door closed behind them she turned to face him. "What are you so nervous about? They don't bite you know."

"I'm not nervous," Jake insisted. "I just can't think of anythin' to say."

"Talk about Matt. Tell them about your ranch."

"Nora," he sighed with disgust. "Your father's a doctor. What does he know about ranchin'?"

"My father loves horses. You love horses. You have that in common."

"I love you. When can we get married?"

"You'll have to come more than once, Jake. Be reasonable."

"That's my problem. I want to come all the time, but how the hell can I if we're not sleeping together?"

Nora giggled as she realized he had deliberately made a pun of her words.

"I can't stand the thought of not sleeping with you tonight." He sounded like a spoiled child.

"Keep your voice down."

"Why?"

"Jake, don't you dare." She didn't trust the sudden wicked gleam in his eyes.

"If your parents found us in some uncompromising position, or maybe overheard some indiscretion, I'll bet we could get married right away."

"Jake!" she warned as she tried to back away but found herself firmly enclosed in his embrace instead.

He was holding her against him, his mouth lowering to hers when she said, "If you love me, you'll do this for me."

"Damn," he groaned as he straightened. His arms still around her, he spoke into her hair. "It better be soon, darlin'. I ain't sure how long I can make it without you. Can't I tell them tonight that I love you and we want to get married?"

"Give them a few days."

"You mean I have to sit through more nights like this? God, I've never been so uncomfortable in my whole life."

Nora grinned. "No. Tomorrow you'll sit through dinner."

Jake groaned and rocked her against him, knowing he'd sit through a hundred dinners if he could have her. "Do you really want a big wedding and a party and all?"

She shook her head. "A small wedding with our families there to hear our promises."

"And a ring?"

Nora laughed. "Well it is customary for a wife to wear one, don't you think?"

"I mean does it have to be diamonds?"

Nora grinned. "Gold will be fine."

"And horses and carriages and gowns?"

Nora pulled back a bit and smiled. "I told you I was teasing when I said that."

"Do you want them?"

"Jake, I want you. Just you."

Jake came the next night and the next for yet another evening of stilted, uncomfortable visits. None of the four were having an easy time of it, but Nora reasoned after the third night, things were beginning to come along. The silent moments didn't stretch on now. Jake managed to answer questions directed his way with more than a "yep," or "nope." He even spoke without being asked . . . now and then. Of course, Jake would never be like his brother, but Nora imagined him to be quite tolerable in both her mother's and father's eyes.

Nora was in their small kitchen peeling potatoes, just about the extent of her kitchen skills, when her mother asked, "Is Jake coming again tonight?"

Nora's eyes darkened with anger at the thought of the man. "Far as I know."

It was easy enough to realize from her tone that she was still upset. "I can't understand why those gifts should have gotten you into such a temper. I would have thought you'd be pleased with his generosity."

"It's not his generosity that upsets me. I'm beginning to think Mr. Brackston and I are not suited after all."

Abigail turned to her daughter with a look of surprise. True there were times when she swore she saw Johnny, but the confusion she suffered at those times did not last. Right now she didn't remember just this morning insisting that her daughter was already married and shouldn't be allowing a man to call upon her. "Why?"

"His arrogance is unbelievable."

320

Abigail laughed. "I often accused your father of the same fault, especially at the beginning."

"Father?" Nora couldn't imagine a more gentle, kinder man. Why she doubted he even knew the meaning of the word.

"Of course you don't see him in the same light, dear, but there were times when . . ." Abigail's cheeks grew to a soft, gentle pink as the memories came.

Nora's eyes widened with astonishment. It was obvious her mother was remembering some intimate moment shared. Nora shook her head wondering why she'd never before imagined her parents capable of loving in much the same manner as she and Jake. It was ridiculous to think they hadn't. Nora knew there was a deep sense of commitment between them, a depth of love rarely seen, for it was openly showed and shared. She smiled at the thought of their love lasting all these years, just as her father stepped into the kitchen.

Her father was a handsome man. The long illness he'd suffered through had not taken away those good looks. Nora could easily imagine her mother being attracted to him. He looked down at his daughter and smiled at her odd expression. "What are you smiling at?"

"Mother just told me how arrogant you were."

Robert Morgan's arm circled his wife's still slender waist and he grinned down into her smile. "Tellin' secrets, sweetheart?" he asked, his voice low, deep, and more intimate than Nora had ever heard before. Her mother's cheeks grew in color and Nora's eyes rounded with astonishment when her father, her

321

own father, laughed just like a man!

"Bob," Abigail said as her cheeks grew bright with color. He laughed again as he nuzzled his face into her neck.

The warmth between her parents brushed over her like warm sunshine and Nora's smile didn't lessen in radiance for a long time.

Keeping his wife close to his side, Robert changed the subject. "What are we having?"

"Chicken."

"Mmm, it smells good."

Nora had promised him that tonight he could ask her father for her hand. He couldn't wait to finish this damn foolishness.

Upon his arrival, Jake felt a definite chill in the atmosphere. Not between Nora's parents and himself. If anything they were downright friendly and getting friendlier with each visit. The chill he felt surrounded Nora. She barely smiled and never looked in his direction. When her mother suggested they have tea, Nora seemed particularly reluctant to leave the parlor. And when Jake offered again to help, she told him in no uncertain terms that she could manage just fine on her own.

Jake ignored her words and followed her into the kitchen. "What the hell's the matter with you tonight?"

Nora turned on him with all the fury she'd kept under control since early that morning. "Didn't I tell you I didn't want horses and a carriage? Well,

322

didn't I?" she asked almost instantly, giving him no real chance to answer her.

"They came?"

"They did." She slammed the kettle on the stove.

"I take it they weren't to your likin'." He sounded oddly disappointed, but Nora was angry enough not to care.

"If you think I'm going to ride around the countryside in something that looks like a hearse, think again. And matching white horses? Whatever possessed you? Where do you think we are? San Francisco? New York City? God, I'd be a laughing-stock."

"What? They sent a hearse? My order musta' got mixed up."

"It didn't get mixed up. I said it looks like a hearse. Are you out of your mind? When would I use such a thing? It's a total waste of money. It's so big, I wouldn't even be able to drive it."

"I expect to hire someone to drive you."

"That's what I thought. Forget it." She pointed a finger at his nose. "I'm definitely not marrying you."

"Why?"

"Because marriage doesn't mean prison."

Their voices began to raise. "What are you talking about?"

"I mean if I married you, I'd never be allowed to walk or ride anywhere without a guard. I can't live like that."

He closed the distance between them and leaned over her, giving her his most threatening glare. "There are no *ifs*, Nora. *When*," he emphasized the word with almost a shout, "you marry me, I expect to keep you safe."

Nora refused to cower. She glared in return. "And that means I'll need a driver?"

"I only want to protect you."

She shook her head. "I can't live like that."

"And I can't live with the fear that something might happen to you."

They were shouting now. Neither giving a moment's care that Nora's mother and father had come into the room to see what all the yelling was about. "I'm not marrying you."

"Yes, you are, goddamn it!"

"Not unless you give up this ridiculous idea."

"All right. You don't want to use the carriage? Fine. I'll have a man follow you."

"No!"

"Nora, be reasonable."

"I am being reasonable. How many women around here have guards?"

"How many have been shot at?"

Nora's mother and father gasped at the news. "Shot at!?" Nora thought her delicate mother was sure to swoon at the very notion. She watched her father reach for her waist.

"What happened?" her father asked.

"Someone tried to kill her." Jake ignored Nora's growl. He knew those words would instantly bring her parents to his side of the argument.

"When?"

"A few weeks back."

Her father shot Nora an accusing look. "And you

said nothing?"

Nora groaned. "It was an accident. I'm sure they meant me no harm."

"Right, that's why they shot her horse and the three of them came tearing down on us. If I didn't happen along . . ." Jake purposely left the sentence unfinished, knowing it could only further upset her parents and add to his cause. Maybe they could get this thickheaded woman to see his point of view.

Abigail gasped.

"The men are gone, Mother."

"We don't know if they're gone."

Nora shot Jake a killing look. He merely grinned.

"Your daughter won't marry me, just because I want to keep a guard nearby until these men are caught."

"That doesn't seem unreasonable, dear," Abigail remarked, obviously concerned.

"You don't know him." Nora shot a fuming glance at the man she loved and right now couldn't figure out why. "Even after the men are caught he'll find some reason to watch my every move."

"I'm not interested in your every move, Nora. I'm only interested in keeping you safe."

"Nora, listen to the man."

Nora groaned. Not her father too! Was there no one to take her side?

She breathed a long sigh before she gave in. "All right. On one condition. After the men are found, no more guards."

"Fine."

"And he'll stay—"

"You said one condition," Jake reminded.

Nora ignored his comment. "And he'll stay far behind me. I don't want the man hovering over me."

"Granted. When can we get married?"

"As soon as you get rid of that obnoxious thing you call a carriage and those two ridiculous horses."

"Tomorrow?"

"Oh, no!" This came from Abigail. "Tomorrow is too soon. We have to make preparations."

Jake sighed his disappointment as he watched his future wife glance at her mother and knew she was going to give into her mother's plea.

"Next week?" he ventured hopefully.

Abigail sighed and offered, "The end of next week?"

Jake nodded and Nora grinned. She hadn't had a thing to say about setting her own wedding date and no one except herself seemed to notice.

Robert Morgan grinned as he led the way back to the parlor. "Shall we leave the ladies to make their plans? I have a bottle of brandy I've been looking to open."

Susie groaned as he slid deep into her body. He was big and vicious with his member and Susie couldn't have enjoyed it more. The trouble was, as usual, he finished within seconds, but Susie didn't mind. She knew best how to find her own pleasure. She smiled as he rolled away. As usual, the moment he was finished, a bottle was in his hand and a cigar in the other. He grinned as he watched her hands move over

326

her body. "Lookin' for more, darlin'?"

"You know me, Johnny. I'm never finished." She spread her legs continuing the manipulation as they spoke.

"You fixin' on leavin' here, ain't ya?"

"You mean with you?"

He shot her a look of annoyance. "'Cause I mean with me."

"Well, I couldn't just up and leave. Not without knowing where my next meal was coming from."

Johnny shrugged. "It wouldn't be for a while yet anyway. I've got some things to do here first." He grinned as he imagined his lucrative future. "I reckon, you won't have to worry about your next meal after I get what I want."

There was a long moment of silence as he drank and smoked, while she did what needed to be done. When she was finished and lay relaxed at his side, he mentioned again the doctor.

Susie made no comment, but decided she'd talk to Jake the next time he came in for a visit and tell him this man was showing unusual interest in that pretty doctor lady, Nora Bowens. Susie might have ignored the mention of the woman's name, if it weren't for the scary way the man looked when he talked about her and Cole.

"Take a ride with me."

"I can't. I promised Mother I'd be back in a few minutes. She has the material for my dress and we're to work on it for the rest of the day."

Jake groaned his disappointment. "I thought you said you wanted a small wedding?"

Nora shot him a puzzled look. "Small or large I have to have something to wear."

"Why? You'll only be wearing it for a few minutes."

Nora laughed. "It couldn't be that you want me naked!" Nora said the words in a scandalous whisper. Jake grinned and responded in all innocence, "Who me? Why the thought never entered my mind!"

They were walking along the wooden sidewalk, holding hands. From the corner of her eye Nora shot him a disbelieving look even as she laughed at his reply. "You know you have a real knack for lying." Her eyes sparkled as she looked his way. "You do it very well."

"Thank you. I can do other things well too."

"I know."

"Do you? Tell me what they are then."

"Riding."

"Uh huh," he agreed with a nod of his dark head. "I can ride very well, especially if I'm riding—"

Nora yanked him to an abrupt stop. "Don't you dare say it!" she snapped, her eyes promising untold suffering if he dared disobey.

"What?" Jake grinned down at her. His blue eyes sparkled with laughter. "What was I going to say?"

"Me," she replied without thinking. "You were going to say especially when you're riding me."

It wasn't until Nora obviously realized that she'd

just said exactly what she'd ordered him not to that Jake pulled her into his arms. Despite the widening of the eyes of more than a few passersby, he kissed her right there on the streets of Glory. Nora's cheeks blazed at his daring. "I love you," he said the moment he raised his mouth from hers.

She moved out of his arms and made a show of straightening her hat and smoothing an already smooth skirt. "Don't kiss me in public, Jake. I'm about to get very upset."

"Are you, darlin'?" he asked with great tenderness. "Well, we won't want that now, would we?"

"No we *wooooouldn't!*" The word came out as a sharp cry when he spun her about and nearly yanked her into a nearby alley.

"Is it all right if I kiss you here, then?"

Nora shot him yet another hard look as she again reached for her hat. "I see we're going to have to get a few things straight between us." Jake grinned and pulled her closer against him. Damn if this woman couldn't act as prim as a schoolmarm in public, while in private she was often as wicked as a man's greatest fantasy. "And the first thing is that I can kiss you whenever I want."

"The first thing is exactly the opposite," Nora countered.

Despite her insistence, Jake's mouth was lowering to hers and Nora wasn't doing a thing to stop it. It was then they both heard the sound of someone clearing her throat.

Nora spun around and Jake's arms held to her waist in a decidedly possessive fashion, pulling her back against him. "I'm sorry to interrupt, but could I talk to you a minute, Jake?"

Jake looked from Susie to Nora and back again. He never realized the low curse that slipped from his lips. What the hell did this woman want? Didn't she know better than to stop and talk to him on the street when he was with his future wife? Jake felt color rush into his cheeks. "Ummm, Nora, this is Susie."

Nora smiled as she moved out of Jake's arms. "I know Susie, Jake. I've been to see the girls at Fancy's a number of times." Nora extended her hand in greeting. "How are you?"

"I'm fine, ma'am. Just heard today that the two of you are getting hitched."

Nora smiled and realized the whole town must know about the coming nuptials by now. "Yes, we are."

"That's good. You're both fine folks."

"Thank you, Susie. That's very nice of you to say."

Jake groaned. What the hell was happening here? Since when did decent ladies converse with whores? He couldn't imagine a more proper conversation if they were sitting down to tea. "Did you want something Susie?" Jake was desperate to see this woman gone.

"Well," she looked slightly uneasy. "I needed to see you."

Jesus. Why me?

"Could you stop by Fancy's place later?"

"I reckon." Jake had never felt more uncomfortable in his entire life. What the hell was Nora going to think? "Ahhh, I'll see you later then."

Jake glanced at the woman at his side and groaned at the sudden wave of guilt that flooded him. A moment later the guilt vanished and was replaced by annoyance. It wasn't his fault that he'd been forced to seek out another. If Nora had been consenting from the first, he'd never have had to look at another woman.

Jake groaned again as he realized how he managed to twist the truth. In all honesty he couldn't blame anyone but himself. Now, all he could do was pray Nora didn't guess that Susie had serviced him often after the first few weeks of her arrival.

The most frustrating fact of all had been that despite the woman's best efforts he'd remained decidedly unsatisfied. It hadn't been Susie or any of the others at Fancy's that he'd wanted. There'd been only one woman who had the power to appease his desire. And now that he had her, there was no way he was going to lose her.

He breathed a sigh of relief as the woman turned a corner. A relief that turned out to be a bit premature.

The first thing Nora felt was pure, unadulterated shock. The man had actually made an assignation with a prostitute and had done it in her presence! But Nora's shock didn't last more than a heartbeat, for rage came instantly to take its place. Never had she known the emotion in such great intensity. It was only by an act of God that she refrained from punching him in his face. Truly it was a miracle she didn't kill him with her bare fists. Nora knew at that moment she possessed all the strength needed . . . and more.

Nora might have led a sheltered life, but she wasn't a fool. She knew Jake and this woman had had a relationship of sorts. Even if guilt hadn't been written all over the man's face, the fact was obvious. But she expected, especially after all the things they'd done together, that other women would be a part of the man's past.

She spun on him the instant Susie disappeared around the corner of the alley. Her lip curled into a sneer. "Are you serious? Are you serious?" From some vague corner of her mind Nora wondered if she had the power to stop asking that particular question. "Are you seriously considering seeing her, after asking me to marry you? Are you seri—"

"But darlin', I ain't gonna' do nothin'. I swear, I'm only goin' 'cause . . ."

Nora's eyes grew wider, almost swallowing her beautiful face. Jake knew he'd be damned, no matter his denials, if he stepped within a hundred feet of the place.

Jake cursed and then growled, "Wait right here."

Jake returned a minute later with Susie in tow. By that time, thank God, Nora had managed to regain some of her control.

Jake returned to Nora's side, his hand snaking around her stiff form and said, "Whatever you got to say, you'd best be sayin' it here and now." Jake could only pray whatever it was had nothing to do with his visits.

"Well," she seemed to hesitate and Jake just knew she was going to be indiscreet. "There's this man."

Jake almost groaned aloud. *Please God. I swear I'll never do it again. I only went 'cause I wanted Nora so bad. Please!*

"He's been askin' questions about the doc here."

"What?" Jake stiffened, Susie's words having snapped him instantly out of his thoughts. He couldn't have been more surprised. Nora grinned as she realized his shock. No doubt he'd been expecting quite a different scenario. No wonder he'd been so nervous. Nora relaxed.

Susie nodded toward Nora. "Well, every time he comes to see me, we . . . you know, finish our business . . . and then he starts askin' me questions about you."

"What does he say?" Jake's eyes narrowed as he watched Susie. Susie shivered at the naked emotion. His gaze promised murder to anyone foolish enough to put designs on his woman. It was easy enough to see that Jake was wild about his lady.

"Oh," she shrugged, "the usual things. He's gonna' come into some money. And he wants me to go away with him when he gets it. And then he asks if I've heard anything about the new doc. Is she and Cole gonna' get married?"

"Why would he want to know?" Nora asked.

Susie shrugged again. "Can't rightly say. All I know is he scares me when he talks about you. He gets a hard, almost evil look in his eyes. And the way he laughs, like he's got this real good secret. It gives me the shivers."

"Goddamn it!"

"Calm down." Nora issued that directive to Jake

and then turned to the woman again. "What's his name?"

She shrugged again. "Calls himself Johnny. Don't know his last name."

"Can you get word to me the next time he comes?"

"Maybe. If Jed ain't busy, I could send him. But he don't usually stay too long. He'd probably be gone by the time you got here."

"Send word anyway."

Susie nodded and then smiled as she wished them both well, turned, and walked out of the alleyway, leaving Nora puzzled and Jake furious.

"It's the son of a bitch who tried to kill you."

"You don't know that."

"Don't I? You tryin' to tell me everybody's been askin' about the doc, with an evil look in his eyes?" He grabbed hold of her, pulling her against him, almost crushing her in his fear for her safety. "I ain't lettin' you out of my sight."

Nora smiled. "Don't worry. We'll be married in four days."

"Like I said, I ain't lettin' you out of my sight."

Realizing his meaning, Nora raised her head from his chest and looked into dark, determined eyes. "You can't stay at my place, Jake. Think of the scandal."

"Then you'll stay with me."

"I can't."

"Look, we're gettin' married in a few days anyway. It don't make no never mind."

"It does. My father won't be able to show his face."

"Then your mother will come with you. She'll be

334

your chaperone." He said the last words with some real dread, and Nora laughed.

She leaned against him and teased, "That means you'll have to do something about those frisky tendencies of yours."

Jake breathed a sigh of despair. "I don't care. I want you safe. Nothing else matters."

Chapter Fifteen

Johnny Bowens watched the young couple from the alleyway across the street and grinned as Jake Brackston took Nora into his arms and kissed her right in the middle of town where anyone could see. So, it was the brother, not Cole, Nora was after. And by the looks of things she had him roped already. Johnny scoffed, the man was a fool. There wasn't a woman alive who had the power to get to him like that, not even his dear wife.

Nora pulled herself out of his arms and straightened her hat. Johnny's mouth turned down in derision. Still the prim and proper miss. Some things never changed. He didn't feel a lick of jealousy at watching his wife with another man. Even knowing they were to be married and would, of course, share the same bed, stirred not a crumb of emotion. No, Jake Brackston could have her. A wicked gleam entered his eyes, but he could have her for a short time at least.

Johnny jumped back into the soft shadows as Jake

suddenly dragged her into the alley almost directly across from him. He slid behind a crate, peeking over the top, lest either of them glance in his direction. Johnny knew he wouldn't easily be recognized, but he wasn't about to take any chances.

Twice he'd seen her dunce of a mother, and twice he'd beaten a hasty retreat. He knew Abigail had seen him, but since Dan was dead and it looked like Pete had run off, probably to Mexico, there was little he could do but come into town himself. The stupid bastard Pete was forever talking about the place, and Johnny hadn't seen him in weeks, not since the day he'd come to town to have Nora take a look at his arm. From the talk around town, Johnny doubted anyone would believe a word Abigail said if she ever mentioned spotting him.

Johnny frowned as he watched Susie enter the alley just as Jake and Nora were about to get down to business. He stiffened at the sight of her. What the hell was she doing? What business could a whore have with those two? Johnny didn't have to wonder for long. There was no other explanation, after all. It didn't take more than a second to convict her and pass down judgment. He sneered his contempt as he watched the three converse. Susie was dead. She just didn't know it yet. And if he was mistaken? Johnny shrugged. What did it matter, one whore, more or less?

He cursed. If she was telling them what he suspected, they'd be more cautious now. He breathed a long sigh and swore to get even. And then it hit him. It didn't matter. One day soon they'd drop their guard. No one could live watching over their shoulder indefinitely. They'd forget for a minute and that's all it would take. A slow smile spread over his mouth. On the day he killed Jake Brackston, he'd claim Nora as his legal wife and have everything he ever wanted.

Even from the porch he could hear them. The house was in an uproar and Jake couldn't wait for the day after tomorrow. Maybe then things would get back to normal. Maybe then he'd be able to talk to Nora without a dozen people watching over them. How had it suddenly become so important that the two of them should never be alone? What could they do in the few days before they married that they couldn't have, indeed hadn't, done before? And how the hell had he lost control of the running of his own home?

Jake groaned knowing he wouldn't find a minute's peace what with neighbors coming by offering their congratulations. It felt like women, by the hundreds, had descended upon him. They invaded his house, each one desperate to see Nora to offer her a gift, and impart a small piece of advice. Thank God, he'd thought to invite Abigail as well. With her mother present, not one could say a word about his wife.

Jake grinned at his thoughts, somewhat surprised to realize that he already thought of her as his wife.

At first Jake had been amazed to find the citizenry of Glory nearly pounding down his door. He hadn't realized that Nora knew so many, but of course she did. For a few months she'd been the only doctor in these parts. And if she wasn't exactly welcomed at first, it hadn't been long before things had changed. It seemed when one was in desperate need, it hardly mattered the sex of the one doing the caring.

Today there were more women than ever. Today Abigail hosted a party for her daughter and every woman he'd ever known or seen in these parts appeared at his doorstep an hour after noon.

It was almost five o'clock and they showed no signs of leaving. Jake had had enough of standing outside waiting to be able to enter his own home.

He walked into his house to the squeals of at least the fifteen or more women who had been chatting happily, drinking coffee or tea as they moved about his kitchen and parlor, enjoying each other's company. Something white flashed just before it was swooped out of sight. The women visibly relaxed, and Jake breathed a sigh of despair. He'd hoped his appearance would send them on their way, only nobody appeared ready to leave yet. He wondered how much longer it would be before he got Nora alone.

His gaze sought her out. Nora was listening to a woman whisper something that brought color to her cheeks.

Jake grinned. He didn't have to think hard to imagine that whatever the woman was saying was a bit racy. What, he wondered, would this group think if they knew he and Nora already had carnal knowledge of one another, and he was eagerly looking forward to further explorations?

He nodded his head over his right shoulder, silently asking her to follow him as he moved down the hallway toward his room.

After a few minutes Nora did just that.

She was moving past his opened door, softly calling out his name, wondering where he'd taken himself off to, when a hand reached out and suddenly dragged her into his room. A second later the door shut behind her and she was pushed up against it, Jake's body pinning hers in place. Thankfully, the women were making enough noise that Nora's small shriek of surprise went unnoticed.

"You scared me."

Jake chuckled a low wicked sound as he rubbed his hips against her belly. "Did I? What did you think I wanted when I signaled for you to follow me?"

Nora grinned. "I thought you wanted to talk to me."

He shook his head. "We do enough talkin' every night. What with your mother, Cole, Matt and the others. God, I can never get you alone."

"And that's what you want? To get me alone?"

"That's a silly question, lady."

"You are a wicked man, Mr. Brackston."

"Am I? Or are you just hopin'?"

"Both."

Jake grinned down at her impish expression. "Ah, darlin', I can hardly wait."

"It won't be much longer."

"It's been too long already. It's been weeks." His mouth was nuzzling the soft skin of her neck as he spoke.

"I'll have to go back home tomorrow. You can't see me before the wedding."

Jake knew he couldn't fight her on this. He sighed,

knowing there was no way she was going without him. "I'll stay in your father's office."

Nora smiled. "Jake. Nothing's going to happen. I won't leave the house, not even for a minute."

"I'll stay in your father's office," he repeated. "Cole can bring Matt to the church."

Her hands left his chest and came to cup his face. "I love you."

Jake groaned. "God, I'm goin' crazy with wantin' you. I keep wakin' up reachin' for you. After only one night with you, I can't sleep alone any more."

"Kiss me before I have to go back."

Not trusting himself to linger overlong, Jake gave her a quick, hard kiss. "Walk with me after dinner?"

Nora grinned. "I'll try."

"What did you tell your mother?"

The night was cool and dark. The air smelled clean with a hint of fall. Above them stars twinkled upon a velvety black bed and Nora leaned against him, his arm close around her waist as they moved from the corral toward the barn. Nora realized their destination and shot him a grin as they neared the back of the building. "I told her that my future husband was a horny toad who couldn't wait any longer and that we were going to the barn to make mad, passionate love."

Jake snorted his disbelief. "A horny toad?"

Nora chuckled a low, wicked sound as she turned from his embrace. Facing him, she walked backwards. "Think I haven't got the nerve?"

"I think you're too nice to purposely give your

mother a heart attack."

"Nice!" She breathed a long sigh of pure disgust. "Lord, how depressingly boring. I think I'd prefer it if you thought anything else but nice."

Jake's grin was a silent telling that he couldn't help what he believed, whether she thought it boring or not.

A wicked gleam entered her eye. "So, you think I'm nice, do you?" A small slightly helpless shrug was her only answer. "You'd better change your mind."

"Or?"

"Or, I'll have to change it for you."

Jake laughed as she swaggered and narrowed her gaze in warning. God, but he couldn't be more pleased with this woman. There were none whose laughter was quite so silky, whose smile was so lovely, whose eyes twinkled with just the right amount of mischief, whose lips were as soft and sweet.

"Would a nice girl do this?" To his amazement Nora moved right up against him, her hand reaching for him. And there in the open, boldly, lustily, she cupped his most private parts, bringing him to an astonished and abrupt stop. An instant later she giggled at his shocked expression, twisted away, and disappeared inside the barn.

"Why you little . . ." In less than a heartbeat he charged after her.

"Little what?" She was just inside waiting for him and nearly scared him to death. He reached for her and pulled her to him. "Nora, for God's sake, I almost knocked you over."

"My, my, we are anxious."

"Witch."

"Jake, darling," she said as she nuzzled her face against his neck, "I swear you're about to turn my head with all these compliments."

"I love you." The words were said in a groan as his arms tightened around her.

"And you can't live without me?"

He lifted her slightly and pressed her fully against him, breathing in her scent. "I can't."

"And you'll always feel the same?"

He was grinding his hips against her, hardly conscious of her words, already lost in the scent and feel of her. "I will."

"And you'll always do as I say?"

Jake groaned as he felt her grow soft and hot against him. He moaned at the deliciousness. "And I'll . . ." Jake pulled back and peered down into her shadowy face. The lack of light couldn't hide her grin. "Nora." The word was little more than a growl and said so sternly that Nora couldn't hold back her tantalizing giggle.

"Yes, dear."

"Don't be a smart ass."

"Oh? Can an ass—?" Her question was cut off by the pressure of his mouth.

The moment he released her lips, Nora laughed in pure naughtiness. "You can't blame me for trying." She danced away from him. "What do you suppose we could do in here? It's so dark."

He moved to stand behind her. "I reckon we could think of something." His arm was around her, his hand moving in slow, aching circles over her stomach. She leaned back against him and sighed as she waited for his hand to come higher.

"You mean if we put our heads together?"

"That's exactly what I mean."

"And how would we do that?"

"Turn around and I'll show you."

His kiss was long and thorough. Before he was done, he'd sampled again the wonder of her special taste and texture. "Ahh, putting our heads together is a very good idea."

"I thought you'd like it."

"I do, but I was thinking maybe we could put other things together." She rubbed herself wantonly against him. "I'm bound to like that as well, don't you think?"

Jake chuckled, delighted by her boldness. "You are a wicked, wicked lady."

She pulled just far enough away to open the buttons of her blouse. "As long as I'm not nice."

It was late. He'd been waiting for hours for the place to settle down. Johnny figured most of the girls were asleep by now and Fancy, who usually stayed up till dawn, was entertaining someone in her room. He figured there was more than a good chance that he could probably come and go with no one the wiser. Johnny shrugged at the thought. It didn't much matter none if he was seen or not. He'd just kill anyone who got in his way.

Johnny figured the damage was done by now. But he wasn't about to let a whore get away with double crossing him. He'd been a fool to talk as much as he had. Silently he swore he wouldn't be making that mistake again.

Quietly he opened the back door and stepped inside. Jed the boy who ran errands for the girls was asleep on a mat near the stove. Johnny crept by and up the stairs without a sound.

Her door was the second on the right. He was inside her room, a soundless shadow in the night.

Mazie had been having trouble with that Willis boy again. He'd threatened her with another going over with his fists; he was back in town again now that the marshal had left. He'd been here again tonight and Mazie had been afraid to stay in her room.

Susie offered the girl hers.

It was very dark. The bed stood as a shadow against the wall. Under the sheet was a dark, slender form. He couldn't see her face, but he'd been here often enough. There was no mistakin' this room.

Mazie muttered a soft cry of surprise when she felt a hand crash heavily upon her mouth. She couldn't see more than a large dark form, but she knew well enough who it was. How had he found her? she wondered.

A moment later her body stiffened as she felt an odd and, for the moment only, slightly painful sensation run across her neck. Five seconds later she realized it wasn't his hand that was hampering her breathing. She struggled, but he'd cut her deep; so deep in fact that there was no way air could enter her lungs. In her panic to breathe, she almost threw him off. Then a minute or so later she no longer felt the need. She no longer felt anything.

It wasn't until one o'clock the next afternoon that Susie went back to her own room. A high, piercing scream rent the entire house, bringing all with pounding hearts from their beds.

Jed came with her, for Susie was terrified to travel alone. She and Jake were standing on his porch when Nora came outside. The woman's face was white, her brown eyes huge with fear.

"Talk has it, it was Willis, but he couldn't have known she was in my room."

"Do you think?"

Susie nodded. "It was him. He musta' seen me talkin' to you."

"What are you gonna' do?"

"I'm gettin' out. I'm dead if I stay. Only I need . . ." Her dark eyes were beseeching as she raised them to his gaze. "Do you think you could . . . ?"

"No problem." Jake nodded. "How much do you need?"

"Enough to get me far away from here."

Nora heard a good part of the conversation. Enough for her to know that Susie was leaving and Jake was giving her the money to do it. She wondered why. "What happened?" Nora asked as she moved to stand at Jake's side.

His arm went instantly around her middle, hugging her roughly against him. "Mazie's dead."

"Oh my God!" Nora couldn't help but remember the young girl, who was barely yet a woman and how afraid she was that she might die. "How?"

347

"Got her throat cut last night."

"Good God! Can't something be done about that man? Can he be allowed to kill as he pleases?"

"It wasn't Willis, Nora. Mazie was sleepin' in Susie's room. Whoever killed her had to think she was Susie."

"Oh my God," she said again. Nora's eyes were huge as they watched the tall full-figured woman.

"I think it was Johnny. I think he musta' saw me talkin' to the two of you."

Nora groaned in horror. It was her fault. If she hadn't acted like a jealous fool, Jake would have met the woman in Fancy's and none of this would have happened. "I'm so sorry."

"It ain't your fault, honey." Susie shook her head and the two of them sat as Jake went into the house for the money.

She left only a moment after Jake handed her the money.

Jake looked at Nora with an almost crushing wave of overwhelming fear and near panic. It was obvious to him that the man who'd been talking about Nora was still in town. His mouth hardened with determination. There was no way that Nora would be going back the night before their wedding or anytime soon after for that matter.

Jake wasn't a man to mince words. He wasn't the type to ask or plead. He wasn't in any mood to worry over Nora's feelings. He took her arm and brought her into the house. Because of his fear, his voice was overly harsh. "I don't care what nobody says. You're not goin' into town, and I don't want to hear another word about it."

It took a moment before Nora realized his meaning. When it did, her eyes narrowed with a threatening glare. Despite the fact that he was obviously worried for her safety, Nora wasn't about to allow anyone the right to tell her what she might do. She gritted her teeth and yanked her arm from his hold. "You are the most overbearing man."

It wasn't exactly the response he was looking for. "Yeah, well, I'll be around for the next fifty or sixty years. I reckon you'll get used to it." His remark appeared to be so intolerant of her feelings, all he managed to do was anger her further.

"Who do you think you're talking to?" Her voice was raising at an alarming rate and there was no way she could control it. "I'm not your child."

"Goddamn it, Nora! You're acting like one."

"Am I?" Nora wasn't sure she could get any angrier. "And how does a child act?"

"They don't take proper precautions. They think nothing will ever happen to them."

Nora glared at him. "Did I say that?"

"I'm only tryin' to protect you and you're always fightin' me."

"That's because you're so unreasonable."

"Is it unreasonable to want to see you safe?"

"It's unlucky to see the bride before the wedding."

"I don't give a shit about luck. You make your own luck. We're getting married here. The preacher and your father can come here."

"I feel like I'm about to step into prison." She was yelling in earnest now.

"Too bad." Jake's voice was no softer. It nearly rocked the walls of the house. "'Cause I've made my

349

decision and you're stayin' here. Have I made myself clear?"

Nora said not another word, but turned and stormed out of the parlor. A moment later her bedroom door slammed shut.

A half hour later her mother walked into the room to see her daughter pacing.

"Didn't I tell you? Didn't I?" she bellowed to her startled mother, who was about to reach for a dress that needed the finishing touches. It was a beautiful dress and Nora was due to wear it the next morning. She glared at the garment, imagining it was nothing more than drab prison garb. "He's an arrogant, aggravating . . . I knew I never should have agreed to marry him. I knew it!"

She glared at the closed door for a long moment before she realized it was not too late. So, he'd made his decision, had he? Well she'd make hers as well. She wasn't married yet, perhaps she never would be. And Jake had no right to order her about, careless of her wants, not even having the decency to discuss the matter. There was no way she was going to allow him to treat her like a child. If he wanted a woman like that, then he'd better look elsewhere.

"Let's go."

"Where?"

"Home. I don't care what he says. I refuse to be married out here."

"Nora, don't you think you're being a little hasty?" Abigail said timidly. She wasn't unaware of the happenings in town and like her future son-in-law feared for her daughter's welfare.

"Mother, I'm going home. Would you like to come

with me?"

Abigail might have been the mother, but she didn't possess nearly the strength of her daughter. Nora was a grown, headstrong woman. There was no way a mother or anyone else could argue her out of a decision once it was made. "Of course, dear," her mother said obediently. If the girl was leaving, there was no way Abigail would allow her to go alone.

Nora threw her things into her bags and then brought them to the front door. She was just depositing the last of them when she heard his voice behind her. "Where do you think you're going?"

"Home." Nora refused to look in his direction.

"Nora I told you—"

"That you did, Mr. Brackston. You told me. No," she corrected, "to be more precise, you ordered me not to leave this house. You commanded that we'd be married here tomorrow. That the preacher and my father could come out here."

Nora took a deep, calming breath. "Now, I'm going to tell you. *If* I marry, it will be in a church. *If* I marry, my father will walk me down the aisle. *If* I marry, it won't be to a pigheaded, stubborn beast. Now, I've made my decision. Have I made myself clear?"

Jake grinned as she repeated almost word for word what he'd said only a half hour ago. Maybe he'd been a bit harsh. Maybe he could have spoken a bit more gently. But he was so scared. Couldn't she understand how much she meant to him? Couldn't she understand that he'd never make it if anything happened to her?

Silently he watched her from across the room. He

didn't dare go near her lest he take her in his arms and carry her into his bedroom. If that happened, they might not be seen for weeks, impending wedding or not.

"All right, Nora," he breathed a long weary sigh, knowing he had no choice but to give into her demands. "Tell me what you want and I'll do it."

"I want you to take me home. You can stay with me, if that's what you want, but on the night before my wedding I belong at home."

He nodded as he moved past her and reached for his hat and gun belt hanging behind the door. He knew better than to fight her on this. Actually he didn't dare. Not until tomorrow. Not until she said the words that made her his. Even then he knew he couldn't control her. Not the way he would have liked. But he would watch her. Nothing was going to happen to this woman. Not if he could help it.

His back was to her when she spoke again. "And one more thing."

Jake stopped the loading up of her bags and waited for her to go on. Her voice was suddenly soft, sweet, heavy with emotion. "I never want you to love me less than you do right now."

Jake dropped the bags to the floor and turned to face her. In a second she was in his arms, hugging him tightly to her.

"Is that an order?"

"Yes."

"I'm sorry I yelled at you darlin'. I'm just so damn scared," he said as he rubbed his face against her hair.

"I know. I'm scared too, but nothing will happen if you stay with me. You can sleep on the couch."

Jake chuckled. "Sounds comfortable. Are you sure I can't share your bed?"

She ignored his teasing. "Tomorrow night I'll massage away all your stiffness."

"Oh God," was the best he could do in the way of a response as his mind took hold of her promise.

Jake watched them from the opposite end of the church. The lady in white and her father were having a private conversation. Jake thanked the Lord that her father was well at last. It had taken a long time, but Nora was no longer needed to work either in his place or at his side.

Jake figured she'd probably see a few people professionally. The ladies especially would no doubt come for her help, but the days of working in town were over. That was a relief. He didn't want to see her traveling back and forth every day. He wouldn't have stopped her if that had been her wish, but he wouldn't have liked it much.

No, Jake had definite plans for this lady and their future together. It didn't include her keeping regular office hours.

This was the first moment in weeks that father and daughter had a chance to speak without a dozen people interfering. Nora grinned as her father leaned close and whispered, "You're shaking like a leaf. It's not too late to change your mind."

"I'm not shaking. You are."

Robert acknowledged the truth of her statement with a low laugh. "Well, it's not everyday that I get to walk my daughter down the aisle. I have every right to be a little nervous."

"Don't faint, 'cause I'll just have to carry you and that will wrinkle my dress."

Robert's eyes sparkled as he grinned. "Anxious, are we?"

Nora bit her bottom lip to keep her laughter at bay. They were in a church, for God's sake. She was about to walk up the aisle and marry the man waiting for her there. This was definitely not the time to laugh. "A little maybe."

Robert nodded toward his soon to be son-in-law. "He reminds me of myself a bit. When I was younger, of course."

Nora smiled as she shot her father a sideways glance. The two men looked nothing alike, but it wasn't looks Robert Morgan spoke of. "I was noticing the resemblance the other day," Nora agreed.

"You're a lot like me, too."

"I know," Nora replied.

"That's bound to make for a few combustible moments." And then as if the thought had never occurred, he stated flatly, "You'll fight."

Nora giggled. "I know."

"But that doesn't mean the man doesn't love you."

Her eyes glowed with happiness. "I know."

Robert grinned. "As long as you know that, you'll be good together."

"I love you, Father."

He smiled as they started down the aisle.

Nora was truly a beautiful bride. She wore a dress of ivory and a mantilla over her red hair. Jake figured he'd never seen anything like her in his life. He silently vowed that this woman would be his forever. Jake had already set about making sure his promise would hold true.

There were three men on their way to Glory— hired guns. Men he'd known when he'd been in the business. They were due to arrive before the week was out. Between the four of them, he figured Nora should be reasonably safe.

They were in her parents' small parlor while half the town came and went offering their congratulations and bringing gifts.

"Did you see Mina?" Nora asked her husband.

"Yeah, she looks nice."

"Nice?" Nora couldn't imagine a more under-stated fact. "She's stunning. I can't remember when I've ever seen anyone half so lovely."

"I can."

Nora smiled at his look of longing.

"When can we leave?" he begged.

"Soon. Cole loves her."

"Not as much as I love you. When can we leave?"

Nora laughed and shot him a teasing look. "You wouldn't be in a hurry, by any chance?"

"I want to get there before dark."

"Where?"

"To the shack."

"Is that where we're going?"

Jake nodded. "Cole will take Matt home. Let's go."

Chapter Sixteen

Jake's gaze was ever watchful, even as he appeared to be listening to his wife's one-sided conversation. Nora shot him another glance and followed the direction of his gaze. Nothing. What in the world was the man looking for? From the moment they had left, he'd been twisting his head every which way.

"All right, repeat everything I just said."

Jake's look was at first startled and then blank. Nora burst out laughing. "That look convinced me, even more than the preacher's words, that we're truly married. You didn't hear a word I said."

"Of course I heard you."

Her look was clearly one of disbelief. "Then what did I say?"

"You were talking about my brother and Mina."

"Good try. That was ten minutes ago. Now what's the matter?"

"Nothing. I just want to make sure nobody's following us."

Nora felt a shiver of fear. "Do you think someone would?"

Jake flashed her a confident smile. "Just making sure."

They reached the cabin at last. Jake gave a sigh of relief after carefully searching out the horizon until he was confident that there was no one within miles of the place. Thank God the mountains were far off to their left. Far enough away that their arrival at the cabin couldn't be seen. By tomorrow, or at the latest the day after, the men would be here and he'd be able to relax a bit.

He and Nora needed time alone and never would have found it at the ranch. A few days of privacy and perhaps he could work out this aching need that never seemed to abate. The one night they'd spent together had not been nearly enough. Indeed, it had merely whetted his appetite. Jake felt as anxious as a boy encountering his first experience with a woman. His heart thundered with anticipation. His yearning left him even more tongue-tied than usual. He needed her so badly, loved her so madly; he wondered if she was aware of how much she meant to him. He smiled at the thought. It didn't matter. He had a lifetime to show her.

He smiled as he took her from the buggy and stood her on the sagging porch. "Wait here for me."

The moment he was finished caring for the horse, he hoisted their bags from the buggy, brought them inside, and came out to gather her in his arms and reenter the cabin. "I hope it's not . . ." she began, remembering the webs, the huge spiders, and the mice the last time they'd been here.

"Don't worry. I sent a few of the men out to clean it up yesterday."

Nora smiled, but her smile turned into a look of astonishment as Jake opened the door, carried her inside, and lit the candle that was sitting on the table. She said nothing but simply stared in amazement at the transformation.

"Like it?"

"Did . . . did you do this for me?"

"Of course, I did it for you." Jake frowned for Nora had as yet to blink and he couldn't tell if she liked it or not.

"I can't believe it," she said, her voice soft with wonder.

"Does that mean you like it?"

Nora grinned as she looked into unsure blue eyes. Jake Brackston unsure? Nora never would have believed it, if she hadn't seen it herself. "No, it doesn't mean I like it." She gave a soft throaty laugh at his instant and obvious disappointment. "I *love* it. But most of all I love you for thinking of it."

Jake put her down and Nora's gaze moved slowly over the refurbished room. Amazing! Who would ever have believed that the bare ugly room they'd used only a few weeks ago could look like this?

It was sparkling clean. Lord, even the rusted stove was polished black. All the equipment that had formerly littered the wall and floor was gone. Gossamer-thin bed drapes hung from the ceiling to the floor at each corner of the narrow bed. It created a lovely, seductive picture as they were each tied back with pink ribbons. Upon the bed were at least three thick, pure white quilts and a dozen satin pillows of the same color.

The floor was covered with rugs and more pillows. The rickety table and chairs were gone. They were replaced by a small, comfortable-looking sofa and a low table that was just about covered with food: Fried chicken, cheese, bread, cookies, small cakes, and a bottle of wine. And to top it all off, there were candles everywhere. They covered every available surface from the windowsills, sink, tables to the floor.

"When did you get a chance to do this?"

"Day before yesterday." He was watching her closely. "While you were busy with the ladies. I had White Moon finish it today."

"You've thought of everything," Nora spoke as if in shock. Her eyes widened when she saw the hip bath. "I can't believe it." The truth of it was, she couldn't believe she'd married so romantic a man.

Nora had known that Jake was a passionate man, but she'd never thought of him in this light before. Now she looked at him with nothing less than astonishment.

"If you don't like it, I could . . ."

She moved into his arms, her own arms circling his neck. "You're amazing. I couldn't have asked for a more beautiful place to spend our wedding night."

Jake had wanted this night to be perfect. Yes, he'd been married before but this felt so different . . . so new. He'd worried all day that this should please her and now felt only unbound relief that it did. "Are you hungry?"

"A little."

"Would you like a bath?"

She nodded and then laughed, her green eyes

flashing wickedly. "You wouldn't be tryin' to get me naked, would you?"

Jake flashed her a smile and for the first time since entering the cabin felt himself relax. "Actually, I was thinkin' maybe you could wear this." He reached for the nightdress that was draped over the bed. Nora's gaze widened. Drape was a good description, for Nora thought that's what it was.

She grinned as he held up the fabric. It was thinner, if possible, than the gossamer drapes that cornered the bed and easier to see through. She fingered the material and then looked up to his expectant gaze. "There's not much to it, is there?"

"Ahhh," he bit his lip. "I was hopin' you wouldn't notice that."

Nora hid her grin and turned her back to him. "Forget I said anything." She looked at the huge pots on the stove, anticipating the luxury of two baths in one day and then pointed to her back. "I'm going to need some help here."

Jake began to work on the long line of buttons at the back of her dress. It took him awhile, but the material soon parted and Nora shimmied it over her hips and stepped out of it. By the time he had most of the water in the tub, her petticoats, chemise, and shoes were gone. She was wearing only her drawers, stockings, and a thin, lacy corset that did a meager job at best of hiding her charms. Actually, all it managed to do was force her breasts up high on her chest, so that they appeared ready to burst free of the garment. The coral tips were barely covered, but Jake could see them clearly through the material. He shuddered knowing he'd never seen anything so

361

erotic in his life and wondered if he wasn't being a bit hasty. He would have liked to see her wear that for a bit and told her so.

"In the bath?" she asked in some amazement.

He shook his head and almost said, "while we eat," but changed his mind. This wasn't the way he'd planned things. Jake swallowed at the sight of her. "What would happen if you took a deep breath?"

Nora chuckled, realizing his train of thought as she followed his gaze. "A lady can't take a deep breath in one of these."

"Too bad," he muttered as he poured another pot of water into the tub.

Nora laughed at his mumblings and reached around her back for the ribbons that would undo the corset. Jake watched in silent, breathless anticipation as the material fell away and left her naked to her waist. God, but she was lovely.

"Take your hair down."

She shook her head. "It will get wet."

"Take it down."

Nora faced his hungry gaze with a soft smile as she reached up for the pins. He didn't dare touch her. He didn't dare come near her. She posed too great a temptation, and Jake wanted to see this night last to the limit of his endurance. He wanted all the teasing of the senses that was his due as her husband.

"Take that off." He nodded toward her drawers.

Nora did as he asked and seconds later stood unashamedly naked, wearing only white stockings that came to mid thigh, held in place by lacy garters. "No, leave them for a minute," he said as he saw she was about to roll them down.

A moment later Jake was on his knees before her, unable to resist the temptation any longer. "Let me." Slowly he rolled the fabric down her legs, his mind dizzy from the scent of her. His hands trembled as his gaze moved over her. Never in his life had he seen anything to compare to her beauty.

With a low groan, his arms reached around her and as he gathered her closer, he buried his face in her stomach. "I can't believe you finally belong to me."

Nora threaded her fingers through his dark hair and smiled, knowing she couldn't love this man more. Idly she wondered how many more facets were there to his personality? She'd never known him to be so tender, so openly loving. Usually he showed his love by yelling and ordering her about. Nora grinned as she remembered their last confrontation, and wondered how many more lay ahead for them. Life with this man certainly wouldn't be easy, but it wouldn't be boring either.

"Why don't you take off these things and join me in the tub?"

He shook his head forcing his needs under control. "Later." His hands released her and moved to his jacket and shirt. Within seconds they joined her things on the bottom rail of the bed. His boots lay beside her shoes. He wore only a pair of black dress pants when he asked, "Where's your brush?"

Nora nodded toward her things. "Small bag."

She was in the tub when he came up behind her. "You're going to spoil me," she warned as he handed her a glass of wine and started brushing her hair. She leaned back with a sigh and her hair almost touched the floor. "Every time I take a bath, I'll be expectin' this.''

Jake chuckled. He watched as she placed her wine on the small nearby table and took the soap and cloth in her hands. A moment later the upper portion of her body was covered with a thin film of fragrant suds. Jake could hardly breathe as he watched the tiny bubbles burst over her creamy wet skin. And then she was rinsing the soap away and her body glowed creamy soft and wet in the candlelight.

Nora sipped at her wine again. ''This is the most decadent thing I've ever done. And you're spoiling me terribly.''

''Every woman should be spoiled on her weddin' night.''

''Lord, it's the best wedding night I've ever had.'' He felt her stiffen. She sat up straighter. The movement cut off the delicious view of her wet, bobbing breasts. She turned to face him, her teeth holding her bottom lip. ''I'm sorry. I didn't mean that. I mean, I did mean that. I just didn't mean to say it.''

She was obviously flustered and Jake laughed. ''I'm not jealous of a dead man, Nora. We've both been married before. I think we can let the dead rest easy.''

He grinned at her enthusiastic nod.

He helped her from the tub and after she was dry and wearing the gown he'd prepared for her, she followed his gaze as it moved down the length of her. ''It doesn't cover much, does it?''

''It covers everything it's supposed to.''

''Which is nothing.''

''Exactly.''

Nora chuckled a low throaty sound and narrowed her eyes. "I wonder, would I have married you if I'd known how truly wicked you are?"

"You knew how wicked I was long before you married me."

Nora grinned, never denying his statement. "Kiss me."

"No." Jake smiled at her obvious disappointment. "If I start that, I won't be able to stop. And I want this night to last for a bit." He took her hand and guided her to the sofa. "We'll eat first."

They fed each other again, making less of a mess of things on this night. Still the eating wasn't any less erotic than the first meal they'd shared here.

Jake's gaze, even as he ate and drank, never left her. He drank of wine and her loveliness; the dual effect was near intoxication. He brought her hair around her shoulders, draped it across her breast and then pushed it back when it blocked his view. After only half a glass, he put the wine aside, fearful that even another sip might be the catalyst that would push him over the edge. He wanted to maintain complete control until there was no possibility for control.

She sat on his lap and Jake touched her whenever and wherever he pleased. He couldn't have been happier. And then Nora went and spoiled it all by asking, "How close were you to Susie?"

Jake groaned. He knew she'd get around to asking him about the woman eventually, but he hadn't expected the question now . . . on their wedding night. "I was never close to her."

Nora bit her lip, hiding the need to grin at the trepidation in his eyes. She left his lap, and Jake sighed with disappointment. His sigh turned into a gasp of surprise as she flung the transparent gown aside and returned stark naked to straddle his hips.

Obviously this woman was no shy miss. Once she set her heart to loving a man, her natural modesty was a thing of the past and Jake couldn't have been more delighted.

"Was she a friend?" she asked as she played with the hair on his chest.

"Of sorts, I reckon." Jake didn't at all like the direction of her thoughts. There were things he wanted to do, things he wanted to say, and none of them had anything to do with another woman. His hands cupped her breasts, bringing them together as he lowered his face to the sweetly scented flesh.

"All right, how often did you see this friend?"

"Nora, please," he almost whined. "Don't go ruinin' everything."

Nora ignored his plea. "Why did you see her?"

His hands never left her breasts and he played with the soft erotic mounds as he spoke, "'Cause I was crazy with wantin' you." He was hard beneath her and Nora smiled as she felt him raise his hips into her softness. "I thought maybe . . ." he couldn't finish. There was nothing he could say that sounded rational. Nothing he could say that wasn't likely to anger her. And her anger was the last thing he wanted tonight.

"She could get your mind off me?" she finished for him.

"Somethin' like that." He sighed in obvious despair and silently begged her to let it go.

"Did she?"

Jake shot her a look of disbelief. His voice lowered to his normal and distinctly unromantic tone. "Be sensible." His hands moved lower, running freely over her midriff and belly, his fingers spread over her hips and rounded rear.

Nora laughed a husky, naughty sound. "I think I'm being very sensible. Did she?"

"Nora, for God's sake." Jake was growing visibly annoyed and Nora grinned.

"Why didn't you want to love me?"

He frowned. "Who says I didn't?"

She ignored his question. "Why?"

Jake couldn't imagine a more ridiculous happening. Here he was with a naked woman sprawled upon his lap, a woman he loved beyond all reason, a woman whose arms were around his neck, whose breasts were brushing enticingly against his chest, leaving him gasping for more . . . and she insisted on talking about the most asinine things. He sighed, helpless but to accede to her demands. "First of all, you have red hair."

"And that reminded you of your mother." A moment later she shook her head. "But you didn't think I was a . . . a . . ."

He shrugged. "Not after a bit."

Nora laughed. "You did! You thought I was a lady of the night?"

"Nora let it go."

"How intriguing." Nora was clearly taking to the notion. "How extraordinarily intriguing." She grinned. "And when you realized I wasn't, why didn't you want to love me?"

"I loved my first wife, and that turned into a mess. I

367

didn't want to love anyone again."

"But you were going to marry Mary Cummings."

"Who says?"

"Everyone. You were seeing her, weren't you?"

"I didn't love her. She's a nice lady. And I needed someone. Matt needs a mother."

"Is that why you married me?" Nora ran her hands from his shoulders down his chest and belly. Jake sucked in a lung full of air as she opened the first button of his trousers. "Because Matt needs a mother?"

Jake shot her a look of astonishment and then laughed a sound of real merriment. "Yeah. The poor kid is desperate."

"What about his father? Is he desperate as well?"

"God," Jake groaned and rolled his hips again, rubbing himself into her softness. "I'm getting there."

Jake had been in a continual state of arousal from the moment they'd entered the cabin. If she kept touching him, it wouldn't be long before he'd find release. Her palm cupped his erection and he groaned. "Don't touch me now."

Nora blinked her surprise. It was more than obvious that he was loving everything she was doing. She couldn't imagine why he'd ask her to stop.

He smiled. "Later. I want to pleasure you first."

Her mouth was a hairbreath from his when she murmured, "Everything you do pleasures me."

"Come up on your knees a little."

Nora did as he asked and then sighed in delight as his wandering fingers slid from her hips and found her most sensitive flesh.

"Do you like that?"

"Mmmm."

He never thought to refuse the prize her rising to her knees offered and Nora's entire body jerked as his mouth drew the tip of her breast deep into a pit of fire. "God."

A moment later, or an hour later, Nora had somehow lost track of time, she was suddenly on the bed. He pushed her back, leaving her legs dangling over the edge. His hands cupped her bottom, lifted her slightly, and brought her aching flesh to the burning heat of his mouth.

He could do the most amazing things with his mouth. Nora had never imagined a mouth could beget such pleasure. Her body was tight, trembling with need as he breathed against her flesh. Her body strained toward him, knowing the pleasure that awaited, greedy for yet another sampling.

Her hands clutched at his hair and his shoulders as she wordlessly urged him on. Soft, whimpering sounds came unnoticed from her throat as a band of pleasure tightened her stomach in earnest.

Her hands balled the soft quilt at her sides. Her head twisted back and forth upon the bed, her breathing was wild and labored. It was coming, the ecstasy only he could instill, and she strained her body against his mouth, eagerly reaching for all she could get.

A low guttural cry slipped from her lips as the aching waves came crashing upon her. She was lost in the throes of the pleasure, knowing nothing but her greediness for still more. Jake groaned at the enchantment that the spasms of her release against his mouth and tongue wrought.

Dazed, she looked up to see his face suddenly even with hers, his eyes telling of a love so intense it took the last of her breath away. "I love you, I love you," she said, and he muttered a curse knowing the words had sent him over the edge of control. No longer able to resist, he slid his body deep into hers.

Nora wasn't sure exactly how many times they'd loved each other. All she knew for sure was she couldn't have moved if the cabin caught fire. She'd never known such total exhaustion. She'd believed their first night together to be everything a woman could ask for, but in truth it couldn't compare to this night. It hadn't been nearly this wild, this savage, this demanding, this giving. She loved him beyond belief, but if he didn't let her sleep . . .

His hand ran over her hip and slid between her legs. She squirmed against it, coming from a short nap with a low groan. "Jake, go away. I need some sleep."

"You've been sleeping for an hour," he said, ignoring her plea.

Nora frowned, knowing by the sound of his voice that he was smiling. She didn't feel like smiling, or talking, or anything else for that matter. She wanted only to sleep. "You can't possibly want more."

"Can't I?" He chuckled softly, his breath tickling her shoulder and neck. "I've been waiting a long time for you."

"You haven't even known me a long time."

"And there's no reason to wait any longer."

"Except for the fact that I'm exhausted."

Nora was in his arms. Sleepily her arms slid

around his neck as he brought them both from the bed. Her eyes were closed, her head rested comfortably against his shoulder when the splash of cold water brought her fully awake.

Nora gave a startled cry and then slapped his chest.

"Ow!" he said at the sting of wet flesh.

She was straddling his hips and both of them were sitting in a tub of now cold water. "That was mean."

Jake chuckled, even as his mouth took hers.

"You know, I was thinking before . . ." she said in a breathless gasp as he released her lips and her head fell to his shoulder.

Jake groaned. "Don't think. Just let me touch you until we both go mad."

"I was thinking that—"

"Nora." His voice was clearly a plea.

". . . that you can do the most amazing things with your mouth."

Jake tucked in his chin and looked down at her devilish grin. "You little vixen."

"I'm serious," she said sitting up again. "You can."

He was silent for a long moment, terrified she was going to ask for the particulars concerning his initiation into the act of loving. Nora grinned, knowing from the flash of panic in his eyes the nature of his thoughts. "Don't worry. I won't ask. I'm only happy that you know what you do."

Jake couldn't hold back his sigh of relief. "It's not what I know that's important. When I'm loving you, I'm using instinct not technique."

Nora smiled, her heart full. Never could she have imagined a love like this. Jake was a quiet man, the

371

kind who kept his feelings to himself; the more he felt the tighter he held to his control. Until now. He forced himself to say aloud his feelings, knowing they both needed to hear the words. "I never thought that there'd come a day when I'd love a woman like this. I never knew a man could."

Nora rained kisses over his face and neck. "One promise?"

"Anything."

"No more prostitutes for friends."

Jake grinned. "I swear I won't even talk to another woman, no matter her profession."

The three days they spent at the cabin were pure bliss. Each morning they'd awaken to find fresh food at their door, and Nora made a mental note to thank White Moon for her troubles. They ate, they drank, they loved until their bodies and desires were replete, only to find the hunger for each other renewed yet again at a look, or a touch.

All too soon it was time to return to the real world. They were dressing when Nora asked, "Do you think we could make a promise to come here once a month or so?"

His smile was tender. "I reckon we could work that out."

There was the sound of a horse coming to a stop outside the cabin. Jake moved quickly to block Nora from harm, his gun already drawn and pointed toward the door. A knock sounded. "Come in."

Nora had never seen the man before. He was tall, with hard features and harder eyes, and stood just outside the doorway. For some reason Nora knew in an instant he posed no threat.

Jake nodded in greeting. "Morgan."

Morgan nodded in return and then touched his hand to the brim of his hat upon seeing Nora and said, "Ma'am." An instant later he looked at Jake again. "Cole's been shot."

Nora gasped.

"How bad."

The man shook his head. "His arm. He'll be all right. We've been making our patrols like you wanted, but what with you two out this far, and Cole gettin' shot, I think it's best if you . . ."

Jake nodded. "I'd be obliged for the use of your horse. I'd like to get her back as soon as possible."

Morgan nodded. "Go ahead. I'll collect your things and see to the buggy."

Chapter Seventeen

With Jake's help, Nora dismounted and hurried through the group of men who stood about the yard and on the porch. Inside, the house was quiet. Her bag was in Jake's room. She made a quick stop on the way to get it. Jake was already at his brother's side and Mina was leaning over his prone figure, worry filling her dark eyes, by the time Nora entered Cole's room.

His voice was low as he comforted the anxious young woman. But the minute he saw Nora he shot her his usual cocky grin. "It took you long enough to get here. What good is having a doctor for a sister-in-law if she's not around when a man needs her."

Nora moved to the head of the bed and lowered the blanket that covered his entire form. His arm was covered with blood. She looked at Jake. "Take off his shirt." And then to Cole she responded with, "I'm not a doctor. And I was with the man who needed me." Jake beamed with pride.

Cole grinned at her saucy return, even as he

groaned with pain at his brother's assistance. "What'd ya' do to her, Jake? In only three days she's got herself a nasty mouth. Is that what happens when a woman makes an honest man out of ya'?"

Nora ignored his comments and examined the wound, looking at the back of his arm for an exit. Nothing. The bullet was still inside. She opened her bag and asked Mina for a bowl and water. The woman was back with the needed supplies within seconds.

"Did you send for my father?"

"I figured you were closer."

"The next time you get yourself shot up, do it when I'm not busy." Nora grinned at Cole's knowing look, surprising herself by not blushing.

"Busy were ya'? Did I interrupt somethin'?" His gaze was comically hopeful.

Nora chuckled. "Just wait until you and Mina get married," she said taking for granted that they would and soon. "Every couple of hours, I'm going to send Matt in to see how everything is going." She was cleaning her hands and then the area around his wound.

"You better not," he warned. "The kid's apt to get himself an eyeful."

Mina gasped. "Cole!"

Nora looked toward the beautiful young woman and winked. "Don't worry, we'll soon shut that smart mouth of his."

"Now, Nora, you know I was only teasin'. You wouldn't purposely . . ."

Nora laughed at his sudden fear. "Apologize."

"I do. I do."

"What happened?" Jake asked, his question putting a stop to the foolishness.

Cole's smile disappeared. "Bushwhacked. I never saw the son of a bitch." And then realizing there were ladies present, he muttered a feeble, "Sorry."

Nora was nearly ready. "You want to sleep while I do this?"

"I'd greatly appreciate it, ma'am."

Nora nodded. A moment later she had a piece of clean cloth over Cole's mouth and nose. Chloroform was dropped on the material and Cole slept. It didn't take long. What with Cole asleep, Nora didn't have to worry about his pain and she soon had the bullet out. She cleaned the wound, sewed it, bandaged it, and cleared away the mess as Cole slept on.

"How long will he be out?"

Nora smiled at her husband. "Not long." She shrugged. "He can't tell you anything, if he never saw who did it."

"He can tell me where."

Her heart thumped as if it were pounding against an immovable object. Nora forgot Mina was in the room. Dread filled her eyes as she faced her husband. "You're not going there?"

"Of course I'm going there."

She was filled with an instant rage. "Jake. I didn't marry you for the sole purpose of giving this family free medical care."

Jake grinned at her comment, but his gaze was totally confident. "I know why you married me."

"I don't want you going out there."

"Do you want me to hide in the house?"

"Why not? It's what you want me to do."

"That's different."

"Right. It's always different." Her voice was filled with disgust.

"Nora, you're a woman."

"And you're a man. So what?" She sneered that he should have made so flippant a response. "Are you trying to tell me a bullet won't do as much damage to a man?" She almost laughed at the absurdity and might have if she hadn't been so terrified. "Well I can tell you, it will. You're a bigger target, easier to hit."

"I can take care of myself."

Nora muttered her distinctly unladylike opinion on the subject and scowled as the words brought a grin to Jake's mouth. "Damn you," the words were hissed between gritted teeth. "If you get shot, I'm going to let you bleed to death." She took a deep fortifying breath. "I won't care. I swear I won't care."

Her eyes were filled with terror and Jake moved to take her in his arms. Holding her close against him, he ran his hands gently up and down her back as he soothed, "Don't worry, darlin', I won't be alone."

The fact that he wouldn't be alone brought little comfort. Nora figured she loved this man far more than she should. If she had any kind of sense she'd stop loving him, or at least love him less. She wanted to hold him close forever and never see him hurt. She wished she could send him out into danger and not feel terror grip at her heart. But she couldn't and knew she never would.

Still she clung to the thought that others would be there. That they would, to a degree, help and protect each other. "You'll be careful?"

"I promise."

She wouldn't act the weak female and leave him to worry about her while he was gone. If he was going, and he was with or without her permission, he'd need all his thoughts on the business at hand. After all, the sooner they found this madman, the sooner they could get their lives back to normal. "Go ask the men. They might know where it happened."

It was dark before Nora heard the sound of riders coming into the yard. Soon after, she heard spurs ringing out as soft footsteps came through the house and stopped just outside his bedroom door. The door opened slowly and Jake grinned to see her sitting in an easy chair, a book in her lap, obviously awaiting his return.

"I thought you might be asleep."

Nora said nothing, but simply stared at this beautiful man, unable to get enough of the sight of him. He moved into the room. She was filled with relief and found herself swallowing again and again lest she give into the need to cry. Until he'd opened the door, she hadn't been positive he had returned. She'd been besieged with terror, imagining the footsteps to be another's. Perhaps one of the men who would bring her the news of Jake's death.

She sat in shadows, a sole candle burned clear across the room. Jake noticed the book and knew she couldn't have been reading. He came closer and knelt at her side. "Are you all right?"

"I'm fine, thank you."

She appeared so fragile, Jake imagined she might break at the slightest touch. "What are you doing?"

She didn't look in his direction. "Sitting here."

"Reading?"

"No."

"Thinking?"

Nora breathed a sigh and looked at her hands which after hours of nervous twisting were finally relaxed in her lap. "Actually, what I was doing was trying to love you less."

His smile was heartbreakingly tender. "Were you? Why?"

"Because I realized today that I've never loved anyone the way I love you." She swallowed again. "And if anything happened to you, it would kill me."

"I know the feeling."

"Do you?" She looked at him for a long moment and then nodded. "I imagine you do. What do you suppose we should do about it?"

"Well, lovin' each other less, or tryin' to, won't help."

"Then what would?"

"Taking care of each other the best that we can."

"But there are times when we can't." Tears were streaming down her face now. "You can't always be with me, nor I with you. Then what?"

"Nora, we can't live our lives in fear." His finger brushed away her tears, but they continued to come. "All we can do is take precautions and love each other while God allows us this time together."

Her eyes closed for a long moment and a tremendous shudder rippled through her body.

"Sweetheart," he said as he lifted her from the chair and sat, settling her upon his lap. "Don't cry.

Please, don't cry.''

But Nora was beyond the point where she could control her emotions. She'd thought she could be brave. She'd thought she could control this terror, but all day the most horrific thoughts had filled her mind. She imagined him dead a hundred times before she heard the sounds of his footsteps outside the door. This fear was too much to ask of anyone; she couldn't stand another minute of it.

Her tears eased after a time and she asked in a weepy voice, "Did you find anything?''

"Someone made camp in the mountains. And we found a body. Looked like it was rolled over the edge and dropped into a ravine. I think there's only one left of the three who tried to kill you.''

Nora shook her head. "I've been sitting here trying to think. Who could want me dead?''

Jake shrugged. "Someone from home? Maybe an old enemy?''

She shook her head again. "That's just it. I haven't got an enemy. At least not one I know of. God, I wish this was over.'' Nora wiped away her tears and sat up straighter. "Will you go looking again tomorrow?''

"No.''

She sighed her relief.

"Whoever is out there comes and goes. He won't be stayin' still now that he's shot Cole.'' His arms tightened around her. "I hired three men. Billy Cully, Morgan and Dakota. You met Morgan this morning.''

She nodded, her face rubbing against his throat. "Who are they?''

"Men I knew a long time ago.''

"Gunslingers?"

Jake smiled. "Yeah, gunslingers, or hired guns. They'll be watching from now on. One of them will always be with you, me, Cole, Mina, or Matt."

Nora stiffened. Matt! Good God, she hadn't thought of that. Matt could get hurt or killed, and it would be her fault. "Jake, I don't know why, but someone wants me dead. Don't you think it would be safer for everyone if I left—"

"No!" He took a deep, shuddering breath and his arms pulled her tighter against him. "No. I'd go crazy wonderin' if you were all right or not. You're stayin' right here."

"But if something happens to Matt."

"Nothing is gonna' happen."

Nora laughed as she pulled her horse to a stop on a cloud of choking dust. An instant later Matt came barreling into the yard, followed closely by Dakota, a dark slender man, whose eyes never stopped moving and whose mouth rarely smiled.

It had been a month since Cole had been shot. A month where nothing unusual had happened. Nora was convinced more and more as each peaceful day went by that they no longer had reason to fear. That whoever it was was gone. Please God, he had to be gone.

"You almost beat me this time. Soon you'll be beating me in riding as well as poker."

Matt grinned as he watched his new mother dismount and reach for him. "I can do it."

"I know. I just want to help."

She reached into her saddlebag for the present Matt had bought his uncle and Mina. It was a silver picture frame. Nora had suggested the belated wedding gift because she knew that Cole and Mina had had a portrait done about a week or so back.

"Can I give it to them now?"

Nora smiled as she noticed Cole's horse tied to the post. Apparently the man was as greedy as was his brother. Most every day found his horse tied outside an hour or two short of quitting time. Today the sun was still high in the sky and he had returned to the house. Her eyes narrowed with impish glee as she nodded, imagining Matt would be interrupting an intimate moment. "Make sure you knock first."

"I know, I know," Matt returned, having been told that very same thing about a hundred times over these last few weeks. He never had to knock before and now he had to knock just about every time he went into any room around here.

Matt did as he was told and waited for a call to enter. His uncle and aunt were in bed, covered to their necks with a sheet. Matt's big blue eyes grew huge as he noticed their flushed cheeks. "Are you sick?"

"No. Just a little tired," Cole said, while silently swearing he was going to start work on his own house this week. "What have you got there?"

Matt looked at the wrapped package in his hand and grinned. "A present."

"For me?"

"And Mina." Matt smiled at the woman and received a gentle smile in return.

"And Nora told you to give it to us now, right?"

Matt nodded his head. As usual his whole body moved with it and Cole grinned. He'd get her for this one. "It's for your wedding."

"That was very nice of you, Matt." Cole handed the package to his wife and she did an amazing job of opening it while never allowing the sheet to fall from around her shoulders.

"You know," Matt said, "the two of you get tired a lot. Why?"

Cole smiled and shot his wife a lusty grin. "Probably because we stay up too late."

"Mamma says everyone should go to bed early. It keeps you healthy." He fidgeted, moving his weight from one foot to the other, and having nothing to do with his hands. He stuck his thumbs in his waistband in a stance much like his father's. "Maybe if you did, you'd have more energy."

"I doubt it," Cole said under his breath, knowing for a fact that going to bed early would only make him more tired. He grinned as he noticed Mina's flushed cheeks. "Your mamma is right. We should all go to bed early." Cole's dark eyes were twinkling as he watched Mina's dusky skin grow even darker in color.

"It's beautiful," Mina said softly as the wrapping finally fell away.

"Mamma said, it would be a real good present. That you've got pictures of your wedding to put in it."

"It is," his aunt agreed. "Thank you."

Cole grabbed the little boy and hauled him upon the bed. Both his aunt and uncle kissed him for the thoughtful present. He hugged them in return, just short of the age where such affection would be embarrassing. He asked Cole, "You wanna go back to sleep?"

"For a little while."

"Can we go fishing when you get up?"

"Sure."

"Shut the door when you go out," his uncle called from the bed.

The moment it closed, Cole turned to his wife and said, "I'm getting a lock on that door. And next week I'm going to starting building us our own house."

Mina smiled. "Why?"

"'Cause I want to make love to you in every room and do it without worryin' if someone like your mother or Nora is gonna' walk in at any minute."

She laughed as he leaned over her. "In every room?" The idea was obviously appealing.

"Especially the kitchen. I want to do it on the kitchen table."

She blinked in innocence. "Really? The kitchen table?"

Cole felt his heart race from the love he knew for this gentle woman. Never in his life had he felt an emotion so powerful, so all encompassing. He loved her madly and gave special, if silent, thanks to Nora and God for allowing him to see what had been right under his nose.

"Tell me again. How long have you loved me?"

"Since I was a little girl."

"I can't believe it," he said yet again. How had he been so blind? "Why didn't you tell me?"

Mina smiled. "I did. Every time I looked at you, but you never saw it."

"Darlin'," he groaned as he took her in his arms. "I was such a fool."

"Make love to me again and I'll forgive you."

Cole grinned, his eyes sparkling at her boldness. He'd been beginning to suspect he'd never get her to tell him of her wants. Slowly, very slowly, she was coming to know her desires. And ever so shyly and gently she was beginning to ask to see them fulfilled.

"I love you," he whispered.

Her eyes were darker than pitch and fire blazed in their centers. She flung the sheet away and boldly lay exposed to his hungry gaze. "I know. Show me how much."

Nora tied her horse to the hitching post outside her father's office. She came into town at least once a week for a visit. No one seemed to notice the dark man who followed her every movement. At times, Nora even forgot he was there. Dakota watched her from perhaps fifty feet away. His gaze moved over the townsfolk as they went about their business. No one looked suspicious or out of the ordinary. Dakota felt the tension he always knew upon entering town ease just a bit.

He leaned against a post that supported the sidewalk's roof as he watched her mount the stairs and figured she'd be inside for the next hour or so. He sighed as he moved to a rocking chair, one of many that lined the sidewalk, and sat down, ready to wait out her visit.

Nora smiled at the laughter she heard from behind the door leading to her family's living quarters. Her father was telling her mother a story. He stopped momentarily when he saw Nora enter their rooms. Automatically he sat her at the small kitchen table, poured her a cup of tea, and began again.

"I was telling your mother about the call I got to the smithy early this morning. It appears there was a problem last night. Seems Jeb heard a noise coming from his daughter's room around midnight and went to investigate."

Nora gasped. "Was Amy hurt?"

Robert shook his head. "She's fine."

"It was dark, so when Jeb opened the door, he only saw a moving shadow. Says he was surprised to see it dash right out the window. I imagine from the bed, although he didn't say it. Seein' as his daughter's room is upstairs and the window a good twenty-five feet from the ground, it was either a courageous or desperate act."

Nora smiled in amusement. "Considering Jeb's reputation, I'd say desperation was the stronger emotion. Did the prowler get hurt?"

"That was the funny part. Jeb got his pants on and ran outside. Figured the guy was either dead or at the very least injured, and sure to be momentarily further injured once he got his hands on him, but he couldn't find a thing."

Nora shrugged. "Lucky he escaped." Nora imagined the hulking giant and the anger he was sure to have known. "I wouldn't want Jeb after me."

"Well, that's the point. He didn't escape."

Both mother and daughter watched him expectantly. "Early this morning, Jeb got ready for work and left his house just as the sun was coming up. As it happens he glanced up at his daughter's window just as he rounds the house and guess what he finds?"

Robert Morgan's eyes glittered with undisguised humor as both his wife and daughter listened with interest.

"The man who jumped?" Nora offered.

Robert laughed. "Right. But he doesn't find him lying crumpled half dead on the ground. He finds him hanging about four feet below his daughter's window. Seems his long underwear got caught on a nail and kept him there for hours. The fella didn't dare move, lest the material rip and he fall to his death. He didn't dare call out for help either, lest Jeb got a hold of him and his prospect for survival become even more precarious."

Nora chuckled and Abigail shook her head even as a smile teased her pretty lips. "What did Jeb do?"

"He got himself a ladder and took the boy down. Luckily it was before the town awoke. And then he called me. Seems his uninvited visitor got his leg slashed on the very nail that saved his life."

"And that's it?"

"Almost. Seems there's going to be a wedding tomorrow."

Nora's eyes widened as she imagined the young girl as someone's wife. "But Amy is only thirteen."

Robert nodded. "And the boy fifteen. They're young, yes, but it appears they're old enough for some things."

"Fifteen. Lord, they're babies. How will he support her?"

"The boy already works with Jeb. I imagine he'll

388

one day take over as the smithy."

Nora leaned back in her chair with a smile of pure contentment and watched her parents. Thank God her father had brought them West. He was finally well again. And her mother, almost her old self at last. Abigail still got confused on occasion. But her confusion seemed only to entail imagining Johnny to be still alive. And that hadn't happened for a while. Nora knew her mother was on the road to complete recovery. Yes, her father's insistence that they come West was the best thing that could have happened to all of them.

"So," her father asked, an expectant look in his eyes. "When are we going to be grandparents?"

Nora felt her cheeks heat up at his grin. "I've only been married three months."

"Three months is long enough. Are you working on it?"

Nora laughed at his eagerness, even as her cheeks grew hotter. "We're working on it."

Nora closed the door behind her and heard the sound. *Psssst*. She looked around, puzzled at the sound. There it was again. Who in the world . . . ?

Nora turned and looked below. Nothing. Who could be making that sound? She walked down the stairs, a frown creasing her smooth forehead. On the sidewalk again she walked around the back of the stairs and gasped as she was suddenly yanked into the alley behind the mercantile.

A hand closed over her mouth as the words, "Don't scream," were whispered above her.

Slowly she was turned to face her captor. Nora's eyes widened with shock as she recognized the man who held her. His hand slipped away. "Johnny! My God, Johnny!" She said nothing for a long moment, her mind unable to take in the amazing fact that her husband was alive. He stood not even a foot away from her. "How?"

Johnny shook his head and smiled. "It don't matter now. The only thing that matters is I'm back."

Johnny figured if he couldn't get to Jake Brackston and he sure as hell couldn't, not with the guard following every move the man made, he'd have to change his plans a bit. He gave a mental shrug. It didn't matter none. He'd shot Cole, thinkin' it was Jake and that hadn't worked either. But he could, if he worked things right, get everything he wanted anyway. He didn't need to kill the bastard she was married to. All he had to do was threaten Nora that he'd tell Jake Brackston that her husband was still alive, and this woman would be apt to give him everything but her first born. Johnny almost laughed aloud at the thought.

"I hear you're married now."

Nora couldn't quite so easily put the startling news behind her. Her mouth hung open, her eyes still wide with shock. "How? What happened? My God, I thought you were dead."

Suddenly she was against him, her arms around his neck, holding him in a suffocating embrace. She couldn't believe it. She absolutely couldn't believe it.

And then the shock began to fade and she realized what he'd just said. She was married to another, while her husband still lived.

"Oh Lord," she moaned as she moved a few steps back. Gone now was her shock. In its place dread filled her green gaze. "I'm married."

"I heard."

"Johnny, I didn't know." She tried to explain. "I thought you were dead. They told me you were dead."

Johnny nodded. "I know."

"Where were you? My God, Johnny, it's been years. Where were you?"

He shrugged. "Around."

Nora gasped at his negligent comment. "Around? Just around? Why didn't you come back?"

"I did. You were gone by the time I got there."

"But . . ."

"And then married by the time I found you again."

"But . . ."

"I reckon, you'll have to tell him that your husband is alive after all."

"I . . . I . . ."

"You ain't sorry, are ya? You ain't sorry I'm not dead?"

"Of course I'm not sorry. It's just that . . ."

"What?"

"I'm married."

"To me."

"No. Johnny, I've married again."

He shook his head. "You know that ain't legal. You're my wife."

"Johnny, it's been too long."

"You tellin' me you love him?"

Nora nodded.

"And I've been searchin' everywhere for you all for nothin'?"

"Johnny, I didn't know. I'm sorry."

"That's it? Just like that, you're sorry, so it's over?"

"What can I do?"

Johnny was starting to enjoy himself. The more clear her distress, the more enjoyment he seemed to find. "Leave him. You belong to me."

"No!" Nora couldn't believe this was happening. How could he be suddenly alive after all this time? How would he expect her to give up Jake? She couldn't. She wouldn't. Not ever!

And then a thought occurred. Her mother had seen Johnny a number of times, including this morning. *Johnny.* The girl at Fancy's had been killed. *Johnny,* a man who had been talking about her.

Her eyes narrowed with suspicion. "How long have you been here?"

"Where?"

"In town. How long?"

He shrugged again. "A while, I reckon."

"A while? A month? A few months? What does a while mean?"

"It means long enough."

It all became clear, and Nora knew beyond a doubt the truth of it. "It was you, wasn't it? You're the one who's been asking questions about me. You're the one who killed Mazie."

"What the hell are you talking about? I never killed anyone."

Nora knew he was lying. It was easy enough to read the truth in his eyes. He didn't try very hard to hide it. Perhaps he wanted her to know what he'd done. But

392

why? Why would he want her to know? Nora was soon to find out. "What do you want?"

His eyes glittered with undisguised madness. The sight of it sent a chill down her back and she knew without a doubt that he meant to scare her. "Money."

Nora closed her eyes on a silent moan. How had it come to this? She'd known Johnny for as long as she could remember. Granted he'd never been a strong man, but his lack of strength hadn't bothered her at the time, for there'd been no evil in that weakness. Where had this evil come from, this near gloating in watching another suffer? Had the war done this? Had it caused him to lose the threads of normalcy and forget what was right and wrong?

She could remember, like it was yesterday, how he had a tendency to blame everyone and anyone for a personal failing. She shivered at the distasteful thought. Why had it never bothered her before?

For a fleeting moment, she couldn't imagine why she'd married him. Had it been because both families had simply wanted and expected the union? Had she mechanically fallen into the relationship like a dutiful daughter? Or had she secretly known his failings and felt a need to be needed? Had that need caused her to make the biggest mistake of her life?

Nora gave herself a mental shake. It hardly mattered now why she'd married him. It was the present she had to deal with. "And if I don't give it to you?"

"Then I'll tell your husband you forgot one little thing before you married him. You forgot to tell him you were *already* married."

Johnny laughed at her horrified expression. "I'll tell him it was a plan we cooked up. That you only

393

married him for the money. That we did it together."

Nora felt a moment's surprise at her own shock. Surely she knew by the maniacal gleam in his eyes and the way he licked his lips and smiled that he was about to say something horrid. Her heart filled with terror. Was the love she and Jake shared strong enough? Would Jake believe her incapable of such deception? "He won't believe you." Nora prayed her words were true.

Johnny grinned. "Yes, he will. And if he doesn't, then maybe I'll just take care of the whole thing by other means."

"What other means?"

"If your new husband was dead, and I came back, I'd own half that fancy ranch."

Nora gave a silent groan. My God, this was a nightmare. This couldn't be happening. "How much do you want?" she asked, her voice dull and lifeless as she realized she'd give this man anything, do anything, if he'd leave them in peace.

"A couple thousand would be good for a start."

"For a start?"

Nora shivered and knew nothing was beyond this man. This wasn't the Johnny she'd married. Something had happened to him. The man she'd known was gone.

Nora knew he'd do exactly as he'd promised. She had no choice but to give him anything he wanted. "When that runs out, I might have to come back for more."

For one wild moment Nora entertained the thought of killing him. She'd never be free as long as he lived. But she'd never be able to live with herself if she willfully ended another's life.

Nora sighed. She had no choice. She'd give this man what he wanted and face the consequences later. Jake would be sure to ask her why she'd withdrawn such a large sum of money. She'd tell him then and pray everything would turn out all right. Nora wondered if he'd believe her. He hadn't had the best experiences with women. What if he didn't believe her? What if he believed she'd married him knowing all along that Johnny was alive? What if he believed they'd planned this together?

For now, she had to get rid of him. She had to see to it that Jake was kept safe.

"I'll get the money."

"When?"

"Now. Wait here."

Nora moved down the alley. Thank God the bank was on the same side of the street. She could reach it easily enough without Dakota seeing her enter the bank or leave it. Mr. Collins gave her a few odd looks. It was obvious people didn't usually walk into the bank and take out three thousand dollars every day. Nora's mind was so filled with terror and fear, she never thought to offer a reasonable excuse as to why she was withdrawing such a large sum. The truth of the matter was, she never would have been able to think of one.

Within minutes she had returned to the alley. In her hand she held three thousand dollars.

Johnny took the money and then sighed in mock disappointment as he counted it. "Three thousand? What am I supposed to do with this, Nora? It's not near enough."

"I can't get any more," and Nora knew she couldn't. Jake had given her access to only one account. The other was for the ranch. He drew from it to pay the ranch expenses. She couldn't touch the money.

"You'd better get more. If you want that husband of yours to stay alive, you'd better get me plenty more."

"But—"

"Tomorrow. I want it tomorrow. Be here."

Nora watched him leave, never bothering to argue that she couldn't. There was no way she could get her hands on more money. There was hardly more than two hundred dollars left in the account. She had to do something. But what?

Nora was on her horse heading out of town before Dakota cursed and came quickly to his feet. She hadn't stayed nearly as long as usual. What the hell did she think she was doing leaving without him? Jesus, all he needed was to let her ride home alone. If anything had happened to her, Jake would probably kill him. Damn, but he'd never seen a man so much in love before. He felt a little jealous sometimes just watching the two of them together. Not that he wanted the woman for himself, though she was a pretty little thing. What he wanted was the feelings they shared. Idly he wondered if he'd ever know them firsthand.

Nora sat at the river's edge for a long time. She knew Dakota was somewhere behind her, but never gave the man a thought. It was Jake who filled her mind. Jake and the worry she knew for his safety. Johnny would kill him. She knew that as surely as she knew her own name. What could she do? Should she kill Johnny before he got the chance? *Could she?*

Nora sighed at the thought, knowing she didn't have it in her. She didn't have the nerve, or stomach, or whatever it was that made a person into a cold-blooded killer. She sighed again.

There was only one answer. She had to leave Jake. If she was no longer married to him, then Johnny couldn't lay claim to anything, and Jake would be safe. It was the only thing she could do.

"Sounds pretty sad, if you ask me. I would have thought a bride of only three months would sound happier than that."

Nora smiled as she turned to find her husband settling himself behind her. His arms around her waist, he pulled her to lean back against him, his long legs stretched out on each side of her, cocooning her with his strength and warmth. "What are you doing out here?"

"Thinking."

"About what?"

"You."

Jake chuckled. "Why come out here to think about me, when you could have come to the house and found me in person?"

"Jake, I love you. I don't want you to ever forget it."

Jake frowned. "That sounds serious. What's the matter?"

"I need some money."

"Take what you want." Jake shrugged. "It's in the bank."

Nora shook her head. "I need more."

"More than three thousand dollars? Why?"

"I can't tell you."

"Yes, you can. Why?"

"I have to leave you." Nora knew her words sounded irrational, but she was so upset she hardly cared.

Jake laughed. "You mean if I won't give you more than three thousand you'll leave me?"

"No, it has nothing to do with the money. I have to leave you."

"That makes sense to me. You love me, so you have to leave."

"I'm serious, Jake."

"You got some explainin' to do."

"I can't."

"Too bad, 'cause you're gonna'." He came to his feet, and brought her to stand at his side. "Let's go."

They rode to the house in silence.

"You're wastin' your time, Nora, you're not goin' anywhere."

"Jake," Nora said as she pushed another skirt into a carpetbag. "Listen to me. I know this is hard to understand, but I have to go."

"And you can't tell me why?"

"If I could, I would."

"You're not walkin' out a' this house."

"You can't keep me a prisoner here. If I want to leave then that's exactly what I'll do."

"Think so? Go ahead and try it."

Nora walked toward the door, only to find herself

lifted and flung back with seemingly no effort at all on her husband's part. She landed on the bed with a bounce. "Want to try it again?"

Nora sighed with despair. He'd never let her go. Not as long as he believed she loved him. And because of her love he was going to die. There was only one way. "I don't love you."

"What?"

"I said, I don't love you."

"I don't believe you."

"Well, you'd better believe me, because it's the truth."

"Since when?"

"What do you mean?"

"I mean, when did you stop? Was it this morning, while you were beggin' for my touch? Was it last night when you had me in your mouth, touchin' me, kissin' me until I thought I'd go crazy?"

"Jake, don't."

"Was it last night? When we sat on the porch and watched the sun go down? And then walked hand in hand to bed? Was it when you were playin' ball with Matt? Or laughing with Mina?

"Was it when I was teachin' you to swim the day before? When was it exactly that you figured out that you don't love me?"

"Oh God." She should have known it was a ridiculous thing to say. She should have known he wouldn't believe her. Not after all the loving between them. Not after the laughter.

"Tell me, Nora. And maybe, just maybe, I'll let you go." Like hell, he silently denied. There was no way this woman was ever going to leave him.

Nora knew a sense of crushing despair. She had no choice. She had to tell him. "It's Johnny."

"Who the hell is Johnny?"

"My first husband. I mean my real husband."

Jake frowned at the word "real", and asked very softly, despite his desire to shout, "What are you talking about?"

"Jake, Johnny isn't dead. He's the one who shot Cole. It wasn't me he wanted dead, it was you. He thought you were Cole."

"When did you . . . ?"

"I saw him in town today." Nora laughed. "Mother has been telling me for months that she'd seen him. I wouldn't believe her. I'm not married to you. Don't you understand? I'm still married to Johnny."

"Like hell. You belong to me."

Nora breathed a deep sigh. "Johnny killed Mazie. He's the one who's been asking questions about me."

"He told you?"

"No. He didn't have to. All of a sudden I realized how horribly evil he is." She shuddered.

"And you were gonna' leave me for him? A man who gives you the shivers?"

"Not for him, because of him." She looked up at his dark, puzzled gaze. "Don't you understand? He's threatened to kill you, so he can take half the ranch. If I'm no longer married to you, and I'm not legally anyway, then he won't kill you. What would be the point?"

"What about the money?"

"He told me he would take it and leave, but when I gave it to him he laughed and said it wasn't enough."

400

She came to her feet and began to pace, twisting her hands nervously as she moved. "He said he wanted more, or he'd get the rest after he killed you. Then he'd claim me as his wife and the half owner of this ranch."

"So you thought you were saving my life by leaving me?"

"Jake, it's the only way. I knew this afternoon that he'd never be satisfied. I'm supposed to meet him tomorrow and give him more. But no matter how much I give him, it will never be enough.

"I thought maybe I could kill him." She breathed a sigh of disgust at her own inadequacies. "But I can't."

"Where are you supposed to meet him?"

"In the alley behind my father's office."

Jake's smile was hard, almost savage, as his thoughts raced ahead to the anticipated meeting. Nora felt a terror unlike any she'd ever known. Deep down inside she knew things wouldn't go smoothly. Somebody was going to die tomorrow.

Neither suspected it would be the most innocent one of all.

Chapter Eighteen

Late that night a lone shadowy figure crept silently into the barn, his hand holding to the reins of the horse behind him. The barn's floor was of earth and covered with straw. Therefore not a sound was heard above the soft soughing of a cool breeze and an occasional whinny of one of the horses within. A dog barked in the distance, but no one took notice for he often did as much. Farther off cows slumbered and those who did not emitted lonely sounds that echoed softly in the night.

Within moments the stranger's horse stood among the others in a long line of immaculate stalls. Seconds later, his saddle was perched among a dozen others and his bridle lined the wall as if it belonged. Johnny grinned as he climbed the ladder to the loft. There was plenty of hay up here. It would make a right comfortable bed. A sight more comfortable than what he'd been sleeping on lately.

Johnny knew better than to trust anyone. He

figured Nora, being a woman and all, would go right to Jake with her problem. In turn, Jake would come to him. The minute he'd walked away yesterday he'd known his plans would have to change again. His eyes glittered in the darkness. Lucky for him he was a man of quick wits and many alternatives. He chuckled a soft sound. In the end he'd outsmarted them both. Johnny had every confidence he'd win.

Johnny lay still and listened, a huge grin curving his mouth at the sounds below. He figured it was real late or real early depending on how a man looked at things. He glanced toward the high window and noticed the position of the moon. He'd been sleeping about three hours.

Silently he rolled over and then inched his way toward the edge of the loft. Leaning over the edge, he watched the men below saddle their horses. He'd been right. She had told the bastard. Lucky for him he had guessed correctly. Now all he had to do was wait and then put his next plan into action.

Just as he'd supposed, his horse was never noticed among the many. The light of their lanterns didn't reach nearly as high as the loft and he knew even if they'd looked right at him, he wouldn't be seen.

His heart was filled with anticipation as he listened to them ride off. He leaned back upon his comfortable bed of straw and imagined what he was going to do with the money. Maybe he'd go down to Mexico. He'd find Pete there probably. Johnny made a snorting sound of pure disgust. After running off on him, Johnny wasn't about to share a nickel with that bastard.

Moments after the sounds of distant pounding hooves was replaced with the gentle humming of cicadas and crickets, Johnny emerged from his hiding place. His intent was to enter the house and take its mistress for ransom. He snickered a silent sound of glee. It would be hours before that bastard returned and her absence would be discovered.

Johnny muttered an obscene word as he moved to the barn's door and saw the vague outline of a man standing upon the porch. Another stood at the far corner of the house where he could see two sides. And another was walking toward the back. All three wore guns strapped to their thighs and rifles held comfortably, easily in their hands. Johnny had been around enough to know these men were hired guns. He'd seen one or two of them in town whenever Nora came to visit her parents. He knew they were perhaps even more heartless than he was. They'd kill him faster than blink and feel as sorry as if they stepped on a bug. He had no chance against any one of them. He cursed again.

The house itself was a blaze of light. It shone from nearly every window, and Johnny knew there was no way that he was going to get near the place. Deep in concentration, he returned to his hiding place. There had to be a way. All he had to do was find it.

A dozen men with tight, hard faces and harder eyes left the ranch before daylight that morning. Upon closer inspection one might have noticed the determined, near savage glitter in every man's eye, the heavy weapons strapped around their waists and secured to their thighs, the rifles sheathed within saddles. Any man who valued his life might have made an abrupt about face upon a chance encounter. But that was only close up. From a distance they looked like any cowboy at home in the saddle, ready for another day of exhausting work. Men at ease with themselves and content with the harsh life they'd chosen.

They left in pairs and in threes. They headed at first in different directions, lest someone watched from a distance and their destination be noticed, to eventually turn south toward Glory.

The men who stayed behind didn't venture out of the yard that day. They watched the house and with it the three women and one small boy who felt trapped inside.

"Why don't we do something?" Nora asked as she watched Mina read to a fidgeting six year old, who wanted desperately to leave the confines of his house and run with his dog outside. "Let's make cookies," Nora offered and then grinned as Matt grimaced remembering her last effort. "Mamma, you have to use sugar when you make cookies."

Mina smiled and Nora laughed, remembering that fiasco. The cookies had certainly looked good enough, but Nora had reached for the salt instead of the sugar while creating the delicious looking batter. After one bite she realized her error. Jake hadn't let her forget it for days and teasingly threatened to force her to eat a cookie, lest she do his bidding. "I know, darling. The trouble is, I needed your help the last time and you were out with your father."

"I'm not very good at it, but Mina can show us how." Matt grinned in hungry anticipation as he imagined his aunt's wonderful cookies. "She makes the best."

Nora looked at the quiet, talented young woman. "Would you like to, Mina?"

"Of course," the gentle woman said.

They were in the kitchen laughing as Matt sampled raw cookie dough, each woman wondering if he didn't enjoy the uncooked version more than the finished product. Suddenly Mina made a soft sound and reached for the table.

"Are you all right?"

"Fine. I'm fine."

White Moon chose just that moment to step into the room. The woman smiled as she watched Nora help her daughter to a seat. "It's too hot in here. You should step outside for a breath of air."

But Cole had warned his wife to stay inside and unlike herself, Nora knew Mina would obey his command to the letter.

White Moon looked into her daughter's eyes for a long moment before a gentle smile curved the older woman's lips. "Your husband serves you well, daughter."

Mina blushed and Nora looked in confusion from one to the other, wondering what she'd missed.

Mina noticed Nora's puzzled look and took pity on her sister-in-law. Out of Matt's hearing she whispered, "I'm going to have a baby." And at Nora's obvious delight she warned, "Don't say anything.

Cole wants to tell all of you tonight."

It was later when the last of the cookies lay cooling upon the table that they heard the explosion.

The men entered town just before daylight. They moved stealthily to their predesignated positions. It wasn't until hours after the planned meeting should have taken place that Jake started to feel nervous. Where was he? Why hadn't he shown up?

Jake was positive no one had noticed their entering town. Lord, they'd come in from four directions. How could anyone have noticed that? And their positions? Most of them were on the roof or under empty crates, with holes punched out for breathing and seeing, or lounging inconspicuously among those who sat by the hour in town watching its slow stream of traffic. No one knew they were there. No one knew unless they'd been watching the ranch and had seen them leave.

Terror clutched at his heart and he breathed an aching sigh of dread. "No!"

"What?" Cole asked, lying on his stomach at Jake's side. The two of them lay close to the edge of the roof. Close enough to the edge so they could watch the comings and goings in the alley below.

"He couldn't have seen us."

"Who? Johnny? No way. We haven't moved half an inch all day. Nobody saw us," Cole tried to calm his anxious brother.

"I mean leave the ranch."

"Jake, we left before light. How could anyone

have seen?"

"I don't know." His brow creased as he tried to understand his anxiety. The sudden terror that gripped his soul. He'd missed something; something he should have realized long before now.

Johnny should have shown up hours ago. They had waited out nearly an entire day to no avail. Why hadn't he come for the rest of his money? Cold tentacles of dread surrounded Jake's heart. Perhaps Johnny had been there all along. Jake couldn't stop the wild thoughts. "Jesus, suppose he was in the barn, or the storage shed, or the smokehouse, or any one of the outhouses, watching everything we did. Suppose he's still there just waiting for the right moment." He didn't finish the thought aloud, but asked in silent dread, *Suppose the right moment had already come?*

Cole shook his head, denying the supposition, even as his heartbeat picked up its pace. "The men are there."

"Yeah, but they'd expect an attack from the outside, not from someone hiding nearby. Goddamn it! Why didn't I think of it before?" Jake was on his feet and running before he finished the last of his words. Cole, his heart pounding with the beginnings of fear, followed closely behind.

The barn was a roaring blaze of heat and color climbing high into the sky. Long, licking red and yellow tongues of fire burst from its sides and climbed up the roof, only to gain speed and heat as it traveled. The hayloft added much in the way of fuel and as Nora watched from the porch of the house, she knew these flames would be seen for miles.

Within seconds of the exploding sound and then the first sign of smoke, the men left behind, including the guards, had formed a long line from the pump to the barn, while others had braved the smoke and flames and freed the few horses still inside.

Twenty minutes passed and it was easy enough to see the fire was winning against all their combined efforts. Still they hurried filled pails of water from one man to the next. The last man throwing what was left of the half spilled container upon the flames. It was an exercise in futility. Nora knew it was hopeless.

The three women and Matt stood in silent horror, taking in the hypnotic scene. The barn's roof groaned as if giving one last cry for help and then succumbed to the flames, only to burst upward with an explosion of heat and roaring flame and just as suddenly collapse in a wild thunder of raging sound. Color shot high into the air; flames burst free, bringing with it large pieces of burning wood and straw. Dakota yelled for the women to move, for more than a few pieces had been flung wide and fallen to the roof of the house. The men quickly changed their direction, lest the flames take hold.

Nora, with Matt's hand in hers, ran into the yard. She shivered, despite the intense heat, as she backed away from the fearful and yet mesmerizing sight of roaring flame. Behind her stood an equipment shack. She backed farther away, guiding Matt from

410

the busy and harried men, so as not to impede them and their work.

Johnny stood behind the shack and grinned as he watched her move closer. Another minute, he promised himself. Another minute and he'd have her.

Gently he rubbed the velvety nose of his horse trying to soothe the animal, although it wouldn't have made much of a difference if the animal had screamed his lungs out. Nothing could be heard above this fire and the wild calls of the men fighting it. Johnny felt the sweat run down his back. It was hotter than blazes and the fire didn't help matters any.

In a minute he'd be out of here. In a minute he'd have her. If Jake Brackston wanted his woman back, he'd have to pay plenty. Johnny cursed his slow thinking. He could have taken her yesterday and been done with it. He shrugged away the thought. It wasn't too late. He'd have her now, and Jake would go crazy with the knowledge.

Nora was almost run over by one of the men as he ran for another ladder. A minute later three men were on the roof, stamping out the small fires that had sprung up from the falling embers. She backed up again, her hand still holding Matt, whose eyes were huge at the sight and smells of fire and fear.

Suddenly she was being pulled back. A startled cry slid from her lips just as a huge hand came to close off the sound. She was twisted around and flung up against the back of the shed.

"Shut up!" The words were filled with hate and the

promise of pain lest she obey. Nora felt a shudder run through her body at the glittering insanity in his eyes. Johnny, my God, how had he managed it? How had he set the fire while the guards watched?

She never realized she still held on to Matt's hand, not until Johnny's mad laughter spilled over them both.

"Did you think to send your man after me? Did you think it would be that easy?"

"What do you want?" Nora was pressed flat against the wall of the shed as she tried to push Matt from her side. The boy was so stunned by the happenings around him, he didn't realize until it was too late that he should have run.

Johnny grinned and took a fistful of Matt's hair. His free hand rested threateningly on the boy's neck. Nora knew he could snap that delicate neck with one vicious twist. "If you scream, I'll kill him. Let's go."

"Matt run," Nora urged the moment Johnny took his hand from the boy's neck.

"I don't think so." Johnny laughed a horrible sound as he grabbed the boy's shoulder and seat and effortlessly flung him high upon the saddle. "If we take him along, I think you'll do your best to cooperate."

"Johnny, let him go. I swear I won't give you any trouble."

"Get on the horse," Johnny ordered, ignoring her plea. Matt sat silently upon the horse, his huge eyes wide with fright. Nora could have run, but knew with one glance at those dark fear-filled eyes that she had little choice but to obey. There was no way that

412

she was going to allow Johnny to take Matt. She had to go too, no matter the danger. There was no telling what he'd do otherwise.

Nora swung herself up behind Johnny, holding tightly to his waist as he swung the horse around. The three of them were just about to ride out when Mina came around the corner of the shed, wondering where the two had taken themselves off to. If she'd been ten seconds later, she might have made it. As it was, she didn't stand a chance. The instant her mouth opened, all three of them knew she was going to scream. In a flash, Johnny took his foot from the stirrup and kicked her with a three inch heel as hard as he could in the stomach.

She fell back against the shed, her head hitting the sturdy wooden structure with a sickening thud. She crumbled to the ground with a soundless, breathless cry slipping from parted lips. Johnny laughed at the ease it took to silence her, while both Nora and Matt watched in horror as her stunned expression fell away and her body lay terrifyingly still.

The men on the ranch wouldn't look up from their work for some time. Not one noticed the horse that rode away from the ranch, for the smokehouse roof was now on fire.

The three raced over the flat area of land that bordered the yard into the wilder country of cactus, hills and gullies beyond. Finally they headed toward the mountains in the distance, where a measure of isolation could be found.

He'd worked things out just right. It was important for Jake Brackston to know terror, for terror

413

caused a man to make mistakes. Johnny grinned at the thought. Maybe he'd make a big enough mistake and Johnny would end up with the ranch after all.

He shrugged at the thought. It made no never mind. Johnny would be satisfied with the money. That was all he really wanted and he didn't much care who he had to kill to get it.

Just a skeleton of the barn remained by the time Jake and Cole thundered into the yard, followed by the rest of the men. It took only a glance at smoke-blackened faces to know that something more than a burned out barn was at fault. Something terrible had happened. Jake could hardly breathe from the terror that taunted him.

Cole shot his brother an optimistic look that promised things would be fine and silently urged him to hold on. He looked toward the house and frowned upon finding White Moon standing on the porch alone. Where was Mina? Why hadn't she come to greet him? He shrugged aside the tiny wave of fear. No doubt she hadn't heard his approach. There was nothing wrong. There couldn't be anything wrong. What could one man do against all these? Besides, Johnny wasn't interested in Mina. He wasn't even interested in Nora. It was money he wanted. If he didn't get it, then he'd think about that later. First thing he wanted to know was where was his wife?

Cole dismounted and handed the reins over to someone. He never looked to see who, his gaze held instead to the woman on the porch. The silence surrounding them was thick. It was as if the ranch were already mourning. Cole refused to acknowledge the thought. Everything is fine. Everything *had to be* fine.

"Where is she?"

White Moon nodded toward the house, unable to mask the pain in her eyes.

Cole wouldn't see it. He refused to see it. He stepped into the silent house and looked wildly from the kitchen to the parlor and back. Where was she? Why wasn't she in the kitchen working over the stove, or sitting in the parlor reading, or playing with Matt, or . . . was she waiting for him? Was she in their bedroom?

Cole sighed with relief at the thought. He smiled as he walked down the long hallway to the last room and opened the door. His smile froze.

He must have made a small sound, for Mina opened her eyes and smiled. Cole almost crumbled on the spot in relief. He leaned against the wall for a moment, willing his legs to hold him. She'd given him such a scare. Lord, he couldn't remember ever being so scared before.

"Why are you in bed?"

"I got hurt," she said softly.

Cole was instantly at her side. He reached for her. Lifting her into his arms. He walked toward the chair beside the fireplace and sat. "What happened?"

"A man came and took Nora and Matt."

"Jesus," Cole muttered as he crushed her against him and buried his face in her neck. There were no words. He couldn't form a rational thought. All he

415

could do was silently hold her against him. His heart bled for his brother, but he couldn't be sorry that Mina was safe. He wouldn't let himself notice the ashen hue of her skin. He refused to acknowledge the white lips.

"I lost the baby, Cole."

"That's all right darlin'." Cole swallowed and choked back tears as he cleared his throat. He hadn't known until this minute how very much he'd wanted that baby. But she couldn't be allowed to see his disappointment, his pain. She'd suffered enough. His hand trembled as he brushed the long black strands of hair from her face. "The only thing that matters now is that you get well. They'll be other babies. I swear I'll give you other babies."

"I love you, Cole."

"I know, honey. I love you too."

They sat quietly for a long time before she spoke again. "I was so happy. Thank you for making me so happy."

Cole couldn't talk. Tears choked his throat. He blinked them back, sniffed, and cleared his throat. He didn't like it when she talked like their love was a thing of the past. "We'll be happy again. You'll see."

"Am I going to die?"

"No!" His arms tightened, nearly crushing her. "Don't ask questions like that. Don't even think it." He breathed a trembling sigh. "I'm going to hold you, darlin'. I won't let you go until you're better."

"If I die, I want you to remember . . ."

"You won't." His arms tightened again. Please God, he silently begged, his terror so intense he was unable to finish the plea. "Mina, you won't."

The room blurred before his eyes as he fought back the tears. "You'll be strong again." He cleared his throat. "I swear. Just hold on to me and you will."

She made a soft sound, sort of a sleepy moan, and Cole tried to smile over his fright.

"I love you. Don't forget that I loved you," she murmured.

He tucked her head beneath his chin and ran his fingers through her hair. "I won't forget. I'll never forget." His breathing was choppy and harsh as he tried to hold back his terror. "Go to sleep darlin'," he soothed through a voice tight with unshed tears. "You'll feel better when you wake up. You'll be much stronger when you wake up."

Only she never did wake up.

Cole watched her for a long time. She was very still, but Cole refused to allow that knowledge to enter his mind. She slept, he swore. She only slept.

Jake came in and knelt beside the chair. White Moon had told him what had happened. She told him that Mina bled and the bleeding couldn't be stopped. For just a moment he had to put aside his own concerns. His brother needed him now. Perhaps he'd never need him quite so badly.

Cole smiled at his brother's concerned, almost pitying expression. "She's all right. She's weak and tired, but she'll be all right."

"Cole."

"Quiet. She needs this sleep," Cole whispered.

"Cole, she's dead."

"Goddamn it! Don't say that." His eyes filled with

417

dread, horror, and then . . . tears. "I could kill you for sayin' that."

He crushed her tightly against him, willing her not to die. Swearing he'd hold her forever if only she wouldn't die. He buried his face in her hair. "She won't die. I'm telling you, she won't."

Jake had never seen a man in the throes of such naked torment. It was almost indecent that he should be witness to it. He tried to look away, but his brother's eyes held him there, willing him to agree. Willing him to say she wasn't dead. That she wouldn't die. And when he did not, the pain was so incredible Jake wondered if any man had the kind of strength he'd need to bear up under it.

Cole might have been fast to smile. He might tease and taunt and act the carefree spirit. But his playful actions belied the depth of feelings that ran deep. Perhaps too deep.

Jake left him to his sorrow, knowing nothing and no one could help him now. It was almost an hour before he came back. The men had returned only moments ago telling him the trail led toward the mountains.

Again Jake entered Cole's room. His brother held to Mina's slender body, unable to let her go.

"I'm going to get him. I thought you might like to come along."

Cole looked up at his brother for a long moment before he nodded. His voice was flat, devoid of all emotions. "I'll be right there."

Cole carefully placed his wife upon the bed. He adjusted her hands over her middle and smoothed the

418

sheet around her still form. Lovingly he spread her hair upon the snowy pillow and kissed her cool white lips. For the very last time.

His eyes held no tears when he left the room, although it was obvious that he had cried. In the place of tears and sadness was now a hatred so powerful and intense, every man who dared to look his way could only shudder, knowing the one responsible for his pain would die a horrifying death.

Chapter Nineteen

Johnny pulled the horse to a stop and grunted, "Get off."

Nora moved back and slid over the animal's rump. She watched as Johnny dismounted, dragging Matt along with him. He was tying the animal to a low tree when Nora came up behind the boy and whispered near his ear, "The first chance you get, run."

"What are you talking about?"

"I asked him if he was all right?"

"That right, boy?" Johnny asked, eyeing the child meanly.

Matt nodded. His small body trembling, his eyes wide with fear.

"I'd better not find out that you're lyin'. Don't cotton much to liars."

"Papa's goin' to be mad at you," he warned in childlike fashion.

Johnny grinned. "I reckon you're right about

that." He nodded over his shoulder. "Let's go."

Matt shook his head. "I can't. I gotta' go home. Papa will be lookin' for me."

"You like your mamma?"

Matt nodded vigorously, some of the fear disappearing from his dark eyes. He almost smiled. "She can't make cookies though."

Johnny ignored the offered information. "You wouldn't want to see her hurt now, would ya'?"

Matt shook his head, again with vigor.

"Then you do what I say, boy, and maybe I won't hurt her."

Nora saw the terror come again to life in the child's eyes and thought to ease his fears. She reached a comforting hand to his shoulder. "Matt . . ."

"Shut up." Johnny's hand flashed out and slapped her hard. She fell back, off balance and toppled to the ground. "Keep your mouth shut or I'll shut it for you. Permanently."

Matt gave a small terrified cry as he watched his mother shake her head in warning and come again to her feet. He cowered behind her, holding to her skirt, hugging her hip. He knew he had every right to be afraid, not knowing why this man wanted to hurt them.

"Let's go," Johnny said as he stepped aside and with another nod of his head pointed out the direction they were to take.

The grade was steep and uneven, their forced ascent hurried along by Johnny's harsh curses and chilling threats. They hadn't traveled a hundred yards before the muscles in Nora's legs began to ache.

By the time they reached a small clearing, the taxed muscles were throbbing and her body was covered with sweat. She sighed with relief as she sat on the ground and looked around her.

They hadn't by any means reached the summit, but a flat nearly smooth ridge less than halfway to the snow covered peak stretching high above them. The clearing appeared to be an outcropping of rock, that had somehow attached itself to the windswept western slope. It was bordered on three sides by trees and thick underbrush. Nora shivered as she realized the fourth side was a sheer drop to a dried up riverbed below. Silently she begged Matt to stay clear of the edge, knowing she dared not say the words aloud, lest Johnny take it into his head to taunt her to madness. She wouldn't put it past him to throw both of them over the edge. She stayed far from the ledge and prayed Matt would follow her lead. He did.

The clearing showed signs of earlier use. At its center, surrounded by small rocks, stood a blackened shallow pit that had once held a fire. Johnny hunched down, watching them closely, as he started another small blaze. Near the fire was stacked broken pieces of tree limbs. He added those and the fire was soon fighting against the cold night.

Nora looked beyond the camp's center. There were blankets and a pail of water, a coffee pot and a cup, plus a few wrapped packages that were obviously supplies.

Nora could only pray that this was the camp Jake had found. When he came for her and Matt, and Nora had no doubt that he would, he'd know then exactly where to look. In the meantime, she had to take Johnny's attention off the boy. Matt had to get out of here and as soon as possible, lest disaster occur.

"How long are we going to stay here?"

"Until I get word to your *husband*," Johnny ridiculed the word. "Once he leaves the money, I'll tell him where to find you."

Johnny watched her for a long moment. He should kill her, he knew, but he wouldn't . . . yet. There was an outside chance that he might yet kill Brackston. If that happened then he'd need her alive to claim her inheritance. Once he got his hands on the money he needed, or maybe even the deed to Brackston's land, it wouldn't matter if she lived or not.

Johnny had brought along a circle of rope taken from his saddle. He smiled now as he ran his fingers over its rough length. "I'm gonna' have to tie and gag you. I gotta' go back and let them know what I want."

His mouth twisted into a sly grin. "Come here, boy."

Nora could see the insanity lurking in his eyes. In an instant she knew his intent. Now that she was here, now that she'd come willingly with hardly a struggle, there was no reason for Johnny to keep Matt alive.

"Johnny—"

"I told you before to shut up."

Johnny reached around her for Matt. His hand on the boy's small arm soon dragged his resisting body from behind his mother. Johnny made a low, horrific sound as he set about his task with undisguised malice. Nora's eyes bulged with fear. "Don't," she whispered the plea. "Please—"

"I told you, bitch," Johnny's hand shot out faster than a striking snake. Again it slammed into the side of her face, but this time it merely rocked her back a bit.

It was then she made her decision. She had nothing to lose. The man was surely mad and had every intent on killing them both. Nora attacked. She screamed a sound of torment as Johnny slung Matt over his shoulder and moved toward the edge of the cliff.

He'd taken no more than three steps before her body crashed into his legs and toppled him, sending Matt's small form sprawling. Her arms wrapped around Johnny's legs, pinning him to her chest. She held on for dear life while Johnny growled his fury, and Matt slipped from his hold. "Run!" Nora screamed. "Go get help!"

Johnny cursed as he reached for the boy only to find a useless piece of Matt's torn shirt in his hands. His eyes narrowed as he watched the boy hesitate at the edge of the clearing. "Get back here, boy, and do it now."

Nora tightened her hold. "Don't listen to him, Matt. Go get your papa. He'll bring help." Nora had no hope that Matt would find his father quite so easily. He might roam the mountainside for days before being found. Perhaps he might never be found, but she had to give him this chance.

"Get back here, or I'll hurt her bad." Johnny

kicked her chest, trying to free his legs.

Nora grunted at the force of his kick, but held his legs all the tighter. "Matt, go. Hurry. Please," she begged. Matt, realizing he had no other choice, did as he was told. Nora almost released Johnny's legs, her relief being so great as she watched Matt dart through the underbrush and disappear into the forest that spread over the mountainside.

"You dirty bitch," Johnny growled as he tore one leg free and kicked her in earnest. Nora groaned as she released him at last. She hadn't the strength or the stamina to take further abuse.

Johnny scrambled to his feet, but his rage was far from lessened at finally being free. He knelt upon her, his knee pressing deep into her stomach. No longer did he use his open hands, but curled them into fists and hit her. It took only three blows before her nose gushed an enormous amount of blood. The mere dribble from a cracked lip went unnoticed.

He looked at the damage wrought and snorted in disgust. Insanity drove him to hit her once again. A moment later he was tearing at her clothes. She was half naked before she realized he wasn't hitting her any longer, but was intent on a different sort of abuse.

She tried to throw him off, but Johnny only laughed at the feeble attempt. Nora was choking on her own blood and couldn't get a deep breath of air. She struggled all the harder and received only another stunning blow for her efforts.

She was naked to the waist now. Her dress having been torn down its center and pushed aside. Johnny

426

reached for her breast and mercilessly pinched the tip. Had Nora not been half dazed by his blows, she might have noticed the pain. As it was she knew only a distant sense of discomfort.

Still, she was more than slightly aware of what he was about to do and knew there was no way that she could simply allow this abuse. It wasn't the first time that she'd fought off an attacker, but she prayed God it would be the last.

His body was already thick with lust, his mind immersed in the soft femininity. Johnny had a constant craving when it came to a woman's breasts. He reasoned big ones to be the best, but any size, exposed to his view, were sure to stir him. He had an excessive need to look and touch. The sight of them was always sure to set his groin throbbing. His voyeurism and lust made all other reality vanish.

Intent on the sight before him, Johnny never realized the movement. He never saw her hand reach for his unprotected gun. Engrossed with the softness of her, Johnny never noticed as it came free of its holster.

A moment later an explosive sound turned the hunger in his eyes to puzzlement, and his harsh irregular breathing stopped altogether.

It took a full ten seconds before Johnny realized what had caused that baffling sound. His eyes widened as he looked down the length of his body. His pants were singed, but the sight of burning cloth went almost unnoticed for he watched in amazement as the inside of his thigh pumped a river of blood over

427

her chest. He could smell fire and the sickening scent of burned flesh. The gun had been less than an inch away when she'd pulled the trigger.

Only then did his mind catalogue the facts. Only then did the pain reach his nerve endings, to register with startling accuracy in his brain. Agony crashed through his body leaving him a mindless, writhing creature as he cried out, rolled off her prone form, and grabbed his shattered leg.

The bitch had done him in. She'd smashed his bone. He could see white chips of it sticking out of his torn and burned pants. He'd been through a war, ridden with Quantrill, and never gotten more than a scratch. Goddamn her to hell! She'd turned him into a cripple! And he was going to kill her for it!

Johnny reached for the gun, determined to turn it on her, but in his pain and rage took hold of the barrel. He jerked it from her grasp. It went off as it left her hand. This time it was his shoulder that took the blow.

He screamed in impotent rage as he again rolled away, blood now pumping from two wounds.

He lay still for a long, silent moment, willing away the worst of his torment. Finally he found the strength to face her again. And when he did, the icy claws of raw terror spread into his belly. She was sitting facing him, the gun that had fallen between them was again in her hands.

Her nose had stopped bleeding, but the lower half of her face, her neck, and her chest were covered with their combined blood. Her eyes were glazed as if she weren't really there. Johnny shivered at her cold empty look and knew he was a dead man. He could smell his own fear as sweat instantly coated his body.

Nora's mind had raced back to the first time. She couldn't for a moment separate the two happenings. How had he returned? She'd killed him, hadn't she? Was it possible that she hadn't? But she'd buried the body. He had to be dead.

Nora shuddered as she realized the whimpering, cringing man before her wasn't a Yankee, but rather her own supposedly dead husband. She couldn't for a minute remember how she had managed to get free, but the weight of the gun in her hands made her feel safe for the first time in hours.

He watched her for a long moment, knowing the next time she fired that gun she'd kill him. Finally, he dared to say, "Nora, don't kill me. Please don't kill me."

Her lips curved into an almost obscene parody of a smile. He knew she hadn't heard him. He knew she was going to kill him. He saw her finger tighten upon the trigger. Johnny screamed as the gun discharged.

Matt ran as fast as his legs could carry him. He stumbled and fell, rolling down a goodly stretch of mountainside. Then he was on his feet, running again. He never noticed the scratches, the bruises. All he knew was he had to get his father. His father would know what to do. Papa would help.

It had taken them the better part of an hour to

climb to the clearing. It took Matt less than fifteen minutes to get to the bottom. For just a second he couldn't think what to do. He started to run, but almost immediately remembered the horse. If he wanted to get home fast, he'd better take the horse.

It took Matt a few minutes, for he hadn't come down exactly where they'd gone up. He couldn't find the horse immediately. The moment he did, he was on it racing toward his home.

Matt hadn't gone more than a mile before he saw the distant movement in the clear, moonlit night.

Jake watched the sun set behind the range of mountain and almost sighed with relief. Silently he prayed for total blackness to hurry, for the night would hide them well. He knew where he was going. All he could do was pray that Johnny had taken Nora and Matt to the same campsite they'd found weeks before. The camp hadn't been disturbed upon discovery. Johnny wouldn't suspect it had been found.

The sound of gunfire echoing over the mountaintops and the desert floor below brought a curse from his grim lips. An instant later muscled thighs dug into Devil's sides as he urged the horse to a faster pace. He was careless of the danger wrought by riding across the rough, uneven landscape at night. He couldn't worry about that now. He had to get to Nora. He had to find both her and his son before it was too late.

Sweat dampened his back and coated his brow despite the fact that it was growing colder by the minute. It was night and as always in the desert, the nights were cold. In the mountains it would be colder still. Jake couldn't think of that now. He couldn't think about Nora shivering. He couldn't think about his son or the terror Matt had to know. If he was to win out against this monster, he had to keep a clear head. He had to think of his next step.

They might have passed each other unseen, had the moon not risen in time. The desert floor might be a vast expanse of near flat barren land, but at night, unaided by stars or moon, it was as dark as the thickest forest.

Matt pulled the horse to a stop, suddenly more afraid than ever. Who could it be that raced ever closer? Was it another man who would take him again? Matt didn't know what to do. He didn't know if he should turn and go back the way he'd come or. . . . Because of his hesitation, the decision was soon taken from him as the group of anxious riders came to surround him.

Up till this point Matt had been more brave than one could expect from a six year old. But upon spying his father, his small voice broke with a desperate cry, "Papa!"

Jake took the boy from the horse and into his arms, pressing his small body against his own in a hungry, thankful embrace. "The man has mamma. He hit her."

Jake forced aside the wild need to go to her without delay. He soothed the boy's tremors for a moment before he asked, "How did you get here? What happened?"

Now that he was safe in his father's arms, Matt couldn't stop his tears of fright for both his mother and himself. "Mamma said run. She said to get you." Matt was crying in earnest now. "She was holdin' his legs, so he couldn't get me." His words were choppy and broken as great sobs tore at his small chest.

Jake's eyes narrowed with rage. "I have to go get her, Matt. Can you show me where she is?"

Matt nodded and pointed toward the mountains straight ahead. With his arm around his son, they were at the mountain's base within minutes. "Up there." Matt pointed again.

"I need you to watch the horses." Jake dismounted and called over his shoulder as he started up the mountain. "Stay here."

Jake was the first to burst into the clearing. By now he was so panicked he couldn't think to be quiet. All he knew was he had to find Nora. The sight that greeted his eyes was horrifying even as it puzzled.

Nora sat across from a whimpering, obviously badly damaged Johnny. Her face, neck, and chest were covered with dried blood, but she held a pistol in both hands steady as she aimed it at the cowering man.

Jake ignored the man, having eyes only for his wife. He knelt at her side. She didn't see him. Very gently he removed the gun from her fingers and gathered her torn, blood soaked dress over her breasts. "Nora. Darlin'. Can you hear me?"

Nora nodded as she raised her gaze to his. "Jake, I'm so glad you came." He rocked her against him for a long moment before she asked, "Is Matt . . . ?"

"He's fine. He's waiting below with the horses."

Nora trembled in relief and knew an exhaustion beyond her ability to bear. "Thank God. And Mina?"

"She died."

"Oh Jake, my God." The tears came then for her sweet, quiet friend. She'd been too busy, too terrified before to allow them. But now, in her husband's protective arms, she gave into the need and clung to his shoulders as sobs tore into her chest.

"Don't let her kill me, please," Johnny begged.

Cole had followed his brother into the clearing. He cursed as he saw Nora's blood-spattered face and walked to where Johnny sat. The heel of his boot flashed out and caught Johnny just beneath his right eye, instantly crushing his cheekbone to splinters. "I won't."

Johnny screamed out and brought his hand up to the throbbing.

"Cole," Jake said in warning.

"What?" Cole asked as he reached down and actually lifted the man from the ground with a powerful and precise shot to his destroyed cheek. This time he was close enough to hear the bone grind upon itself. He sneered his contempt as Johnny cried for mercy. But there was no mercy to be had. Johnny had taken that and more when he'd killed Mina. He'd taken the laughter. He'd taken the tears. There was nothing left for Cole to give, certainly not mercy.

"Leave us," Cole said calmly.

The men behind them instantly moved back. They weren't fooled by his softly spoken words. They knew the look of murder when they saw it and knew as well that this was justice. Cole alone had the right to see this man dead. But Jake knew his brother better than any man alive. He knew that once Cole regained his reason he would be tormented if allowed to kill another cold-bloodedly. Jake cautioned his brother, telling him that the law should see to this.

Cole laughed, the sound raw and aching with pain. "He'd tell them it was an accident. He'd say he didn't mean it."

"Cole, he'll be sent up for a long time."

Cole's dark eyes were hard, harder than Jake had ever seen them. "A long time isn't forever. And that's what he took from me."

Jake shook his head, knowing his brother had made his decision. "You'll have to live with it, Cole."

Cole laughed, the sound as devoid of humor as a wailing cry. "I'll have to live, Jake. That's what I'm afraid of."

Despite the intensity of his agony, Johnny realized the outcome of this almost whispered conversation. The terror of what was to come clutched his heart. There wasn't a doubt in his mind that Cole Brackston was going to kill him. "No! For God's sake, don't leave me with him," Johnny cried as the men moved from the clearing and down the deep slope. Jake gathered Nora into his arms and without another word followed their lead.

"Help me! Please somebody help me!" he

434

screamed into the night to no avail.

The words were cut off as if a fist had slammed into his mouth, leaving only a garbled sound of pain to follow them down the mountain.

Cole hit him again, feeling not a moment's pity for the man who had murdered his wife. He knew before this night was done that Johnny Bowens would wish himself dead a hundred times. When death finally came, he'd welcome the blackness and yes, even the fiery gates of hell, with open arms.

Again he hit him; hit him until there were no more sounds coming from his hated mouth; hit him until the man lay facedown in dirt and moved not a muscle. Cole sat across from Johnny's unconscious body. He added to the fire as he waited. At the first sound of a moan he was on his feet again. And again Johnny felt the mighty punishment of Cole's boot as the other jaw was crushed. He screamed and tried to cover his face, but his hands proved useless against Cole's murderous rage.

He tried to sit up, but the pounding fists wouldn't permit any movement. Again and again they struck his shattered cheeks. Johnny's whole world became only blinding, excruciating pain. He rolled to his stomach, feeling a wave of nausea, knowing nothing in this life could equal such suffering.

He had to get out of here. He had to run, but how could he? His goddamned wife had crushed the bone in his leg.

Johnny begged for mercy. "Please. I didn't mean . . ." The words came out a garbled, toothless mumble as Cole's fists hit him yet again. He rolled to

435

his feet, unable to bear anymore. He had to get away. Every second another punishing blow. It was too much.

Blindly he moved, never realizing the bone in his leg wasn't shattered after all, but only damaged. He could walk. He could limp at least. He tried to run, but the ground tilted wildly and he reached out trying to gain his balance.

Cole smiled and stepped aside as Johnny staggered forward.

Wild to be free of this torment, Johnny hurried his pace. He couldn't see where he was going, but if he could just make it to the woods then this son of a bitch wouldn't be able to find him. He'd hide under the brush. He'd stay there, no matter the pain until Cole Brackston gave up his search and left.

He took another step and another. Cole watched in silent, icy cold fury; never uttering a word of caution as Johnny walked straight off the edge of the cliff.

His horrified scream could be heard for miles.

It was almost morning before Cole came back to the ranch. Inside the house Mina lay clothed in the same white doeskin dress she'd been married in. Surrounding the roughly hewn coffin, white candles burned low, casting the rest of the room into shadows. Cole almost smiled at the sight of her and realized it was befitting that Mina should be surrounded by light. She'd always mean light to him. For what was left of his life he'd know only darkness.

No one was there but White Moon who sat against the wall as if she couldn't bring herself to come any closer. He sat beside his wife and studied her beautiful, still features, trying to imagine she was only asleep. If it weren't for the ache in his heart he might have done it. But the ache wouldn't let him pretend.

Would he ever see her again? Would the day come when he could hold her against him and kiss those sweet lips again? Was she in heaven? Indeed, was there such a place?

He hoped so. He prayed for it to be so.

It felt like a minute or two went by, but it was suddenly light and Jake touched Cole's shoulder. There were people standing all around. He looked at them with some surprise. He hadn't realized he was no longer alone. Their faces were drawn, their eyes sad. Nora, her eye swollen and discolored, was crying. "Cole, it's time."

Cole nodded and allowed them to take her body away. He followed far behind the small parade of mourners to the little hill just outside of town. He waited for the words to be spoken. He waited for them to lower his love into the ground. He waited for the last shovel of dirt to fall, for the last of them to leave before he walked to the top of the hill and stared at the freshly turned ground.

He didn't cry. Perhaps it might have been better if he could. Tears were a balm, a healing of sorts. But he didn't cry. In his chest an emptiness grew, an aching hollow that could never be filled. Cole knew he'd carry it with him until the day he died.

Silently he spoke to her, telling her of his love. He wished her peace and happiness, knowing he'd never have either until the day came when he could join her.

He stayed there until dark. And when he left he knew he wouldn't be back for a long time.

Three weeks later Jake, Nora, Matt and Cole were sitting on the porch watching the sun ease itself behind the distant mountain. The moment it was dark, Cole reached for his nephew. A second later the sounds of the childish shrieks filled the air as his uncle tickled the boy breathless. "Stop!" He laughed with glee as he tried to escape his uncle's hold.

Matt tried to crawl away, but collapsed into another convulsion of laughter as Cole swung him up and over his head. The boy hung on and wrestled his uncle until both were lying on the porch, breathing heavy with exertion. Suddenly Cole said, "I'm going away for awhile."

Matt asked, "Why?"

The adults knew why. Although Cole had seemed to have reconciled himself with his loss, they'd both been expecting it. They made no response.

Cole breathed a long sigh. "I just need to get away for a while." And at his nephew's frown he smiled. "Don't worry, tiger. I'll be back."

"Will you bring me something?"

"Sure. What would you like?"

"Peppermint sticks." Matt grinned, exposing the adorable space where he'd lost his first tooth last week. "I like peppermint sticks most of all."

Cole laughed and hugged him close as he warned, "It might be sometime."

"That's all right. Mamma says I eat too much candy anyway."

"Mamma says, right now it's time for bed."

Matt grumbled his usual bedtime reluctance but hugged his uncle good night and goodbye and was soon following his mother into the house.

"You don't have to go, Cole."

Cole looked out over the yard, his gaze lingering for long moments on the barn as memories flooded his mind. He shook them away. "There are too many memories. Everything I touch or see reminds me of her."

Jake nodded in understanding, wondering if he wouldn't do the same if anything ever happened to . . . he shuddered at the thought and forced it from his mind. "Will you come back?"

"Someday. Maybe." He smiled at his brother. "You're a lucky man, Jake." He said the words with no jealousy or recrimination. They were honest, filled with fondness for both his brother and sister-in-law.

Jake grinned. "I am now." He sighed. "Maybe someday you will . . ."

"Yeah, maybe," Cole agreed, as he came to his feet. But both men knew he didn't believe it.

"Do you think he'll be all right?"

Jake and Nora were in bed later that night. He

hugged her into the curve of his body as he nodded. Nora could feel the movement above her head. "He needs some time, is all. He'll be all right."

"Maybe he should wait a little. Things get easier with time."

"It's not true that time heals, Nora."

"I know. We never forget. It just that the pain gets a little easier. White Moon is better. Sometimes, when I see her laughing at something Matt said, the pain is completely gone."

"Everyone handles pain in their own way. He needs some time alone, time away from here. It will help."

Nora sighed. "Maybe it's better that he's leaving. I was thinking that a new baby might only make him realize his loss all the more."

"You're probably right about that." There was a long pause before he rolled over and lit the lamp at the side of the bed. "What did you say?"

Nora giggled as he turned her onto her back. His gaze narrowed as he read the laughter in her eyes.

"I said, maybe it's better if—"

Jake shook his head impatiently. "After that."

"Oh. You mean the part about the new baby?"

Jake nodded his head.

"Well, I was—"

"Is it fact or theory?"

"Fact."

Jake beamed. The sight twisted her heart with gladness. God, but she loved this man: Lopsided mustache, temper, obstinacy, and all.

"How long?"

"Oh, I expect he'll be about nineteen inches." She measured the space between her opened hands. "That's about average."

"You little . . ."

His hands reached for her and Nora almost choked on the need to stifle her laughter as he tickled her without mercy.

"Six months, six months, six months."

Epilogue

"Let's go down by the river."

Nora glanced at her husband as she stepped from the house. "Are you talking to me?"

"Do you see anyone else around?"

Nora's eyes narrowed with the promise of revenge for that thoughtless and less than gentle remark. Her look brought an instant response.

"I didn't mean it."

She chuckled a low sound of pleasure and sat in his lap. "Why?"

"'Cause I'm scared of you."

Nora laughed again. "I mean, why do you want to go to the river?"

"Oh." His dark look cleared and he flashed her a quick smile. "I thought a lady as smart as you would figure it's time for another lesson."

"It's too dark to swim."

"It's better when it's dark."

Nora chuckled a knowing sound. "Is it? Why?"

"'Cause when it's dark, you don't have to wear any

clothes, while I . . . teach you to swim."

She giggled at his hesitation and the obvious meaning behind it. "Do your eyebrows always go up and down like that right before you teach someone to swim?"

"I don't know. You're the only one I've ever taught."

"You haven't taught me yet." Nora remembered the last time he tried to teach her to swim and blushed at the memory of the two of them cavorting around the banks of the river buck naked. Thank God, no one had come across them playing as uninhibited as children. Nora would have been mortified beyond measure. "You know I think you're just using swimming as an excuse to get me naked."

Jake bit his lip, but his efforts didn't go far toward hiding his humor at her accusation. Still, he shook his head in supposed innocence. "I wouldn't do that."

"Wouldn't you? The last time I ended up naked."

"Did you?" he asked vaguely. "How come I don't remember?"

"Don't remember, hah!" Nora shot him a narrowed look of disbelief. "Remember I was trying to get away and you reached for my shift, and—"

"It ripped." Jake couldn't hide his pleasure at the memory. It was evident in his tone and the sparkle in his eyes. Nora remembered and smiled too, for he hadn't been able to hide his pleasure during the actual happening either.

"You could at least make believe you were sorry about it. That was a beautiful—"

"You wouldn't want me to lie, would you, darlin'?"

Nora rolled her eyes toward the heavens. "You? Lie? Never."

Jake chuckled as he gathered her in his arms and came to his feet. He was walking away from the house before he bothered to ask, "Should I carry you?"

"Maybe you'd better not. I wouldn't want you to get too tired."

Jake nuzzled her neck playfully, and then suddenly looked her straight in the eye. "Why? Have you plans for me?"

"One or two." Nora had to bite her lip to keep from laughing at his hopeful expression.

His gaze moved to her small, rounded belly. "A pregnant lady can swim, can't she?"

"Jake, a pregnant lady can do everything," she returned in her most seductive tone.

She felt him shudder as her hand slid inside his shirt. "Ah, darlin', I'm countin' on it."